Light My Fire

EMMA FOXX

Who knew a blizzard could bring so much heat?

I'm not worried about the freak snowstorm in March stranding me in my brother's cabin in the Minnesota woods. I'm here to drown myself in textbooks—and junk food—and get ready for my big exams, so another couple of days won't matter.

Except, three of my brother's friends are also stranded here with me.

Their guys' get-away started early thanks to my matchmaking grandmother and now we're all trapped together.

Okay, I'm maybe a *little* worried.

Not because I'm scared. Uh…nope, that's not why my heart is pounding so hard suddenly.

Mischievous blue eyes. Flirty grins. Sexy innuendoes. Sweet caregiving. Hunky muscles, tattoos, big…feet.

You get the idea.

I generally find animals easier to deal with than people, especially men. That's why I've been so focused on veterinary school rather than dating. It's also probably why I still have my v-card. (Fine, it's definitely why).

But I've hit the testosterone jackpot and this is the perfect opportunity to practice my flirting. Or get some advice about men. Or maybe even something more.

My inexperience is such a nuisance. But the more time I spend with the cinnamon roll firefighter Wyatt, the golden retriever millionaire Jackson, and the broody fire Chief Luke, the more I think one of them might be happy to help *ahem* expand my horizons.

The problem is, I can't choose between them. So maybe they'll *all* be willing to help a girl out...

CHAPTER 1

Luke

"YOU KNOW, if I'm going to be cuddled up under blankets in front of a fire and snowed in all weekend, there are at least a dozen people I would pick to do it with besides the two of you. And they all look better in lingerie. And out of lingerie."

I roll my eyes. "We gave you three chances to change your mind," I tell Jackson Hill, my buddy Wyatt's best friend from high school, who has also become one of my favorite people to hang out with. "I told you when I called to tell you we were moving the trip up a day, I said it again when we picked you up, and I reminded you right before the plane took off."

We had been planning this guy's trip for about a month. We'd all hoped for some nice weather—or at least sunshine—after the long, cold Chicago winter. We're heading up to northern Minnesota, so it's not like we expected it to be balmy, but the gorgeous cabin our friend, professional hockey player Blake Wilder, owns looks amazing in photos and we figured we'd at least have a sunny deck, cold beer, a boat, and some fishing for our four days.

That plan has changed drastically. There's a big winter storm moving in and it looks like our long weekend is going to consist of hot coffee—maybe with some whiskey in it—and a constantly burning fireplace instead.

"You still came with us," I tell Jackson. "So the lack of skimpy lingerie this weekend is your own fault."

"You do *not* know *twelve* women who would willingly get snowed in with you for four days," Wyatt tells his best friend with a grin.

"Fuck off. I know *at least* a dozen," Jackson tells him. "And I could get three or four of them to come all together." He waggles his eyebrows.

Wyatt laughs. "What the hell am *I* doing going to Minnesota with two dudes for four days of a winter apocalypse when I could be in Chicago with you and *four* blondes in lingerie?"

"Who said I'm sharing?" Jackson asks.

"We've had fun sharing one," Wyatt says. "Think of what a good time we'd have with four."

Jackson grins and nods. "Good point. I've only got one dick, one tongue, and two hands. I could probably use some help."

"That's the spirit," Wyatt tells him, sitting back against the side of the plane that's cruising above the dark water.

Wilder's cabin is on an island accessible only by boat or plane. How the hell did I end up flying from Chicago to northern Minnesota and then taking a chartered private plane to an island where there are only ten houses?

I shake my head. I'm a firefighter. I've lived in Chicago all my life. I hang out with blue-collar guys and gals. I'm happy that way.

But damn, it's nice to have friends with deep pockets, I'll admit.

"Well, now I'm here," Jackson says, tucking his hands further into the pockets of his dark gray overcoat. "I cleared my weekend for this, so I'd better at least get s'mores and hot chocolate out of this sex-less snowpocalypse."

I look at the guy who is twelve years my junior, but has already made more money than I will probably see in my lifetime. "I would think you could afford a decent coat. What the hell are you doing wearing that thing up to Northern Minnesota in March, anyway?"

"I was thinking about sitting out on that fucking gorgeous deck, grilling out, drinking beer, hot tub… just kicking back. I didn't know I would be fighting for my survival."

I huff out a laugh. We're going to a "cabin" that is more or less a mansion in the woods. Heidi, Blake's grandmother, who was the one to call and warn me about the incoming storm and suggest we head up here a day early, promised the cabin was fully stocked. She also said March storms could be brutal but they cleared out after a day or so and we'd have no trouble getting back to Chicago on Monday. We're not going to be hanging out on the deck in the sunshine but we're also *not* going to be fighting for our survival.

"I think we'll be okay," Wyatt tells him. "This cabin is amazing. And we're still getting away. I get that your usual day is pretty cushy but Luke and I deserve this vacation."

Jackson leans back and stretches his legs out. "You two work too hard."

Wyatt laughs. "Next to you, everyone works hard."

"I'll be working hard soon," Jackson says. "When I was developing my app, I worked twenty-hour days for weeks."

"You're not working *at all* right now, though," Wyatt points out.

"I'm waiting for inspiration."

Wyatt grins. "And you're bored. That's why you're coming with us this weekend."

Jackson shrugs. "I also like you two. I can think of worse ways to spend four days."

"But also better," I say. "Blondes right?"

He grins. "There's always time for blondes—and brunettes and redheads—when I get back to Chicago."

"Very accommodating of you," I say dryly. "But fair warning, we *are* playing poker this weekend and I *am* going to take some of your money."

"Bring it on," Jackson says, grinning.

That's exactly what will happen. Jackson is effortlessly brilliant in all things having to do with… whatever he got rich doing. Things seem to just work out for him. Except for poker. At least with me. I beat him every time.

"Here we go," Kenny, the pilot, calls over the engine.

The plane lands on an airstrip that feels more like a suggestion than a legitimate airport. A few minutes later, we're being driven down a bumpy lane to the cabin. It's nearly completely dark but the front porch is lit with soft yellow lights strung from poles.

We unload our bags and a few boxes of supplies—beer from a microbrewery on the mainland Blake recommended, steaks, and Jackson's preferred cold brew coffee… heaven forbid our spoiled baby millionaire not have all of his creature comforts for even four days.

Jackson tips Kenny for giving us a ride, and from the way Kenny's eyes widen, I guess it's a generous amount.

Then we head up the stone path that leads to the cabin.

The wind is definitely picking up and the bite in the air is easily twenty degrees colder than the temps were in Chicago when we left.

"Uh, did Heidi or Blake have someone get the cabin set up for us?" Wyatt asks as we approach the cabin.

I see immediately why he asks. The cabin is lit up. Lights glow from nearly every window on this side of the house and there is definitely smoke coming from the chimney.

"Probably," I comment. "That makes sense." And seems like something Heidi would do. The seventy-something bundle of energy and mischief seems like she would be the ultimate hostess.

"Hallelujah," Jackson says. "It'll be nice and warm inside, and we can start the hot chocolate right away."

He's a millionaire, and twenty-eight years old, but he's been excited about hot chocolate and s'mores since he realized we were not going to be having cold beer and burgers from the grill on the deck.

He might be complaining out loud, but he's actually looking on the bright side.

Which is honestly his personality. He's a happy guy and easy to be around. Of course it's easy to look at life optimistically when everything you touch seems to turn to gold.

He's good for me, if I'm honest. I tend to be a pessimist and it's good for me to hang out with energetic young guys who look on the bright side.

Wyatt too. He's laid-back and goes with the flow. I knew as soon as Heidi suggested we change our schedule that Wyatt would be fine with it. That trait makes him an excellent firefighter where you never know what a shift will bring. He thinks quickly on his feet, is seemingly good at every task thrown his way from working on a stuck elevator, to directing hoses, to comforting victims.

I am definitely the grump of the group. I'm old. And I know things don't always work out the way you want them to. When Heidi called me and told me a storm was coming in, I mentally canceled our trip, and was pissed that I had to spend the next four days off in cold gray Chicago instead of hanging out at the lake with my friends.

But when she said it was simply a matter of leaving early and being snowed in for a couple of days, I adjusted. I'm not an asshole… all the time. I just tend to see things more cynically. Because life often sucks.

We stomp up the steps of the cabin. This side of the house is mostly siding. I imagine the back is glass windows that look out over the lake, with a dock.

I assume we have keys for all of the doors, but I'm not sure which one is which. I pull the keys from my pocket and start to flip through them at the same time Wyatt flips open a covered number pad and types in a series of digits.

We hear a little beep and the distinct sound of a lock opening.

"There's a code for the door?" I ask.

He looks at me. "Obviously."

"And you have the code?"

He grins and pushes the door open with his shoulder, dragging his bag and a box of supplies over the threshold. "Obviously."

We crowd through the door, tossing our bags and setting the boxes down so that we can get rid of our snow covered shoes before stepping further into the cabin.

I shrug out of my coat and toss it, then bend to untie my boots.

I have one off and have started on the other when I hear it.

The distinctly feminine shriek.

I look up quickly and my heart almost stops.

We can see almost the entire first floor of the cabin from the door and the woman standing ten feet away, her hand on her chest, staring at us with wide eyes and her mouth open clearly just came from down the hallway to her right.

But it's not surprise at seeing another human in the space I thought we'd have to ourselves that makes my breath lodge in my chest.

It's seeing *this* particular human.

This gorgeous human woman who is dressed in flannel pajama bottoms and a gigantic sweater over a tank top with her long brown hair piled on her head in a messy bun.

Because she's the woman I've been thinking about for the last several months, no matter how hard I try not to. No matter how many times I tell myself I *can't*. No matter what I try to forget about her.

"Hi, Brooke," I say calmly.

Blake Wilder's sister turns her wide stare on me.

And when our gazes collide, our situation hits me right between the eyes.

We are about to be snowed in with the first woman to get under my skin in years.

Well, fuck.

CHAPTER 2

Brooke

NO, *no, no.*

This has to be a hallucination from sleep-deprivation and isolation.

I *have* been staying up too late studying and I haven't seen another human being in five days.

Plus, now that my spring break is winding down and I feel confident about my finals, I'm half a bottle of wine into my Friday and I had a sex dream last night.

That's why my overtired brain has conjured up three hot guys standing in the entryway of the cabin.

I blink hard.

Nope. Not a hallucination.

They're still here—Luke, Wyatt, and another man I've never met. They're definitely real and not a figment of my imagination. Though both Luke and Wyatt starred in my sex dream the night before, and that wasn't the first time. They've both popped in and out of my thoughts at random intervals in recent months.

I immediately sag in relief that I don't have to defend myself from potential marauding intruders. I almost had a heart attack when I heard the door swing open, followed by men's voices.

"Brooke!" Wyatt Doherty grins at me.

I've only met Wyatt twice, briefly, but I'd recognize him anywhere. He has dark brown curly hair and bright blue eyes, shoulders the width of a football field, beard stubble, and a charming smile. He's a firefighter, and if that wasn't sexy enough all on its own, he has two full sleeve tattoos masking his fair skin. They're covered right now, because he's wearing a black winter jacket and a knit hat, but I saw him roll up his sleeves at my brother's wedding last year and I almost passed out just from that simple act.

I bury my Doritos dust-covered fingertips in the pockets of my flannel pajama pants. "What… how…"

"Brooke," Luke Moody says my name again and my attention is ripped off of Wyatt and straight back to him.

Luke is older, probably in his late thirties or early forties, and he has a low, commanding voice that does something entirely different to me than Wyatt's biceps. Wyatt makes me giggle and blush. Luke makes me hot and uncomfortable. Scared, but in a way that I want to explore, like the thrill of walking through a haunted house. He's thinner than Wyatt, and taller, with a stern jaw and brown eyes. I've never really seen him smile. He's peeling an outer flannel shirt off to reveal his white, muscular arms.

"This is a surprise," he adds.

I notice they've dropped luggage on the hardwood floor.

Luggage.

Oh, God.

They're *staying* here?

I can't tell if Luke thinks it's a good surprise or a bad one.

The stranger-to-me, who has a pleasant and easy smile, is unlacing his boots. He stands back up and eyes all of us curiously. He has a sharp jawline and adorable dimples in his brown cheeks.

"I take it you're Brooke, Blake's sister. Hi, I'm Jackson."

"Uh, hi, Jackson. Nice to meet you. Yes, I'm Brooke," I manage to choke out. "Blake's sister."

I mentally groan at myself. He just said that.

I've never been great at social situations, especially ones I'm not prepared for. I prefer animals to crowds.

Not that this is a crowd, but it certainly feels that way. I cannot believe I'm being confronted by three gorgeous guys and I'm in pajamas with orange fingertips. My hand flies to my head. And a messy bun with unbrushed hair. I try to straighten my bun but all that does is cause it to flop from the right to the left.

It also reminds me that I'm not wearing a bra.

Something Luke seems to have noticed. His eyes drift to my chest. I'm wearing a tight soft gray tank top with a loose granny sweater half-falling off of my shoulders. My tight nipples are clearly visible.

"Sorry we're crashing your party by showing up early," Jackson says, glancing over at my wine bottle and glass.

I have books and unhealthy snacks strewn all over the coffee table.

Sadly, this is the kind of party I have on a regular basis.

Not only am I an introvert, I'm also very busy in my third year of vet school. This is a typical Friday night for me. Just normally, I do it back at my apartment in Minneapolis.

"I'm just here on spring break, studying. I'm leaving tomorrow."

Jackson grins. "That is *not* how I did spring break. Which probably explains why I don't have a college degree, just a lot of dropped classes."

I have no idea what to say to that.

Jackson is wearing an expensive looking winter coat better suited for strolling downtown than hiking in the woods. His boots look brand new. But that's not what is interesting to me about him. It's the easy, confident smile, his sharp cheekbones, and his easy stance. He's both very handsome and clearly self-assured, in spite of his teasing words.

"You're early?" I ask, trying to figure out why they're standing here in my brother's cabin. "For what?"

"Guys' weekend," Luke says.

"Yeah, we're going to fish, hike, drink beer around a bonfire, play poker." Wyatt steps forward in his socks, leaving his duffel bag on the floor behind him. "Your grandma thought we should come early since there's a storm rolling in."

He holds his arms out to me for a hug and I step in automatically, out of politeness, and because this may be my only chance to be this close to a man with this many muscles. I'm not sure our level of acquaintance really warrants a hello hug, but I'm not about to turn it down.

It feels as good as I imagined. He smells like soap and fresh air and he envelopes my body like a weighted blanket has been tossed over me. My nipples press against his sweatshirt, the scraping contact making them even tighter. Over Wyatt's shoulder, I see Luke watching us steadily, intently.

Again, I can't read his expression.

That, and Wyatt's grip tightening on me, his hand drifting down to my lower back, has me pulling back quickly.

Then I register what he said. Wait a second. "My grandmother told you to come early?" I ask, crossing my arms tightly over my chest.

"Yep."

Of course she did.

"Funny she didn't suggest you *leave* early," Luke says, like he doesn't think it's funny at all.

Neither do I.

"Yeah, so funny." Also funny, she didn't call or text to tell me these guys were showing up tonight.

My grandmother thinks she's being clever. She already gave me an earful about spending my spring break alone in the woods when we both know I am fully prepared for my finals and don't really need to study anymore. She thinks I should spend more time with friends and dating. It didn't help that I cried at my brother's wedding, which is totally unfair. A girl isn't allowed to cry at a wedding without it meaning something? I was just happy for him.

And a little sad for myself.

But now that Blake is married, Gran's turned her shady match-making efforts to me.

Heidi Wilder doesn't know the meaning of the word subtle.

I'm both horrified and… intrigued.

A few hours hanging out with three hot guys tonight is intimidating, but also exciting.

Hot guy hugs times three? Go for it, girl.

No, I can't stay here. I'll embarrass myself.

This may be your only chance!

But what if I say or do something awkward?

Jackson interrupts my battling inner voices.

"I hope you don't mind sharing the cabin with three unruly dudes."

"Um, no," I sputter. "Not at all."

Like, honestly, not at all.

Heat spreads across my cheeks, and I search my brain for something to say. This is always my problem. When I'm in my element, with animals, or in a classroom, I always know what to say. I'm self-assured and confident in my knowledge and abilities. Give me a short-hair cat with a UTI or a French bulldog with hip dysplasia and I know exactly what to do.

But men… they're a different beast entirely.

"We'll stay out of your way," Luke says, which further confuses me.

"Um…"

Jesus, how many times can I say "um" in one conversation?

"I'll show you to the bedrooms," I manage to get out. "If you want to put your luggage away. I don't have a lot to eat because I'm leaving tomorrow, but I do have wine and some chips and nuts." I gesture to the table.

Wyatt comes up to me and gives me a smile. "There's a storm coming tonight and tomorrow, Brooke. You're going to be snowed in at least until Sunday. Good thing we brought a ton of food.

You'll be all tucked in here safe and sound with us." He glances at my lips.

My hand goes to my mouth automatically. I probably have a stray chip crumb somewhere. I rub back and forth.

Wyatt takes my hand and holds it out. "Doritos or Cheetos?" he asks, inspecting my fingers.

I swallow hard. But before I can answer, he pops my index finger in his mouth and sucks it lightly. A jolt of pure desire shoots through my entire body. I suck in a breath.

"Doritos," he says. "My favorite."

Then he winks and turns away, bending down to grab his suitcase.

I'm speechless. Especially when Luke's eyes narrow and he glares at Wyatt. He grabs the handle of his suitcase and heads to the stairs without another word. He actually skips the first two steps as he jogs up them.

"First door on the left is available," I call out after him. "Wyatt, you can take the first room on the right. Jackson, second door on the right."

"Thanks, Brooke," Wyatt says, bounding up the stairs after Luke. "Be right back."

Jackson pauses at the bottom of the stairs and gives me a friendly smile. "Yeah, thanks, Brooke. Where is your room, by the way?"

"Down here. I have the primary suite." Thank God. I wouldn't sleep at all if I knew these guys were sleeping a few feet away from me.

Jackson grins. "Probably for the best. Do you like steak?"

"Sure."

"Excellent. We'll fire up the grill in ten minutes." He walks over by the front door and stacks a box on a cooler before picking them both up.

I see they have several bags and boxes. "Let me help."

"Nah. You keep doing what you're doing. Don't let us throw you off your plans."

That's comical.

I'm *definitely* thrown off. I'm so far off I've gone over the cliff.

I still take three grocery bags and haul them onto the kitchen island. Then I realize I really need to wash my hands. I grab my phone off of the dining room table and say, "Be back in a second," to Jackson before fast-walking to my bedroom.

I close the door behind me and head into the bathroom. I wash my hands until they're free of snack food residue and pick up my phone to text my grandmother.

GRAN YOU COULD HAVE WARNED ME

Warned you about what, sweetie?

LUKE, WYATT, AND JACKSON SHOWING UP AT THE CABIN

Why are you yelling? And why would I warn you, just so you could just hop on the first plane out of there before they even showed up?

Yes.

Where's the fun in that?

You're not at all concerned that your granddaughter is alone in a cabin with three grown men?

They're all nice boys. They're Aidan's good friends and your brother likes them, too.

I do trust Aidan, who is dating my brother's wife, and my brother, to not be friends with jerks. But I can't let her comment slide.

Luke is like forty. He's not a boy.

He's a *man*. A man who didn't look thrilled to have me sharing their guys' weekend cabin.

Gran texts back.

> I'm seventy-six. That's a boy to me.

> Not to me!

> So set your cap on Wyatt. I bet the two of you have a lot in common. I understand he's mechanically inclined.

And I like animals and books, so what the heck is she talking about? That has nothing to do with mechanics. The woman makes no sense. I also have no idea how to "set my cap" on anyone, whatever that means.

What makes you think they would even be interested?

I delete that immediately before I hit send. Gran will spend the next twenty minutes complimenting me and giving me a pep talk that will only make me more nervous if I show her any insecurity.

But she doesn't need any encouragement.

> Just have fun. Think of it as practice flirting. You're a beautiful, intelligent, accomplished young woman. They would be idiots not to be flattered by attention from you, Brookey.

The nickname makes me bristle. I don't know why I hate it. I just do.

> A little warning would have been nice.

I'm repeating myself because it's all the ammunition I have with a grandmother hellbent on embarrassing me in the name of matchmaking.

Sweetie, you can't study for everything in life.
Some things need to just happen spontaneously.

She's right. I know she is. But it still makes me want to break out in hives. Though Wyatt did suck on my finger. I'm pretty sure that is flirting. Even I know that.

I glance out the bedroom window. It's already snowing.

How much snow are we getting anyway?

A TON! So much I doubt you can leave tomorrow.

She adds a string of smiley face emojis to that.

If I miss my finals and ruin my career it's your fault.

Relax. It's only Thursday. By Sunday it will be clear and your exams start Tuesday, right?

Yes.

Then enjoy yourself! Get in the hottub. Your neck must be stiff from studying.

There's no arguing with her about that.

You're insane but I love you.

I love you too.

She adds a kiss emoji.

I don't emoji, if that's a verb. It drives her crazy, so normally I will concede with one or two, but not today. She deserves no emoji satisfaction.

It feels too obvious to put on a bra now, so I just button my sweater up. I brush my teeth and then take a deep breath.

My neck is stiff.

My grandmother is right.

I should just try to relax and enjoy myself.

This will never happen again, *ever*. It is a golden opportunity. I could definitely use a little practice flirting. A *lot* of practice. I've only had a couple of boyfriends and those were when I was a teenager.

I've been way too busy to have a relationship in recent years and while I don't regret that, I do feel like I've missed out on one thing I am very curious about—sex.

Being a virgin is starting to feel like a hurdle to future dating.

But to not be a virgin, I have to know how to flirt and talk to men more effectively than I have in the past.

So maybe the solution has just presented itself like man magic in the form of Wyatt, Jackson, and Luke.

CHAPTER 3

Jackson

WATCHING my two best friends with this girl is very interesting. And very amusing.

I've known Wyatt since high school, but I've only been hanging out with Luke for a couple of years. Still, regardless of our differences in age and jobs, for some reason, the three of us just fit.

Luke's a grump, no question, but that's why he needs Wyatt and me. We make sure he kicks back and has fun. Luke is my voice of reason. He gives me advice and if I run an idea past him and he rolls his eyes or says flat out 'don't be a dumbass'—which he definitely will if that's what he thinks—I change my mind.

Our time together is just easy. Our three personalities work together and no matter what we're doing, things just click.

That's why things seem off tonight. And the only new factor in this equation is Miss Brooke Wilder.

I get it. She is gorgeous, and has this sweet air about her that makes you want to ,hug her and, I don't know, brush her hair or something, even while you're imagining bending her over the breakfast bar and fucking her deep and hard from behind.

Or maybe that's just me.

Except watching Luke stomp around the kitchen, and blatantly avoid even making eye contact with her, while Wyatt can't seem to stay more than two feet away from her at any moment, I don't think I'm the only one feeling something here.

"What the hell did you eat here this whole week while you were alone?" Wyatt asks her with a soft smile. "I haven't found any evidence of real food. Please tell me it wasn't just wine and Doritos the whole time."

"Well…" Brooke says.

Yeah, that's going to trip my best friend's protective switch. He's going to want to take care of her for sure. He's an Acts of Service love language guy.

"Brooke," Wyatt says warningly. "Tell me there was a vegetable at *some* point."

Brooke laughs, the sound a light, happy noise that makes me smile. And even as I realize that's cheesy as hell, I can't help it.

"Carrots. They are both vegetables *and* real food," she says.

He pulls a half-eaten bag of baby carrots from the fridge. "This is just sad."

"I didn't have time to cook. And I don't really like vegetables," she says, then gives him a little pout.

Oh, he's a goner.

Wyatt gives her the goofiest smile in return. "I will *prove* to you that you like vegetables. At least when I make them."

Jesus. I have never seen a woman wrap him around her finger so quickly. I am so making fun of him for all of this later.

"I ate soup. And sandwiches," Brooke says. "Not just junk."

"But lots of Doritos," he says, bracing his hands on the counter across from where she's sitting on a stool at the breakfast bar. "I found an empty bag in the trash and there's the half-eaten bag you were working on when we got here."

She nods. "I really like Doritos."

He shakes his head. "Woman, we are feeding you tonight."

She doesn't protest. In fact, her eyes track him as he moves around the kitchen, gathering what he needs for the steaks and baked potatoes.

"How do you like your steak?" he asks.

"However you cook it," she says.

Something in her voice makes me lean forward from where I'm sitting on the stool next to her and study her face.

She looks a little dreamy as she watches Wyatt.

Ah. The girl likes him too.

I know Wyatt and Luke met her previously at her brother's retirement party and again at his wedding. The way they told it before we all gathered in the kitchen is that they flirted with her a bit. Even Luke. I guess he had a few beers in him. Or something. He's acting like he can't stand her right now. But they didn't get her number and haven't been in touch since. Wyatt said he's thought about her a lot though.

Wyatt looks over at her. "I'll make it however you want."

She shakes her head. "I don't really have a preference."

"So you trust me to make it good for you?"

There is definitely something in *his* voice. It's gruff and I know what he's thinking. It's not about steak, that's for sure.

I lift my brows, my eyes bouncing from one of them to the other.

She wets her lips and nods. "Yeah. I do."

This is *definitely* interesting.

Wyatt hasn't been into anybody in a while. He dates a little, but my friend has recently decided that he's looking to get serious. He loves his job and in his mind, the next thing that happens in life is a wife and family.

He's largely given up clubs and bars and has told me that he's now waiting for the right girl to come along.

Does he think that Brooke might be that girl?

Huh.

Well, Wyatt knows me pretty well. There's no way he thinks I'm going to let him flirt with and potentially date this girl without making a play myself.

Our bro code doesn't work the same as many others.

The three of us thrive on competition with each other. It makes the spoils *so* much sweeter.

We can make eating brats while watching hockey into a cut-throat contest. We definitely make things like poker an intense battle. We've been tossed out of three ax-throwing bars. We can be a legitimate menace.

But we've never actually competed over a girl before, other than fun flirtations at a party or something. The last time Wyatt and I were both into someone, we just ended up sharing her for the weekend.

That was a ton of fun.

But I'm guessing Wyatt isn't going to put a ring on a girl we double-team during a snowstorm.

So maybe I'll just test how into Wyatt Brooke really is.

I lean in closer to her and fill her glass with wine. Again. This is her second glass since we got here, and it's obvious she had been drinking before we showed up.

"I'm guessing Brooke is a hot pink center girl," I say.

She turns her head quickly to look at me. "Wh–what?"

I reach up and brush a tendril of hair that has escaped her bun back behind her ear. "Your steak. Medium rare, I'm guessing."

Her cheeks get pink as she studies my eyes, and then her gaze drops to my mouth.

Okay then. Yes, very interesting indeed.

"I don't eat a lot of steak, typically. So… whatever you guys want to give me."

Oh, fuck. My cock perks up a little at that and I can see Wyatt turn to look over at us out of the corner of my eye.

I hope she's submissive.

I'm surprised by the thought that flits through my head.

I don't need a submissive partner. That can definitely be hot, no question, but while I'll get dirty and a little bossy in bed, I'm no dom.

Still, with Brooke…fuck. It's the sweetness about her. Or the fact that she is slightly tipsy. Or that with her hair up in the messy bun, no makeup, and these baggy casual clothes, she seems much younger than her twenty-something. Or something.

She might be feisty as fuck. That's great too.

But I can't get the idea of ordering her around out of my head.

"How do you feel about loaded baked potatoes?" I ask her.

"I'm not sure I have any feelings about them at all," she tells me. The corner of her mouth tugs up. "How do you feel about them?"

I reach over to where her hand is resting on the countertop. I run my finger over the back of her knuckles. "I'm pretty into the excess in all things and will always vote for having *all* the extra goodies," I tell her. "I think that applies to everything from potatoes to life in general."

Her smile grows. "I could get into that philosophy."

I nod. "Yes, I really think you could, Brooke."

Her gaze drops to my mouth again, but comes back to my eyes quickly. "What do you do, Jackson?" she asks. "I know Wyatt and Luke are firefighters. But you're not, right?"

"I'm just rich, charming, and handsome twenty-four-seven," I tell her.

She laughs. "I can see why that might keep you busy."

"Lucky for me, all of those things come very easily, so I do have free time. Just so you know. If you would ever need me for anything."

Wyatt turns away from the sink where he's washing potatoes, but it's not him that pulls my attention. It's the loud *whack* of a knife against a cutting board.

We all look over to where Luke is slicing vegetables for the salad he's making.

"Got an especially *hard* cucumber there, Chief?" I ask him.

He's not looking at us, and he seems to be muttering to himself. "Are you going to be any help at all?" he asks me.

"I'm helping," I say. I grin at Brooke. "I'm entertaining our guest. You find me entertaining, don't you, sweetheart?"

Her lashes flutter, I'm sure involuntarily, at the endearment.

She nods. "I do. But..." She glances at Luke, then Wyatt. "You're really kind of *my* guests. It's my brother's cabin, and I was here first."

I grin. "That's true. I guess that means *you* need to entertain *us*."

She smiles at that, but blushes prettily. Very prettily. The pink flush on her skin is so damned hot.

I hear another sharp *whack* against the cutting board and I have to bite back a laugh.

This is definitely going to be fun. Not only can I flirt with Brooke and tease Wyatt, but I can drive Luke crazy, too. Win-win-win.

"He accidentally got rich and now spends his days fucking around," Wyatt says. He glances over. "That's what Jackson does."

Brooke's gaze comes back to me. "Accidentally? Did you win the lottery or something?"

I chuckle. "Kind of feels that way. I invented an app that took off. Sold it a couple of years ago for a lot of money." I shoot my best friend a look that I know he clearly reads as *game on* and then look back to her. "But I grew up in a working class family. Very normal. Bought my parents a house first thing after I hit it big. I also give a lot of money away to charity. Animals, kids, hospitals. You name it. I have a *huge*... heart." I pause and watch her smile grow. "But I do enjoy life. And if you would ever like to take a spontaneous trip to New York or really anywhere, I'll give you my number. I'll answer for you twenty-four-seven."

She looks at me for a moment, then starts laughing. "Has that ever happened?"

"What?"

"Have you ever said that to a woman, gotten her number, and then has she called you and you've whisked her off to Belize?"

I lean in, tracing my fingers over her knuckles again, and then up to her wrist. "I have never made that offer to another woman."

Her gaze drops to where my finger is rubbing little circles on the inside of her wrist. Her lips part. "Oh."

I love that the simple touch of my finger can take her from laughing to breathing a little faster. And I'm not *just* flirting. I've actually never made that offer to another woman. Even with the ability to charter a private plane on a whim, a trip to an exotic location is committing to at least a couple of days alone with the same person. "The only people I've ever whisked away anywhere are these two." The only two people I could imagine hanging out with for *days* at a time.

Until maybe now with Brooke.

She looks from me to Wyatt and then over to Luke. "I know Luke and Wyatt work together. How do you know each other?"

"Wyatt and I went to high school together. We've been friends since ninth grade. And I met Luke through Wyatt. We're the three musketeers."

I can't read the expression that passes over her face, but I really like her next question.

"So you all do a lot of things together?"

"Almost everything," I tell her.

"That's very interesting," she tells me, her voice softer now.

And I'm suddenly very interested in what she means by that.

Luke comes stomping over with a bowl full of greens and vegetables just then. He sets it down on the counter with a *thunk*. Then he leans over, grabs the glass tumbler in front of Brooke and turns to fill it with more ice water from the fridge. He sets it back down in front of her. "You need to drink more water," he says shortly.

She blinks at him. These are some of the few words he's said directly to her.

I don't know if she's noticed, but I have made a note of the fact that Wyatt and I have continued to fill her wine glass while Luke has been pushing water on her for the past hour.

"Thank you?" she says, though it comes out as a question.

Wyatt has slid the potatoes into the oven and has the steaks seasoned and sitting on a plate ready for the grill.

"I'm going to my room for a minute," Brooke says, sliding off her stool. When her feet hit the floor, she wobbles just a bit, and I catch her elbow.

I can't feel her skin through the thick sweater she's wearing, but I can feel her body heat. And when she looks up at me from this close proximity, I can't look away from her mouth.

So, maybe this isn't just a flirtation to tease my friends. Maybe this isn't just about finding out if Brooke is truly interested in Wyatt.

I would definitely take this girl to Belize and keep her there for a solid week. And I don't think we would actually see much of Belize outside of the hotel, as a matter of fact.

We all watch her leave the room.

As soon as the door shuts down the hall, I turn to my friends. "What the hell is going on?"

Luke hits me with a scowl. "I could ask you the same thing."

"Me? I'm the one being totally *normal*. I'm flirting with a gorgeous girl, who we're stuck with for the next two days."

"How am I not being normal?" Wyatt asks.

"You could turn it on a little bit more. I can tell you're interested in her. But you need to be more direct."

He narrows his eyes. "If you're interested in her, why do you want me to make sure she knows I'm interested?"

"It's her choice," I say, as if it's obvious. It is.

I would happily keep Brooke warm this weekend, but if she chooses Wyatt, good for him. Good for her too. No one knows what a great guy Wyatt is better than me.

"You're flirting with her to mess with me? Or do you like her?" Wyatt asks.

"Both," I tell him with a shrug.

"She's not a game of cornhole for fuck's sake," Luke says.

I can't help but laugh. "You *had* to choose a game with holes, didn't you?"

He glowers at me. "Not everything has to be a goddamned competition around here."

Wyatt and I both look at him.

I'm pleased when Wyatt says, "Why not?"

I nod. "She seems great. We're all stuck here together until Sunday, anyway. We want to get to know her. Why not see who can flirt with her the best?"

"How about you be her friend?" Luke asks. "Why do you both have to think with your dicks all the time?"

Wyatt is frowning, but I'm not taking this seriously. I lean in. "If you want in, Chief, just say so."

Wyatt's eyes narrow as he looks at Luke. "Wait a second, you might want in? You wanna flirt with her, too?"

"No. I fucking don't. She's too young, she probably wants a boyfriend and you both know I don't do that shit, and she's our friend's sister."

Yeah, he's given this *too* much thought for not being interested. "I barely know Blake," I say. I definitely don't consider the hockey player a friend.

Wyatt lifts a shoulder. "I mean, he's a good guy. But I'm not sure I would give up dating Brooke for him."

"So it's just out of the question that you're both gonna keep it in your pants?" Luke asks.

"Not out of the question," I say, looking at Wyatt. "If that's not what Brooke wants, we're not gonna push it. But that doesn't mean we can't make sure she knows she's got options this weekend."

Wyatt nods his agreement. "We'll just be with her. Maybe offer to cuddle if she gets cold." He gives me a grin.

I return that grin. I love our little games. "Exactly. Toast her marshmallows if she asks."

Luke gives a low growl.

"For s'mores," I say. "Obviously."

"Quit trying to get her drunk," Luke says, picking up her wine glass, taking it to the sink, and dumping it out.

"Hey," I protest. That feels like Brooke's choice to make, not his. "Let's not overreact. Neither of us is the type to take advantage of a girl when she's drunk."

Luke takes a deep breath, grips the edge of the sink and lets his head drop. Then he turns. "You're right. Sorry. I'm just a little—"

Brooke comes back into the kitchen, cutting him off. "You're just a little what?" she asks.

Luke just frowns at her.

I roll my eyes. Jesus, he needs *something*, or he's going to have an aneurysm by Sunday.

She looks confused. "Are you okay? Are you sick?" she asks him.

I snort. Her thinking Luke's grumpy face makes him look like he's sick is hilarious.

I know exactly what's wrong with Luke, and I'm guessing Wyatt does, too.

Luke has a thing for Brooke. Maybe a bigger thing than I thought.

But Luke doesn't think he should have a thing for Brooke.

And now Luke knows that he's stuck in this cabin watching his two best friends try to win over the girl he wants.

And here I thought the snowstorm was going to ruin our weekend.

CHAPTER 4

Wyatt

"I'M NOT SICK," Luke grumbles. "Just sick of these two assholes."

That makes me grin. I see what Jackson clearly sees—Luke absolutely is attracted to Brooke and wants in on flirting with her but he thinks she's a relationship type of girl.

Which she probably is.

Or maybe she's too busy with school for that right now, who knows? She *is* here alone on spring break studying.

I'm definitely willing to find out *exactly* what she wants.

Brooke stares at Luke a second longer, but he doesn't elaborate. She looks at me quizzically.

"Don't mind him," I say.

"He doesn't know how to go with the flow," Jackson adds. "Old bachelors are like that."

Jackson really loves to push Luke's buttons and waving his hand in dismissal of Luke right now is tantamount to waving a red flag in front of a bull.

Which is exactly his intention.

The game is more fun if all three of us are in on it.

Not that Brooke Wilder is a game.

More of a case of "may the best man win."

Usually, I would agree. But I don't exactly want more competition.

"Fuck off," Luke tells Jackson.

"I think you need to eat, Luke," Brooke declares. "My brother Blake always gets super hangry. When was the last time you ate? Here, have this."

Brooke, who I strongly suspect is a little tipsy, raises a baby carrot straight up to Luke's lips. His eyes darken and his shoulders go rigid. But when she eases it into his mouth, he flicks his tongue out and pulls the whole thing into his mouth, crunching hard.

"Thank you." His voice is gruff but softer.

Oh, yeah. Luke is melting like the butter I've brushed over our steaks at Brooke's concern.

I feel a ripple of alarm.

Jackson is just fucking with me. Is he attracted to Brooke? Sure. Who the hell wouldn't be? She's gorgeous and really damn sweet. But he's not looking for forever. He's not even looking for a relationship. He's just having a really good time and feels like there's plenty of time for settling down later after he figures out what he really wants long term. Which is fair. We're only twenty-eight. There's definitely time. And Luke is actively avoiding commitment because of the way his marriage ended a decade ago. I don't blame him at all. That was a total shit show.

Neither of them would want more than a hookup.

I'm a different story, though. I'm ready for more than meeting girls in bars or on an app and having casual sex. I want that special someone.

Brooke is exactly what I'm looking for.

So I'll be fucking damned if I'm going to let one of them get the jump on me.

She and I might not click. She might not want to date right now, but I'm going to at least make sure of both of those things before I tap out.

"Luke is right though," I tell Brooke. "You should drink more water and eat." I'm loath to leave these two alone with her while I grill outside, so I invite her to join me. "Want to be my grill master's assistant out on the deck?"

Jackson shakes his head at me. Luke gives me a glare.

I give them both a look in return that I know they interpret correctly: *I'm all in here.*

Brooke nods. "Sure."

We put our boots and coats on, then I take the tray with the seasoned steaks in my hand and head to the back deck. Brooke opens the slider door for me. When we step out, I suck in a sharp breath when a cutting wind hits me. "Damn, it's cold out here all of a sudden."

"It is Minnesota."

"Fair enough."

"It's snowing already," she says, looking nervously at the sky as I turn on the propane for the grill.

The back deck is a sweet setup with a built-in kitchen with a prep area and an overhang. "At least there's a roof over us out here."

"I'm worried about the storm. I have exams on Tuesday."

A glance over shows she's biting her lip and crossing her arms across her chest.

"We'll get you out of here, no matter what." I can't *actually* guarantee that but I'll do whatever is humanly possible to get her home on time. "Where do you go to school?"

"The University of Minnesota. I'm a third year vet student. I'm due to start my clinicals in a few weeks. Assuming I pass my finals."

"How confident are you on a scale of one to ten?" I ask, using tongs to drop the steaks on the grill.

"Nine point nine."

That makes me grin. "Then you'll be fine. That sounds like an amazing career. I love animals."

"Do you have any pets?"

"Nah. I would if I had a different job. But working twenty-four-hour stretches makes it way too hard. That wouldn't be fair to a pet."

"Unless it's a lizard or a snake."

"Exactly. But I much prefer the furry variety of pets. Dogs and cats. How about you—do you have a pet?"

She shakes her head. "No, for the same reason as you. I'm too busy. I'm really looking forward to clinicals for that reason. Lots of opportunities to soothe scared animals. I find that very rewarding. And healing them too, of course, if they're sick."

"I bet you're very soothing." I mean that sincerely, but my voice drops a little. Mostly from a growing desire I have to kiss her but also because the air is so still in this snowfall I don't want to interrupt nature.

She picks up on the tone. Her eyes lock on mine and then suddenly she turns around and steps out into the snow, lifting her head to let fat flakes drift down over her face.

I check the steaks and then join her. "This view is incredible."

It is. It's quickly transforming into a winter wonderland, with the wet snow clinging to the tree branches that surround us at every turn.

"It's beautiful. I love it here." Her tone is wistful and appreciative.

Her cheeks are pink from the cold, her breath coming out in tiny bursts of steam, her eyelashes coated with melting snow that she doesn't bother to wipe away. She turns to me and smiles. "If this keeps up, we can build a snowman."

I think, in that moment, I fall just a little bit in love with Brooke Wilder.

I'll build her a ten foot tall snowman if that will impress her.

"Hell, yeah."

Turning back to the steaks before they're overdone and Luke "I want it practically mooing" Moody hands me my ass for ruining his dinner, I grab the tongs.

The slider door opens. "Hey, guys?"

It's Jackson.

"Yeah?"

"The power just went out."

"What?" Brooke's head whips around and she peers at the suddenly dark house.

With our backs turned, we didn't even notice the lack of light.

Jackson barely has the door cracked and his head is crammed between the frame and the slider, as if that still isn't somehow letting a bunch of cold air into the cabin. "Yep. Flickered, went out, came back on for a hot second, then gone again. Does the fireplace work? Please tell me it's gas."

"It's wood-burning." She puts her hand on Jackson's chest and pushes him back inside. "You're letting all the heat out."

This cabin is easily five thousand square feet. There's no way a cabin this tricked out on an island in Minnesota doesn't have a generator. The fact that the electricity came back on for a second tells me that. I like machinery and tinkering and I have a talent for it. I feel reasonably confident I can solve whatever the problem is.

But as I follow Brooke inside and shut the slider behind me, juggling the platter of steaks, I think better of fixing it immediately. There is something romantic as hell about a roaring fire, a snowstorm, and dinner by candlelight.

Plus, we'll have to stay close to each other for heat. I can't think of anything I'd rather do right now than get under a blanket with Brooke.

"Great. So this is how I die," Jackson says, sounding incredibly unconcerned by that fact.

Luke snorts. "And why is that?"

"We have no heat. Brooke said it's a wood-burning fireplace."

"And Wyatt and I are firefighters. We know how to light a pile of wood." Luke has the flashlight on his phone on and it's providing a decent amount of light.

I set the platter on the kitchen island.

"We're city guys. We don't know how to survive. Our food is going to go bad. I better crack a beer while it's still cold." Jackson opens the fridge in the dark and rummages around, bottles clanking. Something falls on the floor but I can't see what it is.

"Take all the beer out and the rest of the food and put it on the deck," Luke tells him. "It will obviously stay cold out there."

"Brooke, do you have any flashlights or candles here?" I ask her, turning my own phone flashlight on.

"They're right over the refrigerator in that cabinet. I can't reach it though."

That makes me frown. What would have happened if Brooke had actually been here alone? The thought makes me agitated. I'm really fucking glad we got here early.

"Jackson, get the flashlights."

"I'm saving the beer first," he says, standing up with two six packs clutched against his chest. "Hang on."

Luke gives a huff of impatience and retrieves two flashlights himself. He turns one on and hands it to Brooke. He keeps the other one, flicking the switch, and then turning his phone light off.

"Let me start a fire, then we can eat," I say. "We don't want these steaks to get cold."

"Great idea," Luke agrees. "We can eat at the coffee table in front of the fireplace."

Brooke wanders away into the family room, setting her water down on the coffee table. Then she opens the fireplace flue and the glass door, efficiently beginning to lay a fire from the kindling in a basket on the hearth.

"Guess she's got the fire," I murmur to Luke, impressed.

"Guess so." He cuts open the baked potatoes he pulled out of the oven. "These probably aren't done yet but I guess they'll do." He shoots me a look. "Unless you want to take a crack at fixing the generator."

He's on to me.

"How do you know there's a generator?"

"Because I saw it when we pulled up. It's on the south side of the house."

"I'll look at it after we eat. I don't want my steak to get cold."

"Aren't you concerned that Brooke is worried?" His voice is still low, so she can't hear us.

"Does she look worried?" I gesture to her, squatting down in front of the fireplace. Her kindling is already lit, and she's building a log tower over it.

He shakes his head. "I don't know what the hell you and Jackson are doing, but I don't like it. She's way too young."

That makes me laugh. "For you, maybe. Not for me. And have you *looked* at her?"

"More than I'd like to admit."

I grin. "You just did. You *like* her." I'm both amused and a little threatened. Luke has that brooding emotionally unavailable crap going on that women scoop up like ice cream.

He's a real barrier to my plan.

So is Jackson because he's ridiculously good looking, charming, fun, and has bagfuls of cash.

I don't have what either of them does. But I do have a secret weapon—I'm a fucking nice guy.

Brooke seems like a girl who actually appreciates a nice guy.

Especially one who always makes sure his girl comes first. In and out of bed. It matters to me to take care of a woman's needs.

I carry two plates to the family room. Jackson has returned from his mission to save his microbrews and in a minute, we're all eating on the floor at the coffee table. Jackson is complimenting Brooke's fire building skills so effusively she's becoming uncomfortable. She said thank you the first two times but now she's giggling nervously.

"Just eat," I tell him when he makes a third comment.

"What? I'm impressed."

"So you've said. Three times."

"I don't know how to build a fire," he says, picking up his beer bottle.

"Then I guess you'll never win Survivor." I shove a piece of beef in my mouth. He's actually getting on my nerves.

Jackson eyes me. He's wearing a smirk. "My steak is overdone."

I ignore him. "Brooke, do you need anything? I'm going to grab myself a beer."

"No, I'm good, thank you."

"I need another beer," Jackson says.

I'm tempted to tell him to get it himself but I don't want to look petty or childish in front of Brooke. I'm also reluctant to leave her alone with my competition for more than sixty seconds so I retrieve one off the deck as quickly as possible. When I sink back onto the carpet in the family room, Brooke has pushed her plate away.

"I'm full," she says. "That was delicious, though."

"I'm done too." Jackson seems more interested in his drink and Brooke than his steak or salad.

Luke is the only one who's eaten every bite. He also does seem to be in a better mood. Brooke was right—maybe he was just hangry.

"We should push the sofa and a couple of chairs closer to the fireplace," he says. "Maybe we can watch a movie on my phone."

"That's a great idea," Brooke says. She holds her hands out to the blazing fire. "It's really not cold right here."

"Here," I say to Jackson, stacking plates and shoving them at him. "You clean up. Luke and I can move the sofa."

He doesn't protest. Probably because he doesn't enjoy physical labor. He'd rather throw dishes in the dishwasher than lift furniture. He takes the dishes to the kitchen.

Brooke adds more wood to the fire and Luke shifts the coffee table out of the way.

Five minutes later, we're all on the sofa single file, me on the left of Brooke, Jackson on her right. Luke has taken the outside seat, next to the end table. We pushed the sofa forward as much as we could, but I have to admit, the air is getting a little brisk in the cabin.

Brooke found candles in the linen closet so they're scattered around the room.

"The wind is really howling out there," Jackson says. He's put on a sweater and he tugs at the neckline to cover more of his bare skin.

A glance out the window reveals it's nearly whiteout conditions now. The gentle snow a mere thirty minutes ago has ramped up into a blizzard. Fixing the generator is going to be a complete pain in my ass now, so I'd better make this delay worth it.

"It's cooling down in here," Brooke says with a little shiver.

"Here," Luke says, grabbing a blanket from the basket next to the sofa. He spreads it out over me and then Brooke.

His hands brush over her thighs in the process and he yanks them back as if he was scalded. The man has it bad for Brooke, that's fucking obvious.

"I just realized we can't use the hot tub," Jackson says. "That sucks."

"The hot tub sounds amazing right now," Brooke says, rubbing her hands together and shivering.

I take her hands in mine. They're ice cold. I cup them and blow on her skin to warm her hands up. Her eyebrows shoot up and she shivers again.

"What should we watch?" Luke asks, scrolling through his phone. "A Cabin in the Woods?"

"Hell, no," Jackson says. "How about something that takes place in the city? Like Batman."

I let them debate several titles. I wrap my arm around Brooke's waist. "Still cold?" I murmur, leaning down so my mouth is close to her ear.

She shivers again and nods.

"Come here then. I'll warm you up."

I haul her right onto my lap and wrap my arms around her, pulling her back against my chest. Brooke gasps.

"Wyatt, I'll crush you…"

I snort. "Uh, no you won't. The firehose weighs more than you do and I haul that multiple times a week. Just relax back and we'll share our body heat."

She feels incredible tucked up against me, her tight little ass wiggling a bit on my lap. I already have a hard on and it's clear she feels it. She glances back at me, tongue flicking across her bottom lip. But then she faces forward again and relaxes into the hold.

"This is better," she says. "You're very warm."

I pull her long hair back over her shoulder, making sure to brush my fingertips against her jawline in the process. She glances back at me in question.

"Your hair was caught," I lie.

She sighs. It's a sexy sigh, not one of displeasure. "Thank you."

"How about Backdraft?" Jackson says. "The firefighters die in that one."

"Let's watch Fifty Shades of Grey," Brooke says.

"Great choice," I tell her.

Not because I care about some guy and his secretary—I think that's what it's about—but because it tells me Brooke is open to watching sex scenes with us. She's either comfortable or she's flirting.

Luke groans. "Please. No. Anything but *that*."

Jackson shoots me a grin. "We crashed Brooke's weekend. She gets to pick the movie."

"Thanks, Jackson." She smiles at him.

I tighten my grip a little on her waist and prepare to spend the next ninety minutes enjoying the feel of Brooke Wilder on my lap.

CHAPTER 5

Brooke

I DON'T KNOW if I'm proud of myself or horrified that I suggested Fifty Shades of Grey for our movie. How did *that* come out of my mouth?

Wine. I'm going to blame the wine.

Except that I'm sober right now.

Okay, I'm almost totally sober right now. I'm still a little sleep deprived and I've had more wine tonight than I have in months and I'm definitely feeling discombobulated by these three guys showing up and the snow storm and the power outage and everything, but I'm *mostly* sober.

Sober enough to know that watching *that* movie with *these* guys was a bad idea when I can't get to my room and my vibrator for at least a couple more hours.

I'm definitely all hot and bothered now and wishing I'd chosen a silly comedy instead.

Sitting on Wyatt's lap hadn't helped. Especially feeling his erection pressing against my ass the entire time. Not that I had any desire to move. I was very comfortable. His big body is hard all over—muscle on top of muscle—but he's so warm, and the way he wrapped his arms around me, his big hands resting on my thighs, his chin over my shoulder so our cheeks were right against each other made me feel safe and protected and, stupidly, cherished.

I mean, he doesn't *cherish* me. Of course not. That's ridiculous. But being wrapped up and held like that put that word in my head and I can't shake it loose.

It's how I hold scared dogs when they come into the shelter I volunteer at sometimes and how I cradled the three sick kittens my roommate and I found in college and nursed back to health in our dorm room before we had to find them permanent homes. Comforting. You're-special-to-me. I'll-take-care-of-you. All of that seemed to soak into me from his hold on me.

And yes, I'm aware that comparing myself to dogs and kittens probably isn't sexy or even flattering, but I *like* how Wyatt makes me feel and I want more of it.

More of the way his hands would stroke up and down my thighs from time to time. too.

More of the way he eventually shifted so that his hands were resting on my lower stomach.

More of the way his warm breath felt against my neck.

My nipples wanted that warm breath on them. So did my inner thighs. And my pussy.

More of the hard-cock-against-my-ass part, too. Or against other parts of me.

I shift on the cushion where Wyatt left me after the movie ended and he said he was going to take a look at the generator. I would really like to slip down the hall to my room for a little alone time and take care of this horny-as-hell problem I suddenly have.

"Are you okay?"

I look over at Luke. He's still in here with me on the couch, though the second—and I mean the *second*—the movie ended, he'd scooted away from Wyatt and I.

Wyatt had tried to get Luke and Jackson to both come out to look at the generator with him, but Luke had said he knew nothing about generators and Jackson said he didn't have the right boots for tromping around in the snow.

I actually don't believe either of them.

Luke oozes with competence and a take-charge air. He wanted to stay inside for some reason. And I don't think it's because he worries about the cold or snow. Firefighters battle fires in some of the worst conditions imaginable.

Which is so sexy. Whenever I look at Luke, I'm hit by a wave of *God, he's all man.* It's almost hard to look him directly in the eye. I wouldn't call what I feel intimidated exactly, but I can just *feel* how much more experienced and mature he is. I'm sure he sees me as a little kid and if he knew how attracted I am to him, he'd laugh. He'd consider it a crush and nothing more.

Jackson, on the other hand, isn't daunting at all. But he's clearly a flirt and just likes to ruffle feathers. Luke's, for sure. And mine, I think. He likes making me blush. He likes teasing me. But I don't completely buy the playboy persona.

Wyatt says he just fucks around and Jackson said that he's charming, good looking and rich twenty-four-seven, but I can tell there's more underneath all of that swagger. He's comfortable in his own skin. He clearly really likes Wyatt and Luke and has a meaningful friendship with them, and he didn't blink an eye about sitting cross-legged on the floor to eat at the coffee table.

I don't know many millionaires—my brother, who almost doesn't count because I've known him forever and he's a hockey player, not really a business-type millionaire, and now Jackson—but I don't imagine many of them sit on the floor to eat loaded baked potatoes. Jackson also casually played with my hair during the movie. It was hanging down over my shoulder on the side where he was sitting, and I felt a gentle tug at one point and found him twirling the end of a strand around his finger. But his eyes were on the movie. It was almost as if he didn't realize he was doing it. It was strangely sweet.

Still, Wyatt is definitely more my type. He's easy going and just so damned *nice.* He seems to be so aware of me and wants to take care of me without being overbearing. I thought he was going to kiss me out on the deck before the power went out and I'd *wanted* that. So much.

So yeah, if I was going to get intimately involved with one of these guys, it would definitely be Wyatt.

Though they all make my heart beat faster and my body feel more aware and jumpy than I'm used to.

"Brooke?"

Luke's deep voice pulls me from my thoughts and I realize I've been staring at him.

He leans in, a concerned frown on his handsome face. "Are you okay?" he repeats.

I nod. "Um, yeah." My voice sounds scratchy. "Yes. Sorry, just thinking. And I'm…" *Do not say horny. Do* NOT *say horny.* "Tired."

Luke's concerned look doesn't ease. "I don't want you going to bed until Wyatt gets the generator working. It will be too cold in there."

The four of us could snuggle together. Bet I'd be plenty warm then.

I scold my inner voice, who seems to be a bit overeager suddenly. "Right. Yeah, that's true." I force a smile. "I guess I could just sleep out here. By the fire."

Luke looks almost pained by that suggestion. But he nods. "Yeah. We're probably all stuck out here together if there's no power."

Wow, I imagine that's how he'd say 'we're probably all going to need a root canal'.

Jackson soothes my ego, though. "I call Brooke's couch."

I smile at him. "My couch?"

"Wherever you're gonna be," he says with a wink. "You can keep me warm."

I laugh. "Wait, I don't know if I want the pressure of keeping you from getting frostbite."

He grins. "No worries. I'm sure I'll be able to find nice warm spots to put any…extremities… that might be in danger."

I press my lips together as I feel tingles everywhere. Yeah, see, that flirty stuff is really easy for him, almost second nature. But there's also this part of me that wants to dig deeper and find out what's underneath all that charming fun stuff.

Not that charming fun is bad…

Luke makes a strange, low growling noise. "Knock it off."

I look over, and he's glaring at Jackson.

"Hey, you can take her other side," Jackson says. "I'll share. She's not very big, but I'll bet we can both find places to put our *extremities.*"

My tingles now sprout tingles. Because the extremities I immediately think of are *not* fingers and toes, and I'm certain Jackson's emphasis on that word was intentional.

And just when I was thinking that *Wyatt* was my type and Luke thinks I'm just a kid, I'm now imagining myself in a Jackson and Luke sandwich.

I'm suddenly not feeling cold at all.

Luke shoves himself up off the couch and paces over to the fireplace to poke at the fire that doesn't need poking.

"You want to go check on Wyatt and see how the generator is coming along?" Jackson asks him.

"No, I don't," Luke says shortly, his back to us.

I'm staring at his ass as he bends over. I'll admit it.

"He might need some help," Jackson says.

"Doubt it."

"Maybe another pair of hands," Jackson suggests. "I know *I* don't need an extra pair in here."

Luke turns and plants his hands on his hips. "If you're worried about Wyatt, why don't *you* go help him?"

"Because I'm afraid if I leave you alone with Brooke, you might bite her," Jackson says.

I'm watching them toss words back and forth, but I frown at that. Did he mean to say 'bite her head off'?

Luke's gaze finally comes to me and stays for a long moment. I feel my pulse drumming. Shouldn't he be saying something about *not* biting my head off? Or biting me at all?

"I'll be nice," he finally says.

Jackson smirks. "Well, nice is in the eye of the beholder."

Luke's eyes finally leave mine. "I'll be better behaved than you will be," Luke tells Jackson.

Jackson nods. "Oh, I have no doubt of that."

What is going on? There is definitely innuendo here that I'm sensing but not entirely picking up.

Suddenly, the lights flicker on and the hum of the heating system fills the room.

"Fucking thank God," Luke mutters.

"Hot tub!" Jackson says, his grin huge as he pushes up from the couch. He steps forward and holds out a hand. "Let's go."

"Oh, I…" I hadn't brought my swimming suit. I'd sat out in the hot tub the first night I was here, but I was alone, so I'd gone naked, of course. "We should wait for it to warm up, don't you think?"

Jackson reaches over and hauls me to my feet. "There was a lid on it, right? It hasn't been that long. It will be warm enough."

I guess I'll be wearing a bra and panties out there. Because honestly, sitting in the hot tub does sound amazing. Now that the blanket is pooled at my feet, it's *cold* in here.

"Okay," I say. "Let me grab some towels."

"Eureka!" Wyatt declares, coming into the room, grinning widely.

I can't help but smile at him. He's so cute. And it's definitely sexy that he can fix things like generators. I hate to think what I would have done if I'd been here alone, honestly. I could have kept the fire going, but no way would I have been able to do a thing to the generator.

"My hero," I tell him.

His eyes soften when he looks at me. "I like that."

He tosses his gloves and hat on the table, and shucks out of his coat. He's already taken his boots off. His fingers go to the button down flannel shirt he's wearing. As he begins to unbutton, my eyes widen.

Then Jackson strips his sweater off and the shirt underneath, leaving him naked from the waist up.

"Need any help?" Jackson asks me. "Zippers or buttons you can't reach?"

His grin is playful, and I grin back at him. "Um, nope. I actually need to go in and put more *on*."

"You can't wear clothes in the hot tub, sweetheart," he says.

"No, not clothes," I agree, gathering my sweater around my body. "But I need a bra." There—might as well just lay it out there.

"You don't *need* a bra," Jackson says quickly.

"You wear whatever you want," Luke says almost over the top of him.

I give Luke a smile. "Thanks. I'll be right back." I spin on my heel and head for my bedroom.

Yeah, it's freaking *cold* down here. I definitely don't want to sleep in here until it warms back up. So I guess I'm killing time with the guys for the next few hours. No vibrator time for a while, I think, casting a glance at my bedside table.

But the hot tub will be fun.

I'm shaking with shivers by the time I strip, pull on a bra and change my panties so they match the pale blue bra. I know better than to wear white.

Or I could…

Stop being like that! Jackson would be a one-night stand at best and Luke would find that one more reason to think you're ridiculous and be upset you're crashing the boys' weekend.

Wyatt would like it.

Yeah, well… maybe Wyatt and I will have time to explore each other's underwear after this weekend.

And with all of those thoughts straightened out, I wrap myself in the fleece throw from the bottom of my bed and pad out into the hallway and to the living room.

Where I find myself alone.

But I know exactly where they are. They're already in the hot tub. Which means I get to shed the blanket and climb into the tub in only my bra and panties with an audience.

You've worn swimming suits this same size, basically. Who cares?

But I do. Because I want them to care.

There. I said it. I'm very attracted to all three of them and even if nothing is going to happen between me and Jackson or me and Luke, I want them to wish it could.

That's normal. Probably.

I take a deep breath and cross to the door leading to the deck. I slide it open and step out.

And I'm not going to dawdle. The snow is still falling, and the wind is swirling around the house. Though the hot tub is in a protected corner with an overhang, the air around it is blizzard air.

"Ahh!" I shriek as the blast of cold hits me. I drop the blanket and run to the hot tub, practically launching myself over the edge and into the hot water.

Wyatt somehow catches me under my arms and hauls me up before my head goes under.

They're all chuckling, even Luke, and I grin up at Wyatt. "Thanks for the assist."

"My pleasure." He draws me close and sets me on the bench next to him.

He stretches his arm along the edge of the tub behind me.

I settle in, the water coming almost up to my chin, where it hits Wyatt at mid-chest.

I sigh as the warmth surrounds me. Yeah, this is nice.

We all just soak for a few minutes. I tip my head back, watching the snow swirl against the inky sky above us.

It's so quiet out here, it almost seems wrong to talk.

That doesn't stop Jackson, of course.

"Name three celebrities that you'd love to be snowed in with for two days."

Okay, good, a twenty-questions kind of thing. We can relax and get to know each other. Though these guys already know each other very well. I'd still like to know them better. I start thinking about my answer.

"Jenna Ortega, Yara Shahidi, and Danielle Bradbery," Jackson rattles off without waiting for anyone else.

I lift a brow. Wow, he really doesn't seem to have a type.

"Who is Danielle Bradbery?" Wyatt asks.

"Country singer," Jackson says, spreading his arms out to rest along the tub's edge. "Beautiful. Has this very sweet air about her."

He's looking directly at me as he says that.

"You do not listen to country music," Wyatt tells him.

"I listen to everything," Jackson says. "I have eclectic tastes."

I'm still trying to think of my three. I glance at Luke. I can't imagine the grumpy fire chief playing a game like this.

He catches my eye and says, "Gal Gadot, Catherine Haena Kim, and Stephen Colbert."

There's a beat and we all laugh.

And dang, he didn't even really seem to have to think that through either.

"I didn't realize Colbert was your type," Wyatt says.

"You said three celebrities to be snowed in with," Luke replies. "I think Colbert would be funny and interesting to talk to for two days."

Wyatt nods. "Agreed. And now I worry that your standards are higher than I realized and that we might be a disappointment."

Luke doesn't even hesitate before he says, "I worry about the same."

We all laugh again. Luke isn't smiling, but his expression is more relaxed and I like knowing he has a sense of humor.

I also note that the two women he chose are nothing like me. Stunningly beautiful, more curves, far more confident and bold—at least the characters they play are—sexy, and at least ten years older than me.

Got it, Luke. Loud and clear.

"How about you?" I ask Wyatt.

"Okay, Luke had a good point, so I'm going with Stephen King —he'd be interesting to talk to. Dan Levy—because he's Dan Levy, though I think he's way too cool for me—and Josh Johnson —comedian, absolutely hilarious."

I shake my head with a smile. "Not one single woman? Really?"

He lifts a hand and pushes my hair back off my shoulder. "Since I met you, I just can't think of any other women."

I know he's flirting and sweet-talking me and kind of kidding, but I like it. "Aw, well now I feel bad saying that I can't even narrow my list down to just three."

Everyone chuckles and I feel proud of myself. That was very flirtatious for me and the surge of adrenaline it produces is addictive.

Wyatt playfully narrows his eyes and wraps my hair around his hand, tugging me closer and tipping my head back. "Is that right?"

I give what I know is a very fake apologetic look. "Only *three*? When there's all of Hollywood and all the rock stars and don't get me started on the athletes."

Wyatt's gaze drops to my mouth. "Now see, you're just begging me to make you forget about *all* of those guys."

My breath catches in my chest. Yes, yes, I basically am.

"So veterinary school?" Luke asks. "Wyatt said you have exams coming up."

The mini-stare down between me and Wyatt is broken, and he smiles and lets my hair go, but he doesn't let me float away from him.

I clear my throat and think about what Luke asked me. "Yes. I'm a third year. I'll start my clinical rotations soon."

"Why veterinary medicine?" Luke asks.

This is a much easier conversation than choosing celebrities to be stuck with or thinking about how glad I am that I'm here with these three guys instead of anyone famous.

"I love animals," I say. "I was always a good student, excelled in the sciences, and students like that are often encouraged to think about medicine or other healthcare professions. The idea of working that closely with people every day was not appealing at all but then a friend had a dog get really sick and it occurred to me that I could do that."

Luke has watched me throughout my explanation with his typical intensity, and I find myself feeling a strange restlessness. But not an uncomfortable restlessness. This is like a pull to float across the hot tub, straddle Luke, and tell him all my secrets.

Not that I have many, but I feel like I could say anything and I'd be safe.

Geez. What the hell is that?

"How about you?" I ask, trying to cover up that Luke flusters me. "Why did you decide to be a firefighter?"

"Was fascinated with firefighters, fire trucks, all of that since I was a kid," he says.

I'm almost surprised that he answers me without hesitation and with full, complete sentences.

"I told my mom and dad I wanted to be a fireman when I was seven and I never changed my mind. Every birthday cake was a firetruck. They took me on a fire station tour where I got to meet firefighters and climb on the truck when I was ten and they got me a dalmatian puppy when I was twelve."

I am *delighted* by all of that. "Are you close to your family?"

He nods. "Yep. My parents are the best. Everyone still lives in Chicago."

I give him a big smile. I'm so glad he shared that.

I look at Wyatt. "How about you? How did you end up as a firefighter?"

"It's in the family," he says. "My grandpa, my dad, and my uncle, a couple of cousins."

"Wow." I love that too. "That's really cool. And they all live in Chicago?"

"Grandpa and dad and uncle. Cousins have scattered a bit."

I feel the relaxation washing over me. The water, the quiet night, these guys. It's all so *nice*. I'm really glad they showed up.

"So, how many times have you had sex in a hot tub?"

And the relaxation is replaced by tingles and heat just like that. I look at Jackson, waiting for him to answer. He winks at me.

"Twice," Wyatt answers.

"Probably four or five," Luke says.

I look at him with wide eyes. He chuckles and I think my panties might have just dissolved. Damn. I find him very hot when he's broody, but laughing? I'm on fire. And I don't think *that* fireman is going to put the flames out.

"I'm forty," he says. "I've had more hot tub experience."

So he has fifteen years on me. Probably twelve or so on Wyatt and Jackson. I guess he's been making good use of those years.

"And more experience in general, right Chief?" Jackson asks.

Luke shrugs. "Yeah, probably."

"How about you?" Wyatt asks Jackson.

"Twice. Once was with you."

My head turns so quickly toward Wyatt that I feel a little muscle spasm.

"Not *with* Wyatt." Jackson chuckles. "There was a girl there, too."

"Oh." I say that out loud, but my thoughts are now spinning. They've had hot tub sex *together* with a girl.

That's so… hot.

"How about you, Brooke?" Jackson asks. "How many times in a hot tub?"

Oh boy. So, the virginity thing is going to come up right away. Fantastic. I have not had great experiences with this. Some guys think "high body counts" are a turn-off, supposedly, but they also think virginity is some kind of defect. Or maybe it's just the guys I've chosen.

I haven't dated much. I haven't wanted to date much. And when I have, it's never really gone anywhere or lasted long. But the one damned time I liked the guy enough to take my clothes all the way off, I told him I was a virgin and I swear I've never seen anyone put pants and shoes on faster or lie more hilariously on his way out of my room. And out of my life.

"Oh, um… none. Never," I say. That's true. I've never had sex in a hot tub.

To my relief, Jackson takes that at face value. He nods. "You're missing out."

I'm starting to think he's right.

"How about in a tent?" Jackson asks the group. "I know we've got this gorgeous cabin in the woods this weekend, but anyone ever had camping sex?"

"Sure." Luke answers first, to my surprise. "But are you asking about sex while camping or sex in a tent?"

"What are *you* talking about?" Jackson asks.

"Well, camping in a camper or RV is also camping," Luke says. "Though tent camping is superior."

I do not agree with that at all, but I'm not going to say that. I want the sex answer.

"Okay, so both," Jackson says. "How many times have you had tent sex and then camping sex?"

Luke seems to be thinking—or counting—for a moment. "Six times and fourteen times. Maybe more."

Jackson whistles. "You like camping?"

"I like sex." His expression loses some of its openness. "Marci liked camping."

"Ah," Jackson says.

Who's Marci? Now I have to know.

"I've only got two," Wyatt says. "Both in a tent. Same camping trip, actually."

Jackson shakes his head. "None. Not a big camping guy. Unless it's like this," he says with a grin, moving his hand through the bubbly, warm water.

"Me either," I say before he can ask. "Never in a tent." I look at Luke. "Or an RV. Though that sounds better to me than a tent."

His jaw tenses and I regret my comment. I don't know who

Marci is but clearly she's a woman who makes Luke's grumpiness even worse.

"Okay, in front of a fireplace," Jackson says. "That one I've got three. No, four," he adds quickly with a grin. "Yeah, four."

I look at Wyatt and he looks like he's mentally counting.

"Two, maybe three," Luke says.

Jackson frowns. "Dude, you *have* a fireplace."

"So?"

"So why aren't you fucking in front of that thing all the time?"

"Because I have an amazing bed upstairs that's a lot more comfortable than the hardwood floor in front of the fireplace," Luke says.

Jackson shakes his head. "Okay. But beds are pretty basic."

Wyatt laughs. "Well, sometimes having a really soft surface is a plus."

Jackson laughs. "Okay, I hear you. I'm just saying a unique setting can make it more fun."

"Well, I'm boring, I guess," Wyatt says. "I think only once in front of a fireplace."

Jackson looks at me. "How about you?"

"Um, none."

He gives me a half-grin. "None again. So are you a traditional, vanilla, only-in-bed girl?"

Would that disappoint him? I'm not saying I am, but I'm curious if Jackson needs all those extras to be interested?

"If you need fancy settings, maybe you're not as into the woman as you think you are," I say. "Seems like if you're really into the other person, it doesn't matter where you are."

Jackson looks totally surprised. Then he grins. "Maybe, Brooke. Maybe. I would be very into testing that theory."

"So where is the most exciting place you *have* had sex?" Wyatt asks.

Here we go. I really should just put this out there. Get it over with. Put out any sparks between us before it goes too far, and he ends up disappointed.

I take a breath and focus on the bubbles in front of me instead of any of the men. "I've actually never had sex, so I don't know."

There are several seconds of quiet. No one even moves.

Then Jackson asks, "Wait, you've never had sex *anywhere*?"

I finally lift my gaze and look directly at him. "No. I'm a virgin."

Again, several seconds tick by without anyone speaking.

Then Jackson says, "Oh, okay, holy shit. I was not expecting that."

"Way to go," Luke mutters. Then he lifts himself out of the tub.

I'm relieved and disappointed equally to find that he's wearing boxers. He slicks the water off his face and stomps toward the house.

"I, uh…" Jackson blows out a breath. "I'm sorry, Brooke. I didn't mean to make you uncomfortable." Then he lifts himself up out of the tub too. He grabs one of the towels from the stack they brought out with them, sets it up on the edge of the tub and also retrieves the blanket I dropped just outside the door, draping it over the ledge close enough for me to reach. He gives me a smile. "I'll get the hot chocolate started."

I watch him disappear inside.

Then, with another deep breath, I turn to look at Wyatt.

He's watching me with a look on his face I can't decipher.

"I'm sorry we… got into all of that," he says.

"Don't be," I rush to assure him. "I wasn't uncomfortable. It was all just teasing. Good-natured. I know that."

He nods. "It was. I mean…" He runs his hand through his hair. "You're a gorgeous woman. We're all attracted to you. I'm sure that's not a shock. But we would never… expect anything… or want you to think…" He sighs. Then he meets my gaze directly. "We do like to flirt and tease. We, obviously, don't make a secret of it when we're drawn to a woman. But I don't want you to think that I… *we*… any of us… would ever pressure you."

Watching him stumble over all of this makes me realize two

things. One, Wyatt Doherty is a really good guy. And two, me being a virgin makes *everyone* uncomfortable.

"Thanks," I say. "And I know. I'm not uncomfortable," I repeat. "And I trust you guys. I'm inexperienced, but the flirting is fun. So, no worries, okay?"

He looks relieved. "Okay."

He hauls himself up out of the tub and then reaches for the towel and holds a hand out to me.

I rise out of the water and am absolutely *chagrined* when he diverts his gaze as I step out of the tub.

Ugh.

He wraps the towel around me, rubbing my shoulders briskly. Then he reaches for the blanket and also drapes that around my shoulders.

I pull it together in front of me and then we run across the snow covered deck.

Once inside, we all head to the bedrooms to dry off and change clothes.

And I opt for baggy clothes and a bra. Because obviously I'm not seducing anyone this weekend.

Being a virgin is such a pain in the ass.

CHAPTER 6

Luke

A VIRGIN.

Brooke Wilder is a *virgin*.

This has to be some kind of cosmic joke.

Thanks, Universe, for trapping me in a cabin during a snowstorm with the first woman in years I've been interested in and MAKING HER A VIRGIN.

Who wants to watch Fifty Shades of Grey.

For fuck's sake.

As if this weekend wasn't torturous enough, now I have the image stuck in my head that some guy—some random fucking asshole—is going to be the first man to be inside her tight and eager body.

It should make it easier to shut down all thoughts of her and to steer clear of any flirting. Because her being a virgin complicates *everything*. If she's waited this long to have sex, clearly she's waiting for The One. A relationship, marriage, forever.

None of which I can give her.

The thought of marriage should be like a bucket of ice water dumped over my head. And my dick.

Yet, it doesn't seem to be working that way. My brain is fixated on her. She laughs, I want to laugh with her. She smiles, I feel immense satisfaction that she's happy. She sat on Wyatt's lap and my dick got hard. Rock fucking solid hard. I wanted her on my lap wiggling that perky little ass on me and yet, weirdly, didn't mind that it was Wyatt enjoying wrapping his arms around her. At least I know he's a decent guy. He's a great option for her losing her virginity, to be totally honest. He'd be gentle, caring, romantic. Hell, they might end up falling in love and getting married. I wouldn't be surprised. She could do a lot worse than to have Wyatt be her first.

Unlike me, who likes it rough and casual.

Not that she asked my opinion about how and when and with whom she should lose her virginity.

I'm so lost in my damn thoughts, I realize I'm holding a shitty hand when it's time for the showdown in a poker round with the guys. I clearly wasn't bluffing well either because neither folded and I lost twenty bucks.

Brooke went to bed immediately after we got out of the hot tub. I think us scattering like cockroaches after her confession made her uncomfortable. I didn't mean to bolt. I just was in shock and I couldn't think straight. I had to get the hell away from her sweet smile and her nearly naked body, nipples tight in her pale blue bra.

I'd say I blame Jackson and his relentless flirting, but the truth is, we needed to hear she's a virgin. Anything any one of us was thinking before has to be viewed through a new lens. The virgin lens.

"Shit," I grumble, eyeing Jackson's straight. Not even a flush.

He shakes his head. "This is the worst I've ever seen you play poker."

"It really is," Wyatt says. "Maybe Brooke is right and you're getting sick."

"I'm not sick." Irritated, I shove my chair back. "I need to take a piss."

"Got it, Chief," Wyatt says.

He only calls me that outside of work when he wants to get on my nerves.

It works.

I go through the kitchen to the powder room, trying not to think about the fact that Brooke is sleeping in the main bedroom just a few feet away behind that closed door across from the powder room. I lean my forehead against the wood, wishing I could just beat some sense into my brain. What is happening to me? I hate feeling like this—distracted and wrapped up in a woman.

After my marriage to Marci ended in brutal fashion with a DNA test proving my newborn baby wasn't even my baby, I've steered clear of romantic entanglements. I have sex with women who want exactly what I want—a few hours of fun. Nothing more.

Never anything more, ever again.

It occurs to me that if Brooke opens the door I'm leaning on, I will have zero explanation for why I'm doing what I'm doing. Time to pull my shit together.

But that thought immediately evaporates when I hear something from inside her room.

It's a *buzzing* sound. It's soft, but very distinct.

I rear back, horrified.

Then immediately lean back in again, fascinated.

Maybe it's an electric toothbrush or… I can't think of anything else a woman would have that buzzes.

Except a vibrator.

Is she in bed, legs apart, using a vibrator to pleasure herself?

Yes. Yes, she is. Because holy shit, she's *moaning now.* There is no other explanation for what's happening.

Adjusting my dick in my jeans, I try to walk away, but my feet stay firmly planted on the floor right outside her door.

She's panting a little, a sweet soft sound that shreds my resolve to stay the hell away from her. For a split second, I reach my hand out to knock, but then I yank it back instantly. This girl does *not* want me interrupting her fun.

Also, if you play with fire, you'll get fucking burned.

If I knock and she actually invites me in, we'll both wind up a pile of ashes.

She's a nice girl and I'm… not available.

A guy like me has no business taking that sweet girl's virginity. Or anything else from her.

I'm being an asshole. This is a private moment.

But then the vibrator gets louder and faster. Damn, it's like she *wants* someone to hear her. The high whine of the toy still doesn't cover her moans, though, which also seem to be getting louder. I should turn around and go back to the table. That's the appropriate and polite thing to do. I'm forcing myself to turn when I hear her peak with a beautiful cry.

"Oh, God!" she says.

The vibrator goes silent.

Oh, God is right.

Walk away, Moody, fucking walk away.

She gives one last sigh of satisfaction.

I step back carefully, grateful I'm in socks, and praying the damn wood floor doesn't creak. I don't even bother going to the bathroom. My dick is too hard.

Back in the family room, Wyatt is tossing peanuts in his mouth and Jackson is scrolling through his phone.

"I can't believe we can't get cell phone reception here," he says for the fifth time tonight.

"Maybe it's the storm," Wyatt says, also for the fifth time. "I was able to text earlier."

"You should be able to go one night without your damn phone," I snap, stomping to the fridge to grab a beer.

I've barely drank tonight but I feel hot and thirsty. I pop the top off with a bottle opener and chug half of it in one giant gulp. I set it down, gauging if I feel better.

Nope.

Still hot and thirsty.

"What is your problem, seriously?" Wyatt asks when I return to the dining table. "You've been off all night. Does it really bother you that much that Brooke is unexpectedly here with us for a guys' weekend?"

"Yes," I bark.

"Come *on*," Jackson says. "She's so sweet. She's absolutely no bother."

"She's bothering me," I say.

"How?" Jackson says, clearly astounded. "I think she's a little scared of you. She is not going to get in your way."

I fucking want her in my way. Very in my way.

"I just heard her masturbating," I blurt out.

I can't keep it inside. They need to share the horror with me of knowing that in spite of her little mic drop in the hot tub, Brooke is clearly sexual, clearly horny, and clearly not someone I can touch. At all.

Wyatt's jaw drops.

Jackson falls back into his chair. "Are you serious?" he says, and his voice is low, intrigued.

"Yes." I glance toward the hallway, keeping my voice low. "There was no mistaking it. Vibrator, moaning, climax."

"You just stood there and listened?" Wyatt demands. "Jesus fuck, Luke."

"It went very fast," I say in my defense, pacing back and forth. "It doesn't take much to get her off, apparently."

That gives us all pause as we each reflect on a woman who comes quickly.

The silence lasts a good thirty seconds.

"I..." Wyatt starts to speak, then doesn't seem to know what the hell he was going to say.

Jackson's mouth splits into a grin. "Well, *that's* a fun fact about our sweet little roommate."

"No," I say, sharply, pointing at him. "You heard her. She's a virgin. That makes her off-limits."

"Put your finger down," Jackson says, annoyed. "Off-limits to you, maybe. Why does that make her off-limits to me?"

I didn't really expect push back. "Because she's not the kind of girl you just fuck on vacation. She's a virgin. She has expectations."

"Oh, so now you're psychic? You know what she's expecting?" He sits forward again. "I like her. She's smart, she's beautiful. I wouldn't just *fuck* her."

"I want to *date* her," Wyatt says. "I think she's incredible."

I'm both pleased by that and jealous as fuck. "She is incredible," I agree. "Which is why she's off-limits."

"To you," Jackson repeats.

He's right. I'm the one who said it. But I want to hear why he thinks it's true. "Why is she off-limits to *me*?"

He tilts his head. "You're the one who said she is."

"But why?"

"Man, what are we even talking about here? You sound crazy right now."

"I think I am crazy." I run my hands through my hair. "But didn't it freak you guys out that she said she's a virgin?"

"A little," Jackson admits. "I don't think I've ever had any sexual contact with a virgin. Even when I was a virgin."

"Right?" I plunk down in my chair. "There was nothing shy about my high school girlfriend."

"I think it's sweet," Wyatt says. "Plus, it's sexy as hell to know that you can show a woman how amazing sex can be. Help her figure out what she likes and needs. That's pretty damn cool."

He means it. He has a look on his face that is calm and confident. He raises his beer to his lips.

"Wyatt, I think you should be the one." I nod my head firmly. "This is the best solution. You should be the one to take her virginity."

Wyatt sprays beer all over the table. "What the fuck?" He swipes at his mouth. "You don't even know she wants to lose her virginity!"

"Oh, I think what I heard is confirmation she does."

Okay, that's not fair. A woman can use a vibrator, her fingers, whatever she wants on her own body and it doesn't necessarily mean she wants to involve anyone else. She didn't know I was listening. It's not like she was doing that to entice me.

But I can't say out loud that I want to control how and with who it happens because I realize that sounds controlling and, well, insane, but I can't help it. I'm going out of my fucking mind thinking about some idiot twenty-something guy not giving two shits about Brooke's pleasure.

Wyatt stares at me, hard. "You're serious."

"As a heart attack."

"Okay, I'm in."

"What the fuck is wrong with you two?" Jackson asks. "How about you let Brooke decide who she wants to get naked with? Maybe it's neither of you. Maybe it's some guy at school. Maybe it's *me*."

"She just met you," Wyatt says.

"So? You don't know what she wants, if anything. You sure in the hell don't know *who* she wants."

I think about it for a second. Then I turn to Wyatt. "I think it's you."

Jackson throws a beer cap at me. "You didn't hear a word I said."

"I heard everything you said." I snag a peanut from the bowl on the table. "You're right. Brooke *obviously* needs to decide for herself. I didn't mean she doesn't. I just think that if she's interested in having sex, it's better it's one of you two than some random guy we don't know. What if he's an asshole to her and breaks her heart?"

"Or is selfish during sex," Jackson nods. "I get what you're saying." He turns to Wyatt. "We're definitely the best options for her. So turn up the heat. Flirt harder with her."

That makes me feel better in a way I don't care to reflect too deeply on.

Wyatt nods. "I can do that."

"I will too," Jackson says. "Let's give the girl options."

"We have to be very clear about our intention," Wyatt warns. "But no overwhelming her. And whatever she decides, we're all cool with it."

"Deal."

"Deal," I agree. "Now deal the next hand."

This game just got more interesting.

CHAPTER 7

Jackson

"GOOD MORNING," I say, giving Brooke a warm smile as I enter the kitchen. I've chosen not to get dressed, but am still in my lounge pants with no underwear and a white T-shirt.

My sister told me about the gray sweatpants love some women have. She said it's the male equivalent of a sundress. It gives a preview for any interested parties.

I want Brooke to be interested. Curious. Flirtatious.

"Good morning," she says, returning the smile from her stool at the island. Her eyes dart below my waist and her cheeks turn a delightful pink color. She immediately raises her mug to her mouth to hide her expression.

I fight the urge to grin.

"There's coffee or I can make you some tea," she says. She's already put a bra on under her sweatshirt, much to my disappointment.

"I'll have coffee, thank you, sweetheart."

Luke is sitting three stools away from her at the island. A glance in his mug as I cruise past shows he's drinking black coffee. He has a piece of bacon and two eggs on his plate in front of him. "You cooking for everyone?"

"Brooke said she isn't hungry."

"I'm hungry." I head for the coffeemaker.

"There's the stove."

I don't actually expect anyone to cook for me. It's just entertaining to bait Luke. "Where's Wyatt?"

"Probably still sleeping." Luke sips his coffee. He's fully dressed in jeans and a flannel shirt.

If Luke has been this short with Brooke too, she's probably dying for Wyatt to get up. Guess it's up to me to entertain her because Luke certainly isn't trying. Now that I know how he feels about her, though, I know exactly what his issue is. He's fighting the urge to push Brooke against the nearest wall and kiss her senseless.

Which makes me wonder how she would react to that.

I sense she wouldn't object in any way. She keeps darting glances over at him like he intrigues her.

"Do you hear that?" I ask as I press buttons and wait for the coffee maker to do its magic. "What is that?" The sound has just started, but it sounds like *something* walking around on the deck. Not a person. More like a creature. I turn and peer toward the sliding door.

If I see a Sasquatch, I'm going to be really damn excited.

The snow has stopped, and the sun is shining, causing a blinding glare off of the snow that is piled a good twelve inches on the deck. I see a blur of fur pacing back and forth rapidly. "Is that a dog?"

Brooke turns. "Oh! That's the neighbor's dog, Henley. She likes to pop over and say hi. She's so smart that she knows a car in the driveway means someone is home."

She's already standing up to go to the door.

"What kind of dog is she? A Lab?" I love all dogs, but I have a true fondness for Labs. I follow her to the slider.

Brooke is yanking it open and Henley tumbles in, tossing snow up in the air with her snout on her way through the door. Brooke laughs. "Hey, girl. Hi, how are you?" She scratches her behind her ears and bends down to give the dog a kiss on the head.

I reach out to pet her as well, but Henley whines and skitters away. "What's wrong? Don't like strangers?"

"She loves everyone," Brooke says, squatting down to cup Henley's snout with both hands. "Hey, what's the matter?"

I shut the door. Suddenly, Brooke is running her hands down Henley's flank and over her belly, her expression one of concentration. The look alarms me. "What's wrong?"

The dog is shivering, panting, and moving anxiously in Brooke's arms. She's whining again. I can't imagine she's cold because Labs generally love being outside in all weather.

"Um…Henley is pregnant. And I'm pretty sure she's in labor."

"Right now?" I ask, astonished. "Oh, shit! What do we do? Can you call her owner?"

"I'm not dragging her back across the yard. We don't even have a leash and I don't want her running off in a panic. She's only two, so this is probably her first litter. She's nervous."

Suddenly, I'm nervous too. "So, how do we help her?" I bend down and run my hand over Henley's coat. "Hey, sweetie, it's okay. You've got this, girl. Brooke is here to help you." I trust she's in very capable hands.

Brooke is examining Henley carefully from head to tail. "We need a whelping box for her. A safe place for the delivery."

Wyatt comes down the stairs, his hair damp from his shower. "What's going on?"

"We're having puppies," I tell him.

"What? Oh, my God. That's…amazing." Wyatt grins. "Whose dog is this?"

"The neighbor's," I tell him.

Luke has stood up and joined us. "What kind of box do you need?" he asks.

"Something big enough for her and the puppies that we can line with towels," Brooke says, her eyes still on the dog. "I wish we had a dog bed or a kennel but we're going to have to improvise."

"How about my suitcase?" I ask. "It's pretty big."

"It's *absurdly* big," Luke tells me.

"Or the boxes we carried the food in," Wyatt says. "I could cut off the side and tape a few together."

"We don't want to ruin anyone's luggage. The boxes would work," she says. "Jackson, can you get some towels while Wyatt does that?"

"Of course."

Luke has gotten on the floor beside Brooke and Henley with a blanket from the basket by the fireplace and is gently drying her snow dampened fur off.

I jog up the stairs to the bathroom in my bedroom while Wyatt goes into the kitchen to retrieve the boxes. When I come back downstairs with half a dozen towels, Wyatt is already using a pocket knife to splice the sides off of four boxes. Brooke has Henley leaning against her. There's fluid on the floor.

"Did she have an accident?"

"That's vaginal discharge from the contractions. She's in really advanced labor."

I'm not sure I'm ready for this, but I guess I'd better be. "How advanced?"

"A puppy should be here any minute. No more than an hour."

I feel a little queasy as I take in the scene, but I still ask, "Shouldn't she lay down?" I don't even know why I ask that. It's not like I've seen any animal or human give birth other than in movies and on TV. They usually make it seem very dramatic but Brooke looks completely calm and even Henley seems to have settled down.

"She's fine until the box is ready."

I head to the kitchen to grab some paper towels to clean the floor, digging under the sink for some wood cleaner. I find what I need and get to cleaning up the mess.

"Thanks," Brooke says, giving me a smile. "You didn't have to do that."

"It's not a problem. My mother taught me how to clean. She always said she was raising her future daughter-in-law's husband, not a son."

Brooke laughs softly. "I like your mom."

"Me too. She's a great woman." I look out the back door. "Where do the neighbors live? Why would they let this dog out if she's in labor?"

"They must not have realized she was having contractions."

I'm not sure how they could have missed Henley's anxiety. I feel a little judgmental about that but I keep my mouth shut.

"I think this will work." Wyatt and Luke carry over a cobbled together box and set it down next to the fireplace.

"That's perfect." Brooke nods in approval. "Great improvisation."

The sides are secured with duct tape, and when they set it down, I unroll the towels and start laying them inside.

"Do we need to know anything?" Luke asked. "I've never seen this with a dog."

Luke's expression is stern, his face white.

Shit.

Wyatt and I exchange looks. We both know what he's thinking about.

Marci. His cheating ex-wife who let him go through a whole pregnancy, and labor and delivery thinking her baby was his only to have her lover show up at the hospital demanding entrance and a DNA test. It was obviously traumatizing and I can tell he's trying to ignore the feelings it's pulling up.

"Lab litters are big, anywhere from five to twelve puppies, but a first time mom usually has a litter on the smaller side. They'll come every fifteen minutes or so, and Mom will chew off the umbilical cord. We just need to make sure the little guys are all breathing and that they suckle and that the number of placentas that pass matches the number of puppies. We'll need to change the bedding periodically but without disturbing Henley anymore than we have to. But mostly we monitor and she does the work."

I'm impressed with how soothing and calm Brooke is. She helps Henley into the box and encourages her to lie down. I decide to go get her tea and reheat it in the microwave. I bring it over and set it on the fireplace hearth.

"Here you go."

"Thanks. Can someone go look in the linen closet for a heating pad? I think my grandmother keeps one in there. I doubt Blake would have gotten rid of it since he bought the house."

"Sure." Luke is off at a fast pace, clearly needing a task.

"What happens to all those placentas?" I ask, thinking about a half dozen puppies being born and the afterbirth just being... there.

"Henley will probably eat them."

"Holy fuck." I feel my stomach flip.

I turn and go and retrieve my coffee that brewed fifteen minutes ago and take a sip. It's only lukewarm but I don't care. I was going to make breakfast but I've definitely lost my appetite.

Wyatt is laughing at me. "You're not going to faint, are you?" he asks, scraping ash out of the fireplace from the night before.

"No, of course not." I don't think. But me and blood? We're not the best fit.

Henley is licking herself very loudly.

I'm not a huge fan of that either but I just grimace and take another huge gulp of my coffee. Brooke is holding her glass tea mug between her two hands and takes a delicate sip. She looks gorgeous right now, her eyes sharp and intelligent, her gaze firmly on the laboring dog. Her neck is long and graceful and I focus on it so my stomach will stop twisting, fantasizing about kissing along the length of that smooth swath of skin.

"Can I get you anything to eat?" I ask her.

"I'm fine for now. I don't usually eat breakfast."

"That's no good," Wyatt says, reaching out and massaging the back of the very neck I was just imagining touching. "It's the most important meal of the day."

She shrugs. "I don't like to chew first thing in the morning. Where did I put my phone? I should text the neighbors and let them know what's going on. They might be out looking for Henley by now."

Let them look, in my opinion, but I saw her phone on the island, so I just go and retrieve it. She takes it and scrolls, then taps out a text. Then she sets her phone down on the hearth and stands up. "I need to go wash my hands, just in case."

"What happens if something happens while you're gone?" I ask, suddenly panicked.

"I'm just going to the kitchen. Let me know if you see a tail instead of a head, otherwise everything should be fine."

I brave a glance at Henley but I don't see anything other than her pink belly, thank God. I look at Wyatt, but he's set a pile of wood and is now lighting the fire. I squat down and look Henley in the eye. "You're good. I'm good. Everything is good here," I murmur.

She stares at me with soulful brown eyes that melt my damn heart. Her tongue is hanging out, and she's panting, but otherwise she seems chill now. Mom mode activated.

But then I see a burst of fluid and a white… something coming out of her. I slam my coffee down on the floor and yell, "Brooke, something is happening!"

She comes running over with a stack of hand towels.

"Is that right?" I ask her. "Is it supposed to look like that?"

"Yes, that's normal. Puppy is on her way."

I let out my breath and put my hands on my head. "Shit. Okay. Cool." Then I realize the box is only a few feet from the fireplace. "Luke, close that door already. I don't want any sparks popping out."

He does obediently but he also says, "It's five feet. I think it's okay."

"I feel like this should be a more sterile environment." Mostly

I'm just talking because I'm afraid to look at Henley. But then I look because I don't want to miss this. When am I ever going to see puppies being born?

That's exactly what I see. A tiny damp puppy. Henley turns her head and licks the newborn.

"Holy…"

"There we go," Brooke says encouragingly. "Good job, Henley. You're doing amazing."

I'm honestly in awe. It's astonishing how Henley knows exactly what to do.

"Whoa," Wyatt says. "That's incredible. Look at how tiny that little guy is."

"Oh, another one is coming. Let's get this one out of the way." She retrieves the puppy and wraps it in a towel, rubbing its fur dry. "It's a boy. Here, Jackson, just run your hand down his fur to encourage him to breathe and cry."

Suddenly, I'm holding a micro Labrador puppy in a kitchen towel with mushrooms printed on it and it weighs next to nothing. I run my hand down its tiny length, a little overwhelmed at how small and adorable it is. His little head is the size of a chicken nugget. I pet him gently down his back again, drying him off with the towel. The puppy gives a mewling little cry that kicks me in the gut. "He's crying now. We're good."

I cradle him against my chest and decide right then and there once this puppy is weaned, he's mine for the rest of time. I don't care if Henley's owners have promised him to someone or they're going to sell him. I'll pay ten times their offer. I'm fucking in love with this dog.

There's immediately another puppy and Brooke hands him to Wyatt, who looks as enamored as I feel. Then Brooke holds her hands out to me. "Let me give him back to Henley for a minute. There should be a twenty-minute break or so before there is another one."

I'm reluctant to give this pint-sized piece of perfection back, but I do. Henley starts licking the puppy and seems more relaxed.

"Can you go get Henley some water?"

"Sure." Hopefully I miss the whole placenta thing.

"That one is a girl," Brooke says, pointing to the puppy Wyatt is cradling in a cloth.

"She's adorable," Wyatt says. "And Brooke, you're so incredible right now. You're going to be an amazing vet."

"Thanks." She smiles at him as I walk away and I see it—the way they look at each other. With clear affection.

I'm not *exactly* jealous.

More like I'm picturing me behind her and Wyatt in front of her and we're *both* kissing on her. Which would probably overwhelm her on every level. I need to focus on what Brooke needs, not what I want.

I need more coffee. But first I get the water for Henley, wondering if I need to go check on Luke. He's been gone a long time and I know he's in his head right now. But when I'm holding the bowl in front of Henley and she laps a little, he reappears, heating pad in hand.

"Sorry. I had to dig." He bends down and plugs it into the wall without looking at any of us.

"You missed the first two," Brooke tells him. "A boy and a girl."

"No kidding." He glances in the box. Then his expression softens. "Well, damn. Look at that."

"Both Henley and Brooke are actually rock stars right now," I tell him.

"I can see that." Luke squats down and rubs Henley behind the ears. "Good job, girl."

"If you rub my head next, I won't object," Brooke says with a smile.

Luke ignores that.

Her smile falters.

Wyatt leans over and ruffles her hair a little. He clearly means it to be flirtatious and compensate for Luke, but she doesn't react much to his touch. I don't exactly know what to make of that but maybe she's just concentrating on Henley.

We spend the next five hours on the floor by the box, playing cards, snacking, and casually chatting. Henley has three more puppies and Brooke says she thinks she might be done.

"Three boys and two girls." Brooke shifts the boy we've named Tank—because he's way bigger than the other four—away from Henley. "Tank is hogging. We need to let the little guys feed first."

I've named my puppy Nugget. Wyatt named the first girl born Licorice and Brooke the third boy Henry, because she said he looks serious. We're all hanging back waiting for Luke to name the other girl but so far he's kept his mouth shut. He seems to be enjoying this more than I expected, though, so that's good to see.

"I should take Henley outside to go to the bathroom and we should change out the box bedding while she's going potty."

"I can do that." Wyatt is practically falling all over himself to be helpful to Brooke.

I'm fighting the urge to cradle Nugget. Instead, I go one better and pull Brooke in for a hug. "Great job, Dr. Wilder."

She laughs and hugs me back. "Thanks. I had amazing support staff. Henley did all the hard work, though."

Wyatt also hugs her, before she bends down to help Henley up and out of the box.

Once they're out on the deck, I sit down to just watch the puppies, who are wriggling and making noises of discontent. I adjust the heating pad that is wrapped in a towel.

"Hey, you okay?" I ask Luke.

He nods. "I'm fine."

"You sure?" Wyatt has taken a few steps in the direction of the stairs to get more towels, but he pauses.

"Yes." He gestures to the back deck. "Looks like the neighbor is here."

A man is down on his haunches, petting Henley.

"Just the man I want to talk to," I say. "Luke, watch the puppies."

"Don't be a dick," Luke tells me.

"That's classic coming from you. I just want to tell him this little family is all staying here until we leave. That's all."

"Brooke has probably already told him that."

"Then I'll let her know I have her back."

I yank open the sliding door.

CHAPTER 8

Wyatt

I'M PRETTY sure I'm falling in love with Brooke Wilder.

I really liked her the first time I ever met her.

Her sweetness over the past day we've been together has only made me like her more.

But watching her with the dog and puppies?

Stole. My. Fucking. Heart.

She was caring, but commanding when needed. Her confidence and intelligence shone, and kindness just emanated from her.

How is this gorgeous creature a virgin?

No, that is not the most important thing about her. Of course not. But it's *very* fucking hard to stop thinking about.

Yeah, she's a little quiet and shy, I suppose. But God, the way she responds to our flirting, and the way she snuggled into me when I put her on my lap during the movie last night, and the fact that she even has a vibrator and that she openly used it just down the hall from our poker game, makes me think that she has some needs that could use a guy's touch... no, could use *my* touch.

Not just any guy. Not any *other* guy.

Me.

Brooke Wilder should be mine, and I'm going to make sure she knows that.

She can tell me no. She can choose Jackson. Or someone else entirely.

But I'm not giving up easily.

I want her. And not just for this weekend.

Now I just have to figure out how to let her know that.

Satisfied with the state of the fire I've been tending all day, I straighten and turn just as Luke and Jackson both come into the living area. Luke hands Brooke a bottle of water before settling into the armchair perpendicular to where she's curled up in the corner of the sofa.

She has showered and dressed in another pair of comfortable lounge pants and an oversized sweatshirt. These pants are more like leggings, so they fit against her more tightly than the sweatpants from last night, but the shirt hits her mid-thigh and covers her curves.

Her hair is pulled up on top of her head. She's not wearing any make-up. And she looks completely content. A little tired, but also satisfied.

She should. She was magnificent with the dogs.

During dinner—spaghetti with marinara meat sauce, salad, and garlic bread, one of Luke's specialties—we took turns checking on the dogs, but now they're quiet and settled, secured safely in the makeshift box, which we moved to the laundry room so that Henley would feel secure. Though I know that's where Jackson just came from. He's enamored with the dogs. It's pretty cute.

I take a step toward the sofa, planning to settle next to her, but Jackson beats me to it.

"The patients are all sleeping, Doc," he tells Brooke as he effortlessly scoops her up, moves her over slightly and slides in between the arm of the couch and her curled-up body.

She laughs lightly and settles back in against his side, his arm draped around her shoulders.

I scowl at him. He just grins up at me over her head.

Okay, fine. We both agreed we were going to turn up the flirting.

I take the cushion right next to her, my hip pressing into her opposite side. I reach for her stockinged feet and pull them into my lap. Now she is partially draped over both of us.

She doesn't protest, so I press my thumb into the arch of one of her feet, stroking through her sock.

She gives a happy sigh.

Jackson starts rubbing one of her shoulders. "You're pretty hot when you get bossy," he tells her.

She giggles, and the sound shoots straight to my cock.

"Well, that's too bad," she says. "I'm almost never bossy."

"I'm jealous of every veterinarian and tech and volunteer who will ever work around you," Jackson says. "Obviously, you'll get bossy when an animal needs you."

She looks over her shoulder at him, giving him a little smile. "Yeah, I guess so."

The look of pride on her face grips my heart.

"I'm really pissed at your neighbors," Jackson says. "I can't believe they weren't watching her more closely. I don't want them to have Henley back." His voice is tinged with anger.

Brooke looks at him again, her expression soft.

Oh hell no, Jackson's not going to win her over just because he has an obvious soft spot for this dog. I love dogs too.

"We always had dogs when I was growing up," I say. "Can't imagine not knowing where our family pet was at all times. Especially if she was pregnant." I look at Jackson and weigh my next question for a moment. But me and my best friend compete in everything. And this time the prize is this wonderful woman. "How many pets did you have growing up, Jackson?" I ask.

Over the top of Brooke's head, he gives me a look that says clearly he knows what I'm doing. And he will find a way to get me back for it.

"Never really had pets. A hamster once."

Brooke's eyes widen. "You didn't have pets? Your family doesn't like animals?"

"My sister was allergic," Jackson admits. "I think that's why I love them even more," he adds. "I can't wait to have some of my own."

Brooke shifts on the couch so she can see him better. Her calf drags over my lap, and I am certain she can feel my erection. The one that's seemingly constant now that I'm sharing a space with her.

She doesn't react, though.

Well, hell, maybe the girl just thinks that's what size I always am. I don't know much about virgins, but I assume it means they haven't had a lot of experience touching or looking at cocks.

And now I'm thinking about Brooke and my cock and that isn't helping the hard-on in my sweatpants at all.

"Why don't you have pets now?" Brooke asks Jackson.

"Can't have them in my apartment," he says.

"But you're a millionaire, right? You could easily buy a house."

She's looking at him, so I'm able to send him a smirk. Score: Wyatt-1, Jackson-0.

"You know what?" Jackson asks. "That is a really good point. How long till those puppies can leave their mom?"

Brooke arches both eyebrows, and I feel my gut clench. Oh no, he wouldn't…

"At least six weeks."

Jackson nods. "Six weeks is more than enough time to buy a house."

My friend would buy a house so that he can adopt dogs to impress Brooke?

But it makes me want to laugh because that is very Jackson, actually.

And fuck, I can't blame him. This woman is absolutely worth it.

"You're going to buy a house for those puppies?" Brooke asks, her voice definitely full of awe.

Jackson smiles at her. "It's a pretty damned good reason, don't you think?"

Brooke gives a happy little sigh and sits back on the couch cushion.

I exchange a glance with Luke. Luke rolls his eyes at me and shakes his head.

His expression reflects exactly how I'm feeling, a combination of *Jesus Jackson* and *fuck, he's going to get puppies and Brooke's virginity.*

I'm gonna have to step up my game.

"So can I ask you guys a question?" she says after a moment.

I run my hand from her foot up her calf and give it a little squeeze. "Anything," I tell her.

"Well, I'm really glad that you guys showed up here, you've made this thing a lot easier."

"This has turned out really well," I agree.

"I kind of told you something big about myself last night," she says, her gaze dropping to her lap instead of staying on mine.

Luke shifts in his chair and Jackson softly clears his throat. I wonder if our sweet little virgin has any idea how she's affecting the three men in the room with her.

I reach over and tip her chin up with a finger, making her look at me. "You can tell us or ask us anything. No judgment."

She's chewing on her bottom lip and it takes everything in me to keep from running my thumb over that lip.

I can imagine how soft and silky it would feel. But I also know the minute I touch it with any part of my body, the rest of my body is going to want to be involved.

"You guys make me feel really safe," she says.

I know my friends well enough to know that it affects them as strongly as it does me. Luke and I are natural protectors as fire-fighters. Making people feel safe is important to us. But I know Jackson feels that way too. He's a great guy. Maybe a little lost at the moment as far as what to do with his life, but at his core, he is someone who wants the world to be a better place and the people around him, especially the ones he cares about, to be happy.

"That means a lot to us," I tell her, my voice a little gruff.

"So, since we're still stuck here for a little time together, and you know that I don't have a lot of experience with men, I was hoping I could ask you something."

My heart starts thundering in my chest. Oh, sweet Jesus. Is she going to ask one of us to take her virginity? Is she going to ask for some sexual experiences? Sex tutoring?

I will be giving to charity, lighting candles, and going to church twice a week for the rest of my life if the universe dumps this in my lap, I swear to God.

"Of course," my voice even rougher now.

"Whatever you need," Jackson assures her, reaching up and pulling her hair back and over her shoulder.

She takes a deep breath and then says, "So the last time I told a guy I was a virgin, he had a bad reaction too. And I am just wondering, how I should go about talking about this subject with future guys? I mean, is this something I should bring up way ahead of time? Like before we even kiss the first time? Or is this something I shouldn't tell him at all? Just go through with it and he never has to know he's my first?" She looks from me over to Luke and then to Jackson. "I would love to have a male perspective on this."

Several things hit me all at once.

First, Brooke is talking about being a virgin in the future with other guys. That is definitely not a request for us to change that status this weekend.

Second, all of the options that she's laid out suck. She definitely shouldn't keep her mouth shut about it. That's terrible. But she shouldn't be discussing it on the first date.

Then I realize the reason I think those all suck is because I don't want her to have a conversation about sex with any other guy at any other time. Or really sex at all. Ever.

And third, and maybe most disturbing of all, the fact that she's asking us this means something horrible: she considers us friends.

We are people she can talk to about very vulnerable topics. People she can ask advice about things regarding *other* men.

The woman I want to strip down, lay out on the coffee table right now and fuck until she's hoarse from screaming my name, has just friend-zoned me.

Fortunately, Jackson is never speechless.

"No, no, no," Jackson says, leaning in and taking Brooke's chin, turning her to face him. "You don't keep quiet about who you are and what you need. Not for anyone. Ever."

Yeah, that's a good answer.

She presses her lips together and stares at him.

"You understand?" he asks. "The lucky bastard needs to make it special. He needs to understand what a gift you're giving him. But you also don't tell him on the first date. He has to earn even the *potential* to be with you like that. If you tell him you're a virgin upfront, he's gonna think it's a sure thing that he gets to be with you." He strokes his finger along her jaw. "You keep these high standards and hold out for the right guy."

See? Jackson is a good guy.

And fuck. I want to be the right guy he's telling Brooke to wait for.

Hell, Jackson could easily be the right guy. He's kind, definitely knows how to treat a woman right, likes Brooke, sees underneath her sweet shyness. He can make her smile, laugh, blush.

And he's not a stranger to me.

There's something about the idea of her being with some nameless, faceless fuck that I can't be sure deserves her that makes me feel irrational rage. I need to fully vet the guy. I need to be sure he understands how amazing she is.

At least, if it's Jackson, I know she's with someone great. Someone who will treat her right.

"Brooke..." I start. But I'm not sure exactly how to make this offer without sounding like a creep. *You can have me or my best friend.* That just sounds a little weird even if we weren't talking about her first time ever.

"There's an easy solution," Luke finally says, his deep voice calming me for some reason.

Probably because I'm used to Luke taking charge and making decisions for the better of a whole group of people I care about.

We all look over at him.

His eyes are on Brooke. "The easiest way to deal with bringing your virginity up with future guys is to not need to do it."

Her eyes get wide as I frown.

"So just not tell them? I feel like my inexperience will be obvious."

But Luke shakes his head. "No. I mean, make it a non-issue. Don't be a virgin the next time you go out with someone you want a relationship with."

The meaning behind his words slams into my gut.

Yes.

She needs to take care of this before she goes out with anyone else.

Right now. Here. With us.

If I wasn't so close to her, I probably would've missed the way her breath catches.

She swallows hard and then Jackson leans in. I tense because I don't know what he's about to say or do. And I don't know how I'll react if he tells her he wants to be her first. But he looks at me over her shoulder quickly, then meets her gaze.

"Luke's right. You need to lose your virginity to someone that you know and trust. A great guy who really likes you, who knows what he's doing and can make it good for you, and who wants you more than his next breath."

"Ideally, yes, that's what I want," she says, practically whispering.

Jackson gives her a slow smile as he reaches up and traces a finger down her cheek. "And then after you're not a sweet little innocent virgin anymore, and you want to branch out and have a little more fun, maybe try some extras, or some unique locations…" He winks at her as that sinks in. "You know where to find *me*."

His meaning slams into me.

Jackson and Luke are both *very* good friends. I owe them both enormous Christmas gifts this year.

It takes Brooke another second to figure out what he's telling her, but then, she pivots, her gaze colliding with mine.

I just look at her for a long moment, taking in her beautiful face, the flush in her cheeks, the way her breathing comes out in quick little puffs.

Then I lift my hand and cup her cheek. "Brooke?" I ask huskily.

"Yeah?"

"Would you like to go to my room and talk about this some more?"

She wet her lips, then stops my heart by nodding. "Yeah, I really would."

I don't hesitate for even a moment. I stand, bend over, scoop her up, and head for my bedroom.

CHAPTER 9

Brooke

I'M SPENDING the last ten minutes of my life as a virgin.

Okay, I don't know if the sex will start in exactly ten minutes. But I know the next time I walk into that kitchen, the next time I check on the puppies, the next time I sit on that sofa… I won't be a virgin anymore.

I'm making a big deal out of this, I know.

But this feels momentous.

And I don't think it's the losing-my-v-card thing, actually. It's how I'm doing it. Who I'm doing it with. How those amazing men downstairs knew exactly what I needed and just made it happen.

All of that downstairs—having three men basically tell me that I should have sex with Wyatt, and then doing it while two of them hang out knowing exactly what's going on up here—should feel strange.

But on the contrary, I felt cared for.

Am I dreaming? Is this some kind of strange Stockholm syndrome that has set in since we've been snowed in and now delivered puppies together? In my mind it feels like Jackson and Luke were *caring about me* by convincing me to sleep with Wyatt, but is that crazy?

Maybe.

I'm willing to accept that, actually.

I love the feeling that Jackson and Luke actually hate the idea of some guy they don't know taking my virginity. I love the idea that they care that this is good for me. I love the idea that they think Wyatt will be good to me.

Luke doesn't even really like me, so that's just further proof that he's a good guy.

And Jackson *does* like me, but he's willing to step aside and let Wyatt and me be together.

That's really nice. And definitely confirmation that Wyatt is a wonderful choice.

I want to lose my virginity and, *of course,* I want it to be with a guy who knows what he's doing, who is charming and sweet and who I'm *extremely* attracted to. It is a huge bonus that Wyatt also makes me feel safe and cared for, and like *he's* the one who is lucky to be with *me*.

My only concern as Wyatt carries me up the stairs—that is a very hot fireman thing to do, by the way—and down the hall to his bedroom is that he's about to ruin me for all other men.

Will I even *want* to have sex with anyone else ever again after this?

Wyatt Doherty is going to set the bar very, *very* high. And he hasn't even gotten me onto the bed yet.

That changes ten seconds later.

Wyatt strides through his doorway, kicks the door shut behind us, and then lowers me onto the bed. He braces his elbows on either side of my shoulders and just looks down at me.

"Jesus Christ, you are gorgeous," he says, his voice gruff.

I smile. "Thank you."

He leans in and kisses me. It's soft and sweet and just as I'm about to wrap my arms around his neck and deepen it, he lifts his head.

"Okay, my sweet little virgin, here's how this is going to go," he says.

The way he says 'my sweet little virgin' makes my pussy

clench. There's possessiveness there and an edge to his voice that makes me realize he's *really* into this idea of being my first.

"I'm going to try my damnedest to go slow and make this sweet," he says. He kisses me again softly.

I wiggle under him, wanting more. His body is so hard and hot against mine and I moan softly.

"*But,*" he says, lifting his head and moving one hand to my hip, where he grips me, stilling my motion. "It's going to be tough for me. I want you so fucking much." His gaze bounces back and forth between my eyes. "*Christ,* I want you so much," he repeats. "But I *will* make this good for you. We're going to give you *a lot* to like tonight, okay?"

I nod.

"But I need you talking to me," he says. "I need to hear what you like, what you don't like, if you have questions, if you want me to stop or go slower…" His gaze dips to my mouth and it's as if he loses his train of thought. He kisses me again, this time licking his tongue over my bottom lip, then just briefly touching mine, before lifting his head. "Promise me you'll talk to me, Brooke."

I nod. "I promise."

"Okay." He gives me a slow grin. "This is going to be fun."

I can't help but smile back. "I'm looking forward to it."

He chuckles and the low, deep sound rumbles through my body, making tingles dance over my skin. "I'm glad. Especially since you don't even *know* how good it's gonna be."

I wiggle under him again. "Let's get going."

One brow lifts. "Oh, you're not in charge here, darlin'," he tells me. He squeezes my hip. "Though I do appreciate your enthusiasm."

"You're just teasing me now," I say. I try to lift my hips, to grind against him a little, to try to move this along. I feel hot and restless and I *want* his hands and mouth all over me.

He shakes his head. "No. There will be time for teasing, and that can be *very* fun too, but I'm not gonna tease you tonight. Lots of pleasure and absolute *fulfillment*."

I sigh happily. "Yes."

"Do you have any questions for me right now? Anything you want to tell me? Anything you need to know?"

My brain is just saying *get naked, get naked, get naked*. "Can we take our clothes off now?" I ask.

In response, he kisses me one more time, this one deeper than all the others. His tongue strokes along mine, as I feel his hand slide from my hip down my thigh, then up my side to my breast.

He sits back, kneeling between my knees. "Let's see this gorgeous body," he says. "I thought I was going to die last night in the hot tub. Now I can get my hands on you and I can't wait."

He slips his fingers into the top of my pants, snagging my panties at the same time and strips them both down my legs. At the same time, I strip off my sweatshirt and toss it to the floor.

His hot gaze tracks over me as I reach back to unhook my bra. I barely have the tiny hooks undone when he grasps the front and plucks it off my body.

"There we go," he says, scanning me from head to toe.

I always imagined that I would feel shy or embarrassed in a moment like this, but Wyatt makes me feel like a goddess. He's looking at me as if he has never seen anything more beautiful, and it makes me want to stretch and pose for him.

"Holy shit," he tells me, flattening his hand between my breasts and then dragging it down to my belly. "Even better than in my dreams."

I arch up into his touch. "You've dreamed about me naked?"

His gaze meets mine as he cups a breast. I gasp as his thumb drags over the tip. My nipples were already hard, but I seem to be even more sensitive with his hand on me and electricity shoots from my nipple to my clit.

"The first time was after I met you at your brother's retirement party," he tells me, now rolling my nipple between his thumb and finger.

I moan softly, my arousal a combination of his touch and his words.

"Touch me more," I plead.

"Oh, I'm just getting started." He plants the hand beside my head and leans over, licking his tongue over the nipple he just teased, then sucking. I am astonished by the heat that skitters through me. My hand instinctively goes to the back of his head, holding him in place.

He licks and sucks, then kisses his way to the other breast, where he does the same.

My pussy is throbbing, and I feel heat and a knot of need tighten in my lower belly.

"Wyatt," I say softly, not even sure what exactly I'm asking for.

"I've got you, Brooke," he says huskily against my breast. He shifts to the side, leaning on one elbow, sliding his hand over my hip to my belly, running it back-and-forth.

"Damn," he says, his gaze fixed on his hand, and all of me naked below it. "If we'd gone to your room, we could've used your vibrator."

I gasp. "How do you know about my vibrator?"

He looks at me with a wicked grin as his hand travels down my thigh. "Luke heard you with it last night."

My eyes widen, and I feel my cheeks heat. "*What*?"

Wyatt strokes up and down my thigh with his huge hand, lighting little sparks of fire even though I'm grappling with definite embarrassment.

"He heard the vibrator first when he went down to use the powder room. But then he said he heard you moaning. Quickly figured out what you were doing."

"Oh my God!" My hands fly up to cover my face.

Wyatt reaches up and tugs them away. "It was so fucking hot. You have no idea what that did to all three of us. To me, just hearing *about* it."

I swallow hard. "What did it do?"

"Well, I jerked off twice last night thinking of you. And if I know those guys, they did the same."

Wyatt's hand slides up, and now he's cupping my pussy. It's just his full flat palm, but every nerve ending in my body now seems connected to that spot.

I cannot stop thinking about those three men aroused and masturbating, thinking of me.

Wyatt rocks the heel of his hand, pressing in against my clit. "Do you like that?" he asks. "The idea of three men, hands around their cocks, thinking of you and this sweet body, and this tight pussy, and that vibrator and wishing like hell they could be in that room with you?"

I can't bite back the little whimper that comes out of my mouth. It's definitely from the pressure he's applying, but also from the images his words inspire.

"Yeah," he says, pressing again and circling a little this time. "You and this amazing ass and these gorgeous tits and the fantasy of this sweet cunt, combined with your laugh, and your compassion, and your innocence, and just how good and light you make us all feel, has been a hell of a concoction to deal with this weekend."

"Oh my God," I murmur. I didn't expect talk like *this*.

I also didn't expect the way it makes me feel.

"Thank you for letting me be here like this with you," he says, bending over and kissing me softly.

"Thank *you*," I say against his lips, my fingers sliding up his back and into his hair.

"Oh, Brooke, you have no idea what a pleasure this is," he tells me.

His finger is circling my clit and I feel hot and happy and tight and restless all at the same time.

"Now be a good girl and come on my fingers," he says, sliding his thick middle finger into my pussy.

"*Wyatt*," I gasp, the heat coiling tight as he slides it deep.

"Jesus, you're so wet," he says against my jaw. "So tight. You're so perfect, Brooke."

I work on just breathing. His finger is so much better than anything I've ever done to myself.

"How many guys have gotten this far?" he asks, sliding his finger out, then in again.

I wet my lips and shake my head. "None."

He pauses. He shifts over me, so I have to look into his eyes. "None? No one's ever even done this to you?"

I shake my head again. "No. Kissing. Touching my breasts. That's it."

He breathes out, looking amazed. "Okay," he says, almost to himself. "Well, that's a very nice discovery."

"Is it?" I ask. "You all seemed so weird about finding out I was a virgin last night. Is it really nice to know I've never even... done this?"

He moves his finger in and out, leaning in close and dragging his mouth over mine. "Oh, sweetheart, you have no idea. Knowing I'm the first to touch and pleasure and stretch this pretty pussy? The first to get to experience what it's like when you come? This is the best fucking night of my life."

I feel the beginning coils of an orgasm from just that one finger and what he's saying to me.

"Jackson and... Luke," I say. It feels strange to say other men's names when I'm in bed with Wyatt with his finger *there*.

Or I feel like it *should* feel weird. But it doesn't.

In fact, Wyatt's eyes seem to darken a bit.

"What about Jackson and Luke?" he asks, moving that finger in and out in a steady rhythm.

"They acted weird about it."

But Wyatt shakes his head. "Not weird. So fucking turned on they didn't know what to do."

He kisses me deeply as he pumps his finger deep. His thumb rubs over my clit and my orgasm is right there, hovering, needing just a little more speed and pressure. I lift my hips a little, pressing closer to his hand.

When he lifts his head, I can't help but ask, "Really? That was turned on?"

He laughs softly, looking down at his hand between my legs. "The idea of how sweet you are, how all these other stupid men have been walking around and not realizing what was right in front of them, but we were sitting there with you, in your underwear, in a hot tub, far from civilization… yeah, it hit hard."

"Oh." I don't really understand that, but I believe him.

"And they were thinking that it's a lot of pressure to be with a virgin," he says, sliding a second finger inside me.

I moan. The extra stretch is nice. He leans over and sucks on the nipple closest to him and I'm hit by a stronger wave of pleasure.

"Is it?" I ask, somehow. He said he wanted me to talk, and he doesn't seem *bothered* by me asking about Jackson and Luke. "They were… intimidated by it?"

He nods. "They knew it would need to be extra good and special. Jackson likes things to be a little more… playful. Less serious."

His fingers move together a little faster and I feel my pussy tighten around them.

I feel a little bad, but I think about Jackson and what sex with him might be like, how it might be different. But I'm not really sure I get it.

"And Luke," Wyatt continues, adding his thumb back in, pumping and stroking. "Likes it a little rough."

My pussy tightens again.

Wyatt lifts a brow. "Oh? You like that?"

"I have no idea," I tell him, feeling my cheeks flush. "I don't *really* know what that means."

He thrusts a little faster. "It means that he definitely couldn't take care of you the way I can."

The cockiness in his voice and the way he's watching my face as he finger fucks me is hot. I feel my orgasm pulling tighter and tighter.

"Wyatt," I moan.

"Come for me, Brooke. Give me this first one. I need this pussy well prepped before I'm the first cock to sink into this sweet heat."

"Oh god," I moan again, arching my neck.

Then he does something that feels like he's stroking deeper and more firmly, and it's like he hits a certain spot. My orgasm hits all at once, and I feel my muscles clench around him as I cry out.

"Wyatt!"

"That's it," he praises. "Oh yes, that's beautiful."

He keeps his fingers moving as my orgasm washes through me and starts to fade slowly. His rhythm slows, and he lowers his head for a long, deep kiss as he slides his fingers free.

Then he starts kissing down my neck. "You are a dream. So fucking gorgeous," he says. "Let's do that again."

"Ag—"

But he's sliding down my body, between my thighs, and kissing my belly, then my mound, then my clit. The hot, electric shock that shoots through me as his mouth touches me makes me gasp his name.

He looks up at me. "Yes, again."

CHAPTER 10

Brooke

"BUT—" I start.

Wyatt parts my thighs and settles between them. He lifts his fingers, that were just in my pussy, to his lips and slides them into his mouth. He sucks on them, watching me.

My pussy tingles.

"Do you have a question, Brooke?" he asks.

"Um…" Do I? I prop up on my elbows. "Can you take *your* clothes off?" I'd really like to see him naked.

He grins and sits up slightly, pulling off his shirt.

God, that is a gorgeous sight. He's all tan skin, etched muscle, and ink. I want to study the tattoos on both upper arms and shoulders. He's just beautiful and I want to feel all of that against all of me.

"More," I say.

He shakes his head. "Not until I'm ready to fuck you."

I frown. "But we're doing that, right? Tonight? Soon?"

"Damn, I love you greedy," he says, settling back between my thighs. "We are doing that tonight, yes. But how long you have to wait depends on how quickly you come on my tongue."

"Come on your *tongue*?" I ask.

His grin is full and *so* arrogant. "Yes, Brooke. On. My. Tongue."

His brow furrows slightly. "Don't you read romance novels? Or watch porn or anything?"

My mouth drops open, but then I tell him honestly, "I study a lot. Vet school isn't easy. And I volunteer. And I work a little when I can. And I—"

"Okay, shhh," he tells me, kissing up my inner thigh. "I get it. No judgment. I'm so fucking thrilled to introduce you to this."

"This what?"

"Licking your pussy until you come again," he says bluntly. "It's like your vibrator or my fingers. Your pretty little clit is going to love it."

I start to respond—with what I have no idea—but he lowers his head and just shows me what he means.

And… Oh. My. God.

I fall back onto the mattress, my entire body melting, and everything in my world narrowing to Wyatt Doherty's tongue between my legs.

He licks, sucks, licks again, flicks, sucks some more. Then he adds his fingers. Those two amazingly thick, long, knowing fingers.

And I come apart in less than five minutes.

The orgasm feels deeper somehow than the first. It rolls over me, heating every inch of my body, and making me almost sob.

"Wyatt! Oh my god! Wyatt!"

"That's it, pretty girl," he tells me, crawling up my body. "Let 'em hear you."

I slap a hand over my mouth. That *was* pretty loud, and there are two other people in the house.

He pulls my hand away, chuckling. "Oh, no. You scream out my name, girl. It's not like they don't know what's going on up here. I want them to know I'm doing what they sent me up here to do."

I'm feeling the mix of endorphins hit my blood stream. I feel giddy and sexy and *so* excited about what's to come. I wrap my arms around his neck as he stretches out over me, his bare chest finally against mine. His heat seeps into me, the light hair on his chest abrades my nipples, and I kiss him deeply.

I realize I can taste myself on his lips and at first, my instinct is to draw away. But then, for some reason, I open my mouth and slide my tongue into his.

He groans and strokes his tongue deep into my mouth and I definitely taste what he just did.

His hand tangles in my hair, and he pulls my head back, staring into my eyes. "You doing okay?"

"So much better than okay," I tell him, my breathing ragged.

"Good."

I hesitate only a second before asking, "What did Jackson and Luke send you up here to do exactly?"

His grin is slow and sexy. "Rock your fucking world."

I return his grin. "Yeah, you're doing that then."

He kisses me again, but then pushes back, kneeling between my knees again. His gaze sweeps over me. "Damn, but you look good, all soft and sated and wet and pink."

I blush but I don't make any move to close my legs. I couldn't anyway, considering he's positioned between them and doesn't seem at all inclined to move, but also, he's been *very* up close and personal with the part of my body he's now studying. It would be silly to try to cover up now.

Then he pushes off the end of the bed.

"Hey!" I protest.

But his hands go to the waistband of his sweatpants.

"Oh," I say softly as I realize he's undressing the rest of the way.

My heart starts thundering. I prop up to watch.

He pushes his sweatpants down. He's not wearing underwear and his long, thick, hard cock is evident immediately.

I stare.

I can't help it.

I've seen pictures but...

"Is this your first actual in-person view of a cock?" he asks, moving back up onto the bed.

I nod. If it's impolite to stare at a man's erect cock and not look at his face again once he takes his pants off, I'm breaking every etiquette rule here.

So I dive in and ask, "Can I touch you?"

He huffs out a laugh. "Please."

He moves up beside me and stretches out. I reach out and rest my hand on his chest first, running it over the hot skin and hard muscle I've been ogling every chance I get.

"God, you're so hot," I mutter.

"Thanks."

When I look up now, he's grinning.

And now I want to *see* his reaction. He seems very intent on studying my face when he touches me.

I run my hand down to his abs. They jump and clench under my hand. "You're in amazing shape."

"Have to be," he says shortly. He looks like he's gritting his teeth.

I smile and run my hand up and down the bumps of his abs. "Have you ever been on a firefighter calendar?"

"Once." Again, his answer is clipped.

"What month?"

"July."

I stroke my hand a little lower. "Oh, nice. A *really* hot month. That makes sense."

"Brooke," he grinds out.

"Yeah?"

"Wrap that beautiful hand around my cock."

I love when he just says it like it is. I do as I'm told, sliding lower and taking him in my fist.

His breath hisses out and I feel a surge of excitement at how affected he seems. I love that feeling of power.

"Now what?" I ask.

He wraps his big hand around mine and moves it up and

down the length of his cock. "Stroke me," he says. "Squeeze a little."

I do. He groans. "Yes."

"What else?" I ask. I *love* making him feel good.

"So much," he says. "But not now. I need to be inside you. We have all night for other things."

I need to be inside you.

Those six words cause a heat to sweep through me like he dunked me back into the hot tub.

"Okay," I say breathlessly.

He rolls over me. He grins down. "Okay." He kisses me, shifting between my thighs.

I part my legs and he settles against me, the length of his cock pressing against my pussy. That pressure against my clit feels delicious. I shiver and wrap my arms around him, pulling him even closer. I lift my hips and wiggle, instinctively trying to rub against that thick, hot length.

"Hang on, sweet thing," he says. "Hang on." He pushes up.

"Wait, what?"

"Condom," he says, rolling off the bed. He looks back at me. "*Condoms*," he amends.

"Oh." I laugh softly. "Right."

He strides, naked, into the en suite bathroom.

I blatantly gawk at his tight ass as he moves. Damn, this guy is *so* gorgeous.

I would want him to be my first because of how sweet, and funny, and caring, and self-assured he is, but the fact that he is just outright *hot* is such a nice addition.

He returns quickly, carrying a strip of condoms. He tosses them onto the bed beside me, but I barely notice because I can't look away from his cock. And the way he carries himself with such confidence.

He climbs back onto the bed between my legs, his gaze locked on mine. He reaches for a condom, rips it open, and rolls it down the length of his erection.

He blows out a breath. "You ready for me, Brooke?"

I nod. "So ready, Wyatt." I wiggle on the mattress. "Really."

He looks so serious as he leans over me, bracing his hands on either side of me. "God, I'm so..." He trails off. "I'm so glad to be here with you like this."

My heart squeezes. I lift my hand to his face. "I'm so glad I waited until this could be you."

I see emotions flicker through his eyes, then he leans over, kisses me hard, then shifts back, and says, "Guide me in, sweet thing."

I look down at his cock, then reach out and wrap my hand around him.

He groans. "Yes, Brooke, let me in."

I tip my hips a little as I bring him forward. He presses closer and I feel the tip of him at my entrance.

"Might hurt a little," he says. "I think? I'm not sure." He gives me a little smile. "I'll make up for it."

"You already have," I tell him. I put my hands on his ass and pull him close. "I want you, Wyatt. I'm ready."

He breathes out again, and then slowly presses forward. He slides into me. It's a strange feeling. Tight. A stretching. It's good. Then a little painful. Then I shift a little and it's better. Then it gets even tighter. I realize I'm breathing fast. I look up into his face and see how tight his jaw is.

"Are you okay?" I ask.

He's staring at me, and he lets out a sharp laugh. "Um... barely hanging on, to be honest."

"Oh." I frown. "What should I do?"

"No." He shakes his head. "It's not bad. It's... Jesus, you feel so fucking good. You're squeezing me so good, Brooke. God, you're... tight and hot and... I'm working on not thrusting and just... fucking your brains out."

I can't help it. I laugh.

"What?" he asks. "You're *laughing*?"

"I'm just happy," I assure him. "I love that you're so into this. I *want* you to fuck my brains out."

I swear even the bottoms of my feet are tingling.

He groans. "No. I can't. Not this first time." He stops and breathes. "We'll… work up to that."

I laugh again and wrap my arms around him. "Well, how about you just fuck me regular right now then?"

He tenses and I think I said something wrong. But then he drops his forehead to mine. "Hearing this pretty mouth say 'fuck me' is going to kill me."

"No. You can't die before you make me come again."

His groan is louder and longer this time. "Hearing *that* is going to kill me, too."

"Then just do it," I say, feeling a surge of happiness and some kind of feminine power. I lift my legs and wrap them around his waist, and he sinks deeper.

We both groan.

There's a little flash of pain but it fades quickly.

"Jesus, Brooke, baby, I need to move."

"Yes, move," I plead.

"Hang on." He slips one hand under my ass and lifts me slightly.

Then he thrusts and I realize he's just sunk in another couple of inches. And now he's fully inside me. And yeah, wow, I feel *full*. And stretched. And a little uncomfortable.

"Brooke?"

I squeeze my eyes shut. Okay, maybe more than a little uncomfortable.

"Brooke?" He lifts his head.

I take a deep breath. "Just a second."

"Jesus. Fuck. Dammit."

He starts to move, but I clutch at his back. "Just a second."

He stops, breathing hard.

"Kiss me?" I ask.

He finds my lips immediately, kissing me softly, then deeper. I lick my tongue along his lower lip and then slip it inside. He returns the strokes of my tongue and a rumble in his chest vibrates through me and I feel his hand running up and down my side. Otherwise, he's still just like I asked.

I let myself relax. I focus on the feelings of his body against mine. How much he *cares* about this being good. I remember his fingers and his mouth where his huge cock is now, and I feel my inner muscles start to relax and heat.

After kissing for a couple of minutes, I pull back. "You can move now."

He looks concerned. And that right there makes me *sure*.

"I'm sure, Wyatt," I tell him before he even asks.

He holds his breath as he moves his hips in a small stroke.

"More," I encourage, squeezing his ass.

He pulls out further, then sinks back in.

And yeah…that's nice. I sigh. "Oh, yes, like that."

That seems to encourage him. He takes an even longer stroke. I feel my hips arch closer on their own.

Another stroke and I feel the friction start tingles spreading.

"More, Wyatt."

He strokes even longer, then picks up the pace. I gasp. "Oh, *yes*."

"You're good?" he asks, practically panting.

"So good." I look up and meet his gaze. "This feels *really* good now."

"Jesus, thank you god." He laughs lightly, then leans in and kisses me. He drags his mouth to my jaw, then down my neck. "I'm sorry it was so tight, but you're doing so good," he praises. "You're taking me so well."

Those are magic words. My pussy clenches around him and I gasp.

"Oh, you like that?" he asks, against my neck. I feel him smile.

"Yes, talk to me some more," I tell him.

"Gladly. You're so tight and you feel so fucking good."

He thrusts again and I feel the ripples of pleasure deep, deep inside.

"This tight, sweet body is taking all of me now. You're such a good, good girl. I know it's so tight, darling, but god this is so good. You're milking me so well. I just want to fill this hot cunt up over and over again."

Heat and lust rush through me. "Oh, god, Wyatt." I dig my fingers into his ass.

"Yes, sweet thing, that's right. Say it again. Tell me who's fucking you first and so, so well."

"*Wyatt,*" I gasp.

"That's it. The first cock to stretch this perfect cunt is mine and you're not gonna forget that."

He's thrusting deep and slow, and I feel it *everywhere,* I swear.

"Faster, Wyatt," I say. It's just a *feeling.* I want *more.*

He picks up the pace. "Oh, that's my girl," he says.

My whole body feels melty at that.

"That's my girl, taking it all, wanting more."

"Yes, please, harder."

"Jesus," he groans.

But he does as I ask and he starts fucking me faster and harder. His huge hand still grips my ass, lifting me against him as he thrusts forward. I grip his ass and hang on.

"Yes, Wyatt, yes!"

"I could fuck you for days and not get enough of you."

I feel my orgasm gather quickly, tight and hot, deep in my pelvis. "Wyatt!"

He tips me somehow and his pubic bone hits my clit as he thrusts, and after only three more strokes, I'm coming apart.

"Yes, oh! Wyatt!" I call out, loudly, without thought.

"Fuck, Brooke! *Fuck*!" His entire body tenses and he grips me tightly, then he roars my name one more time. "Brooke!"

He holds himself still, breathing hard, staring down at me.

I can't think of anything to say.

Except maybe *when can we do that again?*

I'm sure I'm going to be sore tomorrow, but I don't care. That was *worth it.*

And I want more.

Finally, he grins and lets go of my ass. His hand comes up, and he brushes my hair back from my face. "So…that's vanilla, missionary sex."

I start laughing, and he lowers himself to my side. "I don't believe you. *That* was vanilla?"

"Yep. Seriously."

I look over at him. "Wow. I didn't realize I was such a fan of vanilla. I always get caramel, or lemon, when given a choice."

He rolls in, kisses my neck, and growls. "I'll give you caramel and lemon."

"Oh, good."

"Be right back." He pads into the bathroom. I hear water running. Then he comes back into the room.

He crawls up into bed with me, snuggles in behind me, and pulls me back, spooning me, his hand splayed over my stomach.

"Wait. Are we done?"

He nuzzles his face against the back of my neck. "Give me a chance to catch my breath, greedy girl. Then I'm here to service you all night. Or until your pussy cries mercy."

I grin and wiggle my ass against his cock.

He grips my hip. "Did I create a monster?"

"I think maybe you did. That was…" I sigh. "Amazing."

"Fucking love that," he says against my shoulder.

"Thank you, Wyatt," I say softly.

He squeezes my hip and kisses my shoulder. "Best night of my life, Brooke."

CHAPTER 11

Luke

"WILL YOU FUCKING SIT DOWN?" Jackson demands, exasperated.

I stop pacing long enough to glare at him. "You've been jumping up and checking on those puppies every five minutes so don't come at me for being restless."

"I'm not restless. They're newborn puppies. I'm concerned."

Watching the puppies being born was actually incredible. I've been checking on them periodically too, because they're cute as hell. But Henley and all five puppies have been asleep for several hours. "I think they're good."

"Do you think Brooke is good?"

Jackson is lying on the couch, hands behind his head, feet crossed at the ankles. He's staring up at the ceiling. Again. Maybe he doesn't even know he's doing it, but he keeps looking at the ceiling and glancing up the stairs every time he gets off of the couch.

Brooke has been upstairs in Wyatt's room for *hours*.

They're either talking extensively or having very drawn out sex, or hell, maybe even both.

All I know is they're up there, most likely naked, and I'm fucking down here crawling out of my skin with blue balls and I can't even go to bed because I refuse to walk past Wyatt's room and hear any kind of moaning.

Do I think this is the right move for Brooke, losing her virginity to Wyatt? Yes. Absolutely.

Do I want to hear it happening in real time? No fucking way.

"Brooke is more than good if I had to guess," I say wryly.

Jackson keeps yawning but he's not going to bed either.

"Maybe I should sleep down here by Henley and the puppies," he says now.

"They got moved to the laundry room. You're going to sleep on the laundry room floor?"

"I can bring the box back in here."

That damn fire Wyatt keeps feeding is blazing away, romantic and warm, and I'm stuck here with Jackson. Who I normally enjoy spending time with but we're both off-balance and preoccupied. I need a distraction, but he doesn't even want to play cards.

I yank open the back door and stick my head out for a blast of cold air. "It's hotter than hell in here."

"I think the real heat is upstairs."

I close the door and eye him. "It doesn't bother you?"

"Oh, it's bothering me. I want to be up there. But Wyatt is Mr. Romance. I want Brooke's first time to be special, like we talked about."

Crossing my arms over my chest, I try not to visualize Wyatt murmuring sweet words in Brooke's ear while he moves inside her, but I fail miserably. "You don't think you're romantic?"

"I'm flirty and fun. I can be romantic but I have also been accused in the past of not being serious enough. You know this about me… I get easily distracted."

He does. Jackson goes all in on something, burns himself out, then moves on to the next thing. I would say he does that with women sometimes as well. He likes the idea phase more than the day in, day out of relationships. And he clearly cares about Brooke, just like I do. He wants what's best for her, just like me, but damn, this is harder than I expected.

"A puppy is a big commitment, you know." Jackson made it clear he intends to keep Nugget, at the very least. "You can't get distracted when you have a pet."

Jackson snorts. "Yes, I understand that. Guess I'm starting there. Maybe I'm ready to finally settle down a little bit."

He pulls his phone out of his pocket and holds it up over his head while he's still lying on his back.

If he drops it on his face, I'm going to laugh.

"It's almost two in the fucking morning," he says, after checking his phone. "They're spending the night together, aren't they?"

"Looks that way." I didn't really consider that. I just thought they would have sex and come back downstairs, but that's a me move, not a Wyatt move. "It's a good thing you two are here. If I were here alone with Brooke, I would have fucked this up so bad."

The very thought makes me shudder. Nothing romantic about me and that girl deserves better than I could ever give her.

Jackson turns his head. "Nah. Give yourself a little credit. You're good under pressure."

I grunt. "Thanks. For a five alarm fire or an overdose call, sure. But women? That's a whole different story."

Jackson doesn't press me and I'm grateful for that.

"Should we watch a movie?" he asks. "Something where shit gets blown up and asshole characters die?"

"I can get behind that."

We're discussing options when we hear a door open upstairs. Both of our heads swivel to the staircase. My heart starts thumping way too fast. I don't know if I can handle seeing Brooke in Wyatt's T-shirt and nothing else, looking glowing and satisfied.

Fortunately, it's just Wyatt.

Though I could do without the smug look on his face. I also would prefer it if he wasn't in his fucking underwear.

"I need water," he declares, scratching his bare chest. "I'm dehydrated."

That makes me roll my eyes. "Is Brooke staying in your room tonight?"

He strolls past me with the cocky arrogance of a man who thinks he's performed well. "Yep."

I refuse to ask him anything else. He wants us to and I fucking refuse.

Jackson can't resist. He floats a "So…" out there.

"So what?" Wyatt asks.

"Don't be a dick. Was everything okay, or are we going to have to pick up the pieces with a disappointed Brooke tomorrow?"

"No one was disappointed," he says, taking a glass out of the kitchen cabinet.

"Speak for yourself," Jackson retorts.

Wyatt grins.

"Seriously, though… she had a good time?" Jackson pushes.

"Yes. But I'm not giving you any details, so don't ask." Wyatt drinks the entire glass of water down in two gulps.

I don't know what would make me more angry—him spilling details about Brooke or him not treating her to a good time, so I'm grateful he's keeping his mouth shut.

Besides, I trust Wyatt did right by Brooke.

He wouldn't be wearing that expression if it had gone sideways.

He refills the glass with more water and strolls back toward the stairs. "'Night. Sleep tight, boys."

"You're making breakfast tomorrow," Jackson grumbles. "You owe us."

"I don't owe you shit." Wyatt shoots us a grin and walks up the stairs.

Jackson shakes his head. "I don't know whether to knock him out or shake his hand right now."

I feel the same way. "Maybe we should just go to bed."

"No way. Let's watch the movie. They're still awake up there."

"Good point."

I settle in the club chair next to the couch and we put the TV on over the fireplace, the volume at a normal setting. In spite of thinking sleep will be elusive, I fall asleep after an hour and when I wake up Jackson's asleep under a blanket on the couch and the TV is off. He looks settled in for the night, so I pad quietly up the stairs. I don't even pause outside of Wyatt's room. I just hightail it into my room and to the bed, which I made this morning. I always make my bed. It starts the day off right.

It has the advantage of giving me the opportunity to toss two pillows into the corner and yank the comforter back roughly. I punch the remaining two pillows. More than once.

Then I climb into bed and proceed to not sleep.

All I can think about is Brooke and how fucking gorgeous she must have looked with her expression softened by desire, her mouth falling open in surprise as she learned what exactly makes sex so incredible.

I roll on my side and wish it—and me—and *everything* could be different.

CHAPTER 12

Jackson

I **HEAR** footsteps on the stairs, but can tell by how light they are that it's Brooke coming down.

My heart starts pounding.

I feel like I'm thirteen and have a crush on a girl for the first time. What is this? The woman was just upstairs for the past several hours, having sex with my best friend. For the first time for her *ever*.

Yet I'm lying here on the couch, my stomach twisting, anticipating the chance to talk to her alone in the dark in the middle of the night.

It's four a.m. I know why she's down here. There's a bathroom attached to Wyatt's room, so unless she's hungry after the rigorous activities, she's down here to check on the dogs.

And I already know her.

This is completely about the dogs.

I hear her start across the kitchen toward the laundry room where the dogs were last she knew.

"Brooke," I whisper into the dark, not wanting to startle her.

"Jackson?"

I sit up slowly. This cabin has crazy ass windows. They cover the entire one side of the house and the moonlight, and lights strung across the deck, along with the soft glow of the light over the stove in the kitchen, give us enough light to easily see one another.

"Hey," I say. "They're in here. Closer to the fire."

She starts toward me and I pray to God that she's wearing more than just one of Wyatt's shirts and panties or something.

As she steps into the living area, I sigh with relief, realizing she pulled on her leggings and sweatshirt from earlier.

"You're sleeping down here with them?" she asks, noticing the pillow and blanket on the couch.

"I didn't want them to be alone tonight. Just in case any of them needed anything."

I didn't want to be too close to Wyatt's bedroom, either. I didn't want to hear the two of them through the wall, but it's the truth about the dogs, so I don't feel bad leaving the rest of that out.

"That's sweet," she says softly. She looks at the dogs, sleeping peacefully in the box we made for them. Henley is curled around the puppies and they're all snuggled against one another for heat and comfort.

"How are they doing?" she asks.

I get off the couch and kneel by the box. Brooke joins me on the carpet. "Good. Henley ate a little bit, and I took her out again. The pups have all nursed and have moved around a bit, but mostly everybody has been sleeping."

Henley has awakened with our voices and the movement around her box. Brooke reaches out to the dog, who sniffs her, then gives her hand a lick.

"You're such a sweet girl," Brooke tells her. She smooths her hand over the top of the dog's head. "I wish we didn't have to leave them so soon."

"We're not going to," I tell her. I haven't worked out the details, but I've decided I'm going to offer the neighbors a crazy amount of money for Henley and the pups. I'll figure out some way to get them back to Chicago, even if I need to hang back for an extra couple of days to get it arranged.

Brooke lifts her eyes to mine. "What do you mean?"

"I'm adopting them."

"All of them?" Her voice is a little louder with her surprise.

I reach out and stroke Nugget's back with one finger. I am especially attached to him, but I can't imagine leaving him here for six weeks and I really don't think I can trust him, his siblings, and his mother to the neighbors.

"Yeah. I don't want to split them up."

Brooke is quiet for a moment, watching me pet Nugget. She scoots a little closer.

"Wow. I love that you're doing that."

"I have the resources. It's something I want to do." I shrug. "It feels good."

"Going from zero to six is a lot."

I nod. It is. And I really do have to think about buying a house and stuff. Soon. I've been scrolling the internet for listings, actually, already tonight. But if I take them back to Chicago in just a few days, I'll need to be creative. "Yeah, but…"

I'm looking at the dogs and am surprised when Brooke reaches out and puts a hand on my leg. "What?"

Looking into her eyes, I say, "I think it's time I do something serious."

I don't know if it's the dark, the late hour, the puppies, or just *her*—or maybe a combination—but that came out very easily. And I realize it's true.

She leaves her hand on my leg. "Serious? What does that mean to you?"

"I've been kind of just goofing around for the last few years. But I think it's time I… change some things."

She moves closer. "Like what?"

I cover her hand with mine and love that she turns her hand so we're palm to palm and she slides her fingers between mine.

"Well, like maybe becoming responsible for six dogs." I grin.

Okay, six labs are a lot once they grow and I'm going to either need acreage or I'll need to find them homes, but I definitely want to keep Henley and Nugget long term.

Brooke smiles back. "That is a lot of responsibility. But tell me about these last few years of goofing around. You've been having fun?"

I laugh. "Well, sure. I was twenty-four when I happened to invent something that took off and made me a bunch of money. Then twenty-six when I sold it for quite a few million. That was definitely fun."

She actually looks interested. "But not serious? I mean, being an inventor and making millions seems *very* serious."

I love the feel of her hand in mine. I stroke my thumb over the back of her knuckles. "Nah. It wasn't. The app wasn't serious—still isn't."

"What does it do?"

I smile. "It's a game app. You've heard of Candy Crush and Angry Birds and Monopoly Go?"

"Sure."

"It's like those. It's a package of word games. Anyway—" I shake my head. "It's just fun, and I had no idea I was going to make huge money at it. It's not like I'm solving world hunger, you know?"

"Making people happy, giving people things to enjoy and help them relax, isn't nothing, Jackson."

God, I really like this sweetheart of a woman.

"Thanks. And you're right. But I know I can do more. I'm smart. I know I can do something important. I just need to find…" I sigh.

"Your passion," she fills in softly.

"Yeah." That's exactly it. I feel warm sitting here with her and her understanding me. "So, in the meantime, I've just been goofing around. Like, who am I to take life seriously?" I smile, but I do feel a little niggle of annoyance, at myself, in my chest. "My parents are just normal middle class people. My friends, my extended family… everyone I know and hang out with are just normal people. So, they don't take me as a millionaire too seriously, either. Which is good. They keep me grounded. They remind me that most of the world is like them, not me. Yes, I've taken some amazing trips, my apartment is stupidly expensive, and I really like nice things. But I also paid off their debt, bought my parents a new house—but they didn't want to move too far or get anything too big—and I've invested well."

"Your family sounds great," Brooke says.

I nod. "They're the best." I take a breath. "I've enjoyed the money but I don't feel like I've really done anything *consequential*." I look down at the dogs. "And I'd like to. So yeah, I think it's time for me to get serious. About something."

"Like a new job?"

"Yeah. Or maybe more than that." I meet her eyes. "Maybe a lot of things."

She gives me a soft smile. "You don't have to adopt the dogs to impress me."

I stroke my thumb over her knuckles again. "Is that what you think this is?"

She shrugs. "I've noticed the way you and Wyatt tend to try to one-up each other. Maybe that's how you always are. I guess I thought maybe it was about me." She shakes her head. "God, that sounds ridiculous."

I reach out and tip her chin up with my finger. "It's not ridiculous. It's true. We do tend to compete. We can turn anything into a contest. But you have definitely brought that out in us."

She blinks those big blue eyes at me.

God, she's so gorgeous. Wyatt is such a lucky guy. If it was anyone else, I would feel intense jealousy. As it is, I am envious, but I'm so glad he's the guy who's going to be romancing and taking care of this girl.

Brooke has *marriage material* written all over her, and my best friend is ready to settle down. They are a match made in heaven.

"Well, you don't have to become a dog dad times six to make

me like you." She bites her bottom lip. "I definitely like you. Even before the dogs."

I feel a hot twist in my gut that tells me to be very careful here.

"I'm glad. And yes, the dogs kind of started off as one of our contests. But I'm crazy about them. So even though you're with Wyatt, I'm still going to adopt the dogs."

She frowns slightly. "I'm *with* Wyatt?"

"Well, you sure were for the last few hours," I tell her with a little grin.

Even in the shadows, I can see the slight blush on her cheeks. "Yes. But that was… a favor from a friend."

I chuckle. "If you think Wyatt Doherty thinks of you as a friend, you haven't had very many friends."

She smiles. "I do like him."

"You should. He's a great guy. And he really likes you."

"That's really nice." But she seems puzzled. "I didn't realize that… upstairs… meant we were *together* together. We didn't talk about that."

"Is that okay?" I ask.

She studies my face. "Um, I guess. I can't say I was thinking about beyond this weekend. And…"

"And what, Brooke?" I realize I'm leaning in.

"I just—" She wets her lips. "I like you, too. So I'm just kind of confused about what to do with that."

Well, hell. I'm not sure what to do with that either.

I nod. "You should probably go back up to bed. With Wyatt." I pause. "At least for now."

She doesn't answer immediately. But she nods.

Still, she doesn't move. For several long seconds.

Then she leans in and kisses me.

It's a sweet press of her lips to mine. It's not particularly hot or lusty, but the desire hits me hard and low.

She pulls back after just a few seconds, looks into my eyes, and says, "Goodnight, Jackson."

"'Night, sweetheart."

I don't think I take a deep breath until I hear the door to Wyatt's bedroom shut.

And I don't fall back to sleep the rest of the night.

CHAPTER 13

Wyatt

I'VE NEVER BEEN jealous of Jackson before.

Not because he's good looking. Not because he turned a fun side project into a multi-million dollar paycheck. Not because he has endless free time right now. None of that has ever bothered me because Jackson is my best friend and he's a great guy.

He takes care of his family, is generous with his friends, and even if he doesn't consider himself that serious, he always does the right thing.

But him flirting with Brooke? Her flirting back?

Oh, yeah.

I'm jealous.

I don't have any right to be.

Brooke and I didn't discuss what we are to each other, beyond me being her first.

We were in the moment.

There was no talk about the future.

So, I'm not *upset* with either Brooke or Jackson.

But yeah, I'm a little jealous that they have a spark between them.

It's obvious as Brooke tries to chase Jackson down with a

fistful of snow, both of them laughing in pure delight as the drifting and melting snow makes it nearly impossible to run.

We came outside to get some fresh air and to check on the state of the driveway for our departure Sunday. It became obvious that the tree canopy isn't allowing for a fast melt in spite of the rising temperature and sunshine, which gave Brooke some concern. We probably won't be leaving until Monday. Jackson picked up on her anxiety and decided to perk her up with a snowball to the butt.

Which she loved, even if she pretended to be outraged.

His aim was perfection, nailing her right on the ass that just twelve hours ago I was gripping in my palm as I stroked in and out of her tight, pure cunt.

It feels petty to interject myself into their fun, so I'm hanging back, shoveling the front steps because I have too much energy to stand idly by.

The burn in my biceps is a welcome feeling. It gives me something to focus on, and I don't like to skip arm day anyway, so this heavy wet snow is the perfect solution.

Especially now that even our resident grump, Luke, has decided to join the snowball fight. He nails Jackson on the shoulder and then it's on. They're all bending down to pack snow.

"Jackson, help!" Brooke calls out when Luke lobs a snowball her way, too.

It misses, which was clearly on purpose. Luke has a pitcher's arm normally. He's just teasing her.

"Every man for himself, sweetheart," Jackson says.

"I'm not a man," she says with a giggle.

"Oh, trust me, I've noticed."

"We've all noticed," Luke says.

Brooke blushes a little as she glances over at Luke and smiles flirtatiously. "It's the small hands that give it away," she tells him, holding up her palms. "I can't make big snowballs."

Luke laughs. "Sure, that's it. Not a single other thing on your body or your beautiful face."

That surprises me. It doesn't sound super sexual given his casual tone, but it's still a shift in his attitude. He seems way more relaxed today. Luke must be feeling much more comfortable around Brooke now that her virgin status is history. I can't say I love that either, but clearly Brooke is enjoying herself.

She poses with a snowball for him. "Why, thank you."

Jackson has accumulated three snowballs during Brooke's exchange with Luke. He tosses one up in the air and catches it. "I have *very* big hands," he says. "You know what they say about that, sweetheart?"

Brooke's eyes widen.

I stop shoveling, afraid the metal scraping on the concrete steps will drown out her response. Is she thinking about Jackson's dick size?

"It means you have big balls," Luke says dryly.

"Snow balls or actual balls?" Brooke asks, head swiveling between the two of them.

That makes Luke laugh out loud. Jackson glares at him and throws a snowball at him but Luke easily dodges it.

Luke eyes Brooke. "I mean, he's flirting with you. You know that, right?"

She nods.

"Just checking."

Luke tromps over to me and holds out his hand. "Give me the shovel. Go have fun."

"I'm good."

Luke's eyebrows raise. "You don't sound like it."

I hit the walkway with the shovel and scoop up a load of wet snow. "Your hearing is off."

He stares at me and then just nods. "Okay. Got it."

My gut feels twisted and I'm annoyed by it.

Brooke is now laughing and running away from Jackson, who is pelting her with snowballs. She stumbles and falls in the snow and Jackson falls down beside her, reaching for her. She shrieks and rolls away.

"No, no," he protests. "Truce. I swear. I'm not trying to trick you."

They're both on their backs.

"Promise?" she asks, turning her head to eye him. She looks poised to roll away if necessary.

He touches the tip of her nose in a tender way. "Promise."

Her attention is fixed on him, and that gives my gut another twist. I want her to pay attention to *me*. Which is selfish and something I need to get under control. This is about Brooke, not me, just like last night was.

Brooke starts swinging her arms and legs out in the snow. "Snow angel contest! Luke, judge me and Jackson on whose is better."

"Sure. It's all about the clean exit," Luke says. He shoots me one last look and steps down into the yard again.

Jackson is pretending like he's going to mess up her lines by swinging his legs really wide.

"Cheater!"

Their grins are wide, their breath visible puffs, rising as they laugh and jostle together.

Luke holds his hand out to Brooke. "Here, angel."

She takes his hand and lets him haul her to her feet so she can cleanly jump out of her snow angel without messing it up. She smiles up at Luke but he doesn't return one. The smile on her face falters a little.

"Now who's cheating?" Jackson demands, stumbling out of his and destroying the left wing.

"Brooke wins," Luke says without hesitation. "Now let's go back inside. It's fucking cold out here."

"Agreed," Jackson says, dusting himself off. He reaches over and brushes snow off of Brooke's back. "I need to change into dry clothes." His hand drifts lower. "So do you."

"I'm going to take a hot shower," Brooke says.

She bites her bottom lip. For a second, I think she's going to invite Jackson to join her, but then she seems to remember I exist. She glances over at me, but doesn't say anything.

Luke and Jackson go past me into the house. I'm shoveling like a man possessed when Brooke pauses beside me.

"Are you okay?" she asks.

"I'm fine." Confused as fuck, but fine.

"Is this weird? I don't know how I'm supposed to act. This is all new to me." She crosses her arms over her chest. Her nose is pink from the cold and she looks worried. "Jackson said this isn't a competition but… it still feels that way to me. Jackson is flirting and you look annoyed and you and I didn't really talk about what any of this means, if anything…"

So she and Jackson had a private discussion? I know she left the room to check on Henley and the puppies last night. She must have run into him and clearly they both felt a connection.

I don't really want to have this conversation right now, but I want to—need to—reassure her that the ball is in her court here. I do mean that. I touch her chin and tip her head up.

"Brooke. I like you. A lot. I want to date you after this weekend. Take you out to dinner, go hiking together, spend many nights like last night again with you. But I know this is all new to you. If you want to date Jackson too, or spend the night with him, I'm fine with that. Everything is up to you. It's all your choice, beautiful."

Fine may be exaggerating it, but I understand she's inexperienced. In reality, if she wants to date another guy, I would prefer it be my best friend, who I know will treat her right.

"Last night was so wonderful," she says. "You've really opened my eyes, and it was so special, and I really like you too, Wyatt. I'm just not sure what exactly I want right now. It's all new and a little… overwhelming."

"I'll hang back," I tell her. "I don't want to overwhelm you or put any expectations on you." My heart squeezes just a little, but I have to do what's right for Brooke, not me. "This isn't a competition. This is whatever you want."

I'm willing to wait for however long it takes.

I'm falling hard for Brooke and I want to be with her. Permanently.

But she's not ready for that.

"Are you sure?" She's searching my expression.

"I'm sure." I give her a soft kiss. "Jackson is a good guy."

Brooke puts her arms around my neck and kisses me. "So are you."

She slips past me and into the house.

Why do I feel like I just friend-zoned myself all over again?

Way to go, asshole.

I go back to shoveling, trying to clear out my frustration.

CHAPTER 14

Brooke

I'M HAVING AN AMAZING, fun, flirty, and confusing as hell weekend.

I lost my virginity last night in the most perfect way possible.

Wyatt made it sexy and fun and very, very satisfying for me.

At various moments throughout the day, I'm suddenly reminded of what it felt like to have Wyatt moving inside me, gaze locked on mine, and my body feels tingly all over. The orgasms he gave me… oh my god. I had no idea a tongue could do *that*.

I'm a little sore, but not much. More like just aware that my body was well-loved.

It—and Wyatt—were everything that I could have hoped for in my sexual introduction.

But now that I've experienced it, I feel greedy.

Give me *more, more, more*.

Wyatt made it clear he's happy to oblige.

But… dang it.

Jackson Hill.

There's just something about him. Yes, he's incredibly hand-some and muscular. It's more than that, though. He's so easy to laugh with and he also showed me a caring and compassionate side last night when I found him sleeping by the dogs.

I'm intrigued with the idea of what it would be like to experience pleasure at his hand.

As I change into my last remaining pair of clean leggings and a tank top, I think maybe Wyatt was right—he's created a monster.

My phone pings on the nightstand where I have it charging and I glance down. It's my grandmother.

> Hope you're safe and sound and having fun. The storm didn't look too bad.

I realize my grandmother was matchmaking, but I don't think she intended for me to have quite *this* much fun.

Then again, with Heidi Wilder, you never know.

> Yes, everything is good. :)

I also have a text from my best friend Sophie who is also in vet school.

> Drinks after our exams?

> YES. I have SO much to tell you!

> Ooh, spill the tea.

> I will as soon as I get home.

I don't want to text about my night with Wyatt or my conflicted feelings. That is best discussed over a platter of nachos and some chilled margaritas.

I should be worried about the fact that the snow isn't melting fast enough to get me home on Sunday, but instead I'm totally distracted by the undeniable fact that I'm attracted to both Wyatt and Jackson.

Plus, Luke, if I'm being totally honest.

But Luke doesn't want anything to do with me.

He's been nice. He's polite. He's almost completely stopped scowling. But he's treating me like a kid sister. One who crashed his guys' weekend. He's merely tolerating me.

Grabbing up all of my dirty clothes, I toss them into a laundry basket in the main bedroom's closet and head out into the hallway. I didn't expect to be here an extra two days and I'm out of clean underwear. Though I could probably go without underwear.

That thought sneaks in from nowhere.

Yep. Definitely created a monster.

I still want to do laundry anyway. I hate getting back home to my apartment and having to empty a suitcase full of dirty clothes.

"Oh, sorry!" I say when I push the laundry room open and find Luke in there, bent over.

His butt in those jeans has my mouth turning dry.

He stands up, a scoop of dry dog food in a measuring cup from the kitchen. "Just getting Henley more food. I read online we need to up her calories while she's nursing. Is that okay? I should have asked you first, Dr. Wilder."

I think he means the title to be respectful but it makes me uncomfortable. I'm never sure if he's mocking me or if he likes me just fine. He's really hard to read.

"If she's hungry, Henley should definitely eat." I should step back to let him out but I hesitate. "Luke, I just want to apologize. I know this was supposed to be your guys' weekend and I'm here throwing off the whole vibe."

And having sex with your friend.

He shrugs. "No one planned on a blizzard."

"I know, but…

"Brooke, please. Don't worry about it. I see these two guys all the time. My weekend has not been ruined."

"You seem frustrated." I should let it go but my mouth keeps moving. "I feel like you don't like me."

Luke rubs his jaw. He sets the measuring cup with dog food down on the closed lid of the washing machine. "That's not what this is. I'm sorry if I made you feel that way."

"Then what is it?" I'm genuinely bewildered.

Luke sighs. "It's a self-preservation thing, okay? I like you too much. Way too damn much. I think you're intelligent and sweet and sexy as hell."

My jaw drops and my nipples grow tight. "Oh. But then why…"

"Because I'm all wrong for you. I'm dominating and grumpy and way too selfish for a woman like you."

My whole body suddenly feels warm.

Luke wants me.

There's lust in his eyes, and his shoulders are tense.

I instantly feel relieved and very, very turned on. "Maybe you should let me decide what a woman like me wants."

But he shakes his head firmly. "No. Absolutely not. I was married once, and it ended badly. She cheated on me and lied to me so carelessly that she fucking let me think the baby she was carrying was mine. Never a hint that it might not be." His fists clench and unclench and his voice cracks a little. "She let me watch the baby being born—a little girl who was fucking perfect —and I thought she was *mine*, Brooke. I fell in love with that baby, only to have her ripped away from me."

I'm shocked and absolutely heartbroken for him. I drop the laundry basket, and without thinking, just open my arms and pull him into an embrace. I rub his back gently. "Luke, I am so sorry. That's just horrible. I can't believe you went through that."

My assumption is the baby—who can't even be a baby anymore—is not in his life at all, so I don't pry. I'm grateful he opened up to me and my heart breaks for his pain.

Luke rests against me for a moment, breathing in deeply on the side of my neck. Then he says gruffly, "Thanks. But I can't and

I don't trust relationships anymore. There's a wall up and it's not coming down. Not even for you, angel."

Angel.

He's called me that twice now.

I feel incredible relief knowing he isn't being rude because he finds something about me objectionable. He is building a barrier between us.

"I understand," I tell him, even though it makes me sad. "But if you think I would ever hurt you, you're wrong."

Luke releases me and pins me with a hard stare. "No. I would hurt *you*. That's what I'm afraid of. That would kill me if I did that to you, Brooke. It would break my heart all over again if I destroyed you. I don't want you to *ever* feel this bitterness that I live with."

I nod. I press my lips together. If he feels that way, I'm not going to try to talk him out of it. Given my inexperience, he's probably way more than I can handle, anyway.

I do want to reassure him in some way. "I won't flirt with you, I promise."

"But you will flirt with both Wyatt and Jackson."

He doesn't pose it as a question.

"I like them both," I confess. "It's very confusing. They're both great guys."

Luke has shifted, so he's in the doorway now, putting physical distance as well as emotional distance between us. He leans against the doorframe, looking very masculine and in command.

The word he used to describe himself pops into my head. *Dominating*. Would I like that?

I think I would. From him, anyway.

"Wyatt is ready for a relationship. Marriage, a house, kids."

"I don't know if I'm ready for all that. I haven't explored dating at all. I love spending time with Wyatt, but I don't want to rush into anything."

I realize too late maybe I shouldn't be asking Luke for dating advice.

"You said it yourself. You haven't explored. So explore. Make out with Jackson. Hell, do whatever you want with him. You're young and you should have some fun."

"Okay. Thanks, Luke."

"You're welcome. Now do me a favor and put a sweatshirt on. You're killing me."

I glance down and see my nipples have been standing at attention throughout our entire conversation. Including during that hug.

"Oh!" I cover them with my hand. "Sorry."

Luke grins. "Don't ever be sorry for having needs and wants, Brooke. We all have them."

"But some of us don't get what we want?" I ask softly.

The grin falters. "No, we don't." His voice is flat. He turns on his heel.

"Wait, you forgot—

But he's already gone.

—the dog food." I sigh and bend over to pick up my laundry basket.

Well, that didn't clear up my confusion at all.

I feel like I'm even *more* attracted to Luke.

Who is totally off-limits.

This is why I need to focus on exploring sex, *not* starting any kind of serious relationship.

I dump my laundry and start the washer. I grab the dog food and head back into the kitchen, where Wyatt is making lunch, with a newfound resolve.

My greatest talent is learning. I study like a beast.

I'm going to get as much sex education this weekend as I possibly can.

CHAPTER 15

Luke

THESE TWO ARE DRIVING me nuts.

Okay, these *three* are driving me nuts.

Brooke is abso-fucking-lutely a part of this, but it's Wyatt and Jackson that I want to punch in the face.

They're sitting in the living room, across from each other, acting like the other doesn't exist.

Like brothers who got into a fight and are now giving each other the silent treatment.

And they think I won't notice.

They're such idiots.

And it's all about the beautiful girl stuck with us in this fucking cabin by this fucking snowstorm.

I told Brooke she didn't ruin my weekend. I told her the truth about being attracted to her and that it's just really fucking difficult to ignore it. I told her my whole story, thinking that would push her away.

It didn't.

She's too goddamned sweet for that. She wants to fix me. And hell if I'm not starting to wonder if maybe she could.

I've been living like I'm allergic to warmth and light for years now. I've been telling myself that I'm fine. I've got my job which I love. I've got the guys, who I also love. I've got women whenever I need them.

I've done the marriage thing. I gave the love and trust and forever thing a try.

It's not for me.

But Brooke Wilder is… something else.

She could make me believe again.

And that is the stupidest, most delusional, clearly lust-fueled thing I've ever thought.

I want her, but that's simply because I'm a straight man who loves sex and she's gorgeous and *here* and I know she just had sex for the first time last night and I can *not* stop thinking about that.

But she's innocent and young and trusting. Definitely not my type. At all.

I'm used to women who know the score, can read the signs, who want exactly what I'm willing to give and nothing more.

I just need to last a few more hours and get the fuck away from Brooke and her curves and her smile and her… everything… and I'll be fine. I'll go back to Chicago, call one of my regular hook-ups, or head to one of my favorite bars, and I'll get over this.

But until then, I need some help.

And it needs to come from the two guys I think of like younger brothers, who currently aren't talking to one another because they're just as messed up over her.

"Okay, you both need to knock this shit off," I say over the basketball game that's on TV that none of us care about. "Jackson needs to sleep with her."

Wyatt looks away from the TV, and Jackson looks up from his phone.

Neither of them demand to know what the fuck I'm talking about. Neither of them seem surprised at all.

I sigh from my position in the armchair I've been claiming all weekend to keep myself from sitting on the couch where Brooke always curls up.

"You two are being jackasses. You can't stop talking to one

another because of what happened with Brooke and Wyatt. We all agreed that's what was best." I level a look at Jackson. "You told *her* she should go upstairs with Wyatt."

Jackson nods. "I did. I'd do it again, too."

I look at Wyatt. "Hear that? No one's upset about last night."

He looks at Jackson. "Okay. Good."

"So what's *your* problem?" Jackson asks.

Wyatt frowns. "What? Nothing."

"You've been quiet all day. You seemed kind of pissy outside."

"I'm not. I'm just…" Finally, he blows out a breath. He shoves a hand through his hair. "You two flirting hit me harder than expected. But I know that's stupid. She and I haven't made any plans or commitments."

"Exactly," I say. "And you both like her, so Jackson deserves a chance with her."

And if she's got those two vying for her attention, then she won't be smiling and being sweet with me and pulling secrets out of me and making me think about what-ifs I have no business considering.

Jackson shifts on the loveseat. "I do like her," he admits. "And she told me she likes me, too. And she kissed me last night."

Wyatt sits up straighter. "What?"

Okay, this is good. That clench in my gut is *not* jealousy. I'm here basically advocating for Jackson to take her to bed tonight, for fuck's sake.

Jackson nods. "It was just quick and sweet. Took me by surprise but, yeah. And I want a chance with her too. Not just the sex. To take her out when we get home."

I frown. "She's going to be busy with school. Starting her clinical rotations. You two can't distract her."

They both stare at me.

Yeah, that sounded unnecessarily protective.

And it's none of my damned business.

"I'm talking about here," I finally say, my tone crankier now. "I think Brooke deserves to know all her options *now*."

They're both quiet for several long seconds. Then Wyatt finally says, "Fine."

Jackson blows out a breath. "Yeah?"

Wyatt looks at him and nods. "Yeah. I want her to be happy. To have what she wants. Whatever that is. I know you'll treat her well. So… yeah. If she wants it too, then you should definitely let her know that you're interested."

Jackson gives him a smile. "Thanks man. And you know I'll be good to her."

"You better be."

Yeah, he better be.

I'm feeling that strange restless mix of emotion. I want her, but I can't have her, so I want *these* two to be the ones, but *knowing* they're with her might kill me.

Especially if either of them become serious with her after this weekend.

I could potentially be repeatedly running into this gorgeous girl who's gotten so damned deep in my system I know I'm going to be thinking about her for weeks, if not months, even without seeing her again.

Fuck.

I shove a hand through my hair, then run it down over my face.

Sure, Brooke said she wasn't sure if she was ready for a whole big relationship thing, but these two motherfuckers can be very persuasive.

I just have to avoid her as much as possible until we dig out and get on the plane home. Then I'll worry about getting over her, somehow, once we're back to civilization.

"So you're both going to stop acting fucking weird with each other," I say. It's not a request, it's an order. "You're not going to let a woman come between you. She's amazing, we all agree, but you two aren't going to ruin a friendship because of this."

Normally, I'd think it was ridiculous to think that could even possibly happen. I've never seen these two like this. But now I've also met Brooke. If they'd only *told* me about this woman they'd both met and liked, I'd be really laying into them about letting a piece of ass mess them up. But Brooke's different. I get it. Way more than a piece of ass. And this could become very complicated.

They are slow to answer, but finally Jackson nods.

"Right," he says. "We can't let that happen."

"Agreed," Wyatt says.

Man, I *really* wish they'd both said that with more conviction.

But we'll be out of here soon.

Everything will make more sense once we're back in Chicago, back to our usual routines, back in the real world. All of this is just a crazy, snowed-in fantasy land.

CHAPTER 16

Brooke

I'M down to my panties and bra.

I've even lost both socks.

Of course, the guys gave me the option of quitting the poker game when I ran out of money, but I was convinced my luck would turn. It had to. I couldn't do worse than losing *every single hand*. Could I?

No. But I could *keep* losing every single hand.

And I have.

Jackson was the one who'd suggested we switch to strip poker when my money ran out. Of course he was.

Both Jackson and Wyatt are also now sock-less. And shirtless. And I'm not mad about it.

The only person at the table who hasn't lost a single article of clothing is Luke.

Yet *he* seems mad.

After our laundry room talk, though, I know it's not that he's angry and thinking this is juvenile. He's turned on. He's a little tormented by me sitting here in my panties.

And I like that.

The sex with Wyatt last night, the flirting with Jackson, the confession from Luke has all combined into a warm ball of confidence and sexiness I've never felt before and I want to flaunt it. I want to tease them. I want to turn them on. Tempt them.

I want them to *all* want me so much they can't stand it.

I want them to all remember this weekend for weeks after we get home. Months even.

I look at the cards in my hand. I understand poker, even if my play tonight doesn't prove it.

I know enough that I should absolutely *not* bet on what I'm holding.

"Raise," Wyatt says. Then looks at me.

I look from him, to Jackson—who led—then to Luke, who comes after me. "Call," I say, staying in the round even though I have nothing.

"Fold," Luke says, tossing his cards onto the table.

Jackson grins and turns over a full house.

"Dammit," Wyatt mutters as he turns over only a pair.

I sigh, pretending to be upset as I show my cards.

Jackson chuckles. "Damn, girl, it's almost like you're trying to lose."

I meet his gaze. "Yeah, kind of seems that way, doesn't it?"

His smile dies a little as his gaze grows more intense. "Guess you have to ditch the bra or panties."

"Guess so," I agree.

Luke suddenly shoves back from the table. "I'm out."

Wyatt and Jackson don't seem surprised. "You sure?" Wyatt asks, though his eyes are on me. "Game's not over."

"I'm sure." He grabs his bottle of beer and stomps over to the armchair that he's claimed as his all weekend.

The open concept of the cabin means he's still, basically, in the same room with us at the dining table and him in front of the fireplace and TV, but his back is to us now.

Interesting.

Jackson and Wyatt don't spare him a glance.

"Come on," Wyatt says to me. "Pay up."

I reach under the table for my panties instead of my bra. They won't be able to really *see* my naked bottom half with the table in the way. Wyatt is just to my right but with the way I cross my legs, he won't really *see* anything. Not that he hasn't already seen *everything*. But Jackson is across the table. He'd have to duck under the table to get a look. I hold my panties up, then drop them on the floor next to my chair.

Both men's gazes darken. Heat swirls in my belly.

"Your deal," Jackson says to Wyatt.

"Um, you have to take something else off too," I remind Wyatt.

He keeps his eyes on me as he stands and strips out of his sweats, leaving him in boxers. I let my gaze travel over him as he sinks back into his chair.

He starts dealing again and with only the three of us now, the hand goes a little quicker.

Again, I should fold.

But I don't.

Wyatt folds, and Jackson turns over a pair of aces.

I fight my grin as I turn over my garbage hand.

Jackson leans in, forearms on the table. "Sweetheart, if you wanted to take your clothes off for us, you just had to say so. We didn't have to go through all the dealing and betting, you know."

"It's just a little more fun this way, isn't it?" I ask, reaching behind me for the clasp on my bra. "Builds the anticipation."

The surge of feminine power that shoots through me, as I hear *three* groans in response, has me smiling like a Cheshire cat.

I unhook my bra and also drop it beside my chair.

I note how Wyatt runs a hand through his hair and absorb his muttered, "Jesus."

But I can't look away from Jackson, who's hot gaze blatantly studies me from across the table.

"Yeah," he finally says, his voice low and gruff. "I guess it does. Of course, now the game's over."

I look at the table, then at the two men with me. "Does it have to be?"

"You don't have anything more to bet with," Jackson says.

"Don't I?" I ask, pulling the cards toward me and stacking them. "Don't I have anything else *of value* that you might want if I lose?"

I shuffle as the silence around the table stretches.

"What did you have in mind?" Jackson finally asks.

I meet his gaze. "What do you want?"

"Kisses," he says, his eyes on my mouth. "Maybe… touching."

I nod. "I could live with that."

Jackson looks at Wyatt. "What do you think?"

Wyatt's gaze locks on mine when I look at him. His eyes are hot. "I think that kissing and touching her are *definitely* valuable."

A shiver passes through me and I feel my nipples tighten. I'm certain they notice. I want badly to look in Luke's direction, but I know he's not looking over here. Still, he's listening.

"Okay, then," Jackson says. "Deal 'em."

I pass the cards out and study my hand, holding the cards up in front of my chest. And fighting a smile.

And finally, I have something decent. Interesting.

Jackson bets, Wyatt calls, and they both look at me.

It doesn't matter how this hand goes. This is fun. I'm naked with two hot guys. And I'm having sex tonight. With someone.

"Call," I say.

They both breathe out as if they were worried I was going to fold and take myself out of this hand.

Silly boys.

Jackson lays down three of a kind in queens.

But my straight beats that. I lay mine down with a grin. He arches a brow.

Then Wyatt lays down his full house.

He gives me a wicked grin. "Lose your pants, Jackson," he says, without looking at his friend. To me he says simply, "Come here."

My heart starts hammering, but I swallow hard and stand.

I hear Jackson groan when he sees my full naked body for the first time. I don't look away from Wyatt, though, suddenly feeling flushed and nervous and jumpy.

I'm bare naked in the same room with *three* men. Well, maybe two and a half. Luke isn't participating here and I know he's not going to do anything. Still, he's *here*, and as always, I'm acutely aware of him.

Wyatt reaches out as he scoots his chair back slightly. He pulls me into his lap. He cups the back of my head and brings me in for a deep, long, lots-of-tongue kiss.

My entire body lights up, and I feel hot and tingly from head to toe.

Some of it is definitely the kiss. Wyatt Doherty is a *very* good kisser, but it's also that I know Jackson is watching us. That makes it even hotter. I wouldn't have suspected that.

Wyatt's other hand is on my thigh, and he starts stroking up and down. I part my legs slightly on instinct, wanting his touch higher… deeper.

"Hey now," Jackson says. "Kissing *or* touching, right?"

Wyatt pulls back and gives me a grin. "Right. Almost forgot."

I'm breathing fast and I'm wet and hot and don't care at all about poker suddenly.

"Um…"

But I don't have to come up with any words. Wyatt's big hands settle on my hips and he turns me to face the table. But keeps me in his lap.

Jackson doesn't say anything. His gaze settles on my breasts, and my nipples tighten just from him *looking* at them.

He shuffles and deals without looking at the cards once.

Wyatt can obviously see my cards as I pick them up, but I don't care.

Wyatt is down to his boxers and I can feel his cock, hard and thick, pressing against my ass. Jackson is also now down to boxers only, though I can't see him beyond the edge of the table.

Still, from the mid-ab area and up, he's gorgeous. Smooth medium brown skin stretching over lean muscles that flex as he arranges his cards. He's not as muscular as Wyatt and Luke, but he's still in very good shape. His shoulders, chest, and abs are well defined, and I want to run my tongue over all of them. Then there's his thick, short, curly black hair, his big brown eyes, those lips that I now know are soft, but firm and that I want to feel on so many more parts of my body…

"Brooke," Wyatt says, squeezing my hip. "Your bid."

"All in," I say, not even looking at my cards. I could have a royal flush, and I don't care.

They both give dark, low chuckles.

"What's all in mean to you, sweetheart?" Jackson asks, running the tip of his index finger over the tops of his cards.

"That if I lose this hand, the winner takes me upstairs and gets all the kissing and touching he wants for however long he wants," I say, shocking myself.

The two men at the table both seem to freeze.

"Goddammit."

We all turn toward the muttered curse from the living room area.

Luke has sprung up from his chair and is stomping toward the front door.

"Luke?" Wyatt calls.

"Going for a walk," is his terse response. He jerks his coat from the hooks by the door and yanks the door open, slamming it behind him.

O-k-a-y.

"He's just—" Wyatt starts.

"It's okay," I tell him quickly. "What's in your hand?"

I'm not worried about Luke. This is his decision. He could stay. He knows *I* would be fine with it. This is his choice. If he's all wound-up and upset, that's on him.

Wyatt lays down two pair.

Jackson lays down a flush.

"Okay, then." Wyatt's hands settle on my waist and he

squeezes. Then I feel him kiss the back of my head. "Have fun, you two."

He nudges me up from his lap and toward Jackson.

This is… strange. And exciting. And *god*, I want this.

I really like Wyatt. So much. Last night was amazing. But I also want Jackson so much. I know so many people would judge me for what's about to happen. A week ago, *I* might have judged me for what is about to happen. But these two guys aren't judging. And no one's getting hurt here. We're all consenting adults. We all know exactly what's happening.

So I take one step toward Jackson. "You're the winner," I tell him softly.

"Yeah." He reaches out and takes my hand. "I sure fucking am."

CHAPTER 17

Brooke

JACKSON PULLS ME CLOSE, his hands settling on my hips. He looks me up and down. "Fuck. You're so…"

I put my hand on his face and smile. "You too."

He pulls me into his lap. I go willingly, straddling his thighs. Then he kisses me.

Really kisses me.

It's hot and deep. Different from how Wyatt kisses, but just as hot. Just as all-consuming. His tongue strokes over mine as his hands run over my body. He traces up and down my spine, then over my ass, then up to cup my breasts. His thumbs rub over my nipples and I moan into his mouth.

"Upstairs," I hear Wyatt say, his voice tight. *"Please."*

Jackson pulls back and looks at his friend, grins, then nods. "Yeah, okay." He looks up at me. "My room or yours?"

"Yours." It felt right to be in Wyatt's room last night.

"The toys are in her room, though," Wyatt says.

My eyes widen, and I look over my shoulder at him. "Toy. Singular. And…" I look back at Jackson. "I won't need it, will I?"

He chuckles and runs his big hand down my back again. "Using toys together can be very fun, but that can wait. And I'm definitely a toy guy. And a food guy."

"Food?" I ask, brows arched.

"Whipped cream, chocolate sauce… anything can be fun." He grins at me. "But tonight it can be just you and me."

Using my toy *together*? I didn't think much of it when Wyatt mentioned my vibrator last night. His tongue was distracting me from thinking much at all. But using my vibrator *with* a guy? Isn't it supposed to be a substitute when a guy isn't around? I might want to know more about this.

But suddenly, Jackson is standing with his hands under my ass. I gasp and wrap my arms and legs around him, hanging on.

He starts toward the stairs and I'll admit I'm impressed. "You can carry as much as a firefighter, huh?" I tease, looking at Wyatt over his shoulder.

Wyatt is watching us, but he doesn't really look upset. He looks a little… confused, maybe. Like he's not sure what he's feeling. But he gives me a wink when he catches my eye.

"You're just a little thing," Jackson says. "I couldn't carry their maxes, no way."

"I'm not little!" I protest as he starts up the stairs. "I'm five-seven." My brother is a professional hockey goalie, for fuck's sake.

"Yeah, but you're built like a ballerina or something," he says, jostling me in his arms as we reach the top of the stairs. "You're light." His voice drops lower. "And tight."

I feel goosebumps break out.

We get to his room and he shifts me so he can twist the knob and then push the door open. He strides straight to the bed and drops me onto it. Then he steps back, his gaze taking me in.

"Jesus Christ, you look good on my sheets, sweetheart."

The husky note in his voice has my pussy fluttering.

He goes back to the door and shuts and locks it. Then stops by the bag on the floor by the dresser and digs inside. He comes up with a box of condoms. He stalks back to the bed, tossing them toward the pillows, before climbing up.

I lie back, and he braces himself over me.

"Did you and Wyatt have fun last night?" he asks.

I nod. "A lot of fun."

"Did he take good care of you? Make you come multiple times? Make this sweet pussy nice and hot and wet over and over?"

I whimper softly. "Yes."

"Good." He leans down and kisses me. "So now that you have a starting point, what do you want? What do you want to try now?"

I look up at him. He's the playful one. The one that doesn't take things too seriously.

Except that he wants to. He wants to be more serious, find something more important to do.

That's not about you and definitely not about sex, I remind myself.

"I don't even really know all my options," I tell him truthfully.

"What positions did you try out?" he asks, stroking his hand down my side.

"Just vanilla," I say. "That's what he said."

Jackson chuckles. "You were on your back, him on top?"

I nod. "But I liked it," I say quickly. "It was really good."

"There's nothing wrong with vanilla at all," he agrees. He drags his hand up my thigh and cups my pussy. "Do you want me to fuck you like that, sweetheart? Do you just want to spread your legs for me like this?"

I do without thinking. He runs his middle finger over my clit and then dips just the tip into my pussy.

"So wet," he says gruffly. "Fuck, you're perfect just like this. I'll gladly take you just like this."

He slips his finger in deeper and lowers his head to kiss me again. I grip his shoulders as he slides in and out, then circles over my clit. He runs his mouth from my lips to my jaw.

"You're so tight and hot," he tells me. "I'm aching for you already."

"You can fuck me however you want to," I tell him, breathlessly.

He groans. "Christ, Brooke, you don't even know all the ways I want to."

"Tell me." I love hearing these guys talk in bed like this. Every word seems to amp the temperature of my blood higher.

His mouth moves to my neck where he kisses me, then says, "I want to bend you over the end of the bed so I can hold on to your perfect ass," he says, sliding another finger into me. "I want to put you on all fours in front of a mirror so I can watch your face every time I slam into you. I want to put you at the end of the bed on your back so I can spread your legs wide, but stand while I pound this pretty pussy until you scream."

I'm breathing faster and I know he can feel around his fingers what this is doing to me.

"I want to make you ride me, sitting tall and pretty, your tits bouncing, taking me in, your legs spread wide over my hips." He stops and lifts his head. "That one. That's how I want you."

I kind of lost track. I'm just all in if it involves my legs spread, him inside me, and both of us coming hard.

"You on top." Suddenly his fingers are gone, and he's rolling to his back.

But he brings me with him. I'm draped over him now. He kisses me as he pulls my thighs up on either side of his hips. Then says, "Sit up."

I do. I'm straddling him, his cock nestled firmly against my ass. In this position, I'm on full display. As he proves, his gaze raking over me from my breasts down my stomach to where I'm spread out over him.

"Damn, *that* is a pretty sight," he says, reaching between my legs and sliding his thumb over my clit.

I gasp.

"Yeah, this is full access," he says, grinning a very pleased grin. He reaches up and tugs on one of my nipples. My pussy clenches. "What do you think?" he asks. "You want to be a cowgirl?"

"Cowgirl?" I repeat.

"That's this position." His hands drop to my hips. "You riding me. You can control the pace and depth from here."

"Oh." I wiggle and his breath hisses out. I like even that little bit of power. "Yeah, I might like this."

"You *will* like it," he promises. "But let's do something else first."

"Like what?"

"Did Wyatt eat your pussy last night?"

For some reason, despite everything else that's been said and everything else he knows, and despite the fact I'm sitting on him completely naked, *that* makes me blush hotly.

Jackson chuckles. "I take that as a yes."

I bite my bottom lip. "Yes."

"Did you like it?"

I nod. "Yes. A lot."

"Excellent." Then he's squeezing my hips and moving me up his body.

"What are you doing?"

"Getting a taste for myself."

"What do you mean?"

"I mean, I want to taste your pussy too, Brooke. I mean I want to make you come apart with my mouth before I fuck you. I mean, sit on my face like a good girl until you come."

"I…" Then he settles me over his mouth and his tongue licks me firmly and I grab the headboard to stay upright. "Oh, God!"

"That's right. Just like that," he mutters against me.

Then he starts licking and sucking and I can't help but wiggle and swivel against his tongue and I soon feel the beginning coil of an orgasm.

"Jackson," I gasp.

"Fucking heaven. This is where I want to spend eternity."

I laugh, in spite of the fact that I'm about to lose my mind.

"Play with your nipples," he says, nipping the inside of my thigh.

"I—"

"Brooke," he says firmly. "Pinch those pretty nipples."

Then he sucks hard on my clit and I'm willing to do anything this man tells me. I lift both hands, cup my breasts, and lightly tug on my nipples.

"Good girl," he praises, gripping my ass. "Harder."

So I do. And my pussy clenches and Jackson sucks hard, and my orgasm hits me hard and hot and I cry out. "Oh, God!"

"That's my girl," he praises, immediately dragging me down his body. "Fuck you're amazing." He reaches for a condom and hands it to me. "Want to put it on?"

I nod, my body still buzzing. I open it as he starts playing with my nipples, making the ripples of pleasure continue.

"You're so sensitive. You go off so easy. That's so fucking sexy, sweetheart," he tells me.

I feel like I just performed some amazing act, while in truth it was all him. Still, I'll take the praise. That alone keeps those aftershocks from my orgasm going. I sit up and scoot back, sliding my wet heat over his cock.

He groans. "Fuck. I can't wait to be buried inside you."

I look from the condom to his cock, then up at him. He grins, positions it in my fingers, then helps me roll it down his impressive length. My body shivers thinking about taking him in. Shivers with pleasure.

Yes, they've definitely created a monster.

"Okay, come on up." He takes my hips again, pulling me forward until his tip is at my entrance. "Now you control how fast you take me, how far I go," he says. "Okay?" He brushes my hair back from my face.

I nod. I lift up and take his cock in hand. He sucks in a breath at my touch and I look up at him.

"Go on," he urges.

"I want to make you make that noise again," I tell him honestly, squeezing him.

He closes his eyes and grits his teeth, then his hand wraps around mine. "You will." He chuckles. "You definitely will. Need inside you. You've been working me up for two days. Let me fuck you, Brooke. Then we can play all night."

That sounds *really* nice. I shift again, positioning him, then I start to lower myself over him.

I go slow. I'm still new at this, and he's huge.

His fingers dig into my hips but he doesn't try to hurry me, or stop me. I can tell by looking at his face this is a struggle, though. And I love that he's letting me have control here.

"God," I breathe out. "You're so big."

He lets out a rough laugh. "Jesus. You are so tight, Brooke. God, you feel amazing."

I slowly sink down and unlike last night—because of last night —there's no pain. There's a fullness, a stretch, but it's so good. It's like the two times Wyatt and I had sex *after* that first time.

When I'm all the way down, I wiggle a little, then brace my hand on his chest. His deep brown eyes meet mine. There's heat there, but also an affection that takes my breath away for a second.

"Now what?" I tease.

He blows out a breath. "Now you do whatever feels good."

"Oh." I think about that. All of this feels good. But I lift and lower myself on his length and *yes*, that definitely feels good. "I think I figured it out," I say, my voice breathless as I do it again.

"You have," he says tightly. "Fuck, you look good up there."

I move again. And again. He lifts his hands, cupping my breasts, playing with my nipples. I lift and lower, picking up speed.

"This is good," I say, panting a little.

"It's very good," he agrees. "You are definitely getting the hang of this."

But I need more of… something. "What else?" I ask. I sit up a little straighter, running my hand through my hair. The arch in my back changes the angle slightly and *that* feels really good. I swivel my hips.

"Your clit," he says. He's watching me with dark eyes.

I can see the lust in his expression, the way he's holding on but that it's an effort. That gives me a thrill.

"Oh, yes." I reach between my legs and circle my clit. That's very nice.

Jackson catches my hand and brings it to his mouth, sucking on the finger that was just against my clit. My pussy tightens around him. He swirls his tongue around my finger and when it's wet and slick, he presses it back against my clit.

My eyes on his, I circle and press.

Tingles spread, my pussy tightens, and when I lift up and down, I just want to go faster and faster.

"There you go, sweetheart," he urges. "I'm going to take this vision with me to bed for the rest of my life."

"Have you been thinking about me in bed the last few nights?" I ask.

"Of course."

"What have you been doing while you think about me?"

"Oh, you want to hear how you've disrupted my sleep and made me hard and restless and distracted and turned everything upside down?" he asks.

"Yes," I admit.

He pinches one nipple. "Naughty girl. You *like* having three men all wound up over you, don't you?"

"Yes." My breathing is coming faster now and I'm moving quicker, feeling my orgasm building.

"Well, I've been hard every night, wrapping my hand around my cock, thinking about your mouth, your ass, your breasts, imagining this tight pussy and *wanting* all of it," he tells me. "Even last night when you were with Wyatt."

That makes my pussy clench.

He tugs on my nipple and squeezes my hip. "I've imagined you spread out, bent over, on your knees. Every way to pleasure you. I loved and hated knowing you were getting filled up and stretched out last night. That was so fucking dirty and hot and horrible at the same time."

I'm moving over my clit faster now, lifting and lowering myself faster, fucking him faster.

"But everything about you, everything about your pleasure—whether it's how you take your pancakes to seeing you with those dogs to knowing how to suck on your clit and make you come—has been amazing for me, Brooke. I've loved being here with you. I've loved getting to know you. And *fuck*, this body is *everything* and more than I dreamed of. I'll never get enough of you."

Wyatt had said something similar last night, and it had the same effect. It amped up the lust, but also started a warmer, softer burn that I am very afraid is me becoming addicted to this. To him. To them.

I lower myself so my breasts are against his chest and kiss him deeply. He wraps an arm around my waist, holding me still and taking over, pounding up into me.

I just hang on and let the pleasure rip through me as my orgasm hits.

"Fuck, yes, come on me just like that. Just. Like. That," he says, emphasizing the words with deep thrusts. He groans. "Yes. Yes, Brooke. *Yes!*" Then he stiffens under me, then stills.

I relax against him, my ear against his thundering heart.

After a few minutes, he stirs. He trails his fingers up and down my back.

"You okay?" he asks.

"Very, very, very okay," I tell him, not moving. "But can I stay right here for another hour or so?"

He wraps his arms around me. "You can stay right here forever if you want to."

I don't stay forever.

In my room Sunday morning after forcing myself to leave Jackson's warm and comfortable bed, I take a quick shower and turn on music on the ancient clock radio my grandmother left behind on the nightstand, hoping it will drown out the conversation I need to have with my best friend, Sophie.

After learning that Luke overheard me getting friendly with my vibrator the other night, I don't want to be overheard.

I have to talk to someone about this weekend before I burst, but I don't want any of the guys to know what I'm saying because, well, because I'm about to gush.

"Hey!" Sophie picks up my call right away. "How's studying? Are you back home? We can hang out tonight if you want."

"So… I'm still up north. I kind of got ambushed by friends of my brother." I perch on the edge of the bed and bite my lip. I have no idea how to tell her what exactly has happened because it's frankly a little unbelievable.

"That sounds hot. Are they cute? And what do you mean by ambushed? I'm not following."

"They were supposed to be here for a guys' weekend and came a day early because of a snowstorm. Then I couldn't leave because of the snowstorm. We're all stuck here together until probably Monday."

"Oh shit, but you'll be back in time, right?"

Sophie is also a vet student, and she knows how important this week is for both of us. She's scheduled to start clinicals in Indianapolis in a few weeks.

"Yes, and I feel confident about exams, so it's fine. It's just…"

"You have a crush on one of them?" She sounds downright gleeful. "Please tell me he's a hot hockey player and you're going to date him and invite me to hockey player parties."

"No… Wyatt's a firefighter. Jackson is a self-made millionaire. And Luke is also a firefighter."

Why does my tongue feel two sizes too thick?

Because I want to tell her that I had sex with Wyatt and Jackson but I also want to tell her that I'd love to have sex with Luke, too, and I have no idea how she is going to react. Sophie has been telling me for years I need to "just get the first time over with," so I can enjoy having sex whenever I want, but this is obviously more than that. I didn't just leap, I bungee jumped into being sexually active.

"Which one do you like?"

"All of them." I glance at my closed door, envisioning them in the kitchen, making coffee and laughing and talking. "For different reasons. Wyatt is so sweet. I had sex with him and he was just so gentle and kind and listened to me, knowing it was my first time. Then Jackson is funny and easy to be around and he taught me how to do cowgirl. Then Luke is so... intense and protective. I just honestly like them all."

There's a pause, then Sophie makes a choking sound in the back of her throat. "Hold on. Back the fuck up. You had sex with Wyatt?"

"Yes."

"Well, damn, good for you. It sounds like it was amazing."

I sigh, happily. "It was amazing. I couldn't have asked for a better first time."

"I'm happy for you then."

"Thank you."

"As for Jackson... you do know what cowgirl is, right? Are you telling me you had sex with him, too?"

"Yes."

"At the same time as Wyatt?"

Sophie doesn't sound judgmental, she sounds intrigued. Fascinated.

"No. The next night. Wyatt knew, and they were both cool with it."

"Oh my God, Brooke, you really went for it, damn, girl. I'm super impressed and very jealous right now."

That makes me laugh in relief. "It's just for this weekend, obviously. Kind of a snowed-in unexpected sex fest."

"Next year I'm going to that cabin with you. Holy shit."

"It all just kind of happened, and it's been so much fun. They're really amazing guys."

"What about the third guy, the intense one?"

I close my eyes briefly. "Honestly, I'm really attracted to him too. Is that crazy?"

"No. You're not looking for a husband, you're having fun. If all three guys are hot, they're hot. Bonus points if they're nice guys too."

"Yeah. They are."

"So just have fun. You're all consenting adults. Don't put a label on anything, just embrace the experience. Whatever happens, happens."

"Thank you. I needed to hear that. I don't plan on repeating this with them or anyone else. I just want to live in the moment."

"When life hands you hotties, get naked."

"I can't argue with that."

We end the call, and I take a deep breath.

I want to have sex with Luke, too. I can admit it.

I doubt it will happen, but I am really, really curious as to why the three of them think I need to be shielded from him.

Sophie is right.

Whatever happens, happens.

CHAPTER 18

Luke

TODAY JUST ABOUT KILLED ME.

Brooke is different today.

She's more confident, she's laughing easily, she's walking around in ass-hugging leggings with a sway in her hips that didn't exist before.

She's been thoroughly fucked and loved by two guys, and it *shows*.

It's as if this weekend allowed her to unleash the power of her pent up sexuality all in one big sexy swoop and she feels her own power. She's owning her body and all its needs and damn it, that is so *hot*.

It's fucking with my head and my dick, and everything in between, so yes, even my heart.

Because seeing her glowing—Jesus, she's *glowing*—makes me really damn happy for her.

And really, really angry with myself.

If I wasn't such an emotional black hole, I could be enjoying her smile and her teasing and her body right now, too. Instead, I'm shoving an endless supply of chips and guacamole into my mouth and trying not to say something we'll both regret.

Like "Bend over this couch *now*," or "I bet you look gorgeous on your knees sucking my cock." Or even "Take that dick like a good girl."

I don't know for certain what Wyatt and Jackson have said to her privately, but maybe none of those.

They also probably haven't tied her up, which is something I cannot get out of my head. I want her hands wrapped above her head and her legs spread wide, each ankle secured to a side of the bed. My bed.

I don't think our newly deflowered virgin is ready for all that.

Brooke laughs, a high hearty laugh of pure joy as she accepts a chip loaded with guacamole from Wyatt, him feeding it to her in a way that makes me rage. She flicks her tongue over his finger and his blue eyes darken. Then her perfect pink lips close around his fingers and lightly suck.

I wonder if she's sucked his cock yet. Or Jackson's, wrapping that pretty mouth around a thick erection, learning to open her throat to please a man by taking him deep.

Wyatt pulls his finger away and kisses her.

I turn and head to the refrigerator for a beer I don't need or want.

But I can't watch.

I swear to God, she actually smells like sex, even though she's showered and that's not possible. But it's like the cork was popped and all her endorphins are filling the whole damn cabin and it's not fair that I'm the lone idiot jerking off in my shower while everyone else is fucking.

It's also possible I've passed the point of being rational.

I would actually consider jumping in the lake to cool my overheated ass off if the damn thing wasn't frozen still.

Yanking the refrigerator door open way too hard, all the condiments and beer bottles inside rattle aggressively.

Sixteen more hours, then we can leave this cabin and I can forget all about Brooke Wilder. I'll text a hookup, I'll hit the gym, and I'll stop eating guacamole because now I'll never be able to see an avocado again without thinking of the way she expertly removed the pit today on a half dozen of them and proudly showed us how she makes guac.

Fuck avocados. I don't need them. Salsa is just fine.

But I like guacamole better and therein lies the whole damn problem. I can't have the guacamole or Brooke and I'm stuck with salsa and a potential warm body next to me that I won't be able to stop comparing to Brooke.

Which means I have no business being anything other than celibate for the near future until I can get a handle on my goddamn head.

I grab a beer and slam the fridge door shut again.

Then I unscrew the cap on the beer even though it's not a screw top, scraping the skin on my palm, and toss the cap onto the island in a general "fuck you" to everything.

"I'm going to bed," I announce.

Not that the three of them will care. They're already talking about getting in the hot tub one last time, and I'm not doing that.

"Bed?" Wyatt exclaims. "It's eight o'clock."

"He's old, remember?" Jackson grins as he strips out of his sweatpants. "Next thing you know, he'll be eating dinner at four."

"We're just dropping trou in the kitchen now?" I ask, gesturing to his pants on the floor.

"We told you we're going in the hot tub," he replies. "Come on. It's our last night here since the runway has been cleared for the plane, and hot tubs are good for aging joints."

Something on my face must give him a clue it's not a good time to mess with me because he just shrugs.

"Okay, then. You do you."

It's just an expression that has nothing whatsoever to do with sex and yet all I can think is that they're both *doing* Brooke and I'm doing nothing.

Brooke peels herself away from Wyatt and comes over to me. "Join us. Please? It will be fun."

I shake my head. "No."

She knows why. I explained it to her yesterday.

She's far too tempting.

"I don't want you to be in here by yourself," she murmurs.

"I have the dogs."

"I'm going out," Jackson declares.

"Me too. Brooke, you coming?" Wyatt asks.

"Not yet," Jackson says with a grin.

They all laugh. So now we're just joking about them fucking her? What are they going to do, share her tonight?

Jesus, I do *not* need that thought in my head.

Brooke shoots me one last look but follows them.

I stand in the kitchen for ten minutes, nursing my beer, debating what to do with myself and all my frustration, when Brooke suddenly comes back into the kitchen.

She's not wearing any pants or a bra and she has on Jackson's white T-shirt. It skims her thighs. "I forgot to get my wine."

I don't say anything. I just shift out of the way so she can access the refrigerator. Brooke pulls out a bottle of wine and gets a glass from the cabinet, which makes the shirt draw up. I see she has her panties on still, which is oddly a relief.

I know she's going to have sex with one or both of those guys, yet I don't really want to think about it. Or see any more of her body.

"What are you thinking right now?" she asks me. "You look so…"

"What?"

"I don't know. What are you thinking?" she repeats.

I scoff. "You *really* don't want to know, little girl."

But Brooke leans in closer to me, earnest. "I do want to know. I want to know *you*. The real you. You showed him to me yesterday, and I appreciate that so much. I like you—a lot. But I want more."

"Greedy, greedy," I say, a little amused she's pushing so hard.

As amused as you can be with a rock solid cock.

Brooke stares at me. Her nostrils flare. I've hit a nerve of some kind.

Did one of the guys call her greedy? Was she greedy with

them? Jesus, I hope so.

"I'm not leaving until you tell me what you're thinking right now."

There's a bratty side to Brooke. I didn't expect this. Ironically, it only serves to make her hotter.

"The angel is actually a brat," I muse.

Brooke gasps and pulls back. Then, after a beat, her eyes narrow. "So teach me a lesson then."

Fuck.

That backfired on me.

I shake my head. "No."

"Then tell me the truth. What are you thinking?"

If she wants the truth that much, then fucking fine.

"I'm thinking that I want to see you pull those panties off so I can back you against the wall. I'm thinking that I want to hold your hands above your head so you can't stop me from going as deep as I want when I *fuck you.* When I fuck you against that wall so hard you can't even breathe and your ass dents the drywall."

Her jaw drops.

That should push her away for good.

But instead of turning on her heel and running away, which was my last hope, she just asks, "Which wall?"

Then she licks her lips.

I groan, unable to stop myself. "*No.* I don't want to hurt you."

"You're hurting me now by rejecting me."

"I'm not rejecting you. I'm *protecting* you." What is so damn hard to understand about that?

"I don't need you to protect me from you. I'm a grown woman who knows what she wants. I want *you.*"

It's pure, absolute torture.

Her voice is husky, raw, pleading. She sounds sensual and needy, and I want to give her exactly what she wants.

My self-control is pulled taut like a rubber band and I'm one soft plea away from snapping.

My hands are trembling now with the urge to pick her up and

slam her against the wall, to bury myself to the fucking hilt in her tight body.

"Don't. Go back outside." My voice is rough.

"Please, Luke. I want you to show me." She reaches under the loose T-shirt and peels down her panties. They drop onto the floor.

"Like this? Is this how you want to fuck me?" She backs herself against the wall next to the fridge with a soft thump. Her hands go above her head.

The movement draws the shirt up, so that it just skims the tops of her thighs. Her bare sex is a hint, a promise, a fucking tease that I can't see. So close, yet not mine.

I can look, right? Even if I shouldn't touch.

"Higher," I demand. "Put your hands up higher so I can see your pretty little pussy."

Her breath catches. She obediently does as I ask and there it is —all that sweet juicy goodness bared for me to see. I study the apex of her thighs, imagining what it would feel like to run my tongue over her and have her quiver and buck beneath my touch. I imagine how slick and welcoming her slit would be if I buried myself in her tight heat.

I stand there, rigid, my cock hard in my jeans, and just stare at her.

"Luke," she begs. "*Please.*"

A glance up the length of her shows she is breathing hard, chest rising up and down rapidly, her nipples tight pebbles beneath the shirt, her neck stained pink from desire. Her eyes are pleading, her tongue sliding across her bottom lip. She's gripping her hands together tightly in obedience.

I rake my gaze back down, and she shifts her feet apart in obvious invitation. She even turns one knee out to the side, to open herself for better viewing.

And then, as I watch her, I see the slow slide of her arousal from her pussy down onto her thigh.

The rubber band snaps.

I can't resist her any more.

Hell, maybe I was never going to, anyway.

With a sound that might be a growl or a roar, I don't know, I yank down my zipper, free my cock, and stalk toward her.

"Is this what you want?" I demand, jerking my hand up and down my throbbing dick. "Tell me now if you've changed your mind."

She shakes her head frantically. "No. This is what I want. This is everything I want. Now. Right now."

The little temptress is eyeing my dick with naked curiosity. She actually licks her bottom lip.

Under other circumstances, I would push her down onto her knees, grip her hair, and show her how dominating I can be. But I don't have the patience for that.

Instead, I press against her, crowding her into the wall. I yank her leg up onto my hip. "Last chance to back out, angel."

I'll walk away if she says no now, no questions asked.

Even with her breath warm on my cheek, even with her pussy an inch away from my tip, I'll walk away.

But instead of changing her mind, she pumps her hips forward, seeking my cock. She's sliding all that soft wetness all over me and I bite back a groan at the electric jolt that courses through my body.

She's whimpering right next to my ear. "Show me how you like it, Luke. Show me *fucking*."

I brace myself against the wall with one hand and squeeze her thigh with the other, hard. "You're a dirty little girl, Brooke." I press my forehead to hers, wanting her to understand what it means to be with a man like me. Overpowered. Consumed. "You hid it well. Don't ever hide it from me again."

Brooke is frantic now, bucking her hips to grind against me. She clearly wants to lower her hands and grip my shoulders, but she stays true to the game. She keeps her hands up high.

"That's it. That's my good girl. You ready?"

"Yes! Please!"

Her cunt is right there and all it takes is one hard thrust and then I'm in fucking heaven. Brooke is tight and soaking wet and the minute I complete one slow slide in and out and back in, she's actually coming. She shatters with a muffled scream, biting so hard on her lip it turns white.

"Holy hell, pretty girl," I breathe, overcome with shock and lust. "That's it. Rub that little clit against me." I pause so that she can grind out the rest of her orgasm.

Then I just take her, driving myself into her deeper and deeper, her body like a slick fist squeezing up and down my length. "You're so tight, angel, holy fuck."

"Don't hold back," she begs me. "Do everything you want to me."

"I am. I'm fucking you just like you asked me so nicely for." I run my lips over the softness of her neck, trailing kisses while I pound into her, over and over. "Do you know why?" I murmur.

"No."

"Because you're mine," I tell her. "This is *my* cunt, do you understand? *Mine.*" I thrust balls deep and take great satisfaction at the sound of her ass slamming into the wall.

"*Yes, yes, yes.* Give it to me, yes."

She's actually crying now, great sobs of overwhelming pleasure as she wrings out another orgasm.

I've never felt anything like it as a hot surge of her liquid pleasure soaks my cock.

She's gorgeous in her complete wild abandonment to her arousal, to her body. She's slipping down the wall, only me and gravity holding her up.

"Lower your hands," I urge. "Hold on to me, angel."

Her hands drop to my shoulders and she focuses long enough to lock her gaze on me. "What is happening?" she whispers, her eyes glazed, her cheeks pink. There is dew on her forehead. "Why am I so…"

"So what?" I shift her hip, angling her even higher, opening her more.

"Wet?" Her eyes briefly close.

She's drowning in it, in the pleasure, the overwhelm.

I kiss her then, deeply, teasing at her lips so she'll open for me.

Our very first kiss, while I'm stroking in and out of her and she's just experienced what it's like to come really fucking hard.

"That's because you came, angel. So, so good." We can talk about female ejaculation later. Right now, I need to empty myself into her.

Thank God I don't need condoms. Thank God for that vasectomy I had after Marci ruined my life. Because fucking this girl bare, feeling every inch of her velvety heat clasping me tight is going down as the most pleasurable experience of my life.

"Oh." Her nails dig into my shoulders. "Did you? Come?"

"Not yet." A wave of tenderness rolls over me, in the midst of the greatest pleasure I've ever known. "Do you want me to?"

She nods. "Yes, please. I need to know that I can do that for you."

God, so fucking sweet. So incredible.

I come with a roar I didn't know I was holding back, letting all my hot cum surge deep up inside her as I pound out through the last final strokes.

"You do that for me," I tell her. "You abso-fucking-lutely do that for me."

She's actually wrecked me.

I'm never going to be the same.

Ever again.

I'm panting and leaning against her, easing her thigh down off of my hip. *"Brooke."* I nibble at her ear. "You do everything for me."

The slider suddenly yanks open.

"What's taking you so lo—" Jackson's voice cuts off mid-word. *"Holy shit."*

I half-turn. The guys are striding through the doorway.

"What the fuck?" Wyatt stares at us, in clear shock. Then he glares at me and roars, "Moody, you *fucking asshole.*"

CHAPTER 19

Wyatt

I DON'T EVEN KNOW what I'm feeling right now.

Luke is literally balls deep in Brooke at this very minute. They're both breathing hard. She's flushed pink and looks… absolutely fucking gorgeous.

But I'm feeling the intense, insane urge to punch Luke in the face.

I take a step toward them, but Jackson grabs my arm. "No, man," he says quietly.

"But—" I scowl at him, then back at Luke and Brooke. "What the fuck, Moody?"

Now Brooke is hiding her face in Luke's chest. His hand goes to the back of her head and he says something quiet to her that I can't quite hear. Then he steps back and tucks himself back into his pants.

I'm very fucking glad I can't see his cock from here. *Very* fucking glad.

He turns to face us, blocking our view of Brooke.

That makes my blood boil.

I shrug Jackson's hold off and step forward again. "Knock it off," I tell Luke harshly. "You don't have to *protect* her from me."

"Don't I?" he asks. "You're about to say some pretty heated

things, I'm guessing."

"Not to *her*," I say.

Luke meets my gaze directly. "Good."

Oh really? *Really*? He's *warning me* about how I talk to and treat Brooke?

"I've been *awesome* to her," I say. "You don't have to act like you need to step between us." I look at Jackson. "Or Jackson! We've both treated her like a goddamned queen. *You're* the one who said you weren't right for her. We all know how you like things and we agreed that you shouldn't be with her."

Luke nods. "We did."

"So what the fuck is *this*?" I demand. "I swear to God, Luke, if you pushed her—"

"He didn't," Brooke interrupts. Stepping out from behind Luke. "Of course he didn't." She frowns at me. "You know him better than that."

"Yeah, I know him," I say. Which is exactly why I'm pissed off. Luke's a good man, but he likes sex rough and dirty and *casual*.

Nothing that Brooke needs.

But God, she looks… well fucked. Very well fucked. Not happy and soft and glowy like after she was with me, or even this morning after her night with Jackson, but disheveled and messy and… hot. She looks very hot. Her hair is mussed, Jackson's shirt is hanging off one shoulder, she's got whisker burns along the side of her neck, her lips are swollen from Luke's mouth, and fuck… her thighs are wet. Her thighs are wet because Luke fucked her and *came* inside her.

I see red. "You didn't even use a condom? Jesus Christ! I swear to God if you hurt her I will—"

"Stop it!" Brooke cries, stepping between us. "I'm fine! I'm *fine*, Wyatt." She walks right up to me and puts a hand on my chest. "I wanted it. I *asked* for it. I'm totally okay."

She waits a moment, letting the words sink in. I study her face. She definitely seems adamant. She doesn't seem confused or upset, except with the fact Luke and I are fighting.

I lift a hand to her face, cupping her cheek. "I just… this is all new to you. Jesus, Brooke. We… wanted this to be good. Gentle. Sweet."

She nods. "I know." Her gaze flickers to Jackson and then back to me. "It has been. It *really* has been. I'm so glad it was you who was first. I…" She licks her lips and swallows hard. "There's just something between Luke and me, too."

My chest tightens. Fuck.

I thought Brooke was going to be my girlfriend.

I thought we were going to date and she would meet my parents and we'd maybe take a vacation somewhere together this summer.

But no. She was a weekend fling.

The best I've ever had, no doubt about it, but clearly she's just now spreading her wings and I can't deny her that.

"Okay," I finally say.

"Brooke." Luke's voice is low.

She turns toward him.

"You should go to your room. Clean-up. Whatever. We—" He looks at Jackson and me. "Need to talk."

I wait for her to resist. To tell him to fuck off about sending her to her room like she's a little girl, and he's somehow in charge.

But she steps away from me, crosses to where her panties are still lying on the floor and picks them up.

Then she glances back at all of us one more time before she disappears down the hall.

When her door shuts, Luke crosses his arms and looks at Jackson and me. "Clearly, we have a problem."

"You think?" I ask.

"Do we though?" Jackson asks at the same time.

Luke and I look at him.

He shrugs. "She seems fine. And that's what matters," he says to me. "I wasn't crazy about walking in on that either." He gestures toward Luke and the wall where he was just fucking Brooke. "But she wanted it. We don't get to really have an opinion about that. We both want her. We both knew that Luke wanted her. What they did together isn't really our business."

"He said he wasn't good enough for her," I say, even though it doesn't fucking matter now.

"He clearly changed his mind," Jackson says.

"No," Luke interjects. "I didn't." He sighs. "I'm still too old for her. I'm not the marrying type. I can't give her kids. Brooke is absolutely the settling down type of girl."

I bark out a quick laugh. I don't think Brooke is looking for a relationship right now, even if I wish she was. "The girl who just got with all three of us in three days seems like the settling down type?"

Luke frowns. "Don't you fucking dare slut shame her."

I hold up my hands. "No way. That's not what I'm saying. She deserves to have all the sex she wants to have. I'm saying she's just getting started, and she clearly loves it and wants to learn more. Good for her. I'm just disappointed I can't be the one and only she wants."

Jackson nods. "I'm half disappointed, half turned the fuck on by the fact that she clearly likes all three of us and the different ways we fuck her."

Luke shoves a hand through his hair. "Well, that was *not* supposed to happen with us and it won't happen again."

"She didn't like it?" Jackson asked. "She asked for it, but then you showed her something she actually *doesn't* want?" He looks at me. "Because I showed her a few things, and she was all in on all of it."

This is the weirdest fucking conversation I've ever had. But I nod. "Same."

Brooke is a sweet, eager, curious lover. God, the things I want to still show her.

We both look at Luke. He looks like he's in pain.

"Well, man?" I ask.

"She liked it," he says. "She liked it a lot."

I lift my brows. "Did you go easy on her?" I mean, it was

against the wall but maybe it was a sweet wall-bang? Is there such a thing?

He grimaces. "I... did not."

Jackson whistles. "Okay, then. Our dirty girl is up for even more than we thought."

Jesus Christ. I'm shocked by how my body reacts to Jackson calling her *our* dirty girl.

I shake my head. "This is a mess. Obviously, I'm not going to hold her back. She's discovered a new side of herself and she deserves to explore it."

"What do you mean you're not going to hold her back?" Luke asks, looking pissy.

"I'm not going to ask her out. I won't call her or anything."

"Why not?" he demands.

"Because she's not looking for a *boyfriend*, Luke."

"So you don't want her now that she's had sex with two of your friends?"

It's clear his question hits us all at the same time. It's a very strange thing to have to ask. And the answer should be obvious. *Obviously*, her having fucked my two best friends should turn me off.

It doesn't.

At all.

This weekend was hot. It was confusing and I've felt more jealousy in the past few days than I have ever in my life, but I've also been more turned on than I ever have been. Sharing Brooke with Jackson... and now Luke, as that sinks in... has not been a problem. At least not emotionally. My rock-hard dick that I'm having to take care of on my own more than anticipated is another story.

I don't know what my feelings about all of this mean, but that's the truth.

I blow out a breath. "I'm just saying, the ball is in Brooke's court. I'll make sure she has my number, but I'm not going to reach out."

Jackson nods, but he doesn't look happy. "Yeah. I guess me too."

Luke scrubs a hand over his face. "She's still in school. She's got a lot going on. It's probably for the best."

Yeah, it probably is.

I glance in the direction of Brooke's bedroom. "Should one of us go check on her?"

They both look too. Then we look at each other.

We all seem to agree on the answer silently, but Luke is the one to say, "I think she might need to be alone."

Jackson sighs. "Yeah. Luke's not the hugging and cuddling type. And I don't think we should make her choose between us," he tells me. "I don't know if I could take it when she chooses you."

The thing is, I'm not positive she would choose me. He's right that we shouldn't make her pick between us. That won't be good for any of us. It would put Brooke in a bad position and the emotions are surprisingly raw here. I don't want either Jackson or me to be the one not chosen.

The only solution would be for Jackson and I to go in there together…

But what we really need to do is start to put some distance between us and the gorgeous snow angel who has turned us all inside out and upside down.

We need to get back to reality. Get out of this little snow globe that has entrapped us in this erotic fantasy weekend.

It's been the best three days of my life. Definitely the best sex of my life. Even a strange but undeniable test of my friendship with Luke and Jackson that I think we might be passing?

All in all, a great trip.

So why do I feel restless and empty now as it comes to a close?

Because I'm going home empty-handed.

I let myself start building a white picket fence and a future with Brooke, and now I have nothing.

Which really fucking sucks.

CHAPTER 20

Brooke

AWKWARD.

That's the only way to describe Monday morning with Luke, Wyatt, and Jackson as we all get ready to leave the cabin and return to reality.

I stayed in my room last night after Wyatt and Jackson walked in on me and Luke, and I actually put on a podcast so I wouldn't have to hear what they were saying. I had a feeling it wouldn't be particularly flattering.

As I zip up my bag and drop it to the floor of my bedroom, I know I don't regret having sex with Luke. It was exactly what I wanted—I wanted to see what it would feel like to be treated as an equal, not a delicate virgin. I just regret we weren't more discreet as to when and where.

I don't regret a single second I spent with Wyatt and Jackson, either.

I will always be grateful to Wyatt for taking the time with me to make my first time super special and *very* pleasurable. Jackson showed me a playful side to sex. And Luke helped me wrap my head around why sometimes people just get so turned on they need it *now*.

But these guys are friends and we had communication and an

understanding through all of it until the kitchen with Luke last night and I feel bad about that.

Rolling my suitcase into the living room, I leave it and go over to Jackson, who is on the floor with the dogs. He immediately rises to his feet and holds his arms out for a hug with a smile.

"Take care," he tells me. "You're going to kill it on your exams."

"Thank you. Let me know if you need anything for the dogs. Day or night, you can text me if you're concerned about anything." Jackson is staying behind at the cabin for a week with Henley and the puppies while he makes arrangements to get them all back to Chicago.

I can't believe he's adopting all of them, but at the same time, that's a very Jackson thing to do, from what I can tell. He's impulsive but he's also all in when he decides to do something.

Jackson squeezes me tightly, kisses the top of my head, and releases me. "I will. Thanks for a memorable weekend."

He's being casual, but there's an undercurrent there I don't entirely understand. I just nod. "Thank you," I say softly. "For being you. I had a great time."

He opens his mouth but Luke calls from the front door. "We have to go, Brooke."

Jackson steps back. "Bye, Brooke." He winks. "Make good choices."

That makes me laugh, in spite of my discomfort. "Back to my regularly scheduled Brooke," I tell him. "Books and animals."

At least for now.

I need time to process how I feel about this extraordinary weekend.

Never would I have dreamed I'd have sex with three guys in one weekend and I certainly would never have guessed that I could be attracted to three men all at once.

But I am.

I need time to decide what that means, if anything, given my inexperience with men.

Waving to Jackson, I roll my bag toward Luke, who is waiting patiently by the front door. "Where's Wyatt?" I ask.

"He's in the car already."

"Oh, okay." Wyatt is who I really want to talk to. He was so angry when he saw me and Luke and I want to clear the air, though I'm not sure exactly what to say.

Luke touches my arm lightly. "Hey," he murmurs, leaning in close to me so he can't be overheard by Jackson. "I just want you to know that I had a vasectomy, and I haven't been with anyone else since I was last tested. In case you were worried. I never would have come inside you without a condom otherwise."

The way he talks so openly about coming inside me has my cheeks heating. Which makes me annoyed with myself. These things need to be talked about. It tells me what I need to know about Luke.

He's a good man.

"Thank you for telling me. I am on the pill for my irregular periods but I should have…"

I stop, confused.

What should I have done?

I don't even know right now.

Luke smiles and rubs his thumb across my cheek. "You're a hard woman to forget."

His touch makes me shiver. "But you're going to forget me?"

"I'm going to try, for all our sakes."

My chest feels tight, but I nod.

He's right.

It's the smart, sensible thing to do.

Appreciate this weekend, tuck it away as a great memory, but move on from it.

This is the best way to end things with all of them, really.

The snowed-in intimacy won't translate to the real world.

He opens the door and I head out to the car. Wyatt is in the front seat, and he ignores me.

It hurts more than I would like it to.

Which again tells me I need time and space.

But when we arrive at the airport after the five-minute drive, Wyatt does open the back door for me. He gives me a smile, though it doesn't quite reach his eyes.

"Wyatt—"

I don't even know what I intend to say.

But he just offers me his hand to climb out of the SUV. I take it and step out. The wind whips my hair across my face and Wyatt gently tucks it back behind my ear.

"You don't have to say anything," he says. "And I don't want you to feel bad. I really don't. I'm glad you had a good time."

More like a life-altering, mind-blowing, confusing-as-hell time, but "good" works too.

"I did, thank you."

I can't think of anything else to say because my head is swirling with all kinds of messy and crazy thoughts. I can't just blurt out, "I want to date all of you."

Because I don't even know if I do.

Again, this is all new. Can I trust my feelings?

Time. I just need time to think and I can't do that with any of them touching me.

Fortunately, for all three of us, the plane is small but loud and we have to wear headphones. The flight is only ten minutes across the lake.

Once we're at the airport on the mainland, I'm flying to Minneapolis and they're going to Chicago.

There's a lot of polite door holding for me from both of them and Wyatt rolls my suitcase for me, but yep, it's awkward. Luke and Wyatt haven't said a word to each other. That makes me feel even more uncomfortable.

But I know from my brother and his friends that guys tend to recover from disputes in friendships faster than women do. They'll probably be fine in a day or two.

Or maybe that's just my wishful thinking.

They both do hug me as we're splitting to go to different gates. Just friendly hugs, with lots of space between them and me.

Then Luke says to Wyatt, "Want to grab a beer?"

"Definitely."

We all wave. Then I walk toward my gate. I try to be a cool girl and not look back, but three seconds later I do.

They're not watching me. They're talking to each other, though I can't hear what they're saying, and Wyatt nudges Luke. He laughs.

That makes me feel better.

But then I'm alone at the gate.

No longer a virgin.

And very confused about three very different men.

I get a text from Sophie.

Good luck with your finals! I know you'll nail them! See you soon.

Right. Finals.

That's all I really should be thinking about right now.

Not three hot guys who taught me how incredible sex can be.

I open up my notes app and start studying.

That I know how to do.

CHAPTER 21

Jackson

"I GOTTA ADMIT, this is getting a little boring," I say.

There's no response.

"I know you're probably not bored at all, but I'm used to keeping myself busy and there just isn't a lot for me to do here. You're doing all the work."

Henley eyes me, then reaches down and flicks her tongue across Licorice's back.

"See, that's what I'm talking about," I tell her. "You're settling into mom life and aside from feeding you three times a day, letting you out, and changing the bedding in the box, I'm not really needed full time. Don't get me wrong, I'm glad I stayed. That was one hundred percent the right thing to do but... it's kind of boring."

Lonely is probably a better word for it.

Lonely enough that I'm having entire conversations with a Labrador.

Though Henley is a good listener. She does always appear interested.

I've already asked her if she thinks I should contact Brooke with some bullshit question about the puppies, but Henley obviously just looked at me like I'm an asshole for using her litter as a means to contact a woman.

Or maybe I'm reading too much into a dog's facial expression.

"You're right," I tell her now, just in case she understands me. "Unless there's a real emergency, I can't contact Brooke. She has exams. It would be a real dick move to interrupt her week when we don't actually need any help, do we, girl?"

Henley does glance up at me and I swear she definitely understands me.

So I want to encourage her confidence. "You're a natural at parenthood and everything else I need to know is on the Internet."

Henley moves from grooming Licorice to Henry. Tank is forcing his way in, demanding attention. I pick him up and move him by her haunches.

Tank whimpers in protest.

"Sorry, but you're a straight up bully," I tell him, running my fingers down his back. "Wait your turn."

I will not text Brooke, I will not text Brooke.

It's been three days and I've been tempted at least a hundred times.

Without the guys and Brooke, this cabin is huge and isolated on a damn island. There is no store to run to, no bar to go grab a drink at, no friends or relatives to pop in on and say hello.

Once I get back to Chicago, everything will be fine, but right now I am way too much in my head.

Which means I'm thinking way too damn much about Brooke and how we left things, which was as if it was a casual hookup.

It doesn't feel like that at all.

Brooke is different.

Aside from the obvious, that she's gorgeous and intelligent and sweet, I don't really know why this feels like something that could be something, but it does.

Only I know Wyatt feels the same way.

And Luke fucked her against the kitchen wall.

It's complicated as hell and I've been trying to distract myself from thinking about it too much or too closely.

Today I've played games on my phone, watched a movie, cooked myself a massive omelet for breakfast, done some laundry, and shoveled the back deck for Henley's bathroom breaks. I did a stint in the hot tub, but that only made me think of Brooke—again —so I barely lasted fifteen minutes before I leaped back out. I've gone through the list of houses my real estate agent has sent me and rejected them all for various reasons. Too many steps, back yard too small, outdated kitchen. I'm not looking to do a renovation right now, not when I'm going to be taking care of six dogs.

It's not even two o'clock and I'm contemplating taking a nap I don't even need just to quiet my head.

There's nothing left to do but call my mom.

"Jackson," she says, a hint of censure in her voice. "Son, I love you, but I am at work. I can't be on the phone with you every day just because you're bored."

"Mom, how do you know I'm just bored?"

"Because you've called me every day for the last three days, and you never do that unless you're restless."

I wince at Henley. Guilty as charged.

She's right, I mouth to the dog.

"I am a little bored, I admit it," I tell my mom. "I ordered a bunch of food and supplies for the dogs and they were all delivered and I spent ten minutes talking the ear off of the pilot when I went to pick them up."

My mother laughs. "You've always been a people person, Jackson. Get yourself off that island and come home. Now I have to *go*. I have a job."

"Okay, okay, thank you for picking up even when you know I don't need anything other than to be entertained. I love you."

"I love you, too. Talk to you this weekend. You're coming for dinner Sunday, right?"

"Yes, ma'am. Wouldn't miss it."

We end the call and I set my phone down, reflecting on the fact that my parents have never been bored. Not one single day ever, because they've always been busting their butts to take care of each other and me and my sister.

My parents are both still incredibly hard workers, even though I've bought them a house. They're cruising to retirement so they can collect their pensions and health insurance and live debt free in their golden years. Sometimes I know they think I'm letting too much time drift by but I don't aspire to the grind culture. I want to wait for the right passion project to come along.

But I'm definitely restless.

It isn't just staying alone in this cabin, though that's not helping.

It's wanting to have something to focus my attention on. I'm ready to have a goal to focus on again and I have this nagging feeling it might have something to do with animals.

And it's also Brooke.

She makes me want… more.

I pick up my phone again, snap a picture of Henley and the puppies and send it in our group text with Wyatt and Luke.

Luke, you still need to name the other girl.

It's day five of this puppy not having a name and I'm starting to get worried she'll have an identity crisis. I've been referring to her as Little Miss when I pick her up and cuddle her, but she needs a name.

I've texted them several pics over the last few days and they are responding readily and are definitely interested in the dogs. None of us has brought up Brooke, which is getting on my nerves. We can't just not talk about her.

Or maybe we can.

If we leave it up to Luke, that's how it will go down.

As far as he's concerned, we left all that here at the door when they all departed.

It doesn't sit right with me. These guys are my best friends.

We all like Brooke.

Maybe we can all ask her out and see who she says yes to?

That seems like a crazy idea since two of us will get rejected but it's better than what is happening right now, which is nothing. Wyatt texts me.

> They're growing already, it's crazy.

> I don't have to name her. You pick something.

The text from Luke follows Wyatt's and it's typical Luke. Distancing himself.

> No way. That one is yours.

> Fine. Call her Angel.

That's what I get for pushing.

Angel is what Luke started calling Brooke. I think he thinks we didn't notice, which, of course, we did. We noticed *everything* last weekend.

Or maybe he knows and it's a dig.

Whatever the case, I'm sorry I texted them.

> Angel it is.

I toss my phone aside and lay down on the floor next to the box. "Henley, I think I'm fucked. I can't get this girl out of my head. What do I do?"

Henley ignores me and pulls the newly named Angel over Licorice so she can groom her.

"It's not that easy."

Now I honestly don't even know who I'm talking to or about what exactly.

The worst part of it is I can't call Luke or Wyatt to discuss it.

Instead, I pick up my phone and start researching animal rescue facilities in Chicago. I need something to focus on other than Brooke's sweet smile and her soft cries of pleasure.

CHAPTER 22

Wyatt

THANK God I'm back to work.

I love my job, but it's rare that the first day back after a great vacation is my favorite. This time it's different. I was so damned happy when my alarm went off and woke me up from the dream about Brooke, and I was thrilled to immediately get called to a small structural fire.

After that, we were called to a possible heart attack at a local nursing home. Then we were only back for about thirty minutes when we were called out again to the scene of a three car accident.

I actually wish we could have been even busier. Because every fucking free moment I have, I'm thinking about Brooke. Missing her. Wondering what she's doing and how she is. Is she thinking about me? *Us*? If she is thinking about our weekend together? If so, what is she thinking? How is she feeling? Is she okay? It was a very intense weekend, and I miss her, and wish like hell I could call and just hear her voice. I also want to check on her. Physically, it was a lot. Emotionally, it was *really* a lot.

But I haven't even texted her. Not once. Okay, I've typed out texts four times, but I haven't sent them.

She has her big exams and I don't want to distract her.

Besides, we left it with a goodbye. We made no plans. She didn't say, 'call me', or 'text me.' And she sure hasn't texted me.

She wanted all three of us. That made it pretty clear that she wasn't looking for dinner and movie dates with just me.

I'd rather keep the fun, hot as hell, awesome memories from the cabin than make anyone reject anyone else.

"Doherty, you got my back here, right?"

My attention is pulled back to my present situation.

We're back at the firehouse, and it's been a couple of hours since our last call. We're all lounging in the common area with the Racketeers hockey game on TV, and delicious smells coming from the kitchen.

Luke is cooking. And he's fucking making spaghetti with meat sauce and garlic bread. The fucker.

He couldn't make literally *anything* else? I know it's one of the easiest things to make for a big group, and everyone loves his meat sauce. But we just fucking had it at the cabin. And of course it has me thinking about our weekend. Surely he is too. Right? How could he not? Yeah, he's made it a million other times, but the most recent time was in Minnesota. With Brooke. How could he *not* think about her?

And if he's *not* thinking about her, could he fucking tell her that and then she could get over her crush on him and just want to date me?

"You agree with me, right?" Jason Rasmussen asks me.

I have no idea what they're talking about. "Rarely," I say dryly.

He laughs. "Tucker says Alexsei Ryan is going to be as good as Crew McNeill. No fucking way. Am I right?"

I look at Tucker. "No way," I agree. "Ryan is awesome. And he works his ass off. And him and McNeill together are magic. But he won't ever be *as* good as McNeill."

"Statistically he's just as good," Tucker argues. "Give him more experience and he'll be right there with McNeill."

I shake my head. "He's one of the best in the league, and he'll go down as one of the best in history. But McNeill is a natural. He doesn't even have to try. The guy was born to be a hockey player. You just don't get players like that more than once in a generation."

"We should all just be grateful that we have them both on our team," Rasmussen says.

We all nod. That's the truth.

"Fuck!" Tucker suddenly shouts.

We all look at the television. Justin Travers, the star player for the Dallas Dragons, just scored on the Racketeers.

"Goddammit!" Tucker exclaims. "This new goalie is a piece of shit. Why the fuck did Wilder have to retire?"

The name Wilder seems to punch me in the gut.

God, I miss that girl.

It hasn't even been thirty-six hours and I feel like I'm going crazy.

I glance toward the kitchen at Luke's back. I wonder, for the twentieth time, if he's thinking about her. And if so, what he's thinking.

We haven't talked about her. Jackson and I haven't either. He's been texting us about the dogs, and I love that. I've loved every photo he's sent, and love that my friend is suddenly a dog dad. At the same time, though, every photo reminds me of her. The dogs, of course, but the glimpses of the cabin as well.

I shove a hand through my hair. Fuck, I'm so messed up.

"Hell yeah!" Tucker suddenly exclaims.

I turn back, expecting to see that the Racketeers have scored. Instead, I see something better. Elise Starling is crossing the room with a bakery box.

Actually, it's Elise Starling-Wilder. Elise is married to Blake Wilder, the Racketeers ex-goalie. She also is best friends with Crew McNeill's sister, who owns a bakery.

But even better, she's dating our lieutenant, Aidan Burke. And that means she stops by occasionally when he's working. And she never comes without a bakery box from Books and Buns.

I grin, but as she's greeted by the rest of the firefighters and someone yells, "Burke! Your girl's here!" it hits me that Elise is Brooke's sister-in-law.

And I am again crushed by a wave of missing the sweet virgin who fucking rocked my world.

She's not a virgin anymore.

Of course, that thought follows directly after.

Along with the memories of all the things that made her very much not a virgin anymore.

I'm scowling at the coffee table when Elise stops in front of me with the open bakery box, displaying the assortment of cookies, eclairs, and macarons she's brought for us.

"Hi, Wyatt." She gives me a bright smile.

I look up at her and wonder how often she and Brooke talk. Do they text periodically? Have they gotten to the point of being really good friends along with sisters-in-law? Elise is great and Brooke is amazing. Surely they get along really well. Does Elise know how Brooke is? Did Brooke tell Elise that she was stuck with us? Would she tell Elise she's not a virgin anymore? And how that happened?

Elise snaps her fingers in front of my face.

"What? Sorry," I tell her, forcing myself to focus.

"I asked if you wanted something," she says, jiggling the box. She frowns. "Are you okay?"

I am so not okay. "Yeah. Fine. Why?"

"Because I've been standing here in front of you holding a box of sweets, dressed like this—" she gestures down her body with one hand.

I finally notice the form fitting, pink pinup dress with the black polka dots that really does make her look stunning.

Elise is a gorgeous woman, and the fact that she has a husband and two boyfriends is actually no surprise. Besides being a knockout, she's funny, bright, sassy, and sexy as hell. It doesn't surprise me that she's got enough personality and heart for three men.

"You look fantastic," I tell her.

She props her hand on her hip. "I know. And you haven't even *hinted* at flirting with me. You always flirt with me."

She's right. Even though the first time I ever met her it was her boyfriend, my lieutenant, introducing us. I mostly do it to poke at him, but Elise is very fun to flirt with.

Which is just one more sign that I am beyond messed up over Brooke.

Aidan comes up behind her, wrapping his arms around her and pulling her back against his body. He nuzzles her neck, making her giggle. "What is this I hear about Doherty flirting with you?"

"He's not," Elise says, pouting slightly. "Can you believe that?"

Aidan looks at me over her shoulder. "Maybe he's finally learning that he needs to leave my stuff alone."

She tips her head back and looks up at him. "I'm your *stuff*?"

"Well, mine, Blake's, and Simon's," he tells her.

"I was actually protesting the term *stuff*," she says with an eye roll.

Watching them, I feel a stab of jealousy. Aidan gets to have the love of his life, along with his two best friends.

Actually, Simon, his husband, might be the love of his life. But that would make Blake and Elise his best friends, which totally tracks. Either way, he has the three people he loves most in his life in every way. In his home, in his bed, no worries about someone being left out, or someone being jealous or upset. No one going without one of the other people they love and want and need.

That's actually really awesome.

And of course, Brooke is firmly front and center of my mind again.

As if she ever left.

But I'm also thinking about Jackson and Luke. And their feelings for her. And hers for them.

"Oh my God," Elise says.

I look up, realizing that I've spaced out again.

She's watching me with a glint in her eye.

"What?" Aidan asks.

"He still hasn't flirted with me, and he hasn't taken anything out of this bakery box," Elise says, clearly talking about me, even though I am sitting right here.

"Do you know what that means?" she asks Aidan, looking right at me.

"What?" Aidan asks.

"He's hung up on a girl."

I stare at her. Aidan stares at me.

I consider denying it for about five seconds, then I sigh.

Elise laughs softly. "Not going well?"

"I'm pretty crazy about her, but I'm not sure how she feels. And I haven't told her that I want to see her again."

Elise widens her eyes. "Wyatt Doherty, you are a *catch*. Call that girl and tell her what you're thinking."

I resist the urge to look in Luke's direction. "It's a little complicated."

Elise nods. "Yeah, you really like her."

"Complicated is the sign of real love?" I ask.

"Love seems like the most complicated thing in the world in the beginning," she says. I notice she squeezes Aidan's hands where they are splayed over her stomach. "Until you fall into it with the right person or people. Then it becomes the easiest thing you've ever done."

"So the fact that this is complicated might mean that this isn't right?" I ask.

She shakes her head. "It just means that your brain hasn't caught up with your heart yet."

Aidan kisses her neck and says gruffly, "I think maybe we need to go... *talk* in my sleeping quarters for a minute."

Elise laughs and takes his hand, starting in the direction of the private rooms, where we all sleep when we can.

"If you talk, it better be dirty, and whatever comes with it better take you more than a minute," she tells him sassily. "Or I'll make you watch your husband make it up to me."

I hear Aidan give her a little growl before they move out of earshot.

And yeah, that whole exchange with them wasn't all that helpful.

Because now I have to face the fact that I probably really am in love with Brooke Wilder.

And there are two other men who might have something to say about that.

And I might actually want to hear what they have to say.

CHAPTER 23

Luke

I AM SO FUCKING glad to be done with work.

Going back after a vacation is always kind of hard, but this time I hated every minute of it.

After being stuck in the cabin with Wyatt for three days, then going right back to work at the firehouse with him, I needed a break.

Because every time I look at him, all I can think about is Brooke.

Okay, that's not fair. I am thinking about Brooke anyway. It's not Wyatt's fault. I'm thinking about her whenever I walk into a *kitchen,* for fuck's sake. My own or the one at the firehouse. And that would be true whether I was seeing Wyatt or not.

I can't see a refrigerator without thinking about how it felt to sink into her hot, wet pussy. Or hear her soft, husky voice begging me to fuck her. Or remember what her face looked like as I made her come.

Fuck.

I shove a hand through my hair.

I have got to get this woman out of my head.

I've thought about texting her, just to check in, about a hundred times.

That is so unlike me that I'm actually worried.

She doesn't need me checking on her. She has friends. She has a family. She has a huge, ex-hockey goalie brother. She doesn't need a forty-year-old guy who fucked her against the wall, suddenly becoming an overprotective guardian of some sort.

I'm sure she's fine. She went back to Minneapolis and is taking her exams.

Those are probably going well. She's obviously bright, extremely dedicated, and she's going to be an incredible veterinarian.

There is absolutely no reason for me to text her. Ever.

But if I have to sit in my house by myself, I'm going to do it. And ruin everything.

Which is why I am pulling open the door to one of my favorite bars and praying to God that one of the women that I hook up with from time to time is here and in the mood to have some hot fun.

I need some beer, some darts with buddies, and then I need to fuck Brooke Wilder out of my system.

The heat, noise, and smell of fried food and beer hits me as I step into Eddie's.

The bar is two blocks from my place, so an easy walk after I've had a few. Also easy to walk with a "date" after convincing her to come home with me.

I'm relieved to see that Ben, Gavin, and Mitch are all here. We don't really have a relationship where we text and say, 'hey let's meet up'. But I can usually count on them being here a couple times a week. Ben is divorced, Gavin is still single, and Mitch is married to an ER doctor who works crazy hours, so they're all pretty available and all of them hate sitting at home far more than I do.

Randy, the bartender, sees me coming and opens a bottle of Bud for me and hands it over just as I get to the bar.

"Hey, Cap," he greets.

"Hey," I return as I take the bottle and head for the area at the back where the dartboards are. I know he'll just automatically put it on the tab I pay once a month.

"Damn," Ben says. "You're never here this early."

It's true. As much as I like these guys and hanging out, I'm not a real social guy, so I'm usually the last to arrive and first to leave.

"Your lucky night," I tell him.

Tonight is different because I needed distraction, stat.

And I realize this is a problem.

I'm hoping like hell that with time, thoughts of Brooke will not be a twenty-four-seven problem. Over time, surely her memory will fade. I won't remember her scent, her smile, the silkiness of her skin, how easy it was to make her blush, the tight grip of her body around my cock, the way she begged for me to fuck her…

"Luke," Gavin says.

My attention snaps to him. "Yeah?"

"You're up."

Fuck. Surely with time, this will get better.

It has to.

We play for about an hour before Carrie and a couple of her friends make their way over to us. I noticed them about thirty minutes ago and we made eye contact, but I tried to concentrate on the game.

I was also trying to work up enthusiasm over seeing her.

Carrie is a beautiful, thirty-four-year-old divorcee who I've had three very hot nights with.

She likes things the way I do—a little rough, a lot dirty—and she doesn't expect a phone call the next day. She also doesn't need a lot of sweet talk and flirtation ahead of time.

She is exactly what I need tonight.

And I don't feel one single stir of desire.

I'm pissed about that.

"Hi guys," Carrie greets, as she sets new beers down on the high top table for all of us.

Ben, Gavin, and Mitch all know Carrie and her friends.

"Ladies," Ben says with a grin.

The other women, whose names I cannot remember, start chatting with my friends while Carrie turns to me.

"How's it going?" she asks, smiling the smile I know is actually an invitation.

She looks great. She's also very nice and I know that I could simply say, "let's go to my place," and she would say yes. And I could have some great sex and wake up tomorrow with zero guilt about leading her on.

But as I am standing here in my favorite bar, even having slept with her three times before, I find myself comparing her smile to the one that enchanted me this past weekend. I find myself thinking about Brooke holding the newborn puppies. I think about Brooke making snow angels and how she drowned her pancakes in syrup and how her big blue eyes took in every detail of everything going on around her.

And of course, I think about much less sweet things.

How her nipples look behind the thin cotton of a T-shirt. How she looks warm and wet from the hot tub. How her neck gets pink from whisker burn. How she sounds when she comes.

Fuck.

I can't take Carrie home.

If I can stand in a bar, trying to have a conversation and failing to keep Brooke out of my head for five fucking minutes of small talk, there's no way I'll be able to keep from thinking of her when I'm trying to kiss or fuck another woman.

Has Brooke Wilder ruined me for all other women?

Is it possible that spontaneously fucking a woman who was practically a virgin against the wall could end up making me a damned *monk* for the rest of my life?

I am going to be very pissed if that's true.

But looking at Carrie, who is now watching me with confusion, it feels true.

"It's not going well," I finally answer. And *that* definitely feels true.

"Oh," she says with a small frown. "I'm sorry. Do you want to talk about it?"

Carrie and I are not friends. We are not friends with benefits. We're not even fuck buddies. We've hooked up three times. But she is a nice woman, and we've had some pleasant conversations over coffee the next morning. We're not that far apart in age and we've both been through a nasty divorce.

Maybe that's why I shock us both by saying, "I think I've fallen in love."

Her eyes go wide. "Oh." Then she laughs. "I was not expecting that."

I nod and blow out a breath. "Yeah. You and me both."

"Not with me, right?" Carrie looks amused.

I shake my head slowly. "No."

Just a sweet, beautiful, intelligent girl I have no business falling in love with.

"Phew." She puts her hand to her chest like she's relieved, though she's obviously just teasing me. "You honestly had me scared for a second that I was going to have to let you down easy."

I sip my beer. I don't want to think about Brooke or her rejecting me. I don't want to consider what it means to open my heart back up and allow a woman to own my emotions. Though I strongly suspect I'm not going to have much choice.

The only one letting me down is myself.

"I'm going to head out," I tell her. "Have a good night."

There's nothing at the bar that is going to distract me from Brooke.

Might as well go home.

I've already decided to hell with it.

I'm texting Brooke.

CHAPTER 24

Brooke

I'M EXHAUSTED by Friday night.

My exams went well. I'm completely confident that I passed with flying colors and can move right on to clinicals with no issues.

Instead of being thrilled and pumped up over what's to come, I'm obsessing about the past weekend and the three guys who turned my world upside down.

It's only been eight days since they showed up at the cabin without warning, and yet it's hard to remember what it felt like before that fateful arrival.

Everything is different to me now because what I was hoping would happen—a return to my normal, relatively boring life—hasn't happened at all.

It wasn't just lust or a sexual awakening that had me wrapped up in Wyatt, Jackson, and Luke.

It's *them*.

I have feelings, jumbled, confusing, and complicated feelings, for all three of them, and I have no idea what to do about it.

"Cheers," Sophie says, raising a giant margarita glass up in the air. "To the future Doctor Brooke Wilder."

That makes me smile in spite of my general feelings of frustration and anxiety surrounding my complicated emotions. I raise my own margarita. "And to you, future Dr. Sophie Joplin."

Sophie takes a giant sip of her drink. "Oh, damn, that's good. I was so worried about my exams. I knew you were going to pass with flying colors, but it was a little dicey there for me. You know I get panicked when my whole career and future are on the line."

"I knew you would pull through," I tell her, truthfully. Sophie's always worried about her performance, but then she always does amazing. It's just her personality to really push herself.

The restaurant is hopping, with every table full, and servers racing back and forth with drinks and sizzling fajita platters. It's a festive environment and I should feel on top of the world, but instead the chips are sitting in my stomach like a rock and I keep glancing at my phone sitting on the table.

Wyatt texted me earlier today.

Just a casual, "hope your finals went well, I believe in you."

But it meant the world to me that he was thinking about me and wishing me well. I actually clasped my phone to my chest before answering him with a thank you.

Then Jackson texted me something similar, with a picture of the dogs and also expressing his belief I did well.

I didn't expect to hear from Luke at all.

But his came right on the heels of Jackson's.

> Just wanted to let you know that I've been thinking about your exams all week. I hope you did well. Hell, I know you did well.

I realized they were waiting for my finals to be over before reaching out.

Which was sweet and thoughtful and so *them*.

The relief I felt that they all respected my time this week and yet wanted to communicate with me was… so damn sweet. I had to go into the restroom at the university for a minute to collect myself before leaving for the weekend.

I think I could fall in love with all three of these very different men.

Is that even possible?

It certainly feels that way.

Yet I have no idea what to do about it.

Part of me wants to dive into dating each of them.

But… they're all best friends.

Luke and Wyatt work together. Luke is essentially Wyatt's *boss*.

If they're not happy about me dating both of them, things could get very messy for them at work, and taking personal feelings into the job of a firefighter is downright dangerous. They need to have each other's backs, for the sake of the community they serve in emergencies and for their own personal safety out on calls.

I don't want to be responsible for any tension between them.

Jackson and Wyatt have been friends since high school. I wouldn't want to come between them in any way, either.

"Why do you keep looking at your phone?" Sophie asks. "That's like the fifth time. And you never have your phone on the table."

I bite my lip. There's no denying it. I'm not someone who is glued to my phone normally. Besides, she knows everything and I could use advice.

"I hadn't heard from any of the guys all week, which was what I expected after the way we ended things." I told her on Tuesday that we left it as just a sexy fun weekend and that we'd go our separate ways. "But then today I heard from all three of them. Just a basic checking in. They clearly didn't want to interfere with my concentration this week."

"But now they're free to reach out." Sophie dips a chip into the hot salsa. "Which you like."

"I do." I can't deny it.

My phone buzzes and I jump. My heart starts to race. "It's from Wyatt."

"What does it say?"

My face feels hot as I read it. "I knew you would do well, even if your studying got interrupted." I look up at Sophie. "He added a wink emoji after that. Then he says that he misses my beautiful face and he can't stop thinking about me."

"Nice. He's the one who wants to date you, right?"

"Well, he *did*. According to his friends. I'm not sure how he feels now."

"I'd say he just told you how he feels. The question is, how do you feel?"

"That's the issue. I don't know how I feel. I like them *all*."

My phone buzzes again. I automatically look at it. It's just my phone reminding me I haven't opened the text. I shove a chip loaded with mild salsa into my mouth.

The phone goes off again. It's from Jackson. It's a picture of the puppies. I can see that without opening the text. Then another text pops up.

> One week old today and changing by the minute.

He added six dog emojis at the end, which is pretty adorable.

"You can open it," Sophie says. "It's okay, I don't mind. I'm living vicariously through you right now since I'm big time single."

"I'm single too," I protest.

But I pick my phone up and open the text from Wyatt first and quickly respond.

> Thank you. I felt really prepared and everything went well. I'm thinking about you too.

I hit send before I change my mind.

Did I say enough? Too much?

I have no idea.

While I'm looking at the picture of Henley and the puppies, Wyatt texts again.

> I wish we were cuddling on the couch at the cabin. You on my lap…

I swipe the text away, feeling flustered.

I respond to Jackson.

> They're so adorable! Good job being a dog dad!

Then I get another text from Luke.

I *need* to know what he's saying, so I open the text.

> I can't stop thinking about you.

"Oh, boy," Sophie says. "Girl, your face right now…"

"Let me just answer these really quick and then I'll put my phone away."

"Do you want my advice?"

"Yes. Desperately." I put my phone down and eye Sophie. "Help. I have no idea what I'm doing."

"Just let them know you're out celebrating and you'll be in touch later."

That makes me blink. "That's your advice?"

"Yes. You really are out celebrating. Besides, I think you spent all week hoping they would text you. Now they have. You're caught off guard. Give yourself time to think about what you want to say to each of them."

I nod. "That does seem smart."

I text all three guys the same thing.

I add a smiley face emoji at the end.

Resolutely, I stick my phone into my bag and force myself to smile at Sophie. Determined to change the subject, I say, "I'm going to miss you once I move to Chicago."

"Do the guys know you're moving to their city?" she asks.

So much for redirecting the conversation. "No. I don't think I mentioned it."

I *know* I didn't mention it. And I have no idea how to bring it up now.

Two hours later, I'm home, having walked the two blocks back to my apartment. I had two margaritas and was starting to feel the effects, so I drank two glasses of water before parting ways with Sophie. The last thing I want to do is drunk text Wyatt, Jackson, or Luke. Or all three.

It's tempting to pull my phone back out and check my texts but I don't want to get hit by a bus because my eyes are glued to my phone screen. Just because I'm suddenly head over heels for three men doesn't mean I should be unsafe. Waiting until I'm in my apartment, door locked behind me, I kick off my shoes and dump my purse on the bench so I can dig my phone out. I don't even strip my coat off before I'm swiping.

I have multiple messages from all three guys.

Wyatt has sent four texts.

> Never mind. That's none of my business. You deserve everything you want, Brooke. You're a beautiful person, inside and out.

> I can't stop thinking about last weekend. You felt so good in my arms.

That makes me sigh. This is hard. Too hard.

Wyatt is jealous because I mentioned a friend. If he feels this way over a total stranger, how would he feel if I dated Jackson? Or Luke?

Yet at the same time, it reminds me of how safe and cared for I felt with him. How gentle and understanding he was. Patient as he introduced me to sex. I could imagine myself waking up with Wyatt every morning, knowing I was loved. Feeling safe and secure and happy.

Jackson's texts are playful, flirty. Like him.

> This cabin isn't the same without you. Especially the hot tub. And my bed.

> Henley thinks you need to come visit us in Chicago. Vets still make house calls, right?

Being with Jackson is like the ultimate escape from reality. It's just laughter and orgasms. Which could be very, very addictive.

Luke's next few texts have pulled back. His wall seems to be back in place.

> Enjoy your night out.

> I think I'm going to take the one female puppy. Five puppies are too much for Jackson long term.

Reserved, cautious.

But then his last text just about undoes me.

I named her Angel.

It's just like him to not overtly flirt but to come in with the most powerful text of all—he's reminding me of the nickname he gave me. He wants the puppy he named after me.

Does that mean he wants me?

Luke may think he's rough and gruff but underneath that mask is a man who's been hurt and who continues to hurt because he won't allow himself to love another woman.

A part of me wants to be that woman.

Because I know for a fact he's loyal, and if that wall comes down, I imagine he'd love fiercely and intensely.

It would be incredible to have that kind of love.

I slump down onto my couch, biting my lip.

Without warning, I'm crying.

This is too much.

I can't casually text any of them, knowing this isn't going anywhere.

Knowing this *can't* go anywhere.

Which is my choice. And my reaction right now confirms why I shouldn't be dating any or all three of them—it's overwhelming and I don't know what I'm doing and I'm about to move and start my clinical rotation.

Casual flirting via text feels a little masochistic.

I don't think it's smart.

After I cry for a few minutes, I pick my phone back up and start typing.

I've been thinking and I don't think we should text like this. I have feelings for you and it just makes me miss you and that's too hard. Please, let's just leave it at the goodbye we had on Monday.

I add a kiss emoji.

I delete the emoji.

I add it again.

Then I send it to Wyatt.

Copying it, I then also send it to Jackson and Luke.

Taking a deep breath, I wipe the tears off my cheeks with the sleeve of my sweater.

"You did the right thing," I tell myself out loud. "You need to move on before you're totally heartbroken."

But I realize I might already be heartbroken.

I power my phone off and go to bed.

CHAPTER 25

Wyatt

TWO WEEKS.

It's been two fucking weeks since we got back from the cabin.

Two weeks of dog photos and videos from Jackson.

Two weeks of house and acreage photos from properties he's considering buying. One week of house and acreage photos from the one he actually put an offer on.

Two weeks since I've actually *seen* him, talked about anything else, or mentioned anything that happened at the cabin.

It's also been two weeks since Luke and I talked about anything other than work. When we're at calls, everything is normal. Our teamwork is completely unaffected. Of course it is. I trust him with my life and vice versa. He's the best firefighter I've ever known, and he leads our fire house with integrity, firmness, and heart. There's nothing weird at all when we're doing our job.

But at the firehouse between calls, things are different. If I was going through something like I am about Brooke, I would talk to him about it. But I feel like I can't with this because he's a part of it. He might say otherwise. Hell, he might wish it was different. But, like it or not, he's part of the reason I'm not talking to her every day, not making plans to go see her. Not calling her my girlfriend.

Strangely, it's not even that he fucked her. It's that she has feelings for him. And I'm not mad about it, or jealous. Much. I just know that I need her to have everything she wants, and if that includes Luke, and he's not into that, I'm not going to be happy knowing she's not completely happy.

And, of course, more than anything, it's been two weeks without Brooke. Two of the longest weeks of my life. I've only texted her that one night and that made it worse because she asked me to stop.

And I'm about to lose my shit.

It's my day off. I'm at home, watching one of Jackson's dog videos for the fifth time, and I want to hear her voice with an intensity that I almost can't believe.

This is probably a terrible idea. But I do it anyway.

I press her number and let it ring.

She picks up after three rings.

My heart almost stops when I hear her voice.

"Hello?"

"Hey, Brooke." That's all I manage at first.

I don't know if she has my number programmed in. I don't know if she'll recognize my voice. But suddenly I don't know what else to say.

"Hi," she says softly.

My heart squeezes—as cheesy as that sounds—and my cock twitches, just from that one simple word.

"It's Wyatt," I say.

Her laugh is soft. "I know."

I'm very glad she knows. I blow out a breath. "I maybe shouldn't have called," I say. "But I couldn't resist anymore."

She is quiet for a few seconds, then she asks, "Why would you when I asked you not to reach out?"

"Well, it's not just a friendly call to say hi or to see how you are," I say. "I mean, I really wanted to hear your voice. And I really want to hear how you are. But it's more than that."

My heart is hammering in my chest and my palms are actually

sweating. I don't think I have felt this way talking on the phone to a girl since I was thirteen or fourteen. Hell, maybe not even then. I've always been pretty confident with girls.

I'm just not sure any previous girl has meant as much as Brooke does to me now.

"Well, I'm good. Getting ready to start my clinical rotations in two weeks. My exams went really well, though I think I told you that. And I'm glad to hear your voice, too."

I breathe out, relieved. "That's awesome. I'm glad to hear all of that."

"So what else is this call about?" she asks.

My heart thumps hard, and I swallow, but I am fucking saying this. Consequences be damned. "I want to see you. I can't quit thinking about you. I have feelings for you, Brooke. Feelings I can't get over. I really want to see you again. So I'm coming to Minneapolis. I have the plane tickets pulled up in front of me right now and I am ready to push the buy button. I just wanted to be sure that you're not busy this weekend."

I am definitely all for just showing up, but I'm trying to be respectful. I don't have any idea what veterinary school is like, so if she has more exams or some meeting or something else she has to do, I don't want to fuck that up for her.

The silence stretches for several seconds, and I frown. "Brooke?" My heart is in my throat. "I know how things were when we left the cabin and I know you said it's too hard because you have feelings for me. I know you also have feelings for Luke and Jackson. I get it. I'm okay with that. All I know is how I feel. I just want to see you again. Please let me come to you."

Finally, she says, "It's not that." I hear her take a breath. "I mean, it's maybe kind of that but..."

"Brooke, honey, we can talk about all of that. It doesn't have to be hard, I promise. I really just want to see you. In person."

"Okay," she says. "But don't push the buy button."

I frown. "Why not?"

"Well, I have to tell you something. I wasn't sure if I should. But now…"

I give a short laugh. "After everything you have told me, and everything that happened, you can tell me anything."

Again, she's quiet for a couple of seconds and I picture her gorgeous face with that sweet blush that is so easy to elicit.

Then she says, "I'm in Chicago."

A thrill shoots through me. "Awesome." I slam my laptop shut. "How long are you here? Where are you?" I stand and head for my bedroom to change clothes.

"I'm here for a while. Actually, the next couple of years."

I freeze in my bedroom door. "What do you mean?"

"My internship is here in Chicago. I am living here now."

I let that sink in. Then I pull in a deep breath. "Fuck, yes."

"Wyatt… I…"

"Brooke. Give me your address."

She hesitates, then says, "I don't know if I should."

"You definitely should," I say firmly.

"I like you," she says. "A lot. I've been thinking about you ever since the cabin, too. But I like *all* of you. I don't think I can date just one of you."

I feel like all of the air has been sucked out of my lungs.

But my heart is still hammering.

We can make this work.

I think we *have to* make this work.

"That's not a deal breaker for me," I tell her.

"What do you mean?"

"I mean, I will do whatever you want. Whatever makes you happy. If you want to date all of us, we can make that work."

She's quiet. There's no sound from her end of the phone.

"Brooke," I say firmly, but softly. "We're going to make this work. This isn't over."

Finally she says, "Okay."

"Okay." I pause, then say, "Bye, Brooke. We'll talk soon."

"Bye, Wyatt."

We hang up, but for the first time in two weeks, I'm *happy*. Hopeful.

I don't know how exactly I'm going to solve this, but I am going to see this girl again.

I do know who I need to help me solve it, though.

I send a text to my two best friends.

> We need to talk. About Brooke. ASAP.

Jackson responds first.

> Yeah, we do. In person.

Then Luke texts right on his heels.

> Agreed.

CHAPTER 26
Luke

EYEING WYATT, I ask, "She told *you* to stop texting her too? Damn. I had no fucking clue. I thought for sure she'd want to see you again."

Though now that I think about it, Wyatt's been moping around the firehouse for the last two weeks. I thought he was just giving me space, and I was pretty damn wrapped up in my own complicated emotions. Too busy moping in my own right to notice he was not his usual upbeat self.

"She told me that too," Jackson says, holding his hand up for the bartender.

"Guess she needs space from all three of us," I say. "Can't say I blame her. We probably overwhelmed her by all texting her that same night."

It's actually kind of funny to think we all waited until her finals were over, then we blew up her phone simultaneously. When Wyatt and Jackson both admitted they texted her Friday night, I wonder now why it didn't occur to me at the time we were all doing that.

Then again, we didn't seem to overwhelm her at the cabin.

She was all on board then. But that was flirting and sex.

What happened at the cabin was supposed to stay at the cabin, but it didn't. Not for me, and clearly not for these guys.

We're at my favorite bar, Eddie's, because we finally pulled our heads out of our asses and realized we need to clear the air about Brooke.

"I was texting her about the dogs," Jackson says. "That's a valid reason to reach out to her. If anyone overwhelmed her, it was Wyatt."

"Hey," Wyatt protests.

But he doesn't really deny it.

"I thought you wanted to meet to tell us you're going to Minneapolis to see her. Which I would be cool with, by the way. I know you and Brooke are a good fit for each other." A better fit than me and her.

I've spent night after night turning it around and around in my head and in spite of what I confessed to Carrie about falling for Brooke, it doesn't really change anything if she wants to be with Wyatt. Especially considering she asked me to stop texting her. Which I have respected.

Did it give me a jolt of both love and lust when she said she was catching feelings for me and missed me?

Hell fucking yeah.

Because I miss her too.

And I'm damn sure I'm either falling in love with her or I already am in love with her. Which, for me, is a little terrifying, I'm not going to lie.

Did that text also make me realize that she was right?

It's too hard.

Yep. I agree with that.

"Here's the thing," Wyatt says, sounding excited. He's actually bouncing his knee up and down rapidly, a sign he has too much energy to sit still. "She's not in Minneapolis. She's in Chicago."

My shoulders stiffen, and my heart starts to race.

Here. She's in town and we could see her, touch her?

I envision running my fingers through her silken strands of

hair and leaning in to kiss her, my hand running up the smoothness of her bare thigh.

Jesus. My dick gets instantly hard.

It makes me want to throw all my resolve out the window and drive straight to her.

"Wait, what?" Jackson stops trying to get the bartender's attention, drops his arm and swivels toward Wyatt, who is between us. "She's *here*?"

Wyatt nods. "For the next two years. She's doing her internship here."

I'm stunned. "Wow. Okay. How do you know that?"

"I called her to tell her I had to see her and I was booking a flight to Minneapolis."

Of course he did. I snort.

Jackson throws a look of censure his way. "She asked you not to text her."

"I didn't text her. I called her. She picked up so obviously she wanted to talk to me." He sounds smug.

If I was a dick, I'd point out that she probably would have picked up for me and Jackson too but I don't because Wyatt can say he's not jealous all damn day, but he is. That's why he lost it in the kitchen when he walked in on me with her. Yes, he thought I was being too rough with Brooke, but he was also upset that she was into me, too.

"So if she's in town, why are you at Eddie's with us?" Jackson asks. "I would have thought you'd just go straight to her."

"Because she said she can't date just one of us."

There is a pause while we all digest that.

"So…"

"She wants to date *all* of us?" Jackson asks. "I can get behind that if it means I get to spend some time with Brooke."

"I think we should just tell her she can date Wyatt." I drain my beer in two big swallows.

This doesn't change anything.

"We should do what's best for Brooke," I add firmly.

Jackson looks reluctant. "I don't think we should decide for Brooke what is best for her. That's her call."

"Okay, then this is best for me," I say. "I don't want to date her."

I'm lying and they both know it.

But I need to protect Brooke. I failed at the cabin. I never should have touched her. Because now I want more and I know in the end, I'll only hurt her.

"I think the best thing is if we all talk to her together," Wyatt says. "I can date her solo, or we can all date her. I'll do whatever it takes to spend more time with her. She's the one for me."

His words are simple, determined.

It must be nice to be so confident that you know what you want and it will all work out.

I felt that way once upon a time.

Before I had the rug pulled out from under me.

I rub my forehead. I'm getting a damn headache. "She said she doesn't want to talk to me."

"She said that to me too," Wyatt said. "Then she agreed to see me. So I think what's happening here is she's attracted to all of us and is just not sure what to do about any of it. We should present a united front and make it clear she can have whatever she wants."

I'm going to fucking regret this.

But I'm going to regret it more if I don't do this.

That's pretty damn clear, given the way I've been feeling the last two weeks.

"Okay. Tell her to meet us here."

"I have a better idea," Jackson says. "I'll invite her over to my place to see the puppies. Then we can all talk to her."

"You're going to ambush her?" I ask. "That's fucking rude."

"It will show us all where we stand," Wyatt points out.

"It's not an ambush," Jackson says. "She likes seeing us all together. She likes knowing we're all cool with whatever. Which we are. Right?"

"Don't look at me," I protest. "I'm not cool with a fucking thing right now. But I do want to talk to her. I didn't like the tone of her last text. She sounded upset."

Some guy accidentally jostles me, passing by my bar stool. I glare at him when he doesn't apologize.

He glares back.

"Watch where the fuck you're going." It's misplaced anger, but he's a convenient target for the tornado of emotions I'm feeling. The last two weeks have sucked.

Something about my expression clearly warns him off because he keeps on walking without another word.

I'm torn between wanting to see Brooke alone, so I can get her naked. I've been having a lot of fantasies about tying her by the ankles to my bed, her slim legs spread so that I can see her tight little cunt, her arms tethered to my headboard…

I shift on my stool.

But at the same time, I like the idea of having the guys with me as a buffer, so I *don't* tie her to my bed and keep her there forever.

"She's meeting us—well, me—at my condo in thirty minutes," Jackson says, setting his phone down on the bartop.

"That was fast."

"She must really want to see you." Wyatt blows out a breath, like he isn't sure how to feel about that. He lifts his hand resolutely and indicates to the bartender he wants to close his tab. "Let's go. Brooke awaits."

This is either going to be a fucking disaster or something really incredible.

Might as well see which one sooner than later.

"I'm ready."

"I'll have a drink at home." Jackson is already off his stool.

Half an hour later, Brooke is standing in the doorway of Jackson's condo, frozen.

"Oh, hi," she says after a pause.

It reminds me of the night we came upon her in the cabin, and she was so flustered.

"You know Luke and Wyatt," Jackson jokes as he closes the door behind her.

Jesus. I fight the urge to roll my eyes.

But Brooke gives us a soft laugh and tucks her hair behind her ear. "I thought I was coming over to check on Henley and the puppies. I hope I'm not interrupting a guys' night."

Her tone puts my fears to rest. She sounds flirty, not angry.

"We're here because of you," I tell her. "Let me take your coat."

I hold out my hand, and she peels off her jacket and passes it over to me. I lean in and kiss her cheek. "It's great to see you," I murmur.

Brooke shivers and turns her head quickly so that we're eye to eye. "It's great to see you, too. I..."

"What, Angel?"

But she shakes her head and turns to Jackson. "You could have warned me."

He pulls her into a hug. "Nah. I couldn't risk you saying no. We need to talk, Brooke. We're all tiptoeing around each other and that isn't good for any of us."

"I don't want that."

"Neither do we," Wyatt says firmly.

He goes right in for a kiss on the lips.

Brooke kisses him back, sighing against him as she grips the front of his sweatshirt.

It surprises me how much it turns me on.

I also realize that this might be the perfect solution—I can be with Brooke but if Jackson and Wyatt are dating her as well, it's not all on me. I don't have to be the perfect, full-time boyfriend. I can still have my space and breaks to regroup so that I don't fuck this up.

I can't meet her expectations one hundred percent of the time, but a third? I can manage that.

Brooke pulls away from Wyatt. "No, this isn't… we can't…"

"Why can't we?" Wyatt rubs his thumb over her bottom lip. "Just come inside and see the puppies and let's talk."

Brooke nods and I watch her ooh and ahh over how much the puppies have grown and changed. She examines each of them, and Henley, her fingers gentle but sure, her eyes sharp with intelligence, as she assesses the dogs.

There's no way I can stay away from this woman.

Jackson's condo is bright and light and has high ceilings. There is plenty of room for us to give Brooke space, yet we're all crowded around her. Moths drawn to a flame.

We're jockeying to be the closest to her. I'm not sure Wyatt and Jackson are aware they're doing it, but I certainly am. We all want to be the one this girl turns to and gives a bright smile.

"They're all doing fantastic," she says. "Jackson, I'm so impressed with how you're taking care of them."

Jackson looks like he was just handed the grand prize. "Thanks, Brooke. The instructions you gave me made it easy."

Then because I'm impatient as hell, the second she stands up and goes to the kitchen sink to wash her hands, I follow her.

"There's no reason you can't date Wyatt," I tell her, cutting to the fucking chase. "Look at the guy. He's dying here."

Wyatt glares at me. "I can speak for myself."

"Then speak."

"Brooke, I want to be with you. I have since the first minute I laid eyes on you at Blake's retirement party. I know you said we should leave it alone because you have feelings for me, but that's exactly why we should see where this can go."

Brooke frowns and turns to me. "Is that what you want, Luke?"

No. I want her with me, tied to my bed and gazing up at me with those soft, loving, and very sensual eyes.

"I want whatever you want."

"Jackson?" She turns to him. "What do you want?"

"I want to date you, too. Luke and Wyatt don't have a problem with that."

Wyatt looks pained, but he shakes his head. "No, I don't have a problem with that."

"Me either."

She stares at me again, but I don't say a word.

"How would that work, exactly?"

"Do you want a drink or anything?" Jackson asks. "I should have offered you that sooner."

"No. I'm fine." Brooke leans against Jackson's kitchen island. "This is a lovely apartment, by the way. I love the light."

"Thanks. I think I'm going to rent it out when I move into my house."

"I can't believe you bought a house." She gives him a sweet smile. "You're a good dog dad."

"Gotta give these guys some room to run once they're bigger. Though Luke is taking Angel."

That was a moment of weakness. I don't know what prompted me to offer that.

Though I'm kidding myself.

I know exactly what prompted it. I wanted a reminder of Brooke.

Brooke walks over to me. Her eyes glance over my lips before she stares up at me. "Do you want to date me, too, Luke?"

She slips her hands into mine and I just about drown in her deep eyes. Whatever plan I had to shove Wyatt at her evaporates. Again.

"Yes, Brooke. I want to date you." My voice is husky. "I want to do everything with you and to you. I want to date you, fuck you. *Worship* you."

Brooke goes up on her tiptoes and kisses me. It's sweet, submissive. "So date me," she whispers. "Fuck me."

Her words kick me in the gut.

This woman.

Fuck.

Before I can scrape up a response, she turns and crosses her arms. "What do we do now? You all want to date me and I want to date all of you. I'm not going to choose one of you over the others. I just *can't*. I have feelings for *all* of you. So what do we do about that?"

I guess we're all dating her.

There's no way any of us are going to walk away.

None of us can quit her.

I rub my chin and let Wyatt take it from here.

CHAPTER 27

Jackson

"WE CAN SHARE YOU," Wyatt assures her. "Whatever you want. You can have whatever you want, Brooke. We all want you. We'll… take turns."

He looks at us as if that was really not what he meant to say and he could use some help here.

Brooke frowns. "Take turns? What does that mean?"

"We'll all date you," Luke says. "I'll take you out one night, then another night you go out with Wyatt, then another with Jackson. Equal time with each of us."

Okay, that sounds good. Like a decent solution. Yeah, I'm in.

But Brooke is still frowning and chewing on her bottom lip.

"What's wrong?" I ask, leaning in, forearms on my thighs. "Just tell us what you're thinking. We want this. Just tell us what *you* want."

She looks from me, to Wyatt, to Luke. She takes a deep breath. "To not choose. To not have one of you without the others."

"That's what we're offering," Wyatt says, sounding confused.

"I mean ever," she says, clearly frustrated. "I want you all at once, together. Like how it was at the cabin. I loved when we were all together. Watching a movie, cooking and eating dinner, playing poker." Her cheeks get pink as she clearly recalls how that turned out.

I catch Wyatt's eye and we share a look. Yeah, we remember too.

It was hot. Sure, I got to take her upstairs in the end, but her stripping down to nothing, Wyatt pulling her into his lap, watching him kiss her, knowing he was watching me kiss and touch her, that was all so fucking hot.

"Can I have you all?" she asks, her voice soft. "Together?"

Luke's voice is rough when he asks, "Do you mean in bed?"

She nods. "I think so."

He blows out a breath and shoves a hand through his hair. Then he looks at us. "Well?"

I nod. "Yes. I'm in." Wyatt and I have done this before. We've never had feelings for the girl before. Not like this. But yeah, it's been fun. This isn't a problem for me.

Wyatt is a little slower to agree, but finally he nods too. "Whatever Brooke wants."

Luke pins her with an intense look. "Is that what you want, Angel? All of us at the same time? Touching you? Kissing you?" He pauses. "Fucking you?"

She sucks in a quick breath. She wets her lips. But then she kills me a little when she says, "I want to try it. Can we do that?"

Luke swallows hard. "Yeah, we can do that."

She looks at me. I nod. "You can have whatever you want from us, sweetheart. You're calling the shots."

Finally she meets Wyatt's gaze.

"Yeah," he says, his voice husky. "Of course."

"Come on." Luke holds out a hand to her.

She reaches out to take it, without hesitation. He starts down the hall to the bedroom.

"You okay?" I ask Wyatt before we follow.

"Yeah," he says. Then he meets my eyes and says again, "Yeah. Seriously. I'll do anything for her."

"You know we care about her, right? We'll be good to her."

"I do know that." He claps me on the shoulder. "Yeah, I definitely know that."

I'm relieved. "Good." I grin at him. "Then let's go blow our girl's mind."

He finally lets a grin stretch. "Yeah. Let's fucking go."

We enter the bedroom to find Luke kissing Brooke by the foot of the bed.

They've both already lost their shirts, and he's unbuttoning her pants.

"Oh, we're not wasting time, I see," I comment, stepping in behind her and stroking my hands down her arms. I love her smooth skin and watching the goosebumps rise up in the wake of my touch.

"I think we need everyone to get down to their underwear and then just get our girl used to having three men touching her at once," Luke says, dragging his mouth up and down her neck. "Six hands and three mouths are a lot. Might take some adjustment."

Brooke shivers, her head tipping back, giving Luke more area to kiss. "Yes. God, that sounds so good."

"And we can all get used to it too," Luke says. He lifts his head and looks at me, then at Wyatt, who is still standing a couple of feet away, watching. "Might take us all a bit to adjust to watching the others touching you too, Angel."

She turns her head to look up at me. "Okay."

Luke strips her pants down her legs, and she steps out of them. I immediately palm her sweet ass, squeezing, and loving how she presses back into my hands.

"Let's leave her bra and panties on for now," Luke says. "We'll just work up to everything slowly."

"You've all seen me naked," Brooke says.

I move my hands up her sides and cup her breasts through her bra.

Luke gives her a soft look. "Not all of us have seen you completely naked. But," he says, before she can respond. "Let's just take it slow. This will be fun."

I'm surprised that Luke is the one slowing things down. He's the one who pinned her to the wall and fucked her without even taking her shirt off. But maybe that's why. He wants to make up for that.

Or maybe it's just that he's the natural leader here, and he's taking that responsibility seriously.

I'm good with whatever. As long as my hands get to be on this girl all night, I'm just fine.

Brooke looks over at Wyatt, and she reaches out. "I need you too," she tells him.

He takes a deep breath, but comes close, taking her hand. She pulls him in and lifts her face. He leans in to kiss her.

It's soft and sweet and being this close, watching their lips move against each other's, makes me feel a strange mix of lust and affection.

"Take your clothes off guys," Luke says. "Just down to your underwear."

I shift back, stripping off my shirt, then going to work on my pants. Wyatt does the same, breaking his kiss with Brooke only long enough to yank his shirt over his head and toss it. Then he's kissing her again as he unbuttons, unzips, and shoves his jeans down. He kicks them off, then steps closer to her, cupping her face and deepening the kiss.

Her soft moan makes me run my hands back up her body, cupping her breasts again, toying with her hard nipples through her bra.

The moan is louder this time.

I like that. We're both making her feel good now.

"Up on the bed, sweetheart," I tell her.

I love that she responds to my commands as easily as Luke's. She turns and backs up the one step it takes for her knees to hit the end of the mattress.

Wyatt grasps her waist and tosses her into the middle of the bed.

I crawl up on one side, Luke takes the other, and Wyatt climbs over her, bracing his elbows on either side of her shoulders.

She shivers lightly. "I love being surrounded by all of you."

Wyatt leans down to kiss her, but I'm grateful for his upper body strength that keeps him up away from her body so that I can stroke my hand over her stomach and up to one breast. "We love surrounding you," I tell her.

Luke is kissing her shoulder on the opposite side. I can also see that he's stroking one hand up and down her thigh.

"Wyatt, lift up," Luke says. "Show Brooke that you're okay with us touching her."

Wyatt pushes up until he's kneeling between her thighs, resting on his heels.

He takes in the sight of my hand covering her breast, thumbing over her nipple, and Luke's hand on her thigh, stroking up to cup her pussy.

Luke looks up at Wyatt. "Prove to *yourself* that you're okay with us touching her."

Wyatt's jaw is tight, but he nods. "Make her feel good."

Luke drags his middle finger over her silk-covered clit and as Brooke gasps, I pinch her nipple.

"Oh, god." Her voice is soft.

"You like that?" he asks her. "You like having two men touching you at once?"

She nods quickly. "And one watching."

"How about three touching you?" Wyatt asks, sliding his big palm up her inner thigh as Luke lazily circles her clit and I continue to tease her nipple.

"Yes," she answers breathlessly.

"Not too much for our sweet little virgin?" he asks.

Her cheeks are flushed and her pupils wide. She shakes her head. "Not too much. I want more."

I lean in and kiss the upper swell of the breast I am teasing. "That's right. You're not a sweet little virgin anymore, are you?

Have we made you greedy? Did we find your dirty side, sweetheart?"

She's breathing fast and she nods. "Yes. I think so."

I latch onto her nipple through the bra, sucking gently. "Have you used that vibrator in the past two weeks? Thinking of us? Thinking of how your three men fucked you so good in that cabin?"

"God. Yes."

Luke gives a low groan, and he must press harder on her clit, because she gasps his name.

"Let me help." Wyatt reaches up and pulls the cup of Brooke's bra away from her breast, baring her nipple to me.

The sweet, hard nub brushes my lips, and I immediately lick over it, then suck hard.

Her soft cry shoots straight to my cock.

Wyatt pulls both cups down beneath her breasts, which bares and lifts them perfectly. Then he reaches for her panties, dragging them down her legs. "I think our dirty girl is ready for some direct contact," he says.

Luke immediately starts working her clit in faster circles.

"Fuck, Angel, you're so wet. Are we making you needy?"

"Yes, god," she says brokenly.

"I'm definitely getting okay with seeing you both touching her," Wyatt says. "This is fucking hot. Jackson, you should watch two other men with Brooke."

I lift my head and look down her body where Luke is working her. Wyatt slides his hand up, then slips a thick finger into her pussy.

Her gasp is beautiful.

"*Fuck,*" I breathe out. "That is hot." I look at her face. "You like having both of their hands on you? Is that pretty cunt feeling good, sweetheart?"

Brooke seems to be moving a little beyond the ability to speak. Her eyes are shut, and she's breathing rapidly.

I reach out and brush her hair back away from her face. "Open your eyes, beautiful," I tell her. "Stay with us. All of us."

Her eyes open, and she focuses on me. Kind of. She looks a little dazed.

I lean in and kiss her. Her mouth is desperate on mine, her tongue stroking mine hungrily.

I lift my head, staring down at her. "Give her another finger, Wyatt."

I know when he does because she cries out.

"Suck on her," Luke commands and I know he means me.

I take one nipple in my mouth and roll the other between my thumb and finger.

"Come for us, Angel," Luke tells her. "Come apart for your three men."

A moment later, she cries out, "Oh my *god!*"

Wyatt groans, "Fuck, yeah. "

"Was she a good girl?" Luke asks.

"Oh yeah, very good." Wyatt lifts his fingers to his mouth and sucks them clean.

Brooke is quivering between us. Luke rests his hand on her lower belly, fingers spread wide, gliding slowly back and forth as she comes down.

"Beautiful," Luke says. He leans over and kisses her shoulder then her neck. "Perfect. Such a perfect angel."

I capture her mouth, kissing her deeply again, my tongue stroking along hers. The way she kisses me back is still hungry, but less frantic now. I stroke her hair, kissing along her jaw. "You're so fucking gorgeous."

After a few more moments, her breathing seems to be evening out.

"Now let's get you used to touching three men," Wyatt says. "And I guess the three of us need to get used to seeing your pretty mouth and hand around other cocks."

That sweet little shiver that is a sign of her desire goes through Brooke as he pushes off the bed and strips off his boxers.

Luke and I follow suit.

Brooke's eyes move from Wyatt to Luke, then back to me.

Wyatt crawls back up on the bed with her, reaching underneath to unhook her bra and toss it to the floor. He leans in and kisses between her breasts, then down her stomach, over her mound, pausing on her clit and making her moan, before moving to her inner thigh and giving her a little nip before standing again.

"So what do you guys think?"

"I want you all," Brooke says before any of us can speak.

Luke steps up to the side of the bed and reaches over, brushing the back of his knuckles over her cheek. "What does that mean? What are you thinking?"

"I want you all to fuck me."

I can't help but groan as heat punches me in the gut.

Wyatt sucks in a deep breath and Luke's jaw tightens in that way I've come to understand means he's trying to restrain himself.

Finally, he speaks. "That might be a lot for you in one night."

She looks at Wyatt, then me. "You both fucked me more than once. Would it be different to have three different guys at once, than one guy fuck me three times?"

I honestly didn't know that my cock could get any harder, but it does. I am *aching*.

Wyatt studies her for a moment, and he shakes his head. "Our girl has a point."

Luke clenches his jaw. Then he strokes Brooke's cheek again. "Okay, Angel, how about we just see how things go?" he finally says.

She looks up at him, a smile teasing her lips. She looks a little sassy suddenly. "I know that you'll want to go a little harder than the others, but that's okay. I can take it."

My breath lodges in my throat and I stare at Luke. He gets her harder? Why is that so fucking hot to me?

The look Luke is giving her says he wants to *consume* her.

Holy shit.

"Does that mean you should go first?" I ask him. "Or last?"

Does the super hard fucking need to be first while she's not too sore? Or last, after she's been worked over and warmed up?

I squeeze my eyes shut. "I can't believe I'm thinking the things I'm thinking."

"Well we have a very dirty girl in our bed, boys," Luke says. "I think we're all going to be thinking some pretty fucking hot stuff."

Brooke doesn't look the slightest bit embarrassed.

I can't believe this girl was a virgin two weeks ago.

"Well, if you really think you can take these three cocks, maybe you better get better acquainted with them," Wyatt says, climbing up on the bed between her legs and fisting his cock. "Why don't you use that sassy little mouth on Luke's cock and we'll see if you deserve it in this greedy pussy?"

I have never heard Wyatt talk like this. The times we have played around with the same girl, it's been fun, yeah, a little raunchy, sure, but mostly just straight to business. This is next level. Brooke is bringing out a possessive dirty side to these men that either I didn't know existed or that didn't exist before her.

Brooke looks up at Luke. "Okay." She reaches out and wraps her hand around Luke's admittedly impressive cock. "But you're going to have to tell me what to do."

"Jesus, fuck," Luke mutters. But he sure isn't pulling away.

He gets on the mattress next to her on his knees. Her hand is still around his shaft and he wraps his hand around hers. "Open, Angel."

She turns her head fully toward him and opens. He threads his fingers through her hair and then traces the head of his cock over her lips, like he's putting lipstick on her. His breathing is ragged and his jaw looks as if it's set in stone.

Slowly, he eases the head of his cock past her lips and over her tongue.

"That's right. Take me in. Let me feel this pretty mouth."

He keeps softly coaching her, only letting her take about a

fourth, maybe a third, of his full length. Not only is she new to this, but Luke is a big dude. This is going to take a few lessons.

But fuck, we're all going to enjoy teaching Brooke.

And just like that, I realize that we're all here together, teaching her, enjoying her, pleasuring her, and no one is having a single problem.

This is going to fucking work.

"Put her hand on your cock," Wyatt tells me, his eyes on Luke and Brooke. "Keep her hand busy."

I don't have to be told twice. I take the hand that's not gripping Luke, and wrap it around my shaft. My hand over hers, I stroke up and down, the feel of her touching me like this, even with assistance, fucking amazing.

I hear Brooke moan around Luke's length and look down to find Wyatt settled between her thighs. He's licking her pussy slowly, leisurely, swirling his tongue around her clit, then sucking lightly. We keep all of this up for several long minutes. But Wyatt lifts his head before she comes.

"I think everybody's pretty comfortable," he says, wiping the back of his hand over his wet mouth.

Luke pulls out of her mouth. Brooke's breathing hard.

"What do you want now, Brooke?" Wyatt asks.

"Someone fuck me," she pleads. "Please."

Luke looks at me. Wyatt looks at me.

"No way am I going to argue," I tell them. "So be sure."

Wyatt actually chuckles. "Come on. You heard the girl. She needs to be filled up." He moves out of the way and I crawl between Brooke's thighs.

"That true sweetheart?" I ask running my hands up her inner thighs, admiring the pink slickness Wyatt left for me. "Do you want me to fill you up? Want me to fuck you first?"

"Please, Jackson. *Please.*"

"Oh, I love you begging." I move closer, spreading her thighs wide.

"I need you," she says.

I look at my two best friends. The way they are watching her, stroking her hair, her stomach, her thighs, the way Wyatt links his fingers with hers, the way Luke kisses her all makes up the hottest sight I've ever seen.

I grab the condom Wyatt tosses near my knee. I open it, roll it on, then slide my hands under the backs of her thighs and pull her close as I slide easily into her tight, sweet, hot pussy.

And as her cunt clamps down on me, as she cries out my name when I thrust deep, as Wyatt and Luke hold her and stroke her and tell her how gorgeous and perfect and sweet and hot she is, I realize that I'm never going to get over this.

This is how I want to love this woman from now on.

CHAPTER 28

Brooke

I'M ALMOST EMBARRASSED by how quickly I come. I think Jackson only actually thrusts for about three minutes and my body coils tight and hot and I feel like I explode.

It's not just him, though he's fantastic. It's the combination of *them*.

Their touches, their mouths, their dirty, dirty words.

The way I feel absolutely *worshiped*.

I wasn't completely sure this was going to work.

Now I'm one hundred percent convinced I never want it any other way.

Jackson falls forward, kissing me deeply, then lifts his head. "You're fucking amazing, sweetheart," he says, his voice gravelly.

I breathe out, running my hand over his cheek. "You too."

He pushes up and pulls out and gets off the bed. I assume he heads for the bathroom, but I can't see him with the two other big hot bodies caging me in.

"You're so gorgeous when you come," Wyatt says. "Even when you're coming on another cock."

He says it almost with wonder, his tone sweet despite the dirty words. But I grin.

"Thank you," I say, then giggle. Is that a compliment?

He gives me a half smile. "I admit, I'm surprised how quickly I'm adjusting to this."

I reach up, threading my fingers through his hair. "So you're okay? Really?"

"Turns out, I just really like seeing you lose your mind with pleasure, no matter who's causing it."

"Well, let's be *very* clear," Luke says from my other side.

His big hot hand is resting on my belly, and I turn to look up at him.

"Not just *anyone* gets to cause it. The three of us. This body, your orgasms, your pleasure, belong to the three of *us*."

His possessive tone and the look in his eyes along with those words cause a swirl of heat that makes my pussy clench, despite my recent orgasm.

"You understand, Brooke?" Luke asks.

That firm tone and the fact that he used my first name instead of calling me Angel, has me nodding. "Yes, I understand."

He reaches up, tracing his thumb over my lips. "Good girl."

I'm embarrassed by it, but I can't bite back the soft whimper that evokes.

The flare of heat in his eyes tells me he doesn't mind.

"Why don't you close your eyes and rest for a little bit?" Wyatt asks.

But I don't want to rest. My body is still tingling and hot all over. I know I should be satiated, maybe even sore, but I'm not. This all feels so dirty, forbidden even. I was a virgin two weeks ago. What am I doing lying in bed with two men who just watched another fuck me?

But even thinking about the situation causes a restless energy to go through me and I wiggle, suddenly needing to move.

"I don't think we've worn her out yet," Luke says. He drags his thumb over my lower lip again. "I think we have a very needy girl here who wants another cock in her cunt."

The graphic words shoot heat straight through my pelvis.

Without thinking, I stick my tongue out and swirl it around the pad of his thumb.

His eyes darken. "Put a condom on," he tells Wyatt. "You're up."

Wyatt's hand tightens on my hip briefly and I hear him mutter, "Holy fuck."

I can tell he's turned on. His voice gets that lower husky tone when he is. I can also feel his throbbing erection against my hip.

He shifts and I hear the bedside table drawer open and a condom package rustle.

"Lie on your back," Luke says.

I assume he's talking to Wyatt since I'm already on my back.

I liked the cowgirl position Jackson taught me, so I start to roll toward Wyatt. Luke stops me, his big hands on my hips.

"Come here," he says. He gets off the bed, then drags me to the bottom of the mattress.

"Move to the bottom of the bed," he tells Wyatt.

Wyatt moves until his legs are dangling off the end of the mattress, but he stays on his back. His cock is long and thick and hard, encased in a condom. He strokes his hand from tip to base, over and over, his eyes glued on me.

"Right here." Luke starts to lift me as if I'm going to sit in Wyatt's lap, but I'm facing away from Wyatt.

"I don't get to see her face? Or those pretty tits bouncing while she rides me?" Wyatt asks. I feel his hands settle on my hips.

"You get her tight pussy around your cock," Luke says as they continue talking about me as if I'm not here. "I want to see her face, tits, and the way she looks stretched out over you."

Wyatt groans. "Fuck. Okay. We can always trade places another time because that sounds hot as hell."

Luke's gaze locks on mine. "Yeah."

Luke helps position me over Wyatt's cock, and there's something incredibly hot and deliciously naughty about that.

I feel Wyatt's hand underneath me, where he's holding his

cock, guiding me with one hand on my hip. Luke's hands are on my waist and together they get me into position without me doing anything. I feel like I'm just a toy here for their pleasure and I flush with how much I like that. Then Wyatt pulls me down, slowly, but firmly, and I sink onto his cock, taking his entire length all at once.

He fills me up, and in this position, I feel every inch. I'm grateful for the previous orgasms and Jackson's help in getting me warm and stretched out.

Speaking of Jackson, he strides back into the room as Luke lifts me, then lets me sink down again. I cry out and grip Luke's forearms hard.

"Jesus," Jackson says huskily, stopping a couple of feet away and just taking in the sight.

"Use me for leverage," Luke tells me, drawing my gaze back to him. "Hold on to me while you fuck Wyatt."

Oh, my God. I'm burning up. Wyatt has my pussy full, I'm holding onto Luke as I start to lift and lower, and Jackson is watching me with lust and awe that I swear I can feel seep into my skin.

I move a little faster, and I hear Wyatt swear, and his fingers dig into my hips. My breasts bounce, pulling both Luke's and Jackson's eyes. I tip my head back feeling completely wanton and like the object of every one of these men's sexual fantasies.

It's addicting.

"Jackson," Luke grits out. "Get over here and play with her clit."

"Love to."

Jackson is there beside me a second later, one hand on my back, the other between my legs, circling my clit while Wyatt pumps up into me.

Luke's hands are still on my waist but he's not doing anything more than providing me a firm surface to push on as I lift myself up and down on Wyatt's perfect cock. If I let go, I could brace my hands on Wyatt's thighs, but I like this. I'm able to feel Luke's hard muscles, hot skin, and look into his intense gaze. All while his friend's cock is buried deep inside me.

Oh man, I am so done for.

How can I ever dream of having sex with anyone but these three ever again?

"My god you really do look like a gorgeous fallen angel who is here to steal our souls," Jackson says, brushing my hair over my shoulder. "I will gladly spend eternity in hell for this."

"Jackson," I moan.

"Anything you need, sweetheart."

"Harder. Faster."

He complies, giving me more pressure and speed just as I asked.

I cry out, using Luke's arms to move up and down Wyatt's length faster, my thighs burning.

"That's right, just like that, take what you need," Luke coaches. "Use that cock."

Wyatt's hands squeeze me. "Jesus, Brooke. Fuck me. Yes, fuck me, like that."

I move even faster. I feel my inner muscles start to tighten. But I can't move fast *enough*, or reach quite the right spot.

Luke seems to realize that I need help and he suddenly grips my waist again, lifting and lowering me.

That does it. Three more strokes and I'm hurtling over the edge.

I cry out. I don't even know what I'm saying, as pleasure and heat and the strangest sense of fulfillment wash over me.

A moment later, Wyatt's roar fills the room and he stiffens beneath me as he comes hard.

I slump forward and Luke catches me, wrapping his arms around me. He pulls me forward and helps me sit on the edge of the bed between Wyatt's knees.

Wyatt sits up behind me and wraps his arms around me, under where Luke's hugging me.

Wyatt kisses the back of my shoulder while Luke kisses my head.

I feel Jackson stroking my arm as well.

It's amazing to me that I can tell who's touching me without looking.

I have never felt this good in my life.

Good isn't even a big enough word.

I want more. I want to know I can have this all the time. I don't want a single other man to even hold a door for me and I don't want another woman to smile at any of these men.

I lift my head, wrap my arms around Luke's neck, and pull myself up against him. "Your turn," I say, kissing his neck.

He strokes his hands down my back. "Easy, Angel. You need a minute. Or an hour."

I reach down between us and wrap my hand around his cock. He's huge and hard. "No. I want you now. Right now. Right after them."

I don't care if I'm sore after this. I want them all. Now. Together.

"Angel…"

"Please…" I put a little pleading into my voice.

"Brooke."

He's using that deep, commanding voice that absolutely heats me to my core. I know he's trying to be bossy and thinks that's going to get me to listen to him. What it's really doing is making me need him even more.

"I'll do anything you want, except not have you inside me tonight," I tell him.

I feel an actual shudder go through him and I know it's barely restrained lust.

The power I feel at that is addicting.

I run my mouth up and down his strong neck. "Please, Luke."

I don't know what exactly it is that finally breaks him, but he grips my waist. Then he pulls me back and turns me so I'm facing the bed, where Wyatt is still sitting.

"Hands on Wyatt's thighs," Luke tells me as he bends me at the waist. I feel his big hand stroking up and down my back and over my ass. "This time he's going to need to hold onto you."

Oh my God, I'm still wet, but I feel my pussy respond to the dark promise in his words.

I meet Wyatt's eyes as I brace my hands on his thighs. He covers my hands with his. "You are incredible," he tells me, his voice rough.

Luke's hand is between my legs now, stroking through my wetness, circling my clit. "Last time I'm going to ask—"

He slides two thick fingers into me and I gasp.

"You ready for me?"

"Yes, God yes," I say, making my voice as strong as I can. "I want you, Luke."

Jackson moves against my side, gathering my hair back into a ponytail.

"Fuck, this is the hottest experience of my life," he says to all of us in general.

I feel the head of Luke's cock against my entrance and I push back slightly. The next thing I feel is a sharp sting against my ass.

I gasp. Luke just spanked me.

"Stand there and take what I give you," he says firmly. Then he thrusts.

Even if I was going to say something—sass him or tease him or argue—he just stole my breath.

He didn't ease in, he didn't hesitate, he's deep all at once.

"Oh *God*," is all I manage.

"You can take it," Wyatt tells me, stroking his hands up and down my arms. "Let him have that amazing pussy that Jackson and I just fucked."

"You're doing so well," Jackson tells me from my side, brushing his hand over my face and down my neck. "Such a good girl. You're able to handle all three of your men, aren't you?"

I don't hear anything from Luke except harsh breathing and

the slapping of skin as he thrusts into me over and over. But I feel him in every inch of my body.

Every nerve ending is on fire, and every single one of his thrusts not only fills up my pussy, but I feel like he's filling my entire body with emotions I can't even define.

Having them all three here like this, touching me, talking to me, watching the others take me, feels like a dream. A hot, dirty, erotic fantasy that I didn't even know I had before the cabin and I wouldn't even tell my closest friends about. This is deep dark secret stuff.

But I share it with these men. They're not judging. They're *enjoying* every minute right along with me.

And I will relive it over and over and over again. I know that. But I never want it to end.

"Come for me," Luke commands harshly. He reaches around and finds my clit, circling and pressing.

I'm honestly not sure that I could possibly have another orgasm, but then just like that, like he put a match against a fuse, my body lights up and I feel the coiling tightness again.

"Oh, my God, Luke," I almost whisper, feeling my body start to tighten around his.

"That's right. That's fucking right," he bites out as he continues to thrust into me. "Come on my cock, Angel. Let me feel you."

And as if my body is his instead of mine, I do exactly as he commands. I clamp down, almost harder than before.

He groans, squeezing my hips hard, and empties into me.

I remember then that he's not wearing a condom. The dirty, erotic wildness of all of this is compounded by the fact that when he pulls out, I feel the wet stickiness on my inner thighs.

He leans over and kisses my neck, then mutters against my ear, "One of these times, I'm actually going to be in control of how this goes between us."

I *love* that I can make him snap, so I hope that's not entirely true. Then again, an in-control, taking-his-time Luke would be fun. I did have a glimpse earlier when he was deciding how things should go with Wyatt and Jackson.

Wyatt kisses my forehead and Jackson kisses my shoulder and, despite just doing the absolute dirtiest thing I've ever even imagined, I feel cared for and adored.

I'm saved from having to figure out what to do or say next by Wyatt nudging me back into Luke's arms so that he can stand from the bed. Then he bends and sweeps me up into his arms and strides into the bathroom. He turns on the shower, sets me inside the glass wall enclosure and looks down at me with an affectionate smile. "I'm gonna give you about ten minutes alone to decompress. Then I'm gonna come in here and wash your hair."

He deals with the condom, gives me one last look with a wink, then leaves me alone to breathe, gather my thoughts, and pinch my arm to convince myself all of that actually just happened.

CHAPTER 29

Wyatt

BROOKE IS STILL SLEEPING when I slide out of Jackson's bed the next morning. I try to be stealthy, but then I realize Jackson isn't here, so his leaving obviously didn't disturb her. Even as I stand, I watch her carefully for any sign of movement, but she's still in a deep sleep, her hair splayed out across the crisp white pillowcase, her hands tucked under her cheek in a prayer position, her delicate lips slightly parted.

Her breathing is steady, even.

The sheet has slipped down, exposing her creamy shoulder and the side of her breast. I tug the sheet up to cover her, aware that it's chilly in the bedroom. Jackson keeps his heat down low, which is fine for him, but I worry she'll get cold.

Brooke doesn't stir at all. She's absolutely worn out.

That makes me grin and shake my head.

Damn.

Brooke was incredible last night. So sexy. So obedient. So *willing*.

She came apart for us over and over, fully embracing all her needs and wants. She gave, she took, she loved all of it and us so damn well I know I will never forget a single detail of her on this night for the rest of my life.

I've never experienced anything like what the four of us shared.

Sharing a woman with two other guys was never in my plans. It wasn't even on my radar until Brooke.

But given the choice between no Brooke or sharing Brooke, it was a no brainer. I can't quit her. There was no way to walk away. The two weeks of no contact nearly killed me.

Now, though, it goes beyond just giving into what Brooke wanted.

I *enjoyed* it.

Seeing her be fucked by my two best friends was hot as hell.

And feeling her tight cunt clamped onto my cock while she gripped Luke like she needed him to tether her to the earth or she'd fly away, was hands down the best sex of my entire life.

Every night with Brooke is going to be the best sex of my life.

I can guarantee that.

Grabbing my jeans off of the floor, I step into them and then rub my hand over my hair. It feels like I have bedhead.

Pulling the door softly closed behind me, but leaving it open just a crack so a click doesn't wake Brooke, I go into Jackson's kitchen. He's not there, but Luke is, sipping his coffee and looking about as relaxed as I've ever seen him.

After I took Brooke into the shower, Jackson cuddled her on the couch until she fell asleep, then Luke carried her to bed. Then he returned to the couch to sleep, which didn't exactly surprise me. He likes his space. Physical and emotional.

I didn't give Jackson the option of claiming the bed with Brooke solo. I told him straight out we could each take a side with her in the middle. But Jackson being Jackson, he was fine with it.

"Hey," I say to Luke. "Where's Jackson?"

I'm not a huge coffee drinker, so I just grab a glass out of the cabinet and fill it with water from the refrigerator door.

"He walked next door to the coffee shop to get some egg sandwiches. Neither of us felt like cooking this morning. He's been up for a while. He already took Henley for a walk."

"How was the couch?" I ask him, after taking a big swallow of my water. I'm dehydrated.

"The couch sucks but I was in a good mood, so I got over it."

"You look like you're still in a good mood."

"I am. How about you?" Luke studies me. "You okay?"

I nod. "I'm good. I didn't expect to enjoy last night as much as I did. Seeing Brooke—

"Seeing Brooke what?" a sleepy voice asks.

We turn and see our girl shuffling out of the bedroom, shoving her hair back off of her face.

She's completely naked, her nipples tight pink peaks on her breasts, her arms covered in goosebumps. I drag my gaze over her, wanting to take in every inch of her gorgeous body, from her sleep heavy eyes to her narrow waist, to the soft sweetness of her pussy, and her long legs.

"Seeing you come like a fucking champ," I tell her. I'm already striding toward her. "Did I wake you when I got up, gorgeous? I'm sorry." I pull her in for a soft, tender hug, then I wrap my arms around her. "Good morning."

Immediately, I squeeze her closer, wanting to feel her warm skin and sweet curves.

She sighs and cuddles into my chest. "No, you didn't wake me up. This is when I normally have to get up for school."

I kiss the top of her head, enjoying the press of her bare chest against mine.

She tilts her face up for a kiss, and I'm happy to give her one, brushing my lips lightly over hers.

She wriggles away. "I need coffee."

She eases past me, and I watch the sway of her hips and her tight little ass, hair tousled and heavy down her back. It's a fucking beautiful sight to see first thing in the morning.

Luke blocks her path to the coffee pot. "Go put some clothes on," he tells her shortly. "You're driving your men crazy and we can't fuck you again this morning. You need time to recover."

"But—

"Now." He takes her by the elbow, turns her back to the bedroom, lightly swats her on the ass, and gives her a gentle push. "Go."

My jaw drops. I'm about to ask him what the actual fuck, when to my complete shock, Brooke does as she's told.

She even glances over her shoulder and gives Luke a look shot through with lust, even as she murmurs, "We're going to have to talk about this later. The *bossy* thing."

Luke just smirks. "Get dressed, Angel."

She disappears into the bedroom and I'm overwhelmed with a variety of conflicting emotions I don't understand. I'm outraged that Luke thinks it's appropriate to talk to her like that. I'm jealous that Brooke clearly likes it, even the light spanking. And I'm also very, very turned on. My dick is currently throbbing.

"Don't look at me like that." Luke shakes his head at me. "You agreed to this."

"I know I did. I just think you could be a little less..." *Luke*. He could be a little less Luke.

"No. There's a reason she likes all three of us and it's not because we're the same guy three times over." Luke takes a sip of his coffee. "She's attracted to different things about each of us. Just remember that."

I nod, not trusting myself to speak. I know he's right.

Seeing Brooke happy is fucking everything.

But, damn. I don't know. It's still got me twisted up inside.

Jackson comes into the condo, laden down by brown bakery bags. "Breakfast is served, boys. Where's Brooke, still sleeping?"

"She's getting dressed," Luke tells him.

As Jackson is pulling sandwiches out of the bags, Brooke comes into the room. She's clearly rooted around in Jackson's dresser because she's wearing a baggy Chicago Bears T-shirt and a pair of loose basketball shorts that she's rolled down the waistband on. Her cheeks are damp, like she splashed water on them, and she looks more alert than a few minutes ago.

Jackson lets out a growl of approval. "You look so damn hot in my clothes, baby girl." He strides over to her and scoops her up in a big hug.

Brooke laughs softly. "I didn't want to put my jeans on so early in the morning. I hope you don't mind I went digging in your drawers."

Jackson waggles his eyebrows. "You can rummage through my drawers any time." He gives her a tender kiss. "How did you sleep?"

"Fantastic." She reaches up and kisses him again. "You?"

It's really weird that I'm watching the girl I've fallen in love with easily and happily kissing my best friend. The sex was one thing, but this is affectionate, caring. It's definitely going to take some getting used to.

"Never better. I got some breakfast sandwiches if you're hungry. I know you said you don't usually eat breakfast, but you burned a lot of calories last night." He gives her a grin.

Brooke blushes. "I'll just have coffee, but thank you, Jackson."

There it is again—I'm torn between pleasure at seeing her happy and a little bit of jealousy that it's not directed at me. I really need to get a fucking grip on this or I'm going to mess this whole thing up.

That's the last thing in the world I want because I cannot imagine my life without Brooke now.

"How is this going to work?" I blurt out. "Dating Brooke?"

I need clarity on who is doing what and when so I can work it all out in my head and get right with it.

The three of them look at me, all clearly startled.

"Well," Brooke says, moistening her bottom lip with her tongue. "I'd like to spend time with you all, getting to know you. And I'd like to repeat last night."

That makes my dick hard, but I refuse to be distracted. That's too vague for me.

"Sounds great to me," Jackson says.

Luke nods.

"But how specifically?" I insist. "I want solo time with you," I tell Brooke. "Outside of the bedroom."

I'd like solo time with her in the bedroom too but I sense I would get resistance on that right now. Brooke *really* enjoyed herself the night before.

As we all did.

Brooke comes over to me and smiles. When she touches my cheek with the palm of her hand, stroking down my beard stubble, I feel like a damn cat turning toward the sun. I rub against her. I can't help myself.

"I would love to date you and spend some solo time with you, Wyatt."

It makes me feel absolutely amazing.

It only slightly dampens my mood when she turns to the guys. "And you and you."

"I think we should establish a no sex rule," Luke says. "On solo dates."

Brooke nods. "I like that idea."

"*What?*" I demand. "Why?"

"Because it's about establishing an *emotional* connection with all of you." Brooke's expression is earnest. "Obviously the physical stuff works. I want to get to know you other than that."

Luke gives a cough and then clears his throat.

I realize immediately his plan backfired on him. He wants a no sex rule because he doesn't want to have to break down all his walls with Brooke.

I have no walls and I want to be able to touch Brooke whenever I can.

"I want whatever you want," Jackson says to her.

It mildly annoys me. Can't he ever have an actual opinion?

Or maybe I just want someone to back me up on this.

Sure, watching Brooke come undone for all three of us was incredible, but I want the opportunity to eat her pussy without an audience every once in a while.

Going over the food Jackson has brought, I pick up a flaky

croissant and bite it hard so I don't say something that will get me in trouble.

Jackson shoots me a look of censure. "That was mine."

"Sorry," I say, taking another bite. "Who gets the first date with Brooke? Because I want it."

"I get the first date," Luke says.

"Hey, not fair," Jackson says. "Why not me?"

Instead of being aggravated with us, Brooke beams and takes the mug of coffee Jackson has poured for her. "I love how wanted you all make me feel. We can just play it by ear, according to your schedules."

"No way. Luke and I work the same shifts, and Jackson doesn't have a job."

"I do so have a job." Jackson gestures to Henley and the puppies, who are cuddled up together in a giant dog bed in the corner of the kitchen. "I have a fur family to take care of."

"Forget it. You can be more flexible than we can."

The smile falls off of Brooke's face. "I don't want this to be an issue," she says, softly. "Between all of you."

I instantly feel terrible. "No, no, it's not like that. It's not an issue. I just think a schedule is important."

"Let's just have a little competition," Jackson says. "To work out the rotation."

"You want to compete to see me first?" Brooke asks. She sounds astonished, but also intrigued.

I'm competitive by nature anyway but I'll wrestle a fucking bear for the right to see Brooke first. "Works for me."

"Come on," Luke says, rolling his eyes. "Let's just go from oldest to youngest."

As if Jackson and I are dumb enough to go for that.

"You scared you'll lose?" Jackson says, egging him on.

"Hell, no." Luke sets down his coffee mug. "Bring it on. What are we doing? Arm wrestling?"

"Let's not get violent," Brooke says, sounding a little alarmed.

"Arm wrestling is not violent," Luke assures her. "Especially not the way these two do it."

I finish my croissant and dust off my hands. "Let's go."

"Just relax," Jackson says. "I have a better idea." He smiles at Brooke. "No violence."

"I'm listening," she says.

"We line up and whoever Henley goes to wins."

"No way. You've been taking care of her for two weeks. She'll pick you."

Jackson grins. "Why do you think I suggested it?"

"I agree with Wyatt," Luke says. "I call bullshit."

"Well, we can't do the puppies. Their eyes are barely open at this point. They just wiggle and crawl."

"So put the puppies on the floor mat and see which one gets to the end first. If the puppy you named gets there first, you win," Luke says.

"Or we could arm wrestle." I turn to Brooke. "What do you think?"

"What do I think? I think it's sexy that I have three incredibly hot men who want to spend time with me." Her words are flirty, her mouth turned up in a sexy smile.

God, this woman.

"But the puppies are sleeping," she says. "Let's leave them to it. Arm wrestling opens the door for allegations of cheating. I have a competitive brother, remember? How about we keep it simple and I pick a number between one and twenty?"

Simple but effective. I'd prefer to kick their asses in a physical showdown, but I've protested enough.

"Great idea."

The other guys nod.

"Okay, I have a number."

"One," I say instantly, because it feels right.

"Seventeen," Jackson says.

"Ten."

Brooke's face gives it away the second Luke speaks. Her face lights up. "Luke, you guessed it exactly! How did you know?"

I pick my coffee back up and take a sip to hide my irritated expression. If Brooke's number was ten, that means I came in last.

Luke smiles at her. "Guess I'm just a lucky man."

She beams at him. "So Luke first, then Jackson, then Wyatt. Are we all good with that?"

No.

But it was fair, and this is what Brooke wants.

"Sounds good to me," Jackson says.

"I can't complain." Luke smirks at me.

This is going to make for a hellishly long week. Both at home and at work.

"I'm good," I lie. "Remember, no sex. Your rule, Moody."

His smirk slips.

I instantly feel better.

Brooke sighs happily. "This is perfect. Thank you."

I think complicated is a better description.

But at least going third means I have the advantage of knowing where they took Brooke on their date and I can do one better.

CHAPTER 30

Luke

BROOKE OPENS the door to her loft with a wide smile. "Hi."

I feel myself smiling in return even though I'm still not fully convinced this date is a good idea.

"Hi." My gaze tracks over her from head to toe. She's dressed for the cool March evening in a sweater, coat and scarf, blue jeans that hug her hips, and brown ankle-high boots. She has at least three layers on, and I still feel my body stirring.

"You look beautiful," I tell her. Her hair is down and softly curled. She's put on a little make up, a fact I can only detect because I've seen her with nothing on.

Literally.

And even though I am determined to keep this date PG, it's impossible to look at her and not think of the night she spent with me, Jackson, and Wyatt.

That was, hands-down, the hottest sexual experience of my life. It's been on my mind constantly. How the hell can I stand here with her and *not* think about how soft her skin is, how eager her mouth and hands are, how perfect her...

Fuck.

Tonight is going to be a true test of my willpower.

She steps into the hallway of her apartment building and wraps her arms around me.

Caught off guard, I have no choice but to return the hug. And I certainly don't mind. Feeling her up against me, even with all of our layers of clothes, feels fucking fantastic.

With her arms still around my waist, she tips her head up to look at me. "I'm really looking forward to this."

I am too. Despite the little voice in the back of my mind continually telling me this is a bad idea.

"Have you thought about what you want to do?" I ask her. She smells amazing, and I really want to lean in and bury my nose in her hair.

"I want to kiss you," she tells me.

My body responds before my brain even catches up with what she said. I'm already semi hard.

"I don't know if that's a good idea, Angel," I tell her.

"Why not? Just a little kiss to say hello."

"Because I can't guarantee that I won't back you up against that door and start stripping your clothes off."

Her smile is a little sly and I realize I am going to have an even harder time resisting her if she's going to be a little flirt.

"Well, I think I've made it clear that I wouldn't mind that," she tells me.

I take a breath and blow it out, then set her back away from me. "Tonight is about getting to know each other. Figuring out if we're compatible beyond the bedroom."

"And the kitchen wall," she says.

Yeah, I'm definitely in trouble. It's clear she's feeling good. Confident. Sexy.

And she should. I love that she's discovering this side of herself. I love that I know everything that's been a part of that, including the men.

But, my resistance to her is already paper thin.

"Yes," I finally admit. "But I think we need to figure out if we've got anything going except chemistry."

She tips her head, considering me for a moment, then asks, "Will you kiss me good night at the end of the date?"

I probably shouldn't. I won't want to stop with just a kiss. If I walk her to the door, knowing that her bedroom is just down the hall, and that she would happily invite me in, I don't know if I'll be able to simply kiss her and send her in there by herself.

But looking at her now, even in the harsh lighting of the building's hallway, she's so fucking beautiful that I don't think there's any chance in hell I'm going to make it through this night without kissing her.

"If you're a good girl, I'll kiss you on the sidewalk before we come in."

She pouts for a moment, but then gets a mischievous glint in her eye. "What constitutes being a good girl?"

Fuck. I want to show her all about being a good girl for me. I want to tell her over and over that she is. I want her on her knees, on her back, over the back of her couch. I reach up and tuck her hair behind her ear. "Not tempting me," I tell her honestly.

"How do I do that?"

"No touching, no kissing, and no talking about kitchen walls, bedrooms, or anything that happened the other night."

Her gaze stays on my eyes for a few seconds. "No touching? At all?"

I tuck my hands into my coat pockets. "No touching."

She turns and pulls her apartment door shut, drops her keys into her purse and pulls the strap up onto her shoulder. Then she tucks her hands into her coat pockets too. "Okay, then. I really want at least one kiss, so I guess I'll be good."

I shake my head and fight a smile. She's already a handful, and she doesn't even fully understand just how tightly I'm wound around her finger.

We walk down the hall to the elevator and I punch the button for the lobby. "So what should we do tonight?" I ask.

"You choose. This is your city. I haven't been to Chicago much. When I am here visiting, we mostly stay at my grandmother's, or she'll take us out to restaurants. Of course, I've been to some hockey games." She smiles at me. "But mostly when I see my family, it's when they come to Minnesota."

"Your grandmother lives here too?"

Her smile grows and I can tell that her grandmother is special to her.

"She spends time in Minnesota, Arizona, Florida, and Chicago. She also loves to visit New York."

"You're close?"

"We are. She wanted me to live with her when I moved here but I'm twenty-five." She wrinkles her nose. "Her place is amazing but I need my own space and I definitely don't need my grandmother wondering where I am when I'm not home." She slides me a glance. "Or giving people the third degree when people come over."

I watch the numbers above the door tick down instead of meeting her gaze. I'm trying very hard not to think about where she was the other night and how concerned her grandmother would have probably been if she'd known her granddaughter was spending the night with three men.

"She'll love you."

Now I snap my head to look at Brooke.

The doors swish open just then. I put my hand out to hold them open. "What?"

"She'll love you," she repeats. "My grandmother."

Not she *would* love you but she *will* as if it's a foregone conclusion that I'll meet her.

I swallow. "I'm sure she'll think I'm too old for you."

Brooke just laughs.

She starts across the lobby and I follow, thoughts of meeting her family warring with thoughts of how damned good this girl looks in blue jeans.

I open the door for her, and we step out into the getting warmer but not yet *warm* March night.

I drop the conversation about meeting families. "How about

Millennial Park?" I suggest. "It's pretty with all the lights at night and there's a great brewery close by that I like. We can walk until we get cold and then get dinner."

"I love that," she tells me. "I want to just talk and spend time with you. We don't have to do anything special."

She's so easy to be with. I don't want to go overboard and make this too romantic. I don't want to make or even imply promises of love and forever that I can't deliver but getting to know her, and letting her know me, is important.

She can't be my fuck buddy or my fling.

This either is going to go somewhere real. Or we're going to end it. Before someone gets hurt.

I have an Uber waiting at the curb. I didn't want to drive tonight and worry about parking or having a few drinks. This way I can give her my full attention.

I open the back door and Brooke slides in. I follow her, leaning forward to tell the driver where to drop us off and then settling into the seat next to the girl I want to touch so badly my hand is itching.

As the car pulls away from the curb, Brooke turns to me.

"For the record, my grandmother is lovely and would be completely fine with your age."

"Come on." I give her a smile to cushion my response. "I'm sure she pictures you with someone more like Wyatt."

Brooke frowns. "She'll love Wyatt too. And Jackson. But if you treat me well and make me truly happy and really love me, she would absolutely love you. That's what's important."

My gut clenches. She talks so easily about love and falling into it and relationships developing. Yes, my feelings for her are strong and it happened quickly, but I know well that it takes a lot more than that to make things really *work*.

Still, I love the way Brooke makes it seem simple. Treating her well, making her happy, loving her? Fuck, that not only seems simple, but I can't imagine *not* doing those things.

"She's very open-minded," Brooke goes on. "My brother is in a poly relationship, as you know, and she's thrilled."

"Thrilled?" I ask. That's an interesting choice of words. Accepting maybe, but thrilled?

"Yes," Brooke says adamantly. Then she grins. "She's convinced Blake's so lovable that of course he has multiple partners. I'm sure she'll feel the same about us. I mean, she likes me even more than she likes him."

I chuckle softly. I know her brother, Blake. He's a retired hockey goalie and known to be kind of an ass, actually. At least to reporters and such. *Not* bubbly, sunny, and full of joy, like Brooke. Though he played hockey with the same passion I see in Brooke when she's with the dogs or talking about school and being a vet. Clearly, passions run in the family.

"You and Blake seem pretty different," I say.

"Not really." She tucks her hair behind one ear. "He comes off grumpy and I come off shy. But it's really that we're both introverted. We each have a very small, close inner circle and that's all we need. To everyone else we're quiet and standoffish, but to people who really know us we're happy and talkative and open."

She smiles at me and it hits me how fucking glad I am to be in her inner circle and that she feels comfortable being open with me.

"I think there's some misogyny at play to be honest," she adds. "A guy is quiet and keeps to himself and he's 'broody'. A woman like that is either shy or a bitch."

I can't argue with that though I frown. She's really neither of those things, even shy, and fuck everyone who thinks so. They're just not good enough to get close to her.

"Well, I think it's safe to say you're past any *shyness* with the three newest members of your inner circle," I say.

She grins at me. "Yeah, going from virgin to poly in two weeks isn't very shy, is it?"

Fuck. She knows what she's doing to me, reminding me of… everything. Fucking little flirt.

"Not the word I'd use, no," I tell her.

"I guess it's good I have a sister-in-law who knows exactly what it's like to be with three men."

I hear our driver cough slightly.

I sigh. I guess, if we're really going to do this, we'll have to get used to other people's reactions. And not caring about them.

Brooke reaches over, laces her fingers with mine, and rests our hands on my thigh. "The no touching *at all* doesn't work for me. I'm kind of a touchy person," she says.

"What if I'm not?" I ask, though I make no move to withdraw my hand.

"I think you will be with me," she says.

She has no idea the things I want to be with her. I want the right to run my hands over her ass in public. I want to kiss her anywhere, anytime. I want to make her laugh. I want to be her first phone call when things go right, or terribly wrong.

"But you're right," she adds. "Consent is sexy and it goes both ways. I don't want you to be uncomfortable. Can I hold your hand, Luke?"

Fuck, she can do whatever she wants to me. Even break my damned heart.

"Yes," I tell her. Then I lift her hand and kiss it.

We pull up to our stop a few minutes later and I get out, keeping her hand in mine and helping her from the car.

"Oh wow," she says, looking around.

The lights of downtown shine all around. The buildings are lit up and there are street lamps and lights strung from poles around this section, where it's clear there was some kind of event earlier today.

"It's so pretty," she tells me, after she's spun a three-sixty.

I can't take my eyes off of her, of course. I love my city, but I've lived here all my life. I've seen the downtown lights hundreds of times. Hell, I've fought fires amongst these lights. I love seeing it through her eyes. And I realize that I want Brooke to *love* Chicago. So much that she wants to stay.

"Come on, there's more," I tell her, keeping her hand in mine, completely unwilling to let go of her now.

We start down the sidewalk and I tell her about everything in the park—the fountains and art displays and gardens—and that we're only a couple of blocks from the lake.

"I'll bring you back during the day, when it's warmer too."

She presses close to my side. "I'd love that."

Yeah, I just implied there's a future in the warmer weather. So sue me.

We make it to the main attraction I wanted to show her.

"Oh, that's beautiful!" she exclaims as the Cloud Gate statue comes into view. "I can't believe I've never been this close to it."

We walk up to it. "This is called the Cloud Gate, but it's better known as The Bean," I tell her.

She grins. "I can see why."

The shape of the iconic statue makes that obvious.

The gigantic silver structure reflects the scene around it and at night is aglow with the lights from all sides.

We stand, just watching it and the people around for a few minutes. It's a weeknight, and the weather is still brisk, so there isn't a crowd, but with spring in the air, Chicagoans are starting to come out of hibernation and we're hardly alone.

Brooke shivers slightly and I move behind her, wrapping my arms around her and resting my chin on her shoulder. "Are you cold? Do you want to go to the brewery?"

She snuggles back against me. "I want to stay right here."

I pull her in tighter, unable to help myself.

We stay like that for a few more minutes. I watch the people around us and am acutely aware of how many couples there are. People walking hand in hand or men with their arms around women. People kissing.

People in love.

"Let's go eat," I finally say.

"Okay."

She steps out of my arms and I miss the warmth of her body, but tamp that down.

I do take her hand again though as we walk toward one of my favorite breweries. I don't come here often, but they've got a great selection, and it's got a classy, but laid-back feel.

We're seated immediately at a high table in the middle of the room. I tell myself taking the seat right next to her will make it easier to talk, though I know it's also because I want to be close to her. I love studying the different colors in her hair, the swirls of blue in her eyes, and the various tilts to her lips as she talks and smiles. I'm so pathetically into her I nearly roll my eyes at myself.

I order a local microbrew and Brooke orders a margarita and we peruse the menu quietly, the sounds of conversation and the televisions above the bar filling in the silence.

After our drinks are delivered and we order, she takes a sip and then turns those eyes on me.

"Tell me about your ex."

I nearly choke on my drink of beer. I swallow hard. Then I shake my head. "Nah. We don't need to go there."

She leans in and covers my knee with her hand. "I want to know. I want to know *you* and that's a huge part of who you are. Please."

I study her. Fuck. She's right, of course, but hell, maybe she does need to know. It's the main reason I'm resistant to this thing between *us*. Yes, it's also her age, and her innocence, and the fact that my two best friends are falling for her—a big fucking complication, of course—but Marci is a huge part of my reservations.

"It's not pretty," I say after taking another draw of my beer, then setting the glass down.

"I assumed that was the case. That's okay." She moves her hand from my knee to my hand. She runs her thumb over the back of my knuckles. "So… try to scare me off."

CHAPTER 31

Luke

I **LOOK** from our hands to her face. She's smiling lightly, her eyes open and trusting. Interested.

Fuck, she's so beautiful.

I want her.

Not just physically. I want to be close to her. There's a warmth there, a goodness that keeps reaching out and trying to wrap itself around me. It feels as if I really let it, I'd feel…lighter. Happy. Whole. She could fill in these gaps and cracks that have developed in my heart and my life.

And damn, that's all really woo-woo for a guy like me.

I take a breath. "Marci and I fell in love fast. I met her while I was going through fire school. She was—is—a nurse. We didn't have a lot of money, but we didn't care. We had a simple life that was full of family and friends. We were happy. Or so I thought."

Brooke keeps running her finger over the back of my hand, tracing the veins and tendons. It's strangely comforting.

"We talked about starting a family and I'd envisioned us with three or four kids."

Brooke just watches me, listening to every word, not saying anything.

"So when she told me she was pregnant, I was thrilled." My

grip tightens on my glass of beer. I'd been over the moon. "I went to ultrasound appointments with her, we picked out names, I repainted a room for the nursery, assembled a crib, the whole thing."

Brooke leans closer, her finger still moving on my hand. I don't know if she even realizes that she moves further into my space, but it's comforting not only to have her there, but that she's coming closer rather than shifting away.

"The pregnancy went well. Everything was... perfect." I have to clear my throat to continue. "Her water broke late one night and it was like the movies. I grabbed the bag, loaded her up, drove her to the hospital. We got to the delivery room and the baby was already on her way."

"Her?" Brooke says softly.

I nod. "It was a girl. She was born just two hours after her water broke. Came into the world fast and loud. Yelling her head off." I smile remembering. Jesus, that moment had been incredible. A fucking miracle. "She was eight pounds, totally healthy. Absolutely perfect."

Brooke now curls her fingers around my hand, obviously sensing the story is about to shift.

"I thought everything was perfect," I say, my voice a little scratchy now. "I had my wife and daughter. I couldn't have been happier. And then thirty minutes later, one of the doctors bursts through the door, wild-eyed. He looks at *my wife*, then my *daughter*, and says, "I want a DNA test.""

Brooke sucks in a little breath, but I keep going. I can't stop now or I won't finish.

"They'd been having an affair for almost a year. He claimed he was in love with her. One look at her face when he walked in and I knew she felt the same way. We got the DNA test done immediately and... he was the father."

Brooke's hand tightens on mine, but she still doesn't say anything.

"We didn't even bring the baby home. They went straight to

his house. They hired movers to come get her stuff from our—my —house. We filed for divorce that same week. Because it wasn't contested and we didn't fight over any assets, it went fast and easy."

We sit quietly for almost a minute after I finish.

"How long ago was that?" Brooke asks.

"Almost eleven years."

"Have you ever seen them since?"

I shake my head. "They're not mine."

She starts stroking the back of my hand again.

I look up, and she's watching me. Just looking at her makes my heart rate decrease and I can take another deep breath. I loosen my grip on the glass.

It's another thirty seconds before she says, "Is that why you got a vasectomy?"

Okay, so we're just going to dive into *all* of it. I shouldn't be surprised, I guess. Brooke is a passionate person. When she's into something, she's really into it. School. Sex.

Me.

I feel a warmth in my chest at the idea that I'm something important to her.

"Yeah," I say simply. "I couldn't go through something like that again. I didn't want any accidents and…" This next part won't sound so great out loud, but it's the truth. "I didn't want to put my trust in the women I was sleeping with to handle the birth control. So I handled it. For sure."

She doesn't look offended or even surprised. She nods. "I see."

"Do you want to have kids?" I ask. There's no reason not to lay it all out there. We're here to figure out if this can be something real between us.

She nods again. "Yes. I've always assumed I'd be a mom some-day. I wanted to get through school and start my career first." She laughs softly. "I mean, I wasn't even doing the things you need to do to get pregnant, so it wasn't on my immediate horizon, obviously."

I smile but I do make note that I can't give her something she wants.

"So," I start. "This thing with us then…"

She just lifts a brow.

"Obviously there's an issue there," I say.

"What do you mean?"

"I can't give you kids," I say bluntly.

She lifts a shoulder. "You could have it reversed. Or there's adoption."

I just stare at her. She's so… unbothered. She makes it all seem so easy.

She makes being with her seem so easy.

And a huge part of me is starting to believe that could be true.

She notices something in my face, because she leans in, forearm on the table, her hand flat on mine now.

"Luke, I'm twenty-five. I'm a grown up. I'm in grad school, succeeding in a very demanding program. I'm mature. Intelligent. I know the virgin thing, my inexperience there, probably made me seem really young and innocent, but I'm really not. I know what I can handle. I can make decisions about who I spend time with. I understand things like how vasectomies can impact my future if I fall for a guy who's had one. You don't have to protect me here." She smiles. "I can handle you."

That's hot. All of that's fucking hot. Her confidence. The way she just takes in my story and everything about me and takes it seriously, but also makes it not complicated. And the idea of her handling me… yeah, a huge part of me wants that.

"Okay," I say. "I hear you."

Her smile is bigger now. She traces her finger over my hand again. "I'm really, really sorry all of that happened with Marci."

I blow out a breath. "Well… thanks. I guess."

"Am I a bad person if I say she's an idiot for not realizing how amazing you are, though?" Brooke asks.

My eyebrows arch. "Not at all. I've frequently thought she was an idiot."

"If she had been smarter and held on to you, you wouldn't be here with me right now. You wouldn't have been with me the other night. Or at the cabin. I can confidently say it's her loss, my gain."

I feel a laugh bubble up. "You don't really know me. You have no idea if I'm amazing."

Now she laughs. "Seriously? You're a *firefighter*. You put your life on the line for other people—strangers—every single time you go to work. You are so great with your friends. When you're in a moment with another person, you are all in. Completely tuned in to what other people are feeling, what they need."

I start to respond, but she keeps going.

"I spent three days completely snowed in with you, and I saw a lot that you probably don't realize."

That makes me shift on my stool, suddenly a little uncomfortable. The only people who are truly *close* to me are Wyatt and Jackson. And as much as I love them, I'm not sure how observant they really are. My mom would probably be the only other person who really knows things about me that I don't let show to the rest of the world.

Brooke continues. "You always make sure that Wyatt and Jackson have whatever *actual* things they need, but you also make them aware of how they're speaking to one another and other people. You tell them when they're doing a great job at something. You give them encouragement, but also hold them accountable. You're like this fantastic older brother or something. They really look up to you." She smiles. "And you know it. And you take it seriously. That makes you feel good. I can tell."

Damn. She's right on all of that.

"You're also funny and smart. You're protective. I feel completely safe and comfortable with you. And..." She leans in. "You're so damned sexy I can hardly take a deep breath around you. Until you touch me. Then I still feel hot and tingly, but also... calm, somehow. Like I can just sink into the moment and the feelings and enjoy it. I know you're going to make me feel amazing but I'm totally safe just letting go."

My entire body heats. Not only because of the reminder of all the ways I've touched her, and want to touch her, but because *that* right there is what I want.

That is what I love more than anything. I want people to feel safe when I'm around. I want to make people feel like everything will be okay.

But to do *that* for Brooke, to make it so she can fully be herself and bask in pleasure and happiness and being cared for, that I want more than anything.

"Brooke, you are very fucking dangerous," I tell her, my voice low.

Her laugh is breathless. "Dangerous? Why?"

"Because you make me spill my guts, relive all of that pain, but I come out the other side feeling like a fucking superhero." I lean closer. "A superhero who wants to spend the next twenty-four hours straight making you insane with pleasure."

Her pupils dilate and her lips part. I lift my hand and drag my thumb over her lower lip.

"How can I have just told you *that* fucking story, the lowest point in my life, the darkness that I've been dragging around for years, but two minutes later I'm sitting here feeling cocky as hell and so turned on that I want to bend you over this table right now?"

Her breath catches. "I'm glad," she says softly. "I want to make you feel those things even when there's darkness."

"I—"

Whatever I was about to say is interrupted by the waitress arriving with our food.

That's a relief.

I'm not sure what I was going to say. But it might have been a marriage proposal.

Brooke Wilder has me all twisted up.

Or maybe she has you all straightened out.

I can't help the thought that immediately follows. I don't really feel twisted up. I feel completely clear-headed, as a matter of fact.

I really fucking *like* Brooke. In addition to wanting her more than I've ever wanted another woman.

We start on our meals, but I finish my beer after just a couple of bites and notice her margarita is nearly gone.

I look around but our waitress is nowhere. "I'm going to get us refills," I say, standing and grabbing our glasses.

"Okay. Will you get me an ice water too?" she asks, popping a fry into her mouth.

I want to lean in and lick the salt that lingers on her lip. "Sure."

I head for the bar, taking the chance to breathe deep.

The bar is busy and I'm behind two women who aren't sure what kind of shots they want. But I'm good with a few minutes away. This date is doing exactly what I'd intended, I suppose.

We're getting to know each other.

The way I feel about her isn't just about sex.

It seems that her feelings aren't just about her first sexual experiences, either. She's noticed things about me that she likes and yes, they are things I'm proud of. Things I'm glad she's noticed and paid attention to.

Fuck, maybe this could work out.

I finally get our drinks refilled and turn back to the table, managing the three glasses. I've taken only two steps when I realize that Brooke is not sitting at our table alone.

There are two guys there, one on either side of her, leaning on the table, smiling and talking to her.

Friends from school? They don't look familiar, so I don't think they're hockey players she'd know because of her brother.

I stride to the table and set our drinks down, meeting her gaze. "Hey, everyone."

She looks relieved to see me.

One of the guys straightens. "Oh, hey, man."

The other looks at me, but he's still leaning on the table, close to Brooke.

"What's going on?" I ask.

"Just trying to convince Brooke here to come to the next bar with us," the guy to her left says.

"Do you know each other?" I ask, directing the question at Brooke.

She shakes her head. "They, uh, just came over and introduced themselves."

Seriously? What the fuck? But of course she got hit on immediately. She's gorgeous and sexy and I'm sure they came over and said 'hi' and she was sweet, and friendly and didn't tell them to fuck off instantly. Which, to some men, means 'please get in my personal space and monopolize my time'.

"We're not interested in going anywhere else," I say, trying to be cool and hoping they're able to pick up on subtle 'get the fuck out of here' clues.

"That's fine. We can get her home later."

Well, I guess subtle is out.

I look the guy directly in the eye. He's easily Brooke's age. Maybe even younger. "*I* will be getting her home," I say firmly.

The guy extends his hand. "Sir, I promise you that your daughter will be safe with us."

Right. I should have expected that.

I take his hand, squeezing hard. "There's no way in hell she's going anywhere with you." I pull a little on his arm, making him lean over the table. "You don't go up to women in bars when they're with other people and invite them to leave who they're with to go somewhere with you. What the fuck are you thinking? She'd leave her dad *or* her boyfriend or even her boss or whoever she's with to head out with you somewhere? Use your fucking head."

I let go of him and look at the other guy. "You *never* try to separate a woman from who she's out with, got it?"

He nods, eyes wide.

"And if a woman is *alone* in a bar and you want to talk to her and get to know her, you *stay* at that bar. You don't take women to other places alone. Don't be a fucking creep."

I push him out of the way and reclaim my seat. I reach over and put my hand on the back of Brooke's neck, pulling her close and kissing her. Then I look at the guys. "And don't be assholes and assume an older guy is a woman's *dad*. How about you ask some questions rather than jumping to conclusions?"

The guys look from me to Brooke, then back to me, then to Brooke.

"We just…"

"Sorry, man."

"And I'm sorry to tell you that smart, gorgeous, mature women like Brooke are out of your league. They need older guys who know how to treat them," I say, feeling every bit of the cockiness Brooke has stirred in me tonight.

Brooke leans into me, her hand on my leg. Not saying anything. Just looking very, very content. And beautiful. Always so fucking beautiful.

"Right. Fine," the one guy says. "Sorry."

They start to turn away, but I say, "Hey, treat the other women you meet tonight the way you want men to treat your sisters and friends and mom, okay? Don't be assholes."

They don't say anything, but they nod.

As soon as they're gone, Brooke looks up at me. "See? Amazing."

"You're just feeling like you won because I kissed you before the end of our date," I say, removing my hand from her neck and straightening.

"Well, yes, there's that," she agrees, reaching for another fry. "But also just feeling really good about my taste in men."

"Yeah?"

"Definitely. You were jealous but you turned that into a teaching moment for them. That was impressive." She grabs another fry. "And really hot."

I chuckle, but I'm feeling really good about everything as we finish eating and then head out into the night, hand in hand again.

We walk for a bit, talking about miscellaneous things—how we spent our last birthdays, what I like best about firefighting, what she's nervous and excited about with her upcoming internship.

When we're cold, she wants to go to another bar, but I talk her into heading home.

I could spend twenty-four-seven with her, I realize, and tonight did its job.

I want to keep dating Brooke.

There's something real here.

"So what do you think?" she asks me, stopping on the sidewalk outside her building.

"About what?" I'm thinking I get to kiss her now and that our no sex rule sucks, actually.

"Do we have more than chemistry?"

I move in close and cup her face with one hand. "Yeah, Angel. We do. I like you so fucking much."

She smiles as if I just told her she's won a million dollars. "Me too. I know you've been hurt. But you can trust me." She wraps her arms around me. "I'm a healer. I want to help put you back together," she says softly.

I groan. Fuck. She can do it. I can feel it.

Instead of saying that though, I kiss her. I want it to be sweet. I want it to be emotional and romantic and a promise of more to come.

But about ten seconds in, I'm pressing her against the side of the building. My tongue is tangling with hers, she's moaning, and I'm unzipping her coat and running my hands up underneath her sweater.

Her warm bare skin is heaven, the sweet sounds she makes into my mouth are like a drug, and I'm very seriously contemplating saying to hell with promises and my friendships and anything but being inside this woman for the rest of the night.

I drag my mouth from hers, along her jaw, to her neck as I cup one bra-encased breast in my hand. "You want to put me back together, and I want to make you come apart," I tell her gruffly.

Her head falls back against the building. "Luke," she says breathlessly.

I lift my head and look at her. She's so fucking gorgeous just turning everything over to me, letting me do whatever I want, wherever I want.

For once, for *fucking once*, I'm going to stay in control. And show us both how fun and hot that can be.

"I want you to go inside," I tell her.

Her head comes up quickly. "But—"

"And," I say, pressing my finger over her lips. "I want you to get in bed with your vibrator, and I want you to play. But do *not* let yourself come." I kiss her neck again, giving her a little nip, before I pull my hands from her body and brace them on the wall on either side of her head. "Then I want you to text me."

Her eyes are wide, her lips dark pink from my kisses.

God, I'm never getting over her.

"Okay?" I ask.

She nods. "Okay."

"And when you text I want you to ask me, 'Can I come now?'"

She sucks in a sharp breath. "Oh, my god," she murmurs.

I give her what I know is a wicked grin.

"So we're doing this," she says. "All of this?"

"Yeah, Angel, we're doing this." I lift my hand and drag my thumb over her lips. "And you can *not* come until I say yes in my text, understand?"

She nods. "Yes."

"And if you're my *very* good girl about this," I add. "I promise that you will be very glad next time we're all together."

I'm falling in love with this girl and I'm going to show her in every single way.

She swallows hard. "I'll be good."

"I know you will, Angel." I kiss her again, slow and deep. Then I step back. "Go inside."

She stares at me for a few seconds, then she pushes off the wall and walks quickly to the front door. I watch her through the little window next to the door.

She *runs* to the elevator and I chuckle, even as my cock presses against my zipper insistently.

I get in the Uber, still waiting behind me. At this point, I don't care who has seen what or what they think.

I give him my address and head directly home.

My phone buzzes before I'm even half-way there.

Can I come now?

Jesus. This was a horrible, wonderful idea.

I lean my head back and imagine how she looks. On her bed, legs spread, maybe she didn't even take her sweater off. She's just bare from the waist down. Vibrator and fingers between her legs.

Yes, Angel, you can come now.

There's at least a two-minute delay. I recall how she looks and sounds when she comes.

Finally my phone buzzes.

Thank you.

Jesus. Fucking. Christ.

I'll talk to you soon. Sweet dreams, Angel.

Goodnight, Luke.

Yep. This date was a fantastic idea.

CHAPTER 32

Jackson

"WOW, holy shit, sweetheart, you look amazing."

Brooke is standing in her apartment doorway in a little black dress that hits just above her knees and black heels. The dress has little sleeves that just cover the tops of her shoulders, but the neckline plunges low enough to show a hint of cleavage. She's got her hair pulled back into a fancy twist, with tendrils curling around her face. Her eyes have a smoky shadow on them and her lashes look two inches long. She's also wearing crimson lipstick.

I have found this woman gorgeous since the first time I saw her. But this is next level. I don't need her all dressed up, but the idea that she spent time getting ready for our date makes my heart rate double.

She gives me one of her bright, sweet smiles and turns a three-sixty in front of me. "So this is okay?"

The low back tells me that she's not wearing a bra. Her smooth, creamy skin makes me want to run my hands all over her. Though that has less to do with the dress and more just to do with the fact I haven't had my hands on her in a few days.

No sex rule. No sex rule.

We're such dumbasses.

"You look beyond perfect." I reach out and she slides her hand into mine. I tug her close and kiss her cheek, not wanting to mess up her lipstick. "I'm the luckiest man in Chicago."

She gives me a pretty little smile that makes me want to back her up against the wall and mess up a lot more than her lipstick. I should be focusing on nice romantic things, but this woman brings out a possessive, animalistic side of me that I've never experienced before. I constantly want to touch her, smell her, taste her, *claim* her.

"Thank goodness," she says, her voice a little breathless. "It took me forever to find a dress. I have nothing like this."

I frown. "You had to go get something special?" Shit, I hadn't thought of that. "I'm sorry. I would've happily bought you a dress, sweetheart."

She shakes her head. "No, I called Elise. And since she and her best friend are both with very rich men, they knew exactly what I needed." She smooths her hands down the front of the dress. "Of course, Elise is curvier than me. And she likes the pinup style that isn't really me. And Luna is really petite, so her stuff is too small for me. So nothing they had fit."

"Give me your Venmo. I'm sending you money right now."

She laughs. "I didn't buy anything. Luna's friend Danielle is married to a billionaire and a couple of millionaires." She rolls her eyes even as she laughs. "She needs fancy dresses often. She let me come over and pick whatever I wanted, and we're a pretty close fit. Dani's shorter than me, but I think this still works." Brooke looks down at herself.

I really hate that this was all complicated for her. I honestly had not thought ahead that she might not have something that would fit in at a five-star restaurant. "It works," I assure her. "It *really* works. The only problem is that men are going to be staring at you all night."

"If you're sure."

I am definitely sure. And she's going to have to get used to dressing up. I intend to make her my plus-one for every fancy occasion I have, plus as many romantic, impressive dinners and outings as I can possibly take her to.

I am excited about our date. I haven't planned an entire evening's itinerary with a woman in a very long time, and imagining Brooke's eyes and smile as I show her Chicago in a way she's never seen has me anticipating the evening more than I have anything in a while.

She ducks back inside the apartment and plucks her coat from the coat rack. It's black with a belt and a bright red scarf that matches her lipstick. She grins. "I borrowed this too. My usual coat is way too casual."

"The only way this entire outfit would look better is if it was on my bedroom floor," I tell her with a grin, taking the coat and holding it out for her. Yes, I intend to flirt with her all night. But that's the honest truth as well.

She lets me help her into the coat, then grabs her purse and loops her arm through mine. "This is going to be really fun," she tells me with a confidence that warms me.

I have a town car waiting. I usually like to drive myself, and love my collection of cars, but tonight I wanted to give her my full attention, and not worry about traffic, especially downtown. It's Wednesday night, so I don't expect things will be too crowded but it's still nice to settle into the soft leather, turn to her, rest my hand on her thigh and ask, "So how are you?"

I basically know. We've been texting every day a few times. I send her puppy photos and want to know everything from what she had for lunch to what time she goes to sleep. But I just want to hear her voice and know if there are any details I've missed. I'm addicted to her.

She covers my hand with hers. "I'm good. I'll be perfect if you tell me that we are not going to have a no kissing rule tonight."

I look at her in confusion. "Why the hell would I have a no kissing rule *ever* with you?"

"Luke made that rule when we went out the other night. He said if he started kissing me, it would get out of control. He wanted to focus on talking and getting to know each other. Not just the physical stuff."

Ah, I have been curious about her date with Luke. I wasn't going to ask, but now that she's brought it up…

"Did he stick to it?" I ask, already knowing the answer. There is no way in hell Luke and Wyatt would be able to keep from kissing Brooke if they had her alone. I know them too well, and I know how they feel about this girl.

She grins. "No."

"I'm shocked."

"But almost. A couple of guys hit on me at the bar, and Luke kissed me after that. And then he kissed me at the end of the night."

"A couple of guys hit on you?" I'm not surprised by that either. But I'm a little surprised that Luke left her alone long enough for that to happen. I'm also imagining how I would feel. Then how I expect Luke reacted. "He stayed cool, though, right? Like a dad?"

She giggles. "Pretty much. Or like a disappointed teacher."

Oh, that's a good comparison.

"He stayed cool. But he also made it very clear that we were together."

I lean in closer. "Of course he did. You are definitely the kind of woman that men want to claim, Brooke."

She does that cute little shiver thing. "I liked it."

I can make her feel *very* claimed. "Noted." I look at her mouth. "And no, we are not going to have a no kissing rule."

"Because you definitely have no trouble controlling yourself around me?"

It seems that our not-so-long-ago-virgin is starting to find her inner vixen. And I am here for it.

"Oh, it's not that at all," I tell her. "I just don't care. If someone sees me kissing you or touching you, that's fine with me."

"But you can resist having sex with me tonight?"

I study her. "Actually, I think I can," I say after thinking about it for a moment. "I think you really want to, and delayed satisfaction can be very, very fun."

She swallows. "I do want to," she confesses. "It's like I just discovered strawberry shortcake and I want it *all the time.*"

I grin. "Strawberry shortcake is your weakness, huh?"

"For sure. I will *never* get sick of it. Ever."

I also make note of that.

"But I want to get to know you too," she says.

"You already know me pretty well. I'm not that complicated."

Something softens in her eyes. "I don't know if that's true. But either way, I want to spend time with you. Just us. This will be really nice."

I agree. And I have something I'm excited to tell her about during dinner. "And of course," I tell her. "There are ways of satisfying you that don't involve sex."

Her grin is wide. "I should have known it would be you, the playful, mischievous one, that would come up with a loophole."

I reach up and cup the back of her head, bringing her lips to mine, just barely touching hers. "Yeah, I think we're gonna discuss *loopholes* later." I know she catches my emphasis on the word *loopholes*, my lame attempt to make it innuendo, because she laughs lightly just before I press my lips to hers.

I keep the kiss sweet though because we're pulling up at the hangar where we're getting on the helicopter for our tour over the city.

She doesn't even notice at first.

She lifts her hand, rubbing a thumb over my lip.

"You look good with my lipstick smudged on your mouth," she says softly, and I don't think anyone has ever said anything more seductive in my life.

"I can think of a few other places where I'd like to have that lipstick… and your lips," I tell her.

She grins. "Me too."

We get out of the car and her eyes are wide, taking in where we are.

"A helicopter ride?" she asks. "I thought we were going to dinner."

I lift her hand and kiss it as we cross to where the pilot is waiting. "We are. After. But I want to show you my city."

She puts a hand over her heart, as if she's truly touched. "This is so amazing, Jackson. Thank you."

"Any time, anything, sweetheart."

The flight is perfect. The city lights are gorgeous from above and I enjoy every minute of pointing out landmarks and famous places to her. She asks questions and I promise to take her to the museums, the botanical garden, as well as a game at Wrigley.

When we land and are out of the helicopter, I shake the pilot's hand and exchange a few pleasantries. The owner of the company comes out to greet me as well. I'm used to that since I came into my money.

But as soon as we're on our way to the car, Brooke stops and throws her arms around my neck and kisses me. "That was awesome!"

I hold her against me, hugging her, grinning like an idiot.

I will give all my money to make her look and sound like that every day.

The thing is, I know I don't need to. Brooke doesn't need fancy helicopter flights or dresses to enjoy, and appreciate, a night out. I am going to spoil her and buy her expensive, lavish gifts, and get her anything she ever needs but because I want to. Not because I need to.

"You ready for dinner?"

Her cheeks are flushed. "Yes!"

We take the car to the building on Michigan Avenue where Loretta's, one of the best restaurants in the city, sits on the top floor with a stunning view of the city and the lake.

We're shown to our table and again Brooke gushes about how beautiful everything is. Loretta's really is a great place, but I almost never come. My friends and family like things simpler and my business associates mostly meet online.

We look over the menu for a few minutes after ordering wine.

I look up. "What looks good?"

She smiles. "Um… I'm not sure."

"Not hungry?"

She chews on her bottom lip for a moment. Then folds her menu. "Honestly? I don't know what some of this even is." She laughs softly. "I like a lot of things. What are you getting?"

I was eyeing the steak. Because I know what that is. Some of the other items come with sauces or are prepared in ways that I'm not sure of either. I lean in and lower my voice. "I don't know what a lot of it is, either."

She reaches over and takes my hand. "You know you don't have to impress me, right? I would be completely fine with a burger or pizza or tacos. In fact, I *love* burgers and pizzas and tacos."

I feel a little foolish suddenly. She's a veterinarian. She gets her hands dirty. She cleans up *very* nicely but nothing about this girl has given me any indication that she needs or wants five-star dining. We ate sitting on the floor in front of a fireplace at the cabin and it was fantastic.

"You look *way* too good for burgers," I tell her, stroking the back of her hand.

She studies me for a moment, then looks back at the menu. "How about we get a couple of appetizers and have our wine? Then we can go find some tacos." She gives me a grin. "No one looks too good for tacos."

I'm in love with her.

I realize it in that moment.

I've had inklings before, but in this moment I *know* it. She's so easy to be around. She's so perfect. She can adapt to absolutely anything. Being snowed in, a pregnant dog delivering puppies on the kitchen floor, three men wanting her, hanging out in leggings and a sweatshirt, or dressing up in a sexy black dress.

She doesn't care if I'm a millionaire or if Wyatt and Luke are firefighters. She wouldn't care what any of us do or what we can spend on her. She truly just cares about *us*.

She's everything.

And suddenly tacos sound amazing.

"Yes, absolutely. That's perfect."

The waiter returns and we pick out something with figs and prosciutto—two ingredients we both know and like—and crab puffs.

We sip our wine and chat about nothing in particular as we wait. Still, I feel so close to her. I can imagine doing this every night forever.

When the finger foods arrive, I serve us both and we start to nibble.

"So, I have something to tell you about," I tell her, suddenly nervous. I've been working on this project since two days after getting back to Chicago and it's coming along quickly. That is definitely something about having money that I really like. If you can pay, people are happy to work faster.

"Okay." She looks interested.

I hope she finds this as cool as I do.

"I've decided to buy a place with some land," I tell her. "Plenty of room for the dogs. And maybe even more dogs."

Her brows arch. "Oh, that's great. Luke said he was going to take one of them. Angel." Her cheeks get a little pink.

That's so fucking cute. I nod. "Yeah. But I think I'm going to keep the rest. And… train them for Search and Rescue."

Brooke stares at me. Then she sets her fork down. "Really?"

"Yeah. Those first few days when I felt like I needed to stay home with the dogs, I watched a bunch of animal documentaries, ones about dogs in particular. The ones that I loved most, and that really stuck with me, were the couple about 9-11."

Brooke reaches for my hand again and squeezes me. Her eyes are bright and locked on mine.

"After I saw what the dogs did after the attack on the World

Trade Center, I dug in deeper and learned more about how dogs are trained and incorporated into fire and police departments."

She smiles but just waits for me to go on.

"That obviously really hit close to home because of Wyatt and Luke," I say. "The dogs are amazing and I just think... that would be something important I could do. With a big enough property, I could have a whole training program. We could have different kinds of dogs. Bloodhounds are *especially* good, though I know our labs will be superheroes."

Brooke swallows. When I pause she says, "Who is we?"

I look at her with surprise. "You and me. And Luke and Wyatt. I can own the thing and get training, but you'll be the vet and I want Luke and Wyatt involved as much as they want to be. We'll have to hire others, of course."

Her eyes look a little shiny suddenly. "I love how you call the dogs 'ours'."

I lean in. "They are ours. I can't look at any of them without thinking of you and the guys."

"That plan is... incredible."

"Yeah?" I'm relieved and so happy to hear her say that. "You think I can do it?"

"Of course."

"I mean, beyond paying for it." I suddenly feel a little shy or something. "I'll do that, of course, and hire whoever we need, but I'd like to actually work with the dogs. I'd like to be a trainer."

"So be a trainer," she says. She gives me a big smile. "Absolutely, you should do that. You're *so* great with the dogs, Jackson." She squeezes my hand again. "There is no one who trains dogs who has any special characteristics that you don't have. You'll get trained, you'll learn, but of course you can do that."

"Will you be our vet?"

She grins. "Yes. But I'm not giving you a discount."

I love that grin. I love *her*. I reach over, grasp the bottom of her chair and drag her closer. I put my mouth against her ear. "Bet I could find a way to knock a few dollars off the bottom line."

She giggles. "A *few dollars*? Sir, from what I've seen so far, you could get me to do anything for you."

Heat floods through me. I growl against her ear. "Eat your fancy food, then I'm going to feed you tacos and then I'm going to finger you to orgasm inside your front door, and then I'm going to make you agree to our next date. Which will *not* be sex-less."

She shivers, quickly eats her figs and ham and crab puffs.

We laugh and flirt and talk as we head downstairs, then eat the best tacos from a truck only a block away. Laugh and flirt and talk as she also pulls me into an ice cream shop another block away. Laugh and flirt and talk in the car.

And then I hike her skirt up and make her come hard on my fingers against her front door before leaving her breathless and planning to see me again on Friday.

And I'm not even half-way home before I get a text.

> Thank you for an amazing night. You are going to be as good at raising and training SAR dogs as you are at handing out orgasms.

> And btw, that is VERY VERY VERY VERY good.

I grin and text back.

> I'm addicted to you. Just so you know.

> Good to know. Knowledge is power.

> You don't know anything about the five hundred dollars in cash in my purse do you?

I'd texted my cousin who had accompanied me to the last black-tie fundraiser I'd gone to and asked how much her dress cost because I didn't remember. Then I'd slipped the cash into Brooke's purse since she'd declined to give me her Venmo.

> That's for the dress you'll need to buy next time.

> Not Friday. But sometime I'll need arm candy to some fancy schmancy thing and you're it.

What's your favorite color?

> The color of your skin.

<blushing>

> Yes, the color of your skin when you're blushing.

I want the dress to be your favorite color.

See? She's just so easy. She's not going to fight with me about the money. She's not even making a big deal about a possible future black-tie event. She's making it sweet.

> Blue. Like your eyes. You would look fucking stunning in blue.

Consider it done.

> And blue will look very good on my bedroom floor.

Consider it done.

I pocket my phone with a grin.
I am so fucking gone for this girl.

CHAPTER 33

Wyatt

MY GOAL for our date Friday afternoon is to focus on Brooke.

Not think about Luke and Jackson and what they did with her on their dates.

Sure, I want to know where they took her and if they stuck to the no sex rule and what they talked about and if they are falling in love with her. I'd been fixated on all that stuff all week.

But now that I'm standing outside Brooke's apartment door, I want none of those thoughts crowding my head. I'm sure she had fun with Luke and Jackson. She *deserves* to have fun, to laugh and be doted on and treated like the incredible and special woman that she is.

Now it's my turn to do the same and focus just on her. Not them. Brooke.

I told myself on the way over here that I'm going to just enjoy the opportunity to spend time with Brooke without competing for her attention.

I've never compared myself to other men when it comes to women and I don't like that I've been doing that with Brooke and my friends. It's pointless and is only going to result in me pushing Brooke away, the very last thing in the fucking world that I want to happen.

The bottom line is she likes all of us for different reasons, like Luke pointed out, and I need to be okay with that or she's not going to be okay with me.

That's the pep talk I've been giving myself all week—don't ruin my date with Brooke.

But when she opens her door and gives me a bright smile, I don't need to repeat my mantra or gut check myself.

Everything that's been rattling around in my brain all week disappears.

She's the only thought in my head.

"You look so beautiful," I tell her as a greeting. "Absolutely gorgeous."

She's dressed casually in wide leg jeans and sneakers, with a thick red sweater and an ivory knit hat. She's covered from head to toe and yet, I know what's under all those clothes and just being here, in her presence again, has my heart thumping and my dick hardening. I can never decide what it is exactly about Brooke's facial features that make her so incredibly beautiful, whether it's her long eyelashes or her perfectly adorable nose or her high cheekbones or her wonderfully expressive blue eyes.

It's all of them. But mostly it's the way her smile reaches her eyes and how, when she speaks to someone, she gives them her whole attention. It's how she speaks intelligently, thoughtfully.

It's just her.

She is just a beautiful human, inside and out.

Brooke tilts her head and smiles, her expression a little curious. I must be staring at her like the lovesick fool that I am.

"Thank you, Wyatt. It's good to see you."

"It's good to see you, too. I missed you," I tell her because it's the truth. I'm not going to shy away from my feelings about her.

I lean forward and take her chin with my fingers and sweep my gaze over her lips and up to her eyes. "I know we said no sex but I didn't hear any rules in there about no kissing."

The tip of her tongue sweeps over her bottom lip. "No, there weren't. I'd love a kiss from you."

For a brief second, I wonder if the other guys kissed her, but then I decide, and actually mean it, that I don't care. Brooke wants me to kiss her, and that's all that matters.

I don't have any clear intent to deepen the kiss, but the minute our lips touch, we both get drawn into a passionate embrace. Her arms go over my shoulders and I slide my fingers into her hair, swirling my tongue around hers. It's like we haven't seen each other in months, which is how it feels to me, and now we're hot and heavy and can't get enough of each other.

Finally, Brooke pulls back and grins. "Wow. Hi."

"Hi." I nuzzle along her temple, dropping gentle kisses everywhere I can. "Told you I missed you."

"I missed you too." She glances back at her open doorway. "Want to come in?"

I know a trap when I see one.

"For coffee or more kissing?" I ask her.

"For anything you want." She drags her thumb across her bottom lip.

I almost groan.

Brooke has definitely found her sensuality and she knows how to use it. I can resist a lot of things but our sweet virgin turned temptress isn't one of them.

Part of me thinks the hell with Luke and Jackson.

But I'm also a man of my word.

Unless those assholes broke it.

In that case, I'm sweeping Brooke up in my arms and carrying her into the apartment and laying her down on the nearest surface.

"I want *everything*," I tell her. "But I need to know—did Luke or Jackson break the rules and have sex with you?"

She shakes her head. "No. Just kissing. And maybe a little touching."

I take a deep breath. "Then come here." I take her hand and tug her forward. "We're not going inside, because if we do I'll break my promise to the guys and I'll strip you naked and kiss every single inch of your sexy body."

"I'd like that." Her expression is eager, open.

Now I do groan. "You're killing me. Be a good girl."

She pouts. "Okay, I'll be good, I promise."

Even that pout and those words are ridiculously hot. But I lead her toward the stairs by sheer willpower.

"Where are we going?"

"It's nice outside today. The sun is shining and it's in the fifties. I think spring has almost arrived so I thought maybe we could go to the Lincoln Park Zoo. I'm sure you've been there a million times but it's nice to just stroll through."

"I've never actually been there. I haven't spent much time in Chicago, really. I'd love to go to the zoo."

That surprises me, though I'm not sure why. "I didn't realize you haven't been here much. What made you decide to do your clinicals here then?"

I open the front door of her building for her, and we step out onto the sidewalk. The air smells crisp and clear, yet there's no real wind. It's a perfect day for this time of year.

"My grandmother lives here and of course, my brother and my sister-in-law. My aunt and uncle are here, too. I wanted to experience a different city but without being totally on my own. I can't imagine moving somewhere I don't know a single person. I don't always do well in large crowds or new environments. I kind of shut down."

"I understand that. I've always only lived here, and I have no desire to leave Chicago. This is home. All my people are here." I give her a smile. "Including you. I'm so damn happy you moved here."

"Me too." She's fallen in step beside me, but she glances up. "Are we walking there? I don't have a good sense of the geography here yet."

"No, it's too far, given that we'll be walking around the zoo." I pull my phone out. "We can take a car service." Normally I'd take the bus or the train but then we wouldn't be able to talk as readily.

In the car, we chat casually about movies and favorite foods and how we both come from large extended families but with only one sibling each. I have a little sister who is a pediatric nurse.

"My grandmother told me you're mechanically inclined," she says at one point. "I've been trying to figure out what that means exactly."

That makes me laugh. "Why would your grandmother tell you that?"

"She said we have a lot in common. I think she was trying to matchmake us when you came to the cabin."

"Then I guess I owe your grandmother a thank you. Hell, a giant fruit basket. I'm good at fixing things, especially if they have gears or hydraulics. I'm the guy they send out on elevator rescues. But I'm not sure what that has in common with healing animals."

"Well, we both like to problem solve."

"That is true. I also think we have similar temperaments." More so than her and Luke or Jackson.

She nods. "I agree."

I've been holding her hand in the car, and she squeezes it now.

"Being with you is really easy, Wyatt." She gives me a bright smile. "You feel like home to me."

I couldn't ask for a bigger compliment than that. It drills me straight to the core.

I'm in love with Brooke.

Absolutely, fully, one hundred percent in love with this amazing, caring, intelligent woman.

I almost tell her.

I want to tell her.

But the moment doesn't feel quite right, so instead I kiss her again, passionately.

She sighs into me, into the kiss and I want to capture it, and remember every single second of being with her. If I feel like home to her, she feels like the entire universe to me.

. . .

We kiss in front of the zoo when we arrive and take a selfie together.

I want pictures of us together so I can look at them when I'm not with her. Lots and lots of pictures, documenting a life together, time passing, concrete evidence of a past between us as we flow forward into a future.

"We look so cute together," Brooke says when I show her the picture on my phone. "Text that to me, please."

"Of course." I send her the picture immediately and take her hand as we walk to the gate. "Are you cold?"

"No, I'm good. It's really nice out today. I am from Minnesota, remember?"

"As if I could forget." I grin at her. "I have a whole new appreciation for snowstorms now."

"I've been meaning to ask you… couldn't you have fixed that generator earlier? Why did you wait?"

There is no point in denying it. "I wanted to cuddle on the couch with you under a blanket. I admit it. Also, I didn't know how long it would take and I didn't want to be away from you, even for a few minutes. I still don't."

I mean just generally. It's honestly not even in my head to equate that with Luke and Jackson until she brings it up.

"I know this isn't your first choice, but thank you for understanding that I want to spend time with the other guys."

The right words don't come to me. I don't want to say the wrong thing and upset her or sour our date in any way, so I just bend down and kiss her temple. "Of course. What animal do you want to see first? I personally love monkeys, so I'm going to make a request we stop at the primate house at some point."

"I love primates too. They're such intelligent animals. Let's go there first."

The zoo is filled with families, elderly couples strolling together and twenty-somethings with their phones up, taking pictures of the various animals and the landscape. Spring foliage is just starting to appear with some bulbs blooming.

"Did you always know you wanted to be a vet?" I ask her as we pause to watch the seals zipping around their pool.

One pops his head up and shakes and Brooke laughs. "Yes. I've always loved animals. When other girls were playing with Barbies, I was playing with my vet kit, patching up fictitious boo boos on all my stuffed animals."

"That sounds adorable."

"I was a cute kid," she says with a flirty flip of her hair back over her shoulder. "I imagine you were a true rough and tumble boy, weren't you?"

"Probably. I loved sports, especially baseball. The big treat every summer was when my dad took me to see the Cubs play. I had a little desk calendar in my room and I used to cross out the days until the game we were attending. I would lay out my spirit gear the night before with my mitt, ready to catch a home run. One never came my way though. We should go to a game this summer."

"Maybe this will be your year and you'll finally catch one."

"You can be my lucky charm."

"I don't know about that, but I can guarantee you'll get lucky after the game."

That makes me grin. "Is it April yet?"

Brooke laughs. "I don't think you'll have to wait until April to get lucky."

"Just not today?" I ask, letting my hand drift lower onto her ass as we pause on a path that has no one else in the immediate area. I kiss her and rock her forward onto my hard cock.

Brooke sighs. "I thought I was a rule follower but I don't like this one."

"We'll have to work something out. What if I just eat your pussy?"

"*Yes,*" she breathes, her eyes drifting closed as she presses herself tightly against me. "Please."

I reluctantly release her. "Okay, after we zoo."

She laughs. "That's one way to put it."

We spend two hours making our way through the exhibits nearest the entrance. We don't get far because Brooke likes to read every placard and I like to watch her. I take more pictures of us and we get coffee for her in one of the restaurants.

When I sense she's getting tired and cold, I suggest we save the other half for another day. Brooke readily agrees.

"I'd love for us to come back when all the trees and flowers are in full bloom."

It warms me more than any coffee could to hear her talking as if it's a foregone conclusion we'll be planning and doing things together in the months ahead.

When we get back to Brooke's apartment, she's barely over the threshold before I have the door closed and her pressed up against it. I go down on my haunches and ease her jeans open and down just enough for me to tug her panties to the side and slide my tongue over her clit.

"Wyatt, oh God!"

"I've been thinking about this sweet little cunt all day," I tell her. "You taste so damn good, gorgeous."

Her fingers dig into my hair to hold on to me. "That feels incredible. You make me feel so sexy."

"You are sexy. The sexiest woman I've ever met." Then I tease at her, easing my tongue inside her wet channel over and over, listening to the sound of breathing for clues about what is really getting her turned on.

I find just the right spot when I suck lightly on her clit and press a finger deep into her heat.

Brooke breaks all over me, her thighs shaking as she shudders and cries her way through an orgasm. It's a sound I'm never going to grow tired of.

I let her settle back down to earth, her fingers releasing my head, before I sit back. Staring at her pretty little pussy, I reach out with my finger and stroke over her one last time.

She gives an involuntary, "Oh!" before letting out a deep breath.

I suck on my finger, wanting one last taste of her. When I glance up at her, she's watching me with a hooded gaze, her expression tender, cheeks flushed.

I love you.

I almost tell her again.

But I force myself to stand and give her a quick, hard kiss. "I need to leave or I'm going to fuck you against this door until you can't see straight."

She nods.

Which makes me grin.

I can't tell if she's agreeing that I should fuck her or that I should leave.

Adjusting my throbbing dick, I kiss her on the forehead. "Talk to you soon." Then I shift her away from the door and exit before I do something that will piss off Luke and Jackson.

CHAPTER 34

Brooke

I'M FEELING VERY sassy as I sit at the bar and sip a martini on Friday night.

I don't even know if I've ever had a martini before. I'm not a big drinker in general and I kind of stick to wine and margaritas and the basics when I do.

But this bar with its dark, polished wood, warm lighting, and leather furnishings felt like a place you ordered a martini. I like this one. I had ordered just "a martini" and the woman behind the bar smiled at me, gave me a wink, and said, "We can do better than that. What are you here for tonight?"

I decided *what the hell* and I told her I'm meeting the *three* guys I'm dating here tonight.

Her eyes had gone wide, but she'd given me a big grin, and said, "Yeah, I know what you need."

This martini is chocolate and cinnamon and it's perfect for my mood—sweet and spicy—and I really think I could drink six more of them.

I'm very proud of myself. I'm taking charge tonight with my guys and this is going to be fun.

I'm the first one here, as planned, and I have butterflies in my stomach, but I'm excited.

I pull out my phone to check the time and see if anyone has texted.

I read back through the messages I sent them this morning.

Me to W, J, and L:

> I know we've all made plans for another date, but I have a better idea. I want you all to meet me at The Game Room at 8. Let's do this together. Don't make me choose.

They'd all responded pretty quickly. And pretty much as I'd expected.

> Jackson: See you then, sweetheart. Can't wait. But remember, there's not a no sex rule tonight.

> Luke: I'll be there.

> Wyatt: All of us together on the date too?

Yeah, I'd expected him to be a little pouty about it. But I really want this.

I'm falling for all of them. Equally.

> Please?

It had taken him a little bit to respond but when he had, he'd said, *Of course. Whatever you want.*

I love them for different reasons. They all bring something different to my life. And I love when we're all together. Just eating breakfast the morning after our amazing night together was fun.

I had the best time with each of them one-on-one too, of course. That just deepened what I feel for each of them. But it's not just that I don't want to choose between them. I love *their* relationship. I love watching them interact with one another.

And I can *not* come between them.

I want this to work with all of us together and I think a fun night out, all of us together when we're choosing to do it that way rather than being forced together by mother nature, is going to prove it to them.

The Game Room is a really great bar I found online when I was searching for date night ideas that we'd all enjoy.

It's on the second floor of the historic, classy Chicago Athletic Association Hotel on Michigan Avenue, and it's not just a bar. It's got a number of billiard tables, tables for chess and checkers, shuffleboard, foosball, and Skee-Ball.

I grin as I take another sip of my drink.

It's the perfect place for my guys. Not only are they not the types to just sit around, they're so freaking competitive. I decided the perfect way for us to spend the evening out together.

I've come up with a contest.

And I'm the prize.

I'm already hot and tingly because I know they'll take this seriously and they'll *actually* compete for my attention and what girl wouldn't be all melty for that?

Wyatt, Luke, and Jackson are each a catch. Sexy, intelligent, funny, charming. They're the whole package.

And I get all three.

I somehow feel them before I see them.

I turn on my stool to find them all walking into the bar area together.

Oh, that's nice. I'm glad they came together. I wasn't sure how that would work. I left it up to them but had chosen to meet them here. I'm sensing some tension between them and though they are communicating and making clear what they all want and how they feel, I'm a little worried about their relationship. I'm really glad to see them show up here together.

I smile and lift my hand in a little wave as Wyatt is the first to locate me. They start across the room toward me.

"Damn, girl," the bartender says. "That's them?"

I grin at her. "Yep."

"Whew. Good for you handling all of *that* by yourself."

I laugh. "It's the most fun I've ever had."

"I can only imagine."

"Hey."

Wyatt's husky voice makes my heart trip, and I feel his arms wrap around me and his lips against my neck.

I slide my hand up along his neck. "Hi."

He squeezes me. "You look beautiful."

I'm dressed very casually in a blouse, jeans, and flats. But I did take time on my hair and make-up again tonight. They've obviously seen me *very* dressed down and liked me just fine, but tonight feels special and I wanted to put in the effort.

"Thanks." I smile up at him, then look at Jackson and Luke. "Hi."

Luke gives me a small smile and leans in to kiss my cheek. "Hey, Angel."

"Hey, sweetheart," Jackson says, wrapping me in a hug and pulling me off the stool so he can press me close. "Missed you."

I hug him back and just soak in the happy feel of having them all here.

They seem fine. Comfortable together.

When Jackson lets me go, I look at them all. "Do you want drinks? Food?"

Wyatt shrugs and looks around. "Sure. What's the plan? Hang out for a while, then go somewhere else? Stay here?"

"Oh, stay here," I say. I reach into my pocket and withdraw three slips of paper. "We're playing games tonight."

I hand them each a slip of paper.

They open them and read what I wrote.

Their heads come up quickly, eyes wide... and interested.

"What's this mean, exactly?" Wyatt asks, crowding even further into my personal space.

I'm surrounded by them. Our own personal huddle.

I lean over and look at his paper. It says: *Foosball. Pussy eating.*

I grin at him. "Whoever wins at foosball gets to do that—" I point at the paper. "To me. First."

He looks around. "Where's the table?"

I laugh and point.

"What's yours say?" Wyatt asks, looking over at Jackson's and showing Jackson his.

I look at Jackson's too. His says: *Skee-Ball. Blow job.*

"I fucking love Skee-Ball," Jackson announces.

"Me too," Wyatt says with a frown. "And I'm *good.*"

"I am too," Jackson says. He looks at me. "Is there just one blow job up for grabs here or is it just the *first* blow job?"

I smile and tuck my hands into my back pockets. "We've got all night. We can do whatever after that first one."

I get three low groans and my belly swoops.

"What's yours say?" Jackson asks Luke.

"It says I'm going to get to fuck her first," he says, his eyes on me.

My brows arch.

"What's the paper say?" Wyatt asks.

"Shuffleboard. First cock in pussy," Luke answers.

I had stupidly felt pretty dirty even writing those down and now I love that they've all read them, memorized them, and tucked them into their pockets.

"And you think you're going to win that?" Wyatt asks.

"No question," Luke tells him, still looking at me. "Even if that wasn't the prize. But with those kinds of stakes, there's no stopping me."

I'm finding it a little hard to breathe.

This is probably the best idea I've ever had.

What woman doesn't want to be fought over? And this is safe fighting. Fun. A way to let them all be *them,* but acknowledge our relationship and prove we're all winners here.

Jackson laughs. "The old man is the best one at shuffleboard. That tracks."

Luke doesn't look one bit bothered.

"Have you ever played tabletop shuffleboard?" Wyatt asks Luke.

He shrugs. "No. But I'll be good at it."

"So that's your game?"

"No."

"What do you mean?" Wyatt asks.

"I'll be good at all the games," Luke says easily. "I'll be the one winning *all* of Brooke's prizes."

My body is hot, and the tingles have definitely increased. It doesn't really matter who wins which game to me. *I'm* the ultimate winner here because all of those things are happening to me by one of my guys.

Wyatt shrugs out of his jacket. "Let's go. Foosball first."

I laugh as I watch them head for the game tables, then turn back to my bartender friend. "We're going to need some food and drinks."

She nods and hands me a menu. I place an order for a few appetizers and beer I think they'll like. And another chocolate cinnamon martini. She says she'll bring it all over when it's ready.

Then I go join my boyfriends.

Wyatt and Jackson are already in the midst of a high energy foosball game, trash talking each other, and laughing.

My heart expands watching them. They're so much fun. Jackson is more energetic. Wyatt is steady, more intense, but loves to smile and play. I round the table to where Luke is sitting at a high top table, observing.

"We flipped a coin to see who played first. I play the winner of this game," he says, pulling me between his knees, so my back is resting against him and I can watch the game.

"So you already lost something," I tease.

His hands rest, big and hot, on my belly. "No way. I have to be in the final round to be the *big* winner."

He's got a point.

I can feel the hardness behind his zipper against my back. I press into him. He puts his mouth against my ear. "It's going to be like that all night? You being a fucking flirt? Driving us all crazy?"

I nod. "I did bring you here with the specific goal of making you compete for me."

His hold on me tightens. "That's naughty. And sexy as fuck. And very fun."

I smile and turn my head to look up at him. "I love being with you all. It doesn't have to be about sex all the time, though I love that. But I just want to watch you all together. I know once these initial games are out of the way and we've decided what will happen when we get back to my place, you'll all settle in and joke and talk and just be yourselves. *That's* what I really want." I pause. "I mean, besides getting my brains fucked out by the three hottest men I've ever met."

He growls, then says, "You're brilliant, you know that?"

I lift a brow. "Oh?"

He nods, his expression softening a bit as he looks at me. "This is a perfect group date for us. Those two need to work some energy off when it comes to you. We all need to figure out how this is going to go and realize that it's going to be fine. That there are not actually any winners or losers. We needed a night out all together to unwind and have fun." He squeezes me in a little hug. "You've already figured us out, and that's sexy and sweet as hell."

I wrap my arms over his and settle into him. I love all of that. And I'm glad I made the right call here.

"Your place, huh?" Luke asks.

I nod. "Yeah. I figured neutral turf for you all and…" I bite my lip, then confess. "I want those memories there."

He rubs his cheek against mine. "Another good call. But," he adds, his voice huskier. "We're going to make lots of memories in lots of places, Angel."

Our food and drinks get delivered and the guys all relax even further as they munch on fried cheese curds and wings, and drink.

I'm laughing as I watch Wyatt finally throw his arms into the air as he wins the foosball game. "Fuck yes!"

Jackson shakes his head. "Dammit, Doherty."

Wyatt grins. "I'll let you hold her legs open for me."

Jackson groans and I feel heat swirl through me as they both look over at me with grins.

Luke nudges me forward and slides off the stool. "Not so fast there," he tells Wyatt. He joins him at the table as Jackson comes over to me.

Jackson takes Luke's vacated spot behind me, wrapping his arms around me, too. I take a deep breath of his scent. I love his cologne and I love that each of the guys smell different. I swear I could be blindfolded and still tell them apart.

I shiver with the idea of being blindfolded with them. Maybe we could do that sometime.

"You know I'll happily hold your legs open," Jackson says, almost nonchalantly. "Best view in the house."

Heat and tingles explode in my belly. "Oh my god," I murmur.

He chuckles and nuzzles my neck. "This was a fantastic idea," he tells me. "We're going to have so much fun. I might just throw all the games so that Wyatt will calm the fuck down. There are no losers once you're naked with us."

See, I love how laid-back Jackson is. I love them competing over me, *wanting* me like that, but I know Jackson wants me anyway. He shows me in all kinds of ways.

"You don't have to do that."

He shrugs. "I know. But I just want to play, have fun, hang out. It's all good."

I lean into him. "You're awesome, Jackson Hill."

"Ditto, Brooke Wilder."

We eat, drink, and laugh as we watch Wyatt barely beat Luke at the *very* end of their game.

He grins as Luke grimaces. "Dammit."

"Ah, it'll be okay," Wyatt tells him. "You'll get a turn with her... eventually."

Luke's eyes are hot on me. "I'll be holding her for you. Guess that won't be so bad. I can play with her pretty tits and talk dirty to her."

"I already called that," Jackson corrects him. "You'll be

standing to the side, just watching."

"The fuck if I will," Luke growls.

I laugh. "Okay, okay. There's still two more games to play."

Wyatt moves to stand right in front of me. He slides his hand up into my hair and tugs to tip my head back. He leans in and says, "Oh, there are *so* many games to play. They don't all happen in a bar, you know."

He kisses me and my mind swirls with all the delicious possibilities of what games we could all get up to.

We proceed to the Skee-Ball game, order more drinks, and the laughing and teasing gets louder. They definitely all relax and I fall a little more in love with them all. Their smiles, the way they know each other so well and clearly love one another. They're three completely different people but when we're all together like this, I feel like their personalities combine into one perfect man.

Jackson is out of the Skee-Ball match-up pretty quickly, but he gives me a wink that tells me he did it on purpose. I kiss him as a consolation prize and he murmurs against my lips, "I'm the smartest of the bunch, actually. The less time I'm playing games, the more time I can make-out with my gorgeous girlfriend."

I arch closer to him. "You make a very good point."

Wyatt ends up winning the Skee-Ball game too, barely, and he turns to me with a huge grin. He strides over, picks me up and plants a kiss on my mouth.

Anyone watching us—and we've definitely drawn some attention—is either very clear that I'm here with all of them, or very confused.

"Can't wait to see your pretty mouth wrapped around my cock," Wyatt says, setting me back on my feet, but not giving me any space. He strokes my cheek. "Fuck, you're going to look good on your knees for me."

I shiver. "You'll go easy on me?" I ask, my voice husky.

His thumb strokes over my jaw, his eyes on my mouth. "I don't know about that," he says. "But I promise to be sure you're having a very good time."

I smile. "I can live with that."

"Let's go." Luke claps his hands. "Shuffleboard is next." He hits me with a hot look. "And last."

We pick up our glasses and move to one of the shuffleboard tables. Again, they flip a coin to decide the first two to play. It's Luke and Jackson this time.

Wyatt pulls me up against him, wrapping his arms around me from behind.

"Are you having fun?" I ask, tucking my hands under his arms.

"A *very* good time." He kisses my temple. "Thanks for coming up with this."

"I'm really glad." I angle my head so I can look up at him. "I really want the four of us to be good. Together."

He shifts back so he can meet my eyes. "I know." He sighs. "They make you happy."

I nod.

"And you make them happy."

I smile. "I'm glad." Then I have to ask, "Is that okay?"

He gives me a sweet smile. "How can I be surprised by any of that? They're my best friends. Of course you'd fall in love with them. They're amazing guys. And you're incredible. Of course, my best friends are smart enough to fall for you."

I squeeze his arm. "I didn't expect this. But I like it. A lot."

"I didn't expect it either. But it feels good. And it saves me a lot of time telling my friends all about the cool girl I'm into."

I laugh, feeling a deep sense of relief. I really care about these guys and I don't want any of them upset.

Plus, I really want them all to come home with me tonight.

"Oh darn, I lost again," Jackson says, moving close and pressing me into Wyatt.

I don't mind being in the middle of this sandwich at all. With one hand around Jackson's neck, I stretch the other up around Wyatt's.

They both lean in to kiss my neck at the same time. I have two hands on my waist, two on my hips. I have one hard body behind me, one in front.

I'm pretty much in heaven.

"Come on Doherty. Let me kick your ass quick so we can take that back to Brooke's place," Luke says.

They both lift their heads.

Jackson pulls me closer, away from Wyatt. "I'll keep her company," he says, smirking at his best friend over my head.

Wyatt gives a little grunt. "Just keep her out here. No sneaking off to the bathrooms or something."

"Oh, gee, what were *you* just thinking about?" Jackson says with a laugh.

Wyatt gives me a wink. "I just happened to notice that the bathrooms are all singles and unisex."

"Is that right…" Jackson says, looking at me.

I shake my head. "I have an apartment not too far away. You're *not* getting me naked in a public bathroom."

"Of course not," Jackson agrees. "I only need to get your jeans and panties down part-way. No need for you to be *naked*."

I laugh.

Wyatt says, "No," and points a finger at Jackson. But he's smiling as he turns toward the shuffleboard table.

Jackson lifts me onto the high stool and then leans onto the table next to me.

We watch Luke and Wyatt play shuffleboard and it's not long before Luke is grinning and Wyatt is cussing.

Luke walks over to me and steps between my knees. He's not nearly as into public displays as Wyatt and Jackson but he's suddenly making an exception.

He cups the back of my neck, pulls me in, and gives me a hot, deep kiss. His tongue strokes boldly against mine and I swear I feel it against my clit.

I'm practically a puddle at his feet when he lifts his head and says, "Time to go, Angel. I'm ready to claim my prize."

CHAPTER 35

Luke

IT'S an entertaining ride to Brooke's apartment.

I'm in the front seat next to the driver because I want to prove to myself that I'm in control and I don't need to touch Brooke every second I'm with her.

Let my friends fight over invading her personal space in the backseat.

Jackson is currently making her laugh, while his hand is making inroads to her inner thighs.

Wyatt has his arm around her shoulders and is playing with her hair. He looks fucking besotted and I have to admit, it makes me happy for him. He's been waiting to fall in love for a long time, and it's clear he's there with Brooke. Normally, I think he'd be trying to insert himself more but he's in a great mood, the games and beer doing their jobs to relax him, and he's clearly just feeling good. Brooke has a great effect on him.

I'm not sure it's even registered with him that Jackson threw all three games. He doesn't need to always win, even though he's generally competitive. I think he feels like he's already winning at life, and with Brooke.

He's the most capable of sharing her with the two of us. For me and Wyatt, it's a bit of a head game we have to play with ourselves. Wyatt is only okay with it because Brooke likes it. I'm good with it because it allows me to have a relationship with her without all those expectations I'm not sure I can live up to—living together, marriage, kids. Hell, even being a partner seven days a week.

It's been so long since I've done that it feels chaffing and, well, fucking terrifying.

But this?

This is sexy and fun, and I can just enjoy myself and being with Brooke without pressure.

It's incredible watching her confidence in her sensuality blossom from our attention.

With dizzying speed, Brooke Wilder has embraced her dirty side, and it's such a fucking turn on.

The driver is making small talk with me about how bad traffic is because there is a pop star in town for a concert and a Racketeers hockey game tonight. I'm taking a certain sort of sick pleasure in engaging in conversation with him while being hyper aware of what's taking place in the back seat.

It's making my dick hard and drawing my patience out taut.

I like the wound up feeling and the twitch in my fingers from wanting to strip Brooke naked.

It makes the moment when I actually can all that much sweeter.

Which is why the minute we're in Brooke's apartment, I shut the door behind me with a hard kick from my boot.

Brooke, who is holding Wyatt's hand and dropping her purse on the floor, turns with a startled look. When she sees me, her eyes widen. "That was loud."

"How thin are your walls?" I ask her. "Because it's about to get even louder in here."

"I think they're average. I can hear my neighbor's music when he cranks it but not any conversations or anything."

I move in front of her, sliding my hand along her smooth skin to cup her cheek. "Tell us now if it's going to embarrass you if your neighbor hears you screaming when you come over and over from three guys fucking you. If it does, we can go to my place."

I have no idea who lives in this building but it very well could be other vet students all doing their clinicals. I want to make sure she's taken that into account if that's the case. Sure, she seemed happy to be engaged in public affection with all of us at the bar, but it's one thing to be kissing three guys, it's another to be overheard doing what we're about to be doing.

Brooke shivers. She leans into my touch. Wyatt is still holding her hand and he moves in behind her, lifting her hair on the opposite side of my hand so that he can lightly suck her earlobe.

She shakes her head. "I don't care."

"Are you sure? I'm serious, Brooke. Think about it." I kiss her lips, briefly. "You have to live here."

Her free hand lands on my waist and she tugs me closer to her. "I don't care. We're all adults here."

I nod, satisfied. "Excellent. And yes, we're all adults, but when you're with me, naked, you're my dirty little good girl. So you do what I say, don't you?"

She nods eagerly. "Yes, *I'm a dirty little good girl.*"

So eagerly that I almost moan. My mouth is thick with desire, my dick throbbing.

Wyatt does moan out loud. "*Fuck.* That's so hot, Brooke."

"Very fucking hot," Jackson agrees. He's to her left, taking his shoes and coat off with terse movements.

Then he tells her, "Luke said when you're naked you call him daddy. You've got too many clothes on, sweetheart. Guess we need to change that."

"Wyatt, take off her shirt," I command.

He does so without hesitation, gathering it at the hem and drawing it up over her breasts and shoulders and face, exposing her to me inch by delicious inch. She's wearing a black lace bra. I reach out and flick a finger over the tiny bow between her two breasts. "Feeling fancy tonight, Angel? Dressed up for your men?"

"Yes. Do you like it?"

"I love it." I lean forward and suck the swell of her breast, kneading the other globe with my palm.

Brooke gasps.

Wyatt has her silky shirt in his grip still. I draw back and hold a hand out. "Let me have that."

He does and then undoes her bra. He eases the bra off before teasing both nipples.

Jackson makes eye contact with me as I spin her shirt in my hands. He knows what I have in mind and the look on his face is definite approval.

He shifts behind Brooke, telling Wyatt, "Switch out with me. You need to collect your prize."

"Which one?" Brooke asks.

"Foosball," I tell her. "Wyatt is going to eat your sweet little pussy until you come all over his face."

Her eyes darken at my words and she watches Wyatt moving around her side, his hands trailing down over her belly and drifting lower, barely brushing over the front of her jeans. "Would you like that?" he asks. "For me to taste your cunt?"

"Yes. I've been thinking about it all night. Should we go to the bedroom?"

"No." At that, I take her chin in my grip and kiss her hard. "You got to play your little game at the bar. Now we get to play a little game."

I put her shirt over her eyes. Brooke gasps. "*Luke*, what are you doing?"

She doesn't act resistant. Quite the fucking opposite. She sounds excited. There are suddenly goosebumps on her bare shoulders and her mouth has slipped open on a sharp exhalation of breath.

I tie the shirt behind her head, tight enough so it won't slip, but not enough to give her any discomfort. "It's called Blindfold Brooke."

Jackson taps my hip and silently gestures for me to give him some room. I do, and he leans in and kisses her, teasing his tongue between her lips. She kisses him back, winding her arms around his neck.

When he breaks the embrace, she whispers, "Jackson?"

He nods in satisfaction. "Yes, pretty girl. Told you I was a winner, too. You look so damn sexy right now."

"I do?"

"Yes, you do," Wyatt affirms.

"What should I do?" she asks, quietly. "Tell me how to please all three of you."

"Just be you," I tell her honestly. "And listen to me."

She nods immediately. "Yes, daddy."

I never thought I'd have a thing for that, but with Brooke, I find it to be the hottest damn thing ever. The air is charged between us all with sexual tension, an electric vibrancy that only happens when the four of us are together.

The blindfold is something I've been fantasizing about, partly because I think Brooke will enjoy it, but also because sometimes when we lock eyes the intensity between us is so damn extreme I'm afraid I'm going to lose control. Brooke is still inexperienced, and she isn't ready for all the roughness I can truly bring if I unleash all of the burning desire I have for her.

Yet at the same time, I want to see how far we can push Brooke.

"This is your punishment for making your men compete for your attention." I unbutton and take down the zipper on her jeans. I ease my finger over her clit and deep down into her already wet cunt. "You won't know who is touching you."

"I'll know," she says, simply.

That gives my cock a jolt, and I immediately yank my finger back out of her. "Is that right? Because you're a dirty little girl, aren't you?"

Brooke nods, even as she shifts her hands around in the empty air, trying to find one of us. Jackson shifts behind her and wraps his arms firmly around her waist. "Lean against me," he tells her.

"Put your arms around my neck so you can give the boys a pretty view of your tits."

When she does, I spend a few seconds admiring her. Wyatt is stripping down to his boxer briefs. Jackson is lazily rubbing her nipples between his thumbs and forefingers. Brooke is starting to shift restlessly, cute little sounds of distress coming out of her mouth. She is leaning against his chest and running her hands up and down his cheeks and over his hair, head tilting as she tries to find his mouth for a kiss.

But Jackson evades her, adding to her tease. His eyes are dark, nostrils flared, as she bumps her tight little ass against his cock.

"More," she begs. "Please, Jackson."

"Shh," he says in her ear. "You trust us, don't you?"

"Of course. One hundred percent."

"We've got you," he assures her. "Now stop wiggling against my dick, baby. You're fucking killing me."

She does stop moving, but she turns forward. "Wyatt, where are you?"

He runs his thumb over her bottom lip. She gasps at the soft touch. "Right here, gorgeous."

"Take your prize," she encourages him. "Now, Wyatt. I'm ready. Please?"

That makes me laugh softly. She knows Wyatt is the weak link. She can get him to do her bidding readily.

But to my surprise, he looks to me for permission.

It makes my gut clench.

I know his feelings for this woman.

On his own, he would give in to any and all demands or requests she made of him.

But he's putting his trust fully into me to lead us in taking Brooke to the height of pleasure.

I'm fucking grateful for that.

So, without warning, I reach out and yank her jeans down to her knees.

"Yes," Brooke exclaims, her hips jerking forward from the

motion before she sags back against Jackson for support so she doesn't stumble.

Wyatt lifts one leg and removes her jeans, then the other. He tosses her jeans to the side.

I put a hand on her knee, encouraging her to shift her legs apart. "Spread your legs for your boyfriend," I tell her. "Show him what he won."

She does and Wyatt drops down to his haunches. He leans in and breathes deeply, his eyes closed.

"Jesus," Jackson murmurs, swallowing visibly.

Brooke is trembling already.

I startle her with a kiss. She opens eagerly for me, her tongue tangling hotly and wildly with mine. I know the second Wyatt's mouth touches her pussy because she cries out, right into my mouth, and I get to capture that pleasure. She bucks, trying to pull away, but I wrap her hair around my fingers and tug her tightly against me.

"I've got her," Jackson tells us both.

A glance down shows Wyatt is devouring her with his tongue, his fingers leaving deep impressions on her thighs. Out of the corner of my eye I see Jackson is tightly squeezing her nipple. Brooke is crowded in on all sides, head to toe, and she fucking loves it.

She's kissing me with a fierceness that takes my damn breath away. She's gripping Jackson's hair. She's even rocking her hips forward onto Wyatt.

Close. She's so close.

Then she's bucking and thrashing.

She pauses in kissing me.

Then she cries out onto me as she breaks, coming hard on Wyatt's tongue.

It's mind-blowing how incredible this girl is.

I've never experienced anything like this.

Love and lust and total and complete fucking awe at how amazing she is.

Her warm pants of breath tickle my cheek as she shudders through her orgasm.

When she goes a little limp, I take her hands and help Jackson hold her up.

"That's it, Angel," I murmur to her. "Feel good?"

"So good," she breathes.

"How was that pussy, Wyatt?"

He sits back and wipes his bottom lip. "Fucking perfect."

"That's just the beginning," I tell her. "Ready for more?"

Brooke nods. I can tell she's straining a little to see through the shirt. "Always. *More.*"

So I throw her over my shoulder and fireman carry her to the bedroom.

CHAPTER 36

Wyatt

NO VICTORY HAS EVER TASTED as sweet as Brooke's pussy.

Nothing else will be worth competing for after this.

As Jackson and I follow Luke and Brooke to the bedroom, I register the fact that having Luke take the lead doesn't bother me. Maybe it's because he's a natural born leader. At the station, we all trust his leadership implicitly. He's a damn good chief. It might also be that while I'm absolutely sure of what I'm doing with Brooke one on one, this group dynamic isn't as instinctive for me.

Sure, Jackson and I have shared a woman a time or two, but that was different. That was casual sex. There's nothing casual about what's happening between us and Brooke, and Luke seems to know how to make it even better for her.

I would never have thought to blindfold her, because I like eye contact with a woman, but not only didn't she object, she seems to be enjoying it.

So I'm fine with letting Luke call the shots.

Hell, I'm even cool with her calling him daddy. I get it, and it's actually kind of hot, which I don't totally understand, but I'm determined not to overthink any of this. I'm just going to enjoy watching our girl come apart for us.

I can still taste her on my tongue, and I want more.

Reaching out, I run my hand over the smooth curve of her tight ass. Brooke makes a sound of approval deep in her throat. I squeeze and glance over at Jackson, curious if he's enjoying this view as much as I am.

The answer is an obvious hell yes. He's staring intently at her ass, his hand in his open pants, stroking along his cock.

"Do you know who is carrying you?" he asks her. "I'm enjoying this incredible view of your body, but which of your firemen is carrying you?"

"Luke," she says confidently.

"How do you know?" I ask, curious. "You're right, but how do you know?"

As Luke lightly drops her on her bed, she shrugs. "Well, smell, for one thing. You all smell different. And your hands feel different. You all move in your own way. I don't know. I just *know* you all."

"That's very sexy," I tell her.

Brooke giggles. "Tell me about it."

"I thought of a game for another night," Jackson says. "We'll blindfold you again and you can guess whose dick is in your mouth."

"Oh, that's easy." Brooke waves her hand in dismissal. She's on the edge of the bed, legs dangling over the side, not even attempting to remove the blindfold. "I know I'll win. What do I win if I guess them right?"

"Three dicks in your mouth," Luke tells her dryly, stripping his jeans.

Brooke laughs. Then she pouts. "I should win something else, too." She turns toward me. "Right, Wyatt?"

I'm amazed that she can sense I'm on her right and Jackson is on her left. "Whatever you want, I'll give it to you."

She smiles prettily. "Did you hear that, Luke? Wyatt is going to give me whatever I want."

Luke steps in between her legs. She gasps at the unexpected

contact of his knees nudging hers apart. "I'll give you what you want even before you know you want it." He presses on her shoulder. "Now on your knees, Angel."

Jackson takes his pants off and shifts around next to Luke. "I have something you'll want too, sweetheart."

"Get in front of her," Luke orders me.

I seriously should balk at his bossiness, but I don't. I *want* to be in front of Brooke. I'm starting to realize that when it comes to the three of us and Brooke, there are no bad ideas. I climb on the bed, on my knees in front of her.

"Look at you," I tell her, stroking over her silken hair. "Mouth already open. You want some cock in your mouth, don't you?"

"Yes. I want to suck you, Wyatt."

"Just remember how hard I fought for this," I tell her, shoving my boxer briefs down past my knees and using my foot to flip them off the bed. "I want best efforts, Brooke."

On all fours, she lifts one hand and searches around until she finds my erection. She squeezes the base of the shaft, drawing a hiss from me. "One hundred and ten percent," she promises. "Now come closer."

I do, but I want to delay my own gratification, as well as hers. This is fucking fun, teasing Brooke. I wrap my hand around hers and guide my dick to her lips. I roll the tip around her mouth while Jackson runs his hands down over the curve of her ass. She rocks back against him in open invitation.

"Yes, Jackson, fuck me."

I know he's not going to fuck her, because Luke won shuffleboard. I also know that there is no way Brooke doesn't know it. It also shows she really can sense which of us is touching her.

Jackson lightly smacks her ass. "You know I can't do that, sweetheart. Good guess, though, on who is touching you."

"I told you, I just know." Then Brooke flicks her tongue out and makes contact with my cock. She gives a sound of approval as I jolt from the brief contact. "There you are, Wyatt."

Luke is standing beside the bed, fully stripped now, watching us with hooded eyes. His hand is on his hard dick, pumping up and down with rough, erratic strokes. He looks like he wants to attack Brooke and fuck her into next week.

"Our girl is feeling sassy, isn't she?" I ask. "What do you think, should I let her keep tormenting us or should I fill her pretty little mouth up?"

"She's not going to be able to talk in about three seconds," Jackson declares as he palms her ass and eases her apart. Then he bends his head.

"Oh, my god!" Brooke jerks and almost falls forward.

I hold her up as her hand falls off of my cock and drops to the mattress to regain her stability.

"What are you—oh my god—what—

Then Jackson's prediction comes true. Brooke moans low and deep as Jackson buries his tongue in her ass. I wish I could see her eyes, but I can see enough to know she's experiencing a whole new pleasure. Goosebumps race along her shoulders and she's arching her back. One moan crashes into another one.

I cut off the third by easing my length between her lips. She jolts, then sucks eagerly, as if she needs my cock to ground her. Her hot little mouth feels like fucking heaven over my throbbing dick and I pull back and thrust further, even deeper. She moans around me, opening up to allow me further access.

All that slick heat grabs me and threatens to drown me.

"That's it," I tell her. "You're doing incredible. Take me deep, baby."

She pulls back fully off of me and pants, "I'm trying. Oh, oh, oh, *Jackson*, that feels so... Luke... I *need* you in my pussy. I need to come."

"You will," he assures her, even as he reaches beneath her and cups her breast. "Just not yet, Angel. Enjoy Jackson's tongue for another minute."

Jackson lifts his head long enough to declare, "Minute? Fuck, Moody, I can do this all damn night."

That makes Luke give a sharp laugh, and he drops his hand off of Brooke. "I don't think I can wait all night, but I'll try."

"*No*," Brooke pants. "Why did you all stop?"

I have a clear view of her pouting. I take her chin and give her a little squeeze. "You're the one who stopped the action."

Her jaw drops, which gives me the opportunity to shove my cock back between her parted lips.

I can't with the blindfold anymore. I want to see her eyes.

I shove it back onto her forehead as I start to saw in and out of her hot mouth. She blinks, then raises big blue eyes to me. Her eyes are glazed with desire and approval.

Jackson slides a finger between her cheeks. I'm not sure if he's in her ass or her pussy, but I get my answer when her eyes briefly close and she moans around my cock. Luke is back on her nipples.

"Want two fingers, baby?" Jackson asks. "Don't take your mouth off of Wyatt, just nod yes if you want more."

Brooke's head jerks up and down sharply, taking me with her. My thigh muscles are tense, my teeth gritted. My balls are tightening, but I don't want this to end. I fight through the urge to come, wanting to absorb this view of her, cheeks pink, saliva glistening on her lips, my dick disappearing in and out of her mouth. Her hair is shoved up at a weird angle from the shirt tied around her forehead, and her eyes are starting to water from how deep I'm thrusting.

Luke is swearing under his breath, open palm just pressing his dick against his stomach. I can see the tip gleaming with clear fluid. He's having the same issue I am.

Holding off is fucking impossible with a girl this incredibly sexy.

"You love that, don't you?" Luke asks. "Giving Wyatt his prize? I'm going to collect mine soon, and then that desperate little pussy will finally be full. Until then, let Jackson make you come on his fingers."

Brooke is trembling, pink splotches all up and down her back.

"Here comes three fingers. I want to get you nice and stretched for Luke."

I know when he adds another finger, because Brooke's eyes roll back in her head.

Jackson is leaning at an angle that has to be hell on his thighs but he's as focused on Brooke as we are. Gone is the grinning guy who always has a joke on tap. He looks intense and determined.

I fuck her mouth over and over, and he fucks her pussy. We instinctively match each other's rhythm until she shatters. She bursts, hips dropping, cheeks puffing out as she cries out, but my dick stifles the sound.

"Jesus, fuck," Luke says. He's let go of his cock and Brooke and is clenching his fists. He actually takes a step back from the bed, like he needs distance.

I actually want closer. I hold her head tightly. "Take that dick like a good girl, Brooke. Take my come."

She's still on the tail end of her rocketing orgasm, but she lifts a hand, reaching out for me. She puts her hand on my ass and squeezes, urging me deeper.

That's all it takes.

That permission, that enthusiasm, has my balls tightening.

Then I come hard, shooting hot spurts of cum down her open throat. I let out a ragged groan and pump through the orgasm.

Jackson has eased his fingers out of her and is running his hands over her ass in a calm, soothing gesture. As I try and catch my breath, I can't believe his self-control. I'm not sure if our positions were reversed I would have been able to resist fucking her, Luke's anger be damned.

When I pull back, thighs screaming, I rest on my calves and run a hand through my hair as Brooke swallows my cum. Jackson steps away from the end of the bed and Luke takes his place.

"You're fantastic," I tell her. "Definitely an A-plus blow job."

She laughs lightly and opens her mouth to speak.

But then, without a word, Luke spears his cock inside her.

Her eyes roll back in her head. "*Yes!*"

I shouldn't be shocked by anything Luke does but it seems like a little warning would have been nice.

But then it's obvious yet again he knows what Brooke needs because she grabs my thighs to brace herself and starts to shout out her pleasure.

"Yes, yes, yes!" It's a screaming mantra, each yes in conjunction with a thrust of his dick deep inside her.

Luke looks like he's concentrating on not exploding inside her.

She's rocking onto him, sobbing, and I get hard all over again, watching her being destroyed by pleasure. It almost seems like she's coming on repeat, shuddering her way through multiple orgasms.

Her voice starts to get hoarse from her screams, and I'm absolutely in awe of how free she is in her pleasure.

Jackson is on the side of the bed, and he turns her head, guiding her mouth onto him, muffling her frantic cries. She sucks him eagerly.

"That's it," Luke grinds out. "You're going to take all this dick because you fucking *love* it. You love your tight little cunt getting fucked by me and you love sucking Jackson. You loved swallowing Wyatt's cum."

I'm absently stroking myself to hardness again, so turned on I can't even think straight.

It occurs to me that while I can make Brooke feel amazing by myself, I can never give her this. This is taking her to another fucking planet of pleasure. She's writhing and sobbing and coming on repeat.

It's incredible.

I want her to have as much as she can handle.

Luke is slapping her ass now, a hard, stinging rhythm that has her bouncing a little with each contact. Her eyes are closed, so I slip the blindfold back down, in case she's in sensory overload.

"Brooke, I'm going to come," Jackson tells her.

She nods, and he pulls back and unloads on her bottom lip

and chin, pumping his hand up and down his length. She flicks her tongue over her lip to taste him.

I clap my mouth shut on a hard groan.

"Turn her over," Luke demands then, pulling out.

Brooke gives a cry of disappointment.

I help her onto her back, feeling her trembling as I ease her head down onto the bed. "Blindfold on or off?" I ask Luke, smoothing her hair back off her face, tugging it out of Jackson's cum, which is running down onto her tits.

"On. Hold her hands over her head." Luke tugs her by her right ankle, opening her, then the other.

Even from my angle, it's an incredible view. She's all dewy pink skin, her chest rising up and down rapidly, inner thighs slick, lips and neck and chest glistening. I gently arch her arms up over her head and press them down so she can't move. I shift backwards enough to give Luke room.

Normally I would say I'm seeing more of him than I would like but I can see what this is doing to Brooke, how she's reveling in this attention, and I don't care. Jackson is right beside me too, rubbing his jaw and staring intently at Brooke.

Luke moves between her legs and teases at her entrance. "More?"

"Yes! Please, Luke."

This time when he takes her, he doesn't last long. After a few hard thrusts and listening to Brooke's cries of encouragement, he's groaning.

"This fucking cunt," he breathes. "Angel, you are so fucking *wet.*"

Luke pulls out briefly, teasing the tip of his dick over her clit. Brooke lifts her hips and gives a plaintive cry. When he shoves inside her again, she breaks, shuddering and trying to break free from my grip. I hold her steady and murmur to her, "That's it, baby. You're so good at taking dick."

"I want you to come, Luke," she tells him, ripping her hand

out of my hold and yanking the blindfold off of her head. "Luke. Look at me."

He does, and I see something on his face I feel like I'm not supposed to.

He's in love with her.

It's written all over his expression, from the fierce tenderness in his eyes, to the flare of his nostrils. He looks briefly frozen, then he closes his eyes and roars through an orgasm.

Brooke is crying.

I'm feeling a little dazed.

Jackson looks stunned.

But Luke instantly retreats. "I'm going to win the next game too," he says, voice low and gravelly.

Then he eases out of her and shoves his way off of the bed with a wince. "Jackson, Wyatt, hold her."

He disappears through the bedroom door.

"Where's he going?" she asks, as I pull her up into my lap.

I pet her hair and Jackson climbs in bed with us, and lays his big hand down on her belly. He wipes her chin before kissing her gently.

"He'll be back," he tells her. "Just give him a minute. That was intense."

"It was everything," Brooke says, taking a shuddering breath. "I… I think… oh, my god, I don't even know what I'm saying."

"You don't have to say anything. Just rest." I toss the makeshift blindfold aside and run my fingers over her lips. "Close your eyes, baby."

She does, with a sigh. A smile plays over her lips. "I like giving out prizes."

I laugh softly. "You're the best at it."

"I'm going to go get a warm washcloth," Jackson says, peeling himself off of the bed.

By the time he returns a minute later, Brooke is asleep. I shift down beside her to spoon her body with mine. She stirs a little, giving a "mmm" of approval when Jackson wipes her mouth, chin, neck and chest. She gasps a little in pleasure when he moves between her legs with the washcloth, but doesn't open her eyes.

Then he lays down on her other side and catches my gaze. *On the couch*, he mouths.

I shouldn't be surprised.

Luke's sworn off of love and this was an intense night.

Jackson is running the backs of his knuckles over Brooke's arm and watching her breathe.

Very intense night.

CHAPTER 37
Brooke

I **AM** in the break room at the clinic where I am interning, desperately paging through my notebook. I know I wrote this down. I looked it up two nights ago. I knew we were scheduled to do this surgery today and I wanted to be fully prepared. But now I can't find my notes.

I slam the front of my notebook shut and look at it.

No. Fuck.

This is my red notebook. I took those notes in my green notebook. Which means my green notebook is still at home.

I close my eyes and take a deep breath.

And try very hard not to let my thoughts go to *this is what you get when you stay up too late at night texting your three boyfriends instead of getting your stuff ready for the next morning.*

It's always been my routine to get everything ready and laid out and quick to grab—clothes, books, lunch, whatever kind of jacket I might need for the day, an umbrella if the forecast says it might rain. I *fully* prepare the night before, so in the morning I don't have to rush around and risk forgetting something.

But it seems since I've moved to Chicago that I'm a new person.

You are a new person.

I can't avoid that thought.

And it's true that I feel different in so many ways.

I also know that all of that has to do with the guys I'm dating.

But what I can also attribute to those three is my disorganization this entire week.

I've been at my internship for only two weeks.

The first week, everything went pretty well. My nerves about the internship made me plan ahead, and be strict with Wyatt, Jackson, and Luke when I said I needed to go home early or not get together.

But they are very hard to resist.

This past weekend when we all hung out together and I tried to leave on Sunday early in the afternoon, they talked me into staying. Four different times. I'd given in every time. Happily, I'll admit. It's not like they forced me to stay.

But I ended up getting home far later on Sunday night than I intended. I hadn't gotten to some of the notes I'd meant to review, and hadn't slept as long as I wanted to.

I've felt behind all week now.

They've been texting and calling, just checking in, being sweet. They've each asked me when they can see me, but they have taken my repeated "not tonight" answer in stride.

I'm trying to have a sensible routine. During the week, I go home after work, work out, eat dinner, and spend time reviewing procedures and diagnoses I know are coming into the clinic the next day, so I feel prepared. Then I try to go to bed at a decent time.

I want to do well at this internship. Not only because, for my entire life, I have prided myself on being an excellent student, but because I would really love a job offer at the end of this internship. I want to stay in Chicago.

In large part because of the three men who keep texting me and distracting me when I really need to be paying attention to work.

My phone buzzes as if I summoned one of them.

And honestly, just because it's two o'clock in the afternoon, I can't guess which one it is. I hear from all three of them at all times of the day.

And if I wasn't a little sleep deprived and incredibly stressed, I would find that very sweet.

Now, though, as I am taking a quick break and trying to look something up that I need for my *job*, I'm very tempted to ignore the message.

In the end, I can't. I swipe across the screen and open the message from Jackson.

> Got to work with Bruce today. Totally kick ass.
> I'm loving this.

He attached a photo of him and the German Shepherd I assume is Bruce.

I can't help but smile at it.

My gorgeous, sweet boyfriend who has the personality of a golden retriever, has his arm around a German Shepherd who looks as thrilled to have met Jackson as Jackson is to have met Bruce.

Thank God Jackson has started the SAR training program.

One thing that has saved me a little this week is Luke and Wyatt's work schedule.

They, of course, have had work shifts over the past two weeks, and their shifts are long and can be very intense. The hours following a shift they often need to sleep and decompress.

But then they're off for forty-eight hours.

And then they are blowing up my phone, wanting to see me, sending me flowers and warm cookies at night. And selfies and cute videos. Things that make me miss them and *really* want to see them.

At least they have each other.

Last night the three of them went out together without me.

Which I thought was great. I figured that would entertain them all and distract them from me not being there.

Instead, it made the texts and videos three times extra tempting.

They sent me selfies, a text they wrote together, and a video begging me to come to the bar and meet them.

I actually put my shoes on before I realized it was a bad idea.

I text Jackson back.

> Bruce is the second cutest thing in that photo.

God, I want to hear all about his day, the training, Bruce. Jackson is so into this and I love it. I love seeing him get invested and excited about building something he's proud of and passionate about. The training program and the facility he's building are going to be amazing.

He sends me a line of heart eyed emojis.

> How's your day going?

And see? That's sweet.

It's also a little frustrating. Because they all three ask me that. Which is lovely. Nice. I believe they all really want to know.

But then I end up texting them all the same thing.

One night I cut and pasted the same message to all three of them.

And I felt guilty as hell after I sent it. Who cuts and pastes their interactions with their boyfriend?

A girl with three boyfriends and a very busy work schedule.

But not having a lot of time or mental energy is no excuse.

I'm not being a very good girlfriend to any of them.

Multiplying the guilt and the missing them—and the phone

calls and texts and dates that have been put off—by three is just *a lot*.

And it's starting to make me feel really bad.

"There you are! Need you out here," Tammy, the vet tech, says, poking her head into the break room. "You know, where the animals are?"

Tammy doesn't like me.

"Yeah, sorry, I'm coming."

I stash the notebook in my bag and shove my phone into my pocket.

For the next two hours, I'm busy helping give shots to a new litter of kittens, doing a dental exam on a Great Dane, helping remove stitches, helping put stitches in, and listening as one of the doctors has to deliver news about cancer in a couple's ten-year-old poodle, then listen to a family worry about affording the diabetes medication for their miniature Schnauzer.

By the time I am walking a little girl and her newly adopted cat back to the front, I am feeling the emotional toll. I know this is part of the job and I am prepared for it. But I also know that veterinarians have some of the highest job stress of any profession.

I'm saying goodbye to Haley and her cat Snickers when something on the television in the corner of the waiting room catches my attention. I look up at the screen.

There are firetrucks lining what looks to be the street outside of a warehouse. There are police cars and other emergency vehicles as well. The banner across the bottom of the screen says there was a bomb found in the warehouse.

My heart feels like it turns over in my chest. I look at the receptionist, Kelsey. "Can you turn that up?" I ask.

"Sure." She points the remote at the screen and the sound comes up. I listen for a moment, getting caught up on the story. Apparently, a disgruntled ex-employee planted the bomb. The bomb squad is working on it now. The guy is in custody.

But of course, no one is talking about the firefighters. And no one is saying the name Wyatt Doherty or Luke Moody.

I pull out my phone and send a text to Jackson.

> Do firefighters always get called to bomb threats?

His response comes quickly, thank god.

> Often, yes. They don't handle the bombs though. They're there in case anyone needs medical attention or in case, you know, the bomb goes off.

My heart jumps into my throat.

> Are Wyatt and Luke at the one that's on TV?

No bubbles pop up showing that he's typing. A second later my phone rings.

I answer it, feeling like I can't breathe. "Hi."

"Hey," Jackson says. "Okay, yes, they are there. But like I said, they don't go in unless they're needed. If there's a fire or something else they're trained for."

I'm staring at the TV, mesmerized by the flashing lights.

"Brooke."

I close my eyes and concentrate on Jackson's voice. "Yeah."

"This is their job. They are highly trained and very good at it." He's quiet for a second, then says, "This is part of the deal, sweetheart."

I know he means part of the deal being involved with Wyatt and Luke.

"Don't you worry?" I ask.

"Of course I do. If I think about it too hard. But I just can't. When you go to work, we can't think about dog bites. You're a professional. It's your job and somebody has to do it." He pauses, then says, "They live for this, sweetheart. They love it. They're heroes. But they're smart and they're careful. And they're there together. They have each other's backs. Our job is to be supportive and make sure they work out and get enough sleep and that they don't think about and worry about *us* when they're in there."

I've got it. He's warning me not to freak out about this. That might be distracting for Wyatt and Luke in the future, when they need to be fully focused on what they're doing.

"Okay." I take a breath. "You're right. They're the best at this. Chicago is lucky to have them. They *need* to be there. And you and I need to just give them lots to live for that will keep them careful and smart."

"That's my girl." I can hear the smile in Jackson's voice.

I take another deep breath, letting the words I said really sink in. I swallow. "So… I'll just wait and hear from them later."

"They'll text afterwards. They know that we see this shit on TV. They always text their family and friends when it's over."

I blow out a breath. "Okay."

Tammy comes out into the waiting room, obviously looking for me. She glares at me when she sees me on the phone.

I sigh. "I have to get back to work."

"I can text you after they text me. But I'm sure they'll text you too."

"I won't see it for a while. I'll be working. How about this? Call me if it's anything… bad," I say, hating that. "And call the clinic. Ask for me. I can't have my phone on all the time."

"Understood. But it's gonna be okay. You're gonna get a bunch of texts, I promise."

My heart is racing. No matter how this turns out—and I'm sure Jackson is right that it will be fine—I'm going to want to see the guys tonight. I'm going to want to see for myself that they're fine. I'm going to want to put my hands on them, hug them, kiss them, hear their voices.

I've missed them anyway, and this makes it even worse.

Which means that I won't get my reviews done tonight, and I'll feel less prepared tomorrow. At least tomorrow is Saturday, and the clinic is only open for half the day.

But I'm also going to be distracted for the rest of *today*.

This sucks.

I'm really going to need to adjust to this if I'm going to be involved with Wyatt and Luke.

"Hey, could you maybe somehow turn it into a group text?" I ask Jackson. "All the different texts are really overwhelming. Maybe you could just text them now in a group text and say hey let us know how you are."

He's quiet for a second, then he says, "Sure. Of course. Sounds good."

No, it sounds like I don't have enough time to get texts from my boyfriends, who are right now at a warehouse with a *bomb* inside.

That would be stressful even if it was only *one* boyfriend. This is doubly hard.

Fuck, I know this is their job. And what I'm doing right now is *my* job. Yes, this will get a little easier and I hope I won't have Tammy glaring at me all day every day, but this is still how this is going to be—I'll be busy at work, taking care of sick and injured animals whose families love them very much and are worried and upset. My job deserved my full attention. I'm not able to be texting all day with my boyfriends. While they're doing their very dangerous jobs.

None of this has really hit me before now.

This is a lot.

And I have three people to worry about, not just one. When they're out of town. When they're sick. When they're sad.

I feel the stress, and what almost feels like panic, start creeping up my throat.

You are just overwhelmed by work. You're fine. Stop this.

"Okay, I'll talk to you later," I say to Jackson.

"Yeah. Of course," Jackson says.

"Bye." I disconnect, very aware of the fact that neither of us said I love you.

"Are you okay?" Kelsey asks.

I glance back at the television. "Not really. My boyfriend is a firefighter."

Her eyes widen, and she looks at the television as well. "Oh. Wow. I didn't even know you had a boyfriend."

I know. "Yeah. And his job stresses me out."

"I'm waiting," Tammy snaps.

And *my* job stresses me out.

"I'm coming. Sorry." I take a second to completely shut my phone off, even though it makes my heart drop into my stomach. Then I tuck it into my pocket and head to the exam room.

CHAPTER 38

Jackson

"THIS PLACE IS AWESOME," Wyatt says as we finish the tour of my new house in the kitchen.

Luke nods. "Seriously. Well done."

They've both seen photos of the place as I was deciding between it and another property, but this is the first time they've seen it in person. I just got the keys and signed off on the final paperwork this afternoon.

I love it and I'm pleased that my friends feel the same way. It's an enormous modern farmhouse, sitting on multiple acres, which makes it the perfect place for the four of us to live and to also build the dog training program.

I am fortunate that five of my six dogs are still tiny and not moving much. It won't be long before they need a lot more space, and this place will be perfect.

"I'll let you guys decide who gets which of the other rooms, but I am obviously taking the big one with the Jacuzzi tub in the bathroom," I tell them, leaning back against the countertop and grinning

Luke and Wyatt share a look, then look at me with frowns. "Rooms for what?" Wyatt asks.

"Which room you'll take for your bedroom and which one

Luke wants." The house has six bedrooms, so I'm not worried. Everyone will be able to have a space they love. "I'm even throwing in money for redecoration. Whatever you want. You can pick out the furniture, but I'm paying."

I actually can't remember feeling this good about my money since I bought my parents their house.

Elaborate trips, living in luxury, and not worrying about the future are all great, of course, but I'm never happier than when I'm spending my money on the people I care about. And this house is huge for that. Buying my parents' place felt amazing, but buying a place for me, Wyatt, Luke, and Brooke, is incredible. Contributing to the growth of our relationship like this gives me a satisfaction that is shocking in its intensity.

"Why would I have a bedroom at your house?" Wyatt asks.

I cross my arms and grin. "Okay, I realize that we're probably going to want to be in the same bed with Brooke a lot, but it just seems like each of us having our own space too will be a good idea."

Now Luke also crosses his arms. "Jackson," he says. "Are you thinking we're all going to be living here together?"

Wyatt looks from Luke to me, eyebrows nearly to his hairline. "Wait, what?"

Now I'm the one who frowns. "Why not? This house is huge. And we all want to be together, right?"

"But you're talking about maybe, *eventually*," Luke says. "Like a year from now or something, right?"

"Why would we wait a year?" I ask. "Brooke lives in a *studio*. And we hardly get to see her as it is. I haven't even seen you guys much lately. Why not move in together? It would make her life a lot easier. And I know I want to see her every day. And I can definitely put up with the two of you." My grin fades as I study their faces. I narrow my eyes. "Unless we are not on the same page here."

Luke shakes his head. "We haven't talked about any of this."

Wyatt's scowling. "Of course, I want to see her more often. Have you talked to her about this? Without us?"

"No. Not specifically," I say. "But you all knew I was buying this gigantic house. You've all been excited about it."

"For *you*," Luke says. "We've been excited about it for you. It's a big step. You need the space for the dogs and the new program."

"What the fuck did you think I was going to do with *six* bedrooms?"

Luke lifts one broad shoulder. "Use them for offices. Have trainers stay over. Fuck if I know, man. I didn't know you had one picked out for me though."

I roll my eyes. "I don't. You have five you can choose from."

Just then, I hear a soft voice call, "Hello? Jackson?"

My heart thumps. Brooke is here.

"You invited Brooke? Why didn't you tell us she was coming?" Wyatt asks, straightening.

I shake my head and push off the counter, starting toward the front door. "I didn't know. I thought she was coming over tomorrow."

I meet her halfway down the front hallway. "Hey, sweetheart," I greet. I open my arms and am relieved when she steps into them.

After our phone call this afternoon about the bomb, I felt a strange tension in my gut. She was understandably shaken by the idea that Luke and Wyatt were on site with the bomb. I guess the guys haven't talked through what to expect when being close to a firefighter with her yet. I've had to learn it over the years, but I know Wyatt has had to coach at least one girlfriend through not jumping to the worst-case scenario when there are things on the news.

"I know I said I'd stop by tomorrow. I hope you don't mind," she says.

"Of course not. You're always welcome wherever I am," I tell her. "Is everything okay?"

She pulls back out of my arms and takes a breath. "It's just been a long week. And..." She hesitates and looks down the hall past me. "I just need to see them. I've been thinking about them all day and I know I need to be tough and not let this rattle me, but I just need to put my arms around them."

"Completely understandable," I assure her. "They are going to be very happy to have your arms around them."

And maybe actually having their eyes and hands on *her* will convince them that all of us living under the same roof is a great idea.

I take her hand and lead her to the kitchen.

Without a word, she goes to Luke, who's closest, and steps into his arms. He hugs her close, kissing the top of her head. After a few moments, he leans back and tips her head up with a finger under her chin.

Luke says simply, "I'm okay, Angel."

She smiles at him. "I'm glad. I've missed you."

He kisses her, then turns her and nudges her toward Wyatt.

Wyatt pulls her into his arms, wrapping her tight. "I'm okay, too."

She gives him an extra squeeze, then tips her head back. He lowers his head, kissing her softly.

"I've missed you all so much," she says. She steps back from Wyatt, but he keeps his arm around her shoulders. She looks at all of us. "I'm sorry I haven't been around a lot this week."

"We understand," Luke tells her.

She takes a deep breath. "Thank you."

"I have an idea that could help," I say.

Wyatt sighs. Luke frowns. Still I say, "Why don't you move in here? I obviously have plenty of room and then we could all see each other all the time."

Brooke stares at me. "You're asking me to move in with you?"

"Yes. All of you. The three of you. I think the four of us should live together."

She moves out from under Wyatt's arm and looks from me to Wyatt to Luke. "You've talked about this?"

Luke shakes his head. "Jackson just mentioned it to us right before you got here."

She studies him. "And what do you think?"

I brace myself. I can't put my finger on why exactly but suddenly there's tension in the room.

"I think it's fast," he says.

Brooke crosses her arms. "Because if it was just you and me dating, moving in together, wouldn't even occur to you this soon, right?"

Luke nods. "Right."

"But it's not just the two of you dating," I say. I don't feel like it's butting in. This involves all of us. She's my girlfriend, for fuck's sake, and Luke is the other man she's dating. Well, one of them. This involves all of us. "Hell Luke, if it was just you, you never would've dated her in the first place." I scowl at him. "You wouldn't have even touched her if we hadn't been there, showing you how sweet, fun, sexy, and amazing she is. You probably would've successfully kept your distance, right?"

Brooke tightens her arms against her stomach.

I move closer to her. "Sweetheart—" I start.

But she shakes her head. "No. If that's true, I want to hear it. Were you tempted by me only because of what was happening with me and Wyatt and Jackson?" she asks Luke.

Luke scrubs a hand over his face. "No. I wanted you, Angel."

"But you would have kept your distance?"

He sighs. "Maybe. It probably would have been easier if I didn't know what was happening with you and these guys. If I didn't see how you were opening up and coming alive."

She swallows. "And after the cabin, you would've left me alone," she says. It's not a question.

"I would have thought that was best," he admits.

She turns to Wyatt. "What do you think about us all living together?"

Wyatt looks like he's in pain. "I don't know."

She takes a step closer to him. "Be honest. You do know."

"Okay, it seems really serious. Pretty… permanent."

"And you're not ready for that? For this to be serious?"

"I *am* ready to be serious. You and me," he says, stepping closer to her. "But this idea of the four of us being serious is new to me."

Her eyes widen slightly. "It's been the four of us doing this together from the very beginning."

Wyatt tightens his jaw, then says, "What do you want me to say here?"

"I want you to say the *truth*," she tells him.

"Fine, here's the truth. I would've asked you to move in with me the second we got back to Chicago. I fell hard and fast. I'm crazy about you. And I do consider this serious and I would love to make it long-term. But when I say that, I'm thinking about you and me. The idea of the four of us together is gonna take me a little time to wrap my head around."

He takes a breath. "I thought *this* was in the short term. For fun. Kind of a sex thing. I know that you like them both. I know they both like you. I know the feelings are deeper than I initially expected. But I guess I thought maybe it would run its course."

He meets my gaze. "I don't mean to hurt you. You're my best friend. I just didn't think that you were in the right place for a serious committed relationship."

I don't know how to respond to that. It pisses me off. But also he's not completely wrong. Until I met Brooke and started thinking about the dogs, I wasn't in a place to make a committed relationship work. I can't argue with that except to say that Brooke changed everything.

I'm not sure Wyatt wants to hear that right now.

Wyatt looks at Luke. "And I fully expected you to push her away at the first chance. You've got your emotional walls built up so high I'm sometimes amazed I'm even allowed behind them. Everything you told her is true. You never would've let her close if it wasn't for me and Jackson.

"And I know you. Here in a little bit you're going to start

thinking about the fact that she was worried about you today. That's going to bother you. You don't want people to care about you. I'm allowed because I can be there to actually do something about it. But you hate the idea that Brooke might be sitting at her clinic, watching TV, worried about you. The emotional involvement is something you didn't ask for."

Wyatt takes another deep breath, then looks back to Brooke. "So, I'm sorry, but the idea of us all moving in together, playing house, acting like… I don't know, a couple times four? Like your brother and his people? No, that didn't occur to me."

The kitchen is completely quiet for thirty seconds. Then Brooke says, "This is all really good to know." She turns and walks to the hallway, turning back and addressing us. "I have never had a serious committed relationship with a guy. Not one. And now there are three of you. And frankly, you're overwhelming. I can't even keep up with texting you and working at the same time. And here we are talking about how we have to dig through all our emotions, and define what's going on, and potentially start a poly relationship that clearly Jackson is the only one who's really thought about. And he's the one who supposedly takes things the least serious of all of us." She shoots me a glance. "And I don't mean that in a bad way. I love how laid back and fun you are."

Jesus, I have no idea how to think or feel about anything any of them are saying at this point.

Brooke goes on before anyone can respond. "If I can't even keep up with texts, I don't see how I can possibly think about managing living with all three of you, even if you all wanted that. I *have* to do well at this internship. It's everything I have been working for. It is my future. So… I think we need to take a break."

She stops, letting that hang in the air between all of us. She opens her mouth, then shuts it again. Then shakes her head. "Yeah. I guess that's it. I think we need to take a break. I can*not* come between the three of you. You're best friends. You two have to work together," she says, looking at Wyatt and Luke. "You two have been friends since you were kids," she says, looking at me and then Wyatt. "I can't mess that up. Especially when none of us are really sure about this. So I'm going to go. And I'm not going to come back tomorrow."

She turns and starts down the hallway but stops again and turns back. "And I really, really need you guys to stop texting me."

When she starts down the hall this time, she doesn't stop.

The kitchen is so quiet that we easily hear the front door open and then shut.

It's several more seconds after that before Luke says, "Well, fuck."

Wyatt shoves his hand through his hair. "*Fuck.*"

I really have nothing better to add so I just nod and mutter, "Fuck."

CHAPTER 39

Brooke

I **NEED** sugar and I need advice.

The best place to get both is at Books and Buns, the bookstore and bakery my sister-in-law, Elise, works at. After leaving the guys at Jackson's house and going back to my place, I had spent the next few days trying to puzzle out all of my feelings. I'd wound up cleaning my apartment Friday night for almost two hours and it made me feel more in control of my life. Or at least the illusion of control.

I may be struggling at my internship and with the guys, but I have a clean kitchen. I half expected Wyatt to show up on my doorstep, but he and Jackson and Luke respected my request for space, which left me weirdly feeling lonely.

This isn't what I want.

I don't *want* to end things with them.

Luke, Wyatt, and Jackson are all incredible men, each in their own unique way, and I love being with them.

I just don't know how to manage three relationships and my work responsibilities and once the conversation turned to living together, in a house miles and miles from my clinic, I mentally shut down.

But after scrubbing every inch of my apartment over several

days, sleeping a solid nine hours, and having a drama-free shift this morning, I know I handled the situation from a place of panic and I need to talk to my guys.

After a pastry and some girl talk.

Pulling open the door to the bakery, the bell jingles over the door and the warm air envelopes me. The scent of baked goods and coffee is comforting and I take a deep breath. There's an older couple browsing through the travel books in the bookstore portion and a mom with two little girls in the bakery section, seated at one of the cute little bistro tables.

There is also a couple around my age ordering from Luna, the owner of the bakery. They seem to be struggling to make a choice, pointing to multiple pastries and debating with each other.

I've met Luna a few times because one of her boyfriends is the Racketeers assistant coach and one is a player, so they both know my brother Blake really well. She gives me a cheerful wave.

"Elise is in the kitchen," Luna tells me. "She'll be right out."

"Thanks, Luna."

Elise appears in the doorway, dressed in one of her signature pinup outfits, this one with spring tulips all over the flared skirt and a red, short-sleeved sweater. I have no idea how she bakes dressed like that, but Elise treats every day like a pinup pageant. I admire her style, but the thought of wearing high heels on a regular basis makes me shudder.

"Brooke!" She comes around the counter and gives me a big hug.

I sag against her in relief. She's going to understand exactly how I'm feeling.

"Coffee? Tea?"

"Coffee. And one of everything in that case."

I'm only half-joking.

Elise laughs but gives me a look of concern as she pulls away and studies me. "Your face tells me this is a chocolate situation, not something subtle like lemon."

"The more chocolate and the gooier the better," I agree. "Can I help?"

"No, go sit. Text your brother and tell him we're hanging out. He'll love that. He is a little offended he has only seen you once since you've been in Chicago."

That makes me wince.

I saw Blake at lunch with my grandmother when I first arrived, but since then, it's been work and Wyatt, Jackson, and Luke. This is my first time seeing Elise and I've barely texted with Sophie and my other friends. I had one video call with my parents and some texts. My time management skills are being tested, and I'm failing miserably.

I text Blake and he responds with a brief, "Bout time. Hope work is going well."

That makes me feel even worse. Granted, that's how Blake texts.

Elise sets down two coffees and a plate piled high with various sweet treats. "I got us a sampling." She sits down and immediately takes a bite of a chocolate eclair. "So… how's work?"

"It's fine. I love the work and I love the animals, but I feel a bit over my head dealing with the staff. I'm not used to that kind of fast-paced environment. School is totally different."

"Is your boss an asshole?"

"Well, the veterinarians have been mostly cool to me. One is a little brisk, but I think that's his personality. But there is a tech, Tammy, who hates me. She's very snarky to me."

"There will always be a Tammy at every job. You have two choices—ignore her or shut her down. I vote for shut her down."

"I don't know how to do that," I tell her, honestly. "I don't want to make an enemy."

"She's already made herself your enemy. Maybe she's jealous of you."

"I don't know… I'm not really sure what the issue is. She hates that I get texts from the guys at the clinic." I sip my coffee. "Which stresses me out."

"The guys?"

"Luke, Wyatt, and Jackson."

Elise's eyebrows raise. "So that's an ongoing thing?"

I had briefly told Elise about our weekend, without a lot of details. I didn't tell her I've been seeing them since I arrived in Chicago. I'm not sure why. Maybe it just seemed like I was living in the moment, or maybe it seemed weird to text my sister-in-law and announce I'm dating three men. Maybe I didn't know what it was exactly, other than a lot of sexy fun.

"I've been seeing them. First separately, then together." I choose the other chocolate eclair off of the plate and set it on my napkin. "It's been so much fun. I really like all of them."

"And the sex?" Elise asks, striving for casual but looking *very* curious.

"Amazing. It's incredible. Mind-blowing." I let out a breath, thinking of the nights I've spent in their arms, surrounded by all three of them worshiping my mouth, my body, my pussy.

I'm not blushing, but I do feel warm.

"But it's a lot?" she guesses. "Trying to juggle three boyfriends and a new job?"

I nod, grateful she understands. "Yes. It's so much. Then Jackson suggested moving in to his house, which is nowhere near the clinic, and then Luke and Wyatt had their own reservations and issues, and I just got overwhelmed. I left and told them we needed a break."

Elise doesn't say anything for a second. She just carefully watches me and sips her coffee. "That is soon to move in together. You just started dating. But I married Blake really quickly so I can't say much about that. What I can say is this—you all need to be on the same page if you want a poly relationship to work long term. If that's even what you want—for it to work long term."

"I didn't think about it. I haven't had a serious boyfriend since high school and in comparison that was just kid stuff. Wyatt wants me alone, truthfully, and Luke is on the fence about a serious relationship, period. Jackson is all in on me and the other two being with me. We're all over the place. And then yesterday I found out that Luke and Wyatt were out on a bomb call, and it was just something I've never even considered. It all just became too much, and I know it wasn't the right thing to do to walk away without talking it all out, but I just don't want to come between their friendships when I don't even know what I want."

Without warning, there are tears in my eyes.

"Shit," I say, vehemently. "I don't want to cry."

"You're allowed to cry. That's a lot to unpack. First of all, let's start with the easy one. If you're going to date firefighters, or even a single firefighter, you have to accept it's part of the job. They're highly trained and they know what they're doing. But yes, there are risks. I worry about Aidan, but this is more than his job. It's his passion. So you have to decide if you can live with partners who sometimes have to put their lives on the line."

Running the tip of my finger around the top of my coffee mug, I nod. "I know that. I do feel like I can handle it. It's just been such a whirlwind and I guess I never expected to have feelings this strong for any of them."

"Do those feelings include love?" Elise asks, gently.

The tears return full force. "Yes. I love all of them. I didn't even think that would be possible, but they're amazing men. Jackson is so upbeat and enthusiastic and easygoing. He'd give you the shirt off of his back. Wyatt is loyal and kind and has nothing bad to say about anyone ever. Luke is intense and commanding and passionate. I love them all. I can't choose between them."

The thought drives a lump into my throat. "But I would hate it if we tried to be a foursome and it failed and they weren't friends anymore."

"I think that's for them to decide individually if they want to take that risk or not. They're grown men."

Wiping my eyes with my napkin, I take a deep, shuddering breath. "You're right."

"What *you* need to decide is if love is worth the risk. It's new. You all need to learn how to effectively communicate. I can tell you from my own experience that's what will trip you up. You have to make major decisions together. I went and married your brother without telling Aidan and Simon, and that almost ruined everything. If this just happened, it's salvageable if you want it to be. It's as simple as do you want to be alone or do you want to be with them? Picture your life both ways, with all the pros and cons of each. Take some time to really think about it."

I envision my life with just me, going to work, coming home, hanging out with co-workers or friends here and there. Not dating because how could I ever date another man after I've experienced what I have with these three?

Then I picture them with me, cooking dinner, walking Henley and the puppies, laughing over a board game, skin on skin at night in bed, waking up together.

It hits me like a clap of thunder. There's no comparison. One future is just fine. One is rich and full of love and passion.

"I don't need to think about it," I declare. "I'm in love with them." Somehow, somewhere between that first moment they showed up at the cabin, and now, I fell completely and totally in love with Wyatt, Jackson, and Luke. "I want to be with them."

Elise smiles. "Then tell them that. But first, finish your eclair."

"Thank you," I tell her, sincerely, even as my mind is whirling with ideas of how to approach them, how to apologize for bolting, and how we can create a relationship that feels good to all of us. "I appreciate you, Elise."

"I appreciate you too, Brooke. I'm thrilled to have a sister."

That touches me wholly. I stand up and go around and hug her. She hugs me back, hard.

"What's the plan?" she asks when I sit back down, tears gone.

"I think I have a few ideas..."

"Spill the tea."

An hour later, I leave Books and Buns feeling determined and confident.

I want my guys.

CHAPTER 40

Luke

I AM FORTY YEARS OLD. A twenty-five-year old girl should
not be able to get to me.

But three days after Brooke told us she needed a break, I have
finally come to the conclusion that it doesn't matter what my head
says… she did anyway. She got to me so much that I'm doing
something that I *never* thought I would do.

As I start the third day without Brooke Wilder, I realize that I
do actually want it to be true that she can be someone I fall in love
with and someone who loves me back.

Do we make sense? Maybe not entirely.

Was Jackson right when he said that I would never have
touched Brooke or gotten close to her if it wasn't for him and
Wyatt getting close to her? Maybe. But that seems less true the
more I think about it. If I had spent time with her, no matter the
circumstance, I would have seen her light and warmth and I
would have wanted it. What I feel for her is more than physical
attraction and that allowed her to sneak past my defenses even
with her age and with Wyatt and Jackson in the picture. And with
my past.

But these past few days have shown me that there is no use in
lying to myself. I'm miserable without her. I'm miserable not

knowing how she is. I'm miserable not knowing if her internship is going well. I'm miserable not being able to text her things I know will make her smile. I'm miserable not being able to ask her out for a simple dinner.

And I definitely miss holding her, kissing her, being covered in her scent, being a part of making her come undone with pleasure.

It feels like my right to do all of those things and it feels completely wrong to be apart from her.

I want her back. But I know that there's something I have to do before I can tell her that.

I need to fix my shit so I can move on and be happy.

I'm tired of being miserable. I'm tired of being angry. I'm tired of assuming I am going to end up in pain.

And yes, I'm forty years old. Which means I'm fucking old enough to know how to fix this.

That's why I'm walking across the grass toward a play area in a picturesque old Chicago neighborhood.

Marci is sitting on a bench near the slides where several young children laugh and run and play.

She lifts her hand in a little wave, but as I draw closer, I can see the trepidation in her expression.

That's understandable. I haven't seen or spoken to my ex-wife in over a decade.

I take the seat next to her on the wooden bench. "Hi," I say simply.

"Hi." She gives me a smile.

"Thanks for meeting me."

"Honestly, I almost said no, but my curiosity got the better of me."

It had taken me a little work to get her number. My mother still exchanged Christmas cards with Marci's mom and she was able to get Marci's cell number from Janet.

To my mother's credit, she simply asked if everything was okay when I asked for that favor. I had confessed that I met someone special but that I felt I needed some closure with Marci before I could fully commit. The fact that my mother took that at face value and helped me, tells me that my mom agrees I need that closure.

We sit quietly for a couple of minutes, watching the kids play. I know none of these kids are the baby girl I thought was mine. Her name is Audrey, and she is in dance class in the studio across the street from the park. Marci said this was the best time and place for her to meet me because of that dance class. I don't blame her for wanting it to be a public, neutral space, and for there to be a timeline on our meeting.

I finally look over at her. The ten years that have passed have been good to her. Her long blond hair is pulled back into a pony-tail, she only has light makeup on, and she's wearing jeans, tennis shoes, and a simple tee with a zippered hoodie over the top. She looks like a very casual mom at the park with her kids.

"Do you have more than one?" I ask her. Obviously, one of the children playing is hers.

She nods. "Two more. Boys. They're seven and four."

I'm surprised that I don't feel anything when she tells me that. I would have expected that to be painful.

"Are you still with Ryan?"

"I am," she says. "He's still at the hospital. We're going to cele-brate our anniversary with a trip to Europe next spring."

I look over to find her watching me. Her expression is difficult to read. She seems curious.

"Are you happy?" I ask. I hadn't intended to ask her that. I suppose I didn't think I cared. But now, I realize I hope the answer is yes. Because if she blew everything up the way she did, and we were both miserable, that would be a big fucking waste.

"I am," she says, her voice soft. "I feel like I should feel bad about that."

I blow out a breath and meet her gaze. Again, I would have expected looking directly at her to be like a punch in the gut.

It's not. She's just a woman that I used to know. A woman I don't know anymore. She has an entire life that has nothing to do with me. She probably doesn't think about me more than possibly a handful of times in a year. We were married so I have to think there are dates, or places, that remind her of me. But she has plenty of other things occupying her life. Her mind. Her heart.

"I don't know why exactly you wanted to see me," she says after a long moment. "But there is something that I've wanted to say to you for a long time."

I open my mouth to tell her that whatever it is it's not necessary but she stops me.

"Please let me say it."

I don't have to. I don't owe her anything. But I feel my head nodding. "Okay."

"I'm sorry," she says. "I've never really said that to you. And I do mean it. What I did was selfish and stupid. And I know you might not believe me, but when I got pregnant, I really hoped she was yours. I made a mistake having the affair, and then I… got caught. And I'd hoped that maybe I'd be able to get out of it. If she was yours, we could've just moved on."

I absorb that. Do I believe her? I think I do. I might not have if she'd told me she was sorry six months after it all happened. Or even a year. But now? She's had time to think about it, to grow up. So yeah, I accept that.

"I forgive you," I tell her.

She seems to sigh with relief.

"And it's worked out, right?"

She sighs again. "Yes. You and I would have too, I'm sure. But I am happy and I can't regret how it worked out. And I hope that you're the same way."

Now I feel the punch to the gut.

But it's not her fault. I realize that it's mine.

I don't feel the same way. I haven't moved on. I'm not happy. At least, not as happy as she is.

Not as happy as I could be.

I *let* her take that from me.

I take a deep breath. "I needed to see you because…"

Suddenly now sitting next to her, it hits me how ridiculous it is that I haven't moved on.

What she did to me was awful. Selfish, heartbreaking, painful. I had every right to be angry and hurt at the time. But it's been ten years, and I have been holding myself back from relationships and happiness because of a choice *she* made. A mistake that she made. It wasn't my fault. I had been a good husband to her. I had wanted to give her children, build a future. She knowingly, purposely, slept with someone else and took all of that away from us.

It was her choice to cheat. But it's been my choice to let it color my life and every relationship for the past ten years.

"I've met someone," I tell her. I'm getting more and more used to saying that out loud. It comes easily this time.

Her eyes widen. "Just now? You're still single?"

"Yes. Well, no," I say, thinking about Brooke. "I'm not single now. Because of her. But I was up till very recently. And I realized that I've been holding on to a lot of resentment and fear about relationships."

I can see in Marci's eyes that she feels bad about this revelation. "And you're here to ask me what happened with us?" she asks.

"I was," I admit. "But I realize now that I'm here that it doesn't matter. We're different. She and I are not you and I. And I realize that what happened between us was a choice you made. Not me."

Rather than getting angry or defensive, Marci nods. "Exactly. It was me. And in all relationships, there are two sides, of course, and I could say that you worked long hours and were gone a lot or something like that. But in our case, it was that I was immature and didn't fully appreciate you and committed to you before I was really ready."

"I appreciate you saying that," I tell her. I feel a huge weight lift off of my shoulders. And my chest. I can take a deep breath and it feels like it's been *years* since I could really do that.

"How about your new girl?" she asks. "Does she know what she wants?"

I smile thinking about Brooke. Our angel definitely knows herself. "She does," I say. "Probably better than I do."

"And will she be honest with you about what she wants and needs?" Marci asks.

My smile grows. Yeah, I don't have to worry about that. "She definitely will."

I know Brooke is feeling overwhelmed with everything, but she's been honest about what she's wanted from the very first day we met her. She wanted us to leave her alone and she told us that clearly. When we are all together, she's very good about telling us how she's feeling and what she's thinking.

We just have to be sure to prove to her that we're listening. She doesn't have to feel overwhelmed with us. She just has to tell us what she wants and needs from us. We'll deliver every time.

"Then you definitely need to stop being afraid," Marci says. "I'm sure she's not selfish like I was."

Selfish is the last word I would ever use to describe Brooke Wilder. I shake my head. "No, she's not."

"And she won't take you for granted?"

In fact, I've always felt completely appreciated and cared for with Brooke.

I swallow hard. "No."

Marci gives me a smile. "Don't let some dumb girl from your past affect your future happiness."

I study her. She looks a little like the woman I married, but there is a calm and a confidence there that I don't remember. I'm glad she found that, even if she needed someone else to help her discover it.

"You're right. Thanks again for meeting me."

She reaches over and squeezes my hand. "It's the least I could do. I really do wish you the very best."

I actually am able to squeeze her hand back and say, with honesty, "I'm glad you're happy, Marci."

"I'm glad you're going to be happy, Luke."

I take a deep breath and stand. I am really glad I'm going to be happy too.

Now I just need to go find my best friends and figure out what we're going to do to convince our girl that *we* are what is going to make *her* happy.

CHAPTER 41

Jackson

"I ABSOLUTELY LOVE IT, SWEETIE," my mother says as we step back into the house after the tour of the new area we've just finished for the dogs behind the house.

My parents are seeing the house for the first time, but they have previously met my dogs, including the puppy that my mother has been carrying around since she arrived, dropped down onto the floor cross-legged with the puppies, and Tank crawled into her lap.

It's very possible that Angel will be living with Luke and Tank will be living with my parents rather than turning into search and rescue dogs.

We settle into seats in the living room and my mom asks, "Do you have a plan for this huge house?"

Most of our conversation has revolved around the plan for the dog training program, including adopting more dogs and bringing on staff.

Of course, the subject of the house is a sore one. It's been a week since Brooke and the guys stood in my kitchen, and all acted as if the idea of moving in together was the stupidest thing anyone had ever said.

I miss them all like hell.

I haven't seen any of them and have only exchanged a few texts with Wyatt. I've been leaving Brooke alone as requested, even though she is constantly on my mind.

"Actually, I had offered to let Brooke, Wyatt, and Luke move in."

My parents look up at me at the same time. They seem confused.

Before either of them can ask any questions, I dive in. "All three of us are dating Brooke. Together. We kind of are thinking about trying, maybe, to have a relationship all together."

I take a breath. I hadn't intended to dump all of this out there, but I need to talk about it and my two best friends are part of the problem so it looks like mom and dad get to be the sounding boards today. "Not that I think that matters to you," I feel the need to add. "I just thought you should know. We all fell in love with Brooke and she likes all of us. At least she did. Then we all got to be kind of too much for her and she's asked to take a break. But we *were* all dating her. Sometimes one on one, sometimes we would all go out together. Anyway, I thought it was working. I was really happy with it. So I bought this house and thought it made sense for us to all live here together."

My mom is watching me, clearly just waiting for me to finish talking. When she realizes I'm done, she says, "This is really far from the city for all of them."

That's all. She doesn't ask more questions about how the three of us are all dating the same woman. She doesn't delve further into this break we're taking. She doesn't even seem overly shocked by any of it. Her comment is more of a common sense statement.

"It just felt like it would be easier if we were all living together," I tell them. "The three of us guys are best friends. I love being with them. We get along great. If we're dating the same woman, it seems like it would be easier on all of us if we were in the same place, a lot of the time."

My mom nods. "It does make sense. The part I think is a

little odd is that you would expect two firefighters and a veterinarian—all of whom need to be close to work and able to get there with very little notice at times—to drive to and from this house." She looks around. "It's gorgeous. But it's not very practical."

"So your relationship advice to me is to be *practical*?" I ask her. I am smiling though.

I love my parents. They are such down to earth, laid-back, normal people. They were not overly impressed or shocked by my windfall of money. They told me they always expected I would be successful, but my mother's first question to me was if I enjoyed my work and if I was proud of what I was doing. That was more important to her than how much I had in the bank.

I realize now that's what has been niggling in the back of my mind. I'm not ashamed of the money I've made, but I wouldn't say I'm particularly proud or that I feel I've made the world a better place with my app. These two people have led a great life, and I value their opinion very highly.

"My advice," my mother says, "is to be yourself. I know that Wyatt and Luke love you for who you are. I want Brooke to love you for who you are, too. Not because of your money or a big house."

"She does," I say. Then I frown. Actually, Brooke hasn't said I love you. We haven't done a big declaration of emotion or talked about our feelings. But I know she likes me. I know she has feelings for me and I do feel like she knows me. I know for *sure* she's not with me because of my money.

"You don't need to try so hard, Jackson." My mom is still rubbing the puppy's head, and he's falling asleep on her chest. "It comes from a good place. It comes from wanting the people that you love to know you love them. It comes from wanting to take care of all of us. But you need to realize that you're enough. You can take care of us just by being yourself. You don't have to buy us houses or vacations or *things*. We want *you* to love us. Your ability to make anything fun, your ability to roll with the punches life throws, your ability to see the bright side of almost any situation is your gift. Not your money."

I look around the house. "You think I bought this to impress them?"

It's my dad who answers. "You did it to take care of them. You bought this as a way to contribute to your relationship. But you don't need to do it this way. You don't need to buy the house. You just need to be a part of the relationship. You have a lot more to contribute than money and the things money can buy."

He's right.

That's exactly how this felt. I was trying to contribute something meaningful. Something that would show Brooke, Wyatt, and Luke that I was serious. That they could depend on me to make our relationship a major priority.

That realization hits me right in the chest.

"I just wanted to give them something they needed that only I could provide. I want to take care of them."

"But *this* isn't actually what they need," my mom says. "In fact, it's out of the way and too far for them and their work."

"But the dogs need this place," I say.

"Do they?" mom asks. "If Luke takes one and we take one and your sister takes one, and Wyatt takes one, that only leaves you with Henley and Nugget. You could easily keep them at your condo."

I widen my eyes. "What about the training program? I want to be a trainer."

"So be a trainer," my dad says. "You'll be great at that. Build a training center, house the dogs, hire staff. But you don't have to live there too. It doesn't have to be *this* place."

My dad is a really smart guy. "I guess maybe I could try that," I say with a smile.

"And if you buy a reasonable house your money will last longer," he says with a grin.

I laugh. "Are you afraid I'm going to run out of money and have to come live in your basement or something?"

Dad chuckles and shakes his head. "Not at all. You have a serious girlfriend who has two other boyfriends. I think those three are going to take very good care of you now."

My heart squeezes in my chest.

Fuck. I hope that's true.

I need to call my friends and we need to figure out how to convince our girl that we understand her boundaries and we promise not to be too overwhelming.

Or convince her that she likes us even when we're overwhelming.

Or convince her that she can handle us even though we're overwhelming.

Or something.

Whatever it is, I know the four of us can figure it out. Together.

CHAPTER 42

Wyatt

I FUCKED UP.

I knew I would, and I did.

I thought it was going to be my jealousy that pushed Brooke away.

It was, partly. But it was also the fact that it never, ever occurred to me that Brooke might want a long-term relationship with Luke and Jackson.

That this wasn't just her exploring her newfound sexuality with men she trusts.

That when she said she couldn't choose between us, she meant that forever.

I treated my two best friends like extras in my relationship with Brooke and I was so far off base it's clear to me now I was only seeing what I wanted to see.

I've been unfair to all three of them and it's taken me days of missing not just Brooke, but my friends, to realize that.

Pacing in my apartment, I keep glancing at my phone. I texted both Luke and Jackson and asked them to come over. They agreed, but now that I've officially pulled my head out of my ass, I'm impatient to make it right.

Sure, we've texted casually the past few days, but none of us have discussed what happened at Jackson's new house the other day when Brooke unexpectedly showed up, then dumped all three of us.

Okay, to be fair, she said she needed a break, not that she never wanted to see us again, but it was still a shock.

I didn't handle Jackson's suggestion of living together well.

Or Brooke's assertion that we've been a foursome all along.

Damn.

She's right.

We have been a foursome all along, and it was *good*. Really fucking good. Not just the sex, which was amazing, but how we could all hang out together and just be ourselves.

It can be even better if we all just commit to a conversation where we lay out our feelings and come to an understanding. Together.

Being without Brooke has been hell.

I'd never forgive myself if I lost not only her forever, but if I damaged my friendships with Luke and Wyatt in any real way.

I'm not sure exactly at what moment I realized I needed to fix this. Somewhere between stunned shock on Friday to waking up alone this morning with no Brooke in the bed with me.

And nothing in between but one work shift and a whole lot of lonely as fuck time spent in my apartment going around and around in my head.

Finally, there is a rapid knock on the door. It's Jackson's knock. It also turns it into a musical rhythm. This is clearly the Jaws theme song.

I open my door and give him a sheepish look. "Thanks for coming over."

"You know I'm always here for you," he says mildly, strolling into my living room. "Even if you insulted the fuck out of me by saying I don't take anything seriously."

That makes me wince. "I'm sorry. I didn't mean that to sound so harsh. I didn't mean it as a blanket statement. I just didn't think you were looking for a relationship."

"I wasn't," he says simply. "But there was Brooke and it was done. I fell in love with her, Wyatt. I thought that was kind of obvious, but I guess not. To you or to her, apparently."

There's another knock on the door. Normally, Luke's knock always sounds a little angry, but this one is just a normal rap, which gives me hope that he's not irreparably pissed off at me.

"Hey," I say.

"Hey." He puts his hand out for a fist bump. "So what are we going to do to reassure Brooke this can work? I'm assuming that's why you summoned us, right?"

"Well, yes. One hundred percent. But I also wanted to clear the air. Do you guys want a beer or anything?"

"I'll never say no to a beer."

"Do you have craft beer or just domestic?" Jackson asks.

I give him an are-you-fucking-kidding-me look. "No."

"Fine. I'll just take a bourbon."

We get our drinks and settle into the living room. Jackson is on the couch with me, Luke in the club chair.

As I'm debating how to say what I need to say, given how complicated all of my feelings have been, Luke speaks first.

"I went and saw Marci."

Jackson chokes on his bourbon. "No shit?"

"No shit."

We both stare at him. When he doesn't elaborate I ask, "Why?"

"I needed closure. She did apologize for what happened, which was good to hear. Funny thing is though, when I saw her, I realized I didn't need closure from her. I could get it on my own if I just allowed myself to move on. To trust Brooke and what I feel for her. I'm in love with Brooke."

"Damn, I'm happy for you," Jackson says. "Betrayal is a hell of a weight to carry around all these years."

"It is. So I put it to bed. One woman's selfish actions don't define all women. Or me. Maybe I could have been a better husband. It doesn't excuse what she did, but I didn't hear what she was asking me for, you know what I mean? I worked a lot. I spent most of my free time with friends and not with her. Maybe I wasn't ready for marriage or maybe she just wasn't my person."

"Brooke is your person," I say, already knowing the answer.

He nods. "But the thing is, she's yours too, and Jackson's. She belongs to all of us, and all of our hearts belong to her. We need you to be okay with that."

"That's why I called you here. I owe you both an apology for making assumptions that you both weren't invested in Brooke or our relationship. And I do mean *our* relationship. This only works if it's all four of us and I guess I needed what happened Friday to be the thing that knocked me over the head and made me understand it."

"So you're willing to commit to it being the four of us, permanently?" Jackson asks. He's eyeing me carefully. "Are you absolutely sure?"

"Yes. I realized that we all give something different to Brooke that she needs. But more than that, we're best friends. We're a team. I'm the kind of guy who goes all in on a relationship and I have to admit, I would have a hard time dragging myself away from Brooke for time with friends. Now I don't have to. I have the best of both worlds."

Luke grins suddenly. "Only you would see it that way. But you're right."

"I thought through some things too," Jackson says. "I'm in love with Brooke. But I shouldn't have made assumptions and sprung living together on her or either of you. I need to communicate more effectively. If and when we all move in together, the three of you should be in on that decision, anyway. I'm going to sell the house. It's too far out of town for all of you."

My jaw drops. "You just bought it!"

He shrugs. "So? It's not right for my people. It's already on the market. I had to compete with like ten other buyers so it won't be a problem to unload it. I want to take care of Brooke but this isn't the way to do it. I'm going to take my time, get certified as a trainer, and look for a commercial property to run a rescue shelter out of. I also don't need six dogs. I'm giving Tank to my mom and dad. Luke, you can take Angel if you want. She's almost weaned now."

"Damn. That sounds like a great plan," I tell him. I really mean that. "You're good at anything you put your mind to, man."

"Thank you. Now can we put our minds to helping Brooke work through what just happened? How do we reassure her that we understand she's feeling overwhelmed and that we're all in, but we're also willing to take it slow and by her rules?"

"I've been wracking my brain for two days," I admit. "And I don't. Just tell her?"

"We can't text her," Luke points out. "She told us not to."

"I thought about flowers, but that's so… ordinary," Jackson says. "I want something better than that."

We all sip our drinks.

There's a knock on the door.

We all sit up straight. "What if that's Brooke?" Jackson asks.

"Why would it be Brooke?" I stand up and go to the door. I look through the peephole. It's an expedited mail delivery man. I open the door. "Hi. Can I help you?"

"For Wyatt Doherty."

"That's me."

He hands me an envelope.

"Thanks."

I shut the door and see the return address is from Brooke. Heart racing, I rip it open. For a split second, I'm terrified it's something terrible, but then I grin as I quickly scan it.

I hold it up. "Guys, we're in business. Brooke invited me to the cabin."

"What?" They both jump up and race over. They read it over my shoulders.

"Brooke Wilder requests your attendance at a private poker tournament," Jackson says out loud. "Buy-in is one sex toy to be used on the organizer at competitors' discretion. Rules are as follows: Brooke deals every hand. RSVP to Brooke via text."

My dick is instantly hard. My heart soars. "I think we're in business. This is in three days. Our girl is telling us she's going to be in charge. Are we all good with that? Because I sure as fuck am."

"Hell, yeah," Jackson says.

"I'm all in," Luke says firmly. "I'm going to assume both me and Jackson have an invitation waiting for us at home?"

"I'm sure of it."

I pull my phone out and text Brooke.

> Thanks for the invite. I'll be there. Considering my buy in options now.

She responds immediately.

> I trust you.

It means the world to me.

We're all on the same page now, and Thursday can't get here fast enough.

CHAPTER 43

Brooke

I'M NERVOUS, but also so excited.

My guys are on their way.

After my talk with Elise, I'd realized that I needed to make the next move. I need to be the one that says 'yes, I'm ready to do this'. I had asked for a break and the guys have given me that. But now I'm ready to go ahead. I know what I want. I want to be with them—even when it's complicated or overwhelming.

In fact, being able to say I need time and space and having them give that to me, after the cabin when I was dealing with exams and now, has shown me exactly how well my guys listen and that they respect my needs.

I also can't stop thinking about what Elise said about imagining my life both ways—with and without the guys.

I can do that, but my life without them is sad, lonely, and cold. I don't want that. And I know I'll never find another man, or men, like them.

Life with Wyatt, Jackson, and Luke might be a little chaotic and busy at times, but they've proven that I can get time and space when I need it.

And… I love them.

So it's time to tell them all of that. And I've chosen the perfect place—the cabin where it all began.

I look around the room.

I have the table in the kitchen set up like a poker table with a green felt tablecloth, poker chips, and cards. I even found a cute party banner that says Poker Night to hang on the cupboards. It's silly but I'm feeling… festive.

I've got some finger foods, and their favorite beers and drinks.

But I think their favorite part will be the dealer. And the prizes.

I'm currently dressed as a casino poker dealer in a white shirt, black bow tie, black vest—though I did forego a bra and this shirt is a little see-through, not by accident—and a short black skirt with sheer black stockings that leave some thigh bare between the top of them and the hem of the skirt. Probably not found on the floor in most public casinos, but tonight it's a private party and we're going to have fun. We all have things we need to say, things we need to figure out, but we also need to be together. In all the ways we want to be together.

I've started a fire in the fireplace—it's the end of April but nighttime is still chilly in Northern Minnesota—and just put on some low, sexy jazz music when I hear a knock on the door.

They don't have a key to let themselves in this time.

I smile, and press my hand to my stomach where the butterflies are suddenly swooping. I cross to the door and take a deep breath before swinging it open to find all three of them standing together on the front step.

My smile is big and genuine. "Hi. Welcome."

Wyatt is in front. His smile is sweet, but he seems a little nervous. Jackson is right behind him. His smile is big and bright. Luke is at the back. Not smiling, but he meets my gaze directly, his eyes full of heat. They all seem strangely relieved. To be here? To see me? That I'm smiling? It's only been six days but it feels longer. If they're unsure of what's going to happen here tonight—

and that it's all going to be very good—I will soon assuage their doubts.

"Hi," Wyatt says. He looks back at the other two as if not sure what to say or do. "We're here."

I push the door open and move back. I feel three sets of eyes track over me from head to toe. I let my lips curl up, feeling confident and powerful.

"I've been waiting for you," I tell them as they each step through the door. I'm just out of reach and I can tell they're not quite sure what to do but they all also want to touch me.

I hold out one hand. "I'll need your entry fees upfront, please."

They all kick off their shoes and shrug out of their jackets. Everything gets piled just inside the door.

Then Jackson steps close and hands me a long thin box wrapped in bright red paper. He gives me a grin and a wink. "I know you already have at least a couple of these. But the three of us picked this one out together."

Tingles dance through my body. Obviously, it's a vibrator or dildo, but the idea of these three picking it out together is hot.

I smile. "You can choose your seat," I tell him, gesturing toward the table across the room.

"No kiss hello?" he asks, crowding close.

The important thing about tonight is to remind myself that I have control. Even when it's all of us together and I have a big surgery on Monday morning to prepare for, I can spend a weekend away with my guys and call the shots.

I smile. "I'll explain the rules in a little bit."

He shakes his head, but looks curious. That's Jackson, always up for anything and willing to go with the flow. He saunters over to the table and chooses the middle of the three seats I have set up across the table so that I can stand on one side and deal to them.

Wyatt is next. He moves in close, towering over me and doesn't hesitate to lift his hand and cup my cheek. I give him a warning look.

He grins. "Okay, I can wait to hear the rules." He loops a gift bag over my wrist and I hear the soft sound of metal clinking. He winks. "But let's get this going."

Then he turns and heads for the table as well, sitting to Jackson's right.

Luke is last, but certainly not least. He steps close, taking up even more of my personal space than Jackson or Wyatt did. He hands me a small black box with a red bow on top. "I love playing, but I've missed the hell out of you, so let's not drag this out."

I love that they are impatient. I've missed them too. Especially when the time apart was filled with uncertainty.

But this is going to be fun. My guys love to compete, and after all, they are the ones that taught me that delayed satisfaction can be oh so delicious.

I take my gifts and cross the room, setting them on the counter, then turn to face them.

They are all blatantly studying me in my very short skirt and stockings.

"You don't want to open your gifts?" Jackson asks.

I shake my head. "I know that I will love them. You guys picked them out for me. And we'll be using them together. So I know it's going to be fun and wonderful. I don't need to know anything ahead of time. I trust that whatever happens will be perfect."

Obviously there is a lot of underlying meaning to my words, and I love that I can look into their faces and see that they understand that.

I take my place across the table from them. In poker, obviously, the players don't sit right next to one another, but in this kind of poker, it won't matter. I pick up the deck of cards and shuffle them. "Does anyone need anything to eat or drink?" I ask sweetly.

"Let's just do this," Wyatt says, a little gruffly. "Whatever has to happen before I can kiss you."

I lift a brow at him. "We're going to have fun," I promise him. "Tonight is very important."

"If you need to direct this a certain way you go right ahead, sweetheart," Jackson says, giving the other guys a look. "We're so excited to see you and be here together. You'll have to forgive these two."

I smile at them. "I'm really happy to see you too. I promise it will all be worth it."

"Tell us what's going on, Angel," Luke says, his tone also a little short, but I know it means he's just impatient.

I shuffle again and tell them, "I'm going to deal five cards. You have the chance to exchange up to three cards just like in five-card draw. Winning hand gets the first prize."

Wyatt sits forward. "No bidding?"

I shake my head. "Luck of the draw."

"And what does each winner get?" Luke asks, his gaze sliding to the gifts they've brought me.

I grin. "Those are for later. Winner gets to hear me say something very important to him, gets to say whatever he wants to me or anyone else at the table, and then…" I look at each of them with a little smirk. "I'll take one piece of clothing off."

They all sit forward, and Luke growls, "Deal the cards."

The way they want me is addictive. My body is already hot and tingly, and the tiny thong I am wearing is already wet.

"How do we know when the game is over?" Jackson asks.

"When I've said everything I need to say," I tell them.

"What if you're bare-assed naked and Jackson hasn't won a hand yet so you haven't said anything to him?" Wyatt asks.

Ah, yes, my less competitive, plays-poker-only-for-fun boyfriend. I smile at Jackson. I love all of their different personalities so much.

I lift a shoulder. "We're all a team now. If we all have an ultimate goal in mind…" I glance over at the gifts sitting on the countertop, then back to them. "Then we need to come up with a way to get to it. Together."

I'm making a point here but also counting on the fact that while they do love to compete, they love our team more.

Luke smacks the table with an open palm. "Deal the fucking cards, Brooke."

Oooh, Brooke, not Angel. He *is* impatient now.

I grin and start tossing cards down in front of each of them.

They turn them over, Luke asks for two new ones, Jackson wants three new ones, and Wyatt stays.

They turn them face up and Wyatt wins.

I smile and round the table. I slide into his lap and actually feel him shudder as he pulls me close and puts his face against my neck.

God, this man.

I slide my fingers into his hair and hold him close. "Wyatt, I'm in love with you."

His head comes up quickly, his gaze clashing with mine.

I nod. "I'm madly, completely in love with you. The way you love me, the way you make me feel like a queen, the way you always put me first. And the way you love Luke and Jackson. I can't imagine my life without you. Without you taking care of me, without trying constantly to think of ways to take care of you and having you always get there first, but still wanting to try because you deserve that. Just being in your orbit and being the recipient of some of this amazing heart. I want to be with you. I know that now for sure."

He looks like he is about to say something, then pauses. "Can I talk now?" he asks.

I smile, feeling tears prick at the back of my eyes. "See? Even when I know that it's taking everything you've got to hold back, you're still putting me first, and really listening." I press a kiss to his lips but then pull back before it gets deep. "Yes, you can talk now."

"I am madly, completely in love with you, too. And as I guess you figured out, I will do anything for you. I have realized that seeing you happy is the most important thing to me, and I want to make you the happiest woman in the world. And I realize that to do that, I need Jackson and Luke. So I'm in. I'm all in with this. With us. All of us. However, you want that to go."

I wrap my arms around him and give him a huge hug. "How I want it to go, is all of us together, starting right now."

I push back and stand, though.

I look at all of them. "Now that the talking portion has started, I do want to say to all of you, I do think eventually we will end up living together. But I think for now, we take it slow. We keep our own places, but stay together whenever that feels right. We go on group dates more often than individual. Or we just stay home. But sometimes individual stuff makes sense. And sometimes it will be the three of you without me. And maybe sometimes it will be me with two of you and not one because he's off doing something else. And all of that is okay. We'll just take this day by day, but I want us to be together, committed, and monogamous…" I laugh softly. "Or whatever it is when I only have three boyfriends."

They all, thankfully, chuckle.

"We can do that," Wyatt says.

I breathe deeply and then start to round the table back to my dealer's position.

"Um, excuse me," he says, reaching out and grabbing the back of my skirt. "I believe you're supposed to take something off."

I lift a brow, then look down at his hand. "The zipper's right there. Help me out."

He gives a little growl and the next thing I know, the zipper on my dress has been yanked down and my skirt is lying in a black, silky pool at my feet.

I step out of it and saunter back to my position behind the table. But I know all of my guys got a very good view of me in only my black thong, garters, and black stockings.

"Jesus Christ," Luke mutters.

"Please tell me she's keeping the stockings and garters on later," Jackson says, his eyes glued to me.

"That can definitely be arranged," Wyatt agrees.

I pick the cards up and shuffle again, then deal five cards to each man.

They look at their hands, exchange a few cards, then lay them down.

This time Luke wins.

I round the other side of the table. He shoves his chair back and practically yanks me into his lap. One big hand cups the back of my head, fisting my hair, and he brings me in for a hot kiss before I can protest or lay out any further rules. As his tongue plunders my mouth, his other hand grips my thigh and he turns me so I'm straddling his lap.

His hand strokes up and down my thigh, his thumb coming close to my center three times before his thumb finally brushes over my clit through the black silk.

I gasp and pull back. I stare into his face. "You're cheating," I say, practically panting. "This is supposed to be for talking."

He gives me a jerky nod, then says, "I saw Marci."

My eyes widen.

He goes on before I can come up with words.

"I'm good. I got the closure I needed. Years too late maybe, but just in time for you. I'm ready, Angel. Ready to move on, ready to let you in, ready to love you with everything I've got."

My heart flips, my stomach swoops, my pussy clenches, and I swear my brain blanks for a moment.

He brings me in until our foreheads are touching. "Please tell me I haven't completely fucked this up. I tried to hold back, but I couldn't. You're way too strong a force. And I'm so fucking grateful for that."

I cup his face with both hands and pull back so I can look at him. "I love you, Luke. I love your strength, I love your loyalty, I love that you are our rock, our leader. You make me feel safe, and I can't imagine facing the storms of life without you as my anchor."

He takes in a deep, shuddering breath, then crushes me to his chest. "Thank God. I love you so much, Angel."

With my cheek pressed against his heart, I can see Wyatt and Jackson watching us. They're looking on with a mixture of relief, happiness, and affection.

I squeeze Luke, and after another moment, he lets me go.

I stand and he holds both my thighs.

"Vest, tie, and shirt," he says.

I lift a brow. "That's three things."

"You want out of them as much as we want you out of them," he tells me. "And that will leave only this soaking wet, tiny little thong for Jackson."

I look at Jackson. "You are so sure he's going to win next?"

Luke reaches up and tugs my tie, unhooking it and tossing it to the floor. "Yeah, I am."

I certainly hope so. I step back from Luke, unbutton and shrug out of the black vest, then slowly unbutton the white shirt.

I enjoy every second of teasing my men, especially the low groans when they see for sure I'm not wearing a bra.

I let the shirt slip down my arms and toss it to the side.

Now I am standing in front of them in only the thong, stockings, and heels.

"She's keeping the shoes on too," Wyatt says.

"Fuck yeah she is," Jackson agrees.

I move behind the table, shuffle the cards, trying to ignore how tightly beaded my nipples are and the fact that I can barely make the cards stack together because of the adrenaline pumping in my system now. A mixture of love and lust, relief, and giddy happiness is coursing through me.

Somehow, I manage to give them each five cards.

No one asks for any additional cards and Luke places his face down on the table. "I'm out," he says.

I frown and start to reply when Wyatt does the same. "I'm out too."

I realize quickly that they are throwing the hand so Jackson will win and I meet his eyes and grin.

He turns over five cards that amount to absolutely nothing in poker. He smiles and sits back in his chair. "Come here, sweetheart."

I start around the table and Wyatt shoves his chair out of the way so I can get to Jackson in the middle.

I sit on his lap, and he pulls me around to straddle him. He slides a hand through my hair, then cups my cheek. "What do you want to say?" he asks, letting me go first.

"I love you so much, Jackson. You are happiness and fun and goodness all rolled up into one amazingly hot and sweet man. And I can't live without your smiles and your heart and your sunshine. I need you in my life and I need you in the lives of the other two men that I love with all my heart."

His smile is bright and full of love. "Well, that's a good thing, because I'm not going anywhere. I love you too, Brooke. You've helped me find passion and purpose, and I look forward to all of the amazing projects and causes we've all got ahead of us." He looks from side to side at the other two. "Together."

My eyes well up, and I have to blink rapidly. I wrap my arms around his neck and give him a long hug, then pull back and press my lips to his.

I stand and take a deep breath. "So we're doing this? The four of us, for good, no matter what? We can be honest when we need little breaks or when having a relationship with three other people gets to be a lot. We can also be honest when we need each other for something and someone isn't stepping up." I give them all a pointed look. "Even if that someone is me? You guys have to tell me when you need something I'm not giving you."

They all nod.

"We'll all keep our own interests and schedules and space for now, but we'll also combine our lives and our families and our time as much as we're able."

They all nod again. Such agreeable sweethearts. I almost laugh.

"We're all yours, Brooke," Wyatt says. "We all revolve around you like you're the little sun in our universe. You call the shots."

I smile slightly, and then hook my thumbs in the top of my thong. I start to push it over my hips. "Well, that sounds great. With one exception. I really like being bossed around in the bedroom and I am really hoping that the clinking noise I heard in that gift bag means you brought handcuffs."

My thong drops to the floor.

I hear three growls, three chairs scraping, and then I am scooped up, thrown over a fireman's shoulder, and carried into the living room.

My millionaire gathers the gifts.

Wyatt puts me down on the sofa.

"We're not going upstairs?" I ask as he kneels before me and spreads my knees. Not that I'm complaining.

"We're bringing this all back to exactly where it started," he tells me with a smirk. "This living room, this couch, in front of this fireplace."

Suddenly, all the lights go off.

I gasp, but the fireplace gives off enough light that I can see Wyatt and Jackson, both grinning. And I realize that Luke isn't in here with us.

Jackson starts opening my gifts and lays out a vibrator, a pair of soft fuzzy handcuffs, and... oh my god... nipple clamps.

Luke strides into the room with two flashlights and two burning candles.

"The only disadvantage to our plan is that we won't be able to see every gorgeous inch of her," he says, setting the candles on the two end tables.

Wyatt grasps my legs and pulls me down so I'm lying along the couch. Then my guys gather around.

"Well, I guess it's a good thing that we've got forever then," Jackson says. "Plenty of time to love this girl in so many ways, and so many places."

That's so sweet and romantic...

I feel the handcuffs circle my wrists and then hear little clicks as Luke cinches them. I tug and find he's fastened them to something solid, probably the side table.

Sweet, romantic, and really fucking hot.

Luke leans over me and says, "Yeah, we're definitely doing this again with the lights on." Then he kisses me deeply.

And then, in the firelight, with the three loves of my life, I lose track of who is touching me where and who is saying what, because it doesn't matter in this moment. I'm surrounded by love and happiness and pleasure beyond my wildest imagination.

I came to this cabin initially to study so I could pass my exams. But it turned out that I'd learned even more—about myself, love, and life.

And I really think that together the four of us are going to get an A+ on any tests to come. It's all a group project now.

Thanks for reading Light My Fire!
Want to see where your fav foursome are a year in the future?
Read a free bonus scene at https://tinyurl.com/mr3wmpbz

Meet Emma

Emma Foxx is the super fun and sexy pen name for two long-time, bestselling romance authors who decided why have just one hero when you can have three at the same time? (they're not sure what took them so long to figure this out)! Emma writes contemporary romances that will make you laugh (yes, maybe out loud in public) and want more…books (sure, that's what we mean ).

📷 ♪ g

www.ingramcontent.com/pod-product-compliance
Lightning Source LLC
Chambersburg PA
CBHW031847310726
48972CB00005B/1450